PRAISE FOR

The

KING'S
MISTRESS

"A well-written, comprehensive view of the period in which women were marginalized, their glittery, gem-laden gowns reflecting the corruption of the times." —*Historical Novels Review*

"An absorbing story with a valiant and engaging young heroine, trying to make her way through the maze of court intrigue that surrounds her." —*BookLoons.com*

"A dynamic fictionalization of the life of Alice Salisbury . . . an empathetic but realistic portrait of a colorful and, if Campion is to be believed, misunderstood woman." —*Publishers Weekly*

"A first-rate historical novel . . . The author is the world's foremost Alice Perrers scholar, and this knowledge makes the narrative shine." —*Capital Region Living* (Albany)

"A sumptuous pageant of castles and royal courts and countryside." —*Bellingham Herald*

"In *The King's Mistress*, Alice Perrers at last comes into her own as a keen observer, not a villain, of English history. The High Middle Ages, the role of women, court intrigue, lust and love, all come alive through Alice's eyes. Yet the panoply of powerful people flaunting their influence and toying with other people's lives sounds amazingly modern. This is a rich novel to enjoy and ponder." —**Karen Harper**, author of *The First Princess of Wales*

The
KING'S
MISTRESS

The

KING'S
MISTRESS

A NOVEL

EMMA CAMPION

BROADWAY PAPERBACKS

NEW YORK

Copyright © 2009 by Candace Robb
Map copyright © 2009 by Charles Robb

All rights reserved.
Published in the United States by Broadway Paperbacks,
an imprint of the Crown Publishing Group,
a division of Random House, Inc., New York.
www.crownpublishing.com

Broadway Paperbacks and its logo, a letter B bisected on the diagonal,
are trademarks of Random House, Inc.

Originally published in hardcover in slightly different form in the United
States by Crown Publishers, an imprint of the Crown Publishing Group,
a division of Random House, Inc., New York, in 2010.

Lines from *Troilus and Criseyde* are based on *The Riverside Chaucer,*
Oxford University Press.

Library of Congress Cataloging-in-Publication Data
Campion, Emma.
   The king's mistress : a novel / Emma Campion.—1st ed.
      p.   cm.
   1. Great Britain—History—Edward III, 1327–1377—Fiction.
   2. Edward III, King of England, 1312–1377—Fiction. I. Title.
PS3568.O198K56   2010
813'.54—dc22   2009053739

ISBN 978-0-307-58926-2
eISBN 978-0-307-58927-9

Printed in the United States of America

Book design by Barbara Sturman
Cover design by Laura Duffy
Cover photographs by Yolande De Kort/Trevillion Images (background)
   and Cereinyn Ord (woman)

10 9 8 7 6 5 4 3 2 1

First Paperback Edition

for Alice

Dramatis Personae

Royal Family

Edward II*—King of England, overthrown by Queen Isabella and lover Roger Mortimer

Isabella of France—Edward II's queen

Roger Mortimer*—Isabella of France's lover

Edward III—King of England, son of Edward II and Isabella

Joan of Scotland—daughter of Edward II and Isabella

Philippa of Hainault—Edward III's queen

Edward of Woodstock—Prince of Wales and Aquitaine, eldest son of Edward III and Philippa

Lionel of Antwerp—Earl of Ulster, then Duke of Clarence, second son of Edward III and Philippa

John of Gaunt—Earl of Richmond, then Duke of Lancaster, third son of Edward III and Philippa

Edmund of Langley—Earl of Cambridge, then Duke of York, fourth son of Edward III and Philippa

Thomas of Woodstock—Earl of Buckingham, fifth son of Edward III and Philippa

Isabella of Woodstock—favorite daughter of Edward III and Philippa

Mary and Margaret*—younger daughters of Edward III and Philippa, died of plague

John de Southery—bastard son of Edward III and Alice Perrers

Edmund*—Earl of Kent, half brother of Edward II

Joan of Kent—Edmund's daughter, eventually wife of Prince Edward, eldest son of Edward III

---

*Mentioned, not appearing.

Elizabeth de Burgh—Countess of Ulster (in her own right), first
  wife of Lionel of Antwerp
Blanche of Lancaster—Duchess of Lancaster, first wife of John of
  Gaunt
Constance of Castile—Duchess of Lancaster, second wife of John
  of Gaunt
Katherine Swynford, née de Roët—Duchess of Lancaster, third
  wife of John of Gaunt

Other Historical Figures

Master Adam; Robert Broun (though I have no proof of more than
a business relationship between him and Alice); Geoffrey, Philippa,
and Thomas Chaucer; Jean Froissart; Dom John Hanneye; Simon
Langham; William Latimer; Robert Linton; Richard Lyons and
Isabella Pledour; John Neville; Henry Lord Percy and Mary Percy;
Alice, Joan, and Jane Perrers (and perhaps Isabella and Joanna);
Janyn Perrers; John Perrers (called "Martin" in the book); John
Salisbury; Nicholas Sardouche; Richard Stury; William Wykeham;
William and John Wyndsor (Windsor)

Mentioned in THE KING'S MISTRESS

Alice's properties

① Ardington
② Crofton
③ Fair Meadow
④ Gaynes
⑤ Radstone
⑥ Southery
⑦ Tibenham

Royal residences

1 Berkhampstead Castle
2 Castle Rising
3 Eltham
4 Havering
5 Hertford Castle
6 King's Langley
7 Queenborough Castle
8 Sheen
9 Windsor Castle

● Extent of properties
managed or held by Alice

★ Cities
■ Royal residences
● Alice's properties

WOODSTOCK
⑤ OXFORD
1
6 5
⑥
4
③
④
9 3
8 LONDON
ISLE OF
SHEPPEY
7

WELLS

② WINCHESTER

N

0 10 20 30 miles
0 10 20 30 40 kilometers

© 2009 Charles Robb

BOOK

I

AN INNOCENT ENCOUNTERS THE WORLD

1

Right as oure firste lettre is now an A,
In beaute first so stood she, makeles.
Hire goodly loking gladed al the prees.
Nas nevere yet seyn thyng to ben preysed derre,
Nor under cloude blak so bright a sterre

—Geoffrey Chaucer, *Troilus and Criseyde*, I, 171–75

WHEN HAD I *a choice to be other than I was? Should I have been more selfish, more stubborn, more rebellious? Have I been too compliant, too quick to give the men in my life what they thought they wanted? Am I a fallen woman, or am I an obedient handmaiden? As a female I was acceptable only as a virginal daughter, a wife, or a widow—unless, of course, I took vows. I have been all three— daughter, wife, widow—and one other, mistress.*

My lover is now long dead, and I sense death drawing near for me. I write this for my children, praying that they might understand.

I began my life in a quite acceptable fashion, but the royal family laid such snares in my path that those who would throw the first stone are certain that I can never right myself even now. Yet when had I a choice to be other than I was? This is the argument of my life.

• 1355 •

DURING THE week our parish church of St. Antonin on Watling Street, east of St. Paul's in London, hummed with chantry Masses. Ours had long been a parish of wealthy merchants who worshipped under the stricture of Christ's teaching that it was easier for a camel to go through the eye of a needle than for a rich man to gain the kingdom of God, and so they bequeathed great sums for Masses to be said for their souls after death. The chantry priests were kept busy with almost continuous prayers, for it was an old parish and had buried many wealthy men and their wives, anxious for redemption.

I loved to spend time in St. Antonin's on ordinary days. It was the only place I had permission to go without a companion, a guardian, and I felt safe there. The priests' murmured prayers embraced me, and the familiar paintings and statues of our Savior, His Blessed Mother, and the saints reminded me that as long as I said my prayers and obeyed my elders I need never fear the devil. I was happily naïve, an innocent in the ways of the world.

On Sundays and important feasts the atmosphere of the little church lacked this womblike comfort, for on those days all parishioners except the bedridden attended Mass. The wealthy merchants flaunted their success by parading with their elegantly dressed families, while the gossips made note of any changes in the attendance or indeed in the attendees—a swollen lip, a swollen belly hiding beneath an uncharacteristically voluminous skirt, an outrageously expensive new headdress—so that all observations might be debated and settled after the service and for days to come. I basked in the light of my handsome family on these busier days.

I must have long been aware that on Sundays St. Antonin's was also a marriage market, but with that gift we have as children for ignoring what does not affect or fascinate us I had paid no attention to that aspect of the day. Until it was my turn.

I begin my story with my first appearance as a vendible in that place that was my sanctuary during the week. It was the autumn after my thirteenth birthday.

It had come as no surprise to me that I was expected to wed at a suitable age. I have no memory of a time when I had not understood that as a girl my worth to the family was my marriageability, either to a mortal man or to Christ, and my parents had never spoken of the possibility of my entering a nunnery. Father was a respected member of his guild, a trader in fine cloth and jewels, and a partner in a shipping concern. My marriage should bring him even greater prosperity, or status, or, preferably, both.

I suited my parents' plans. I was pretty, well formed, well behaved, quick witted but not openly opinionated. As presentable as Father's luxury wares. I was willing and eager to be betrothed, believing that my life would only then begin; and the outcome of the Sunday I am about to recount certainly shaped the rest of my life, for good or ill.

That my moon cycle had recently begun had been fair warning to me that my parents would begin to discuss my betrothal to someone of use to the family. But I had not expected them to take action quite so soon. Mother explained to me in her usual chilly wise that I was now of an age to assume my role in the family, to link it with another successful merchant family, and therefore she saw no reason to delay.

"The money we have spent for the grammar school you attend is better spent elsewhere. You shall not return to it."

She did not willingly waste anything, particularly affection, on me, saving that for my brother John, the eldest. Indeed, she had declared her milk used up by nursing him, and before my birth engaged a wet nurse. My two younger siblings had in their turn been handed over to wet nurses, and when weaned we were all cared for by Nan, a servant who saw to our every need with affection and devotion—but she could not entirely make up for Mother's indifference.

Father was my champion. He had insisted on my time at the grammar school, and, unbeknownst to Mother, had also taught me much about the qualities and grades of cloth, as well as how to negotiate a good price and keep accounts. With his encouragement I often hid behind the curtained doorway in our home's undercroft, where he stored and displayed his merchandise, and listened to his negotiations with customers; afterward he would explain his tactics. He seemed to enjoy my precocious suggestions. I enjoyed sharing this secret endeavor with Father and told no one about it, not even my best friend Geoffrey Chaucer.

On that fateful Sunday, I sensed that the household woke holding its collective breath. Father nervously whistled and twice asked Nan the whereabouts of his boots as he paced in the hall. John was ready early and restless as well.

My gown and surcoat had been made for me from Mother's latest castoffs, an azure gown—of escarlatte, the finest wool—and a green surcoat. Unlike her usual instructions to make my gown shapeless, she'd had her maid fit this one to my blooming breasts and slender waist. Nan's hands trembled as she dressed me with the help of another maid, who was also subdued. No doubt they were anxious that Mother should judge my attire satisfactory and not find occasion for an angry outburst.

Although I sat quite still while Nan combed my hair I was aquiver with anxiety. I distracted myself by trying to divine what prosperous merchant Father would favor for me. I knew he would not content himself with the most handsome man with the sweetest temperament, for the goal of my marriage was an alliance of our successful house with another, preferably even grander, one. Nor could I hope for someone my own age.

I had once thought that my best friend Geoffrey might be the one, but his parents had recently sent him off to serve as a page in a noble household. Seeing my disappointment, Father had reminded me that though the Chaucers were sufficiently wealthy and respectable, their son was but thirteen years old. Before he might wed, a young man must have a position or inheritance that could support a household, and Geoffrey had neither.

I was distracted from my brooding when Nan motioned for me to turn around so she might check that all was buttoned and tucked. She clapped her hands as I spun about, but when I turned to face her again I saw that she was crying.

"Nan, what is wrong?"

"You will have a dozen marriage proposals by evening and be wed by Christmas," she cried. "And then I'll not see you again. You'll forget your old Nan."

I hugged her so tightly she squealed and pushed away. "I love you too much to forget you," I said, and meant it with all my heart.

"You will undo all my work," she protested, but I could see that she was well pleased.

As I stepped into the hall my brother John broke off his pacing to stare, then dropped his gaze, swinging his head slightly as if looking for something on the floor.

"What is it?" I asked.

He looked up again, his eyes drawn to my now-flushed face, then my long neck, which was quite bare.

"I hardly know you, dressed so," he mumbled, turning toward Father, who had joined us.

"For pity's sake, Alice, do not bite your lip." Father drew me aside. "You have nothing to fret about. This is your day to revel in your youth and beauty, eh?" He took one of my hands and bowed to it, kissed it, then stepped back to have a good look at me. "God's blood," he swore under his breath. He did not smile, but neither did he frown.

"Do I look beautiful, Father?" I asked, confused by his expression.

"You do indeed. Your mother will be proud of you today. We all will be."

"Now will you tell me who will be watching me most closely as I pray today, Father? I know you have spoken to someone."

He took off his hat and dabbed his forehead, sweating despite the chill in the hall. "You will see him soon enough, Alice, soon enough. Walk meekly and smile sweetly to those who greet you. It will be all the better if there are suitors in reserve, eh?"

He raised his hand to pat my shoulder, as was his wont, but suddenly corrected himself and dropped it. I realized that, like John, he found me changed and somehow untouchable. I felt hot and sick and wanted to flee.

But Mother had just entered the hall from the solar above. She paused at the door with such an air of grace and command that I felt as if I were my five-year-old sister Mary, grimy and underfoot.

"Walk toward me," Mother commanded.

I did so, shivering under her hard scrutiny.

"Turn around."

Again I obeyed as if I were a doll she manipulated from afar.

She sighed. "We have no time to fuss. There is no remedy."

"Margery, what are you saying? Alice looks lovely," Father protested.

"You would think so," Mother said with a withering look at him. "I can only hope that your chosen prey thinks likewise."

Was it possible she was as much in the dark as I regarding Father's choice?

"Come, John, Will." She sighed at my little brother's mussed hair. "Where is Nan? Has she not finished dressing Mary?"

Mother did not look my way again. I stood in the hall, embarrassed and feeling discarded. It was Nan, dear Nan, who saved the day for me.

Placing Mary's dimpled hand in mine, she said, "Tell your sister what you told me, Mary."

As I looked into my little sister's wide eyes, I realized that I was seeing love, admiration, all that I had hoped to see in the eyes of my parents and John.

"You are so beautiful," Mary declared. "I want to look just like you when I grow up."

Tempted to reach down and press the dear child to my heart, I forced myself to be satisfied with a peck on her momentarily clean cheek and a press of her hand.

"Will you walk with me to church, my lady Mary?" I asked, and my heart melted at the delight in her eyes.

"You are beautiful as a spring dawn," Nan whispered. "Your mother does not like to be outshone, while your father has realized his daughter is about to leave his household. Do not judge them for their simple feelings, Alice."

And so I relaxed, once more noticing how soft the escarlatte felt against my skin, how it draped with such a liquid weight and movement that I felt graceful.

I bent to Mary. "Hold your head high, little sister. The Salisbury girls will turn all other heads this morning. You look so pretty in your gown."

Once the family was assembled in the hall I took my cloak from the peg on the wall, but Mother shook her head and handed me one of her own, gray, lined in gris, a fine fur made from the winter hides of squirrels—only the lovely backs. On her it was more of a short cape, but it reached below my knees and felt wonderfully soft and caressing.

"Take it off as you enter the nave," she instructed. "I do not want to have wasted the fine cloth of your robe by hiding it beneath a cloak. I purposed to show that your body is ready for bearing children."

Her words embarrassed me, as if I were about to parade naked through the city. I must have had tears in my eyes, because Father patted me on the shoulder—now sufficiently covered—and whispered that Mother had a headache and did not mean to be curt.

I nodded to Mary and grasped the hand that she offered me. "Let us be gone!" I said with forced cheer.

It fooled Mary, and she giggled and hopped along beside me as I headed toward the door. Will suddenly charged ahead and opened it with a sweeping bow. Now I, too, giggled and was grateful for my younger siblings.

The autumn morning was damp with a river mist that would rise by midday but for the moment made me glad of the gris lining in the cloak. Such a damp, chilly morning usually inspired complaints on my part, but today it was comforting, as if I could be private a little longer. I tried to remind myself that I was merely on display to potential suitors. It might be a year or more before I walked to the church porch to be wed. But I could not shake the sense of stepping off the edge of the world known to me and into a void without boundary, without bottom. I shivered and pulled the cloak tighter round me with my free hand.

Mary still skipped along beside me. I pressed her hand, wondering how often I would see her once I was a wife, how much of her life I would know.

At the church door Nan took the cloak from me and reached for my sister's hand, but I held firm. "She will steady me, won't you, Mary?"

My sister tugged on my hand and nodded with such a gladsome smile that I took heart. Stepping into the nave I felt the reassurance of the familiar. I could not begin to count how many times I had stepped through those doors. The expanse of stone above me seemed to lighten my step.

"Master Janyn Perrers! Good day to you," Father exclaimed.

My heart danced. He was a widower, wealthy and exceedingly handsome, who at one time had been a frequent guest at our table. But he'd not graced our hall in a long while, and I'd imagined he had wed. He was as I remembered—olive skin, dark eyes, and lustrous, curly hair. He had a deep, resonant voice, and his face lit up when he smiled. He wore his elegant clothes with ease. Next to Father, Master Janyn was my ideal man.

"Master John Salisbury. *Benedicite.*" Janyn Perrers bowed. "And Dame Margery." He bowed again, but I noticed that he did not look Mother in the eyes as he did Father. Now he looked my way. "And is this Mistress Alice? Surely this is not the child I last saw playing in your garden? She cannot have blossomed into such a beautiful woman overnight!" His eyes were so friendly that I could not help but smile.

I curtsied to him and was startled by his warm hand suddenly grasping mine. Looking into my eyes as if I were the only person in the nave, he bowed over my hand, brushing it with his lips. I felt myself blush to my fingertips. I could not seem to find my voice but stared at him as he bowed once more to my parents and moved away into the crowd.

"What is he doing here this morning?" Mother hissed at Father. Her head trembled on her delicate neck.

"He occasionally worships here, Margery, you know that."

"Not for a long while."

"That is true. But we spoke the other day and are once more at ease with one another."

"God's blood, if you are planning what I think you are, I'll wring her neck before I let her marry him."

Now I was horribly aware of eyes following us, but could not be certain whether I was the focus of interest or whether it was Mother.

Her pale face was stained with unbecoming splotches of crimson emotion and she held her head so rigidly that her veil shivered like a delicate insect wing.

She would wring my neck before she would let me wed Janyn Perrers? That could not be what she meant. Surely. I did not like my suspicion that Father had not consulted her.

After Mass, the Chaucers paused to greet our family and Geoffrey told me that he had not guessed I could be quite so beautiful as I was that morning. I tried to laugh at his confusing compliment, but managed only a weak smile.

"You look frightened," he said. "Are you?"

"This day is not unfolding as I'd dreamed it would," I said, irritated to feel tears start.

"This will not do," Geoffrey said with a most sympathetic look. "Straighten up and meet the eyes of your fellow parishioners. You are worth all of them." He groaned as his mother's voice intruded, calling him away. "She is worried that we will defy them and pledge our troth."

Other families with eligible young men were now approaching us, and Father proudly introduced each one in turn to me. Many of the young men I already knew, although they behaved toward me quite differently than they had in the past.

BY THE time my family and I walked out into the churchyard the mist had been burned away by a warm midday sun the deep gold of autumn. The sudden brightness blinded me, and I stumbled on the shallow steps leading from the porch. I was caught up and set back on my feet by someone with strong arms yet a gentle touch.

"God bless you," I said, a bit breathlessly as I smoothed out my gown with one hand, shading my eyes with the other. I discovered my savior was Janyn Perrers.

But I doubt he heard me, for Mother had already pulled him to one side and was berating him in an angry whisper. I did not rush to his defense, for fear of her reaction.

Father said something beneath his breath to Nan and she called to her four charges, hurrying us across the square to our house.

John heaved a loud sigh as we stepped into the hall. "Whatever upset her, Mother will be testy for the remainder of the day."

Will started toward the garden door, but Nan pulled him back, tidying his wild hair.

"Let us quietly await your parents," she said.

Mary fought back tears. "Why is Mother so angry?"

I hugged her and promised it would prove to be nothing.

When Mother and Father arrived, they were hissing at each other, faces flushed with emotion. Inside the door Father grabbed Mother's elbow and roughly pulled her closer to have the last word. She snatched her arm from him, gathered her skirts, and rushed out again. I could hear her stumble up the outer stairs to the solar. The boards creaked overhead.

With a tug at his clothes and a twist of his neck, as if to ease it, Father affected calm as he joined us.

"Your mother took offense at Master Janyn Perrers's behavior. She did not realize he had saved you from a nasty tumble, Alice, and chided him for being so rude as to touch you, a young girl. It is most unfortunate, for he is to dine with us today and your mother is now too shamed by her discourtesy to join us. She believes we will all be more at ease with you presiding over the table as mistress of the house."

Though I felt uneasy about his lie I could think of nothing to say but, "Yes, Father."

It was a strange and most uncomfortable afternoon. In celebration of the lovely weather, Cook and Nan had set up a trestle table by the door to our small courtyard. The flowers were all spent, but as the sun warmed the plants their fragrances mingled with the delicious smells on the table. It would have been delightful—but Mother loomed large in her absence. I did not feel prepared to play hostess in her place. I was not the only one discomfited. Father was too loud and jovial. Janyn's parents, Master Martin and Dame Tommasa Perrers, were plainly ill at ease.

But not Master Janyn. He was as charming as he had always been in our home.

Will and Mary had been bustled off to the kitchen with Nan, and a part of me yearned to be in there with them, at ease and at peace. I felt as if all that was familiar and reassuring had been packed in a cart that was pulling away too fast, much too fast, and I wanted to protest that I must have it all back at once, all in place, all as usual.

But Master Janyn made certain that I did not feel that way for long. While the other adults talked in stilted courtesy to one another, he entertained John and me with stories of his travels to Lombardy, Naples, Calais, Bruges. I found myself doubting Mother's suspicion that he meant to wed me, for he knew so much of the world, he was about twenty years my senior and so grand he could not possibly want a child like me to be hostess in his home.

And yet . . . from time to time he would look at me with a curious expression, as if wondering about me, perhaps trying me out in different settings or different clothes. He inquired as to my preferences—colors, foods, even feast days—and listened with such concentration that he several times echoed my exact words to himself, as if determined to remember them. After an account of a journey or some other event he would glance at me as if gauging whether or not it had been to my liking. He did not treat John in such wise. I believed it to be the behavior of a man paying court.

At some point the dinner was over, and I was at last at the door of the hall bidding our guests farewell. Dame Tommasa touched my cheek and said that she hoped to see me again very soon. Master Martin was deep in discussion with Father about reports of a mutual friend's ship lost in the Channel. Master Janyn took both my hands in his and looked deep into my eyes. He was much taller than I was, but in that moment I felt as if our eyes were so close I might feel his lashes if he blinked. His skin was warm to the touch, and he smelled very pleasant. But he seemed too much a man, too knowing and strong, too able to bend me to his will. If we were to wed my life would be swallowed up by his. Alice would be no more. I wanted to tell him to go away and not return, and at the same time wanted him to lean closer and kiss me on the lips. As the thought occurred I felt myself blush.

Janyn smiled, and for a moment looked quite mischievous, which suited his face. "I believe you have stolen my heart, Mistress Alice. I pray you be gentle with it." He kissed my hands, each in turn, and then bowed and let go of me.

I was terrified and thrilled. After our guests had departed, Father asked me how I liked Master Janyn.

I hesitated. "He is so much grander than I am. Such a man of the world," I began.

"Ah, so he did not please you." He shook his head at the sound of Mother moving about up in the solar. "Has she poisoned you against him? Did she say aught to you before he arrived?"

"I *do* like him," I protested.

But he did not seem to be listening. In spirit he was already continuing his argument with Mother. I had been depleted by the effort of playing hostess without preparation, and felt like a pawn in a chess game, unimportant, simple to move, easy to lose.

"She said nothing to me after church," I added, and, muttering some excuse, fled to the kitchen, seeking Nan.

I lay in bed that night comparing my previous night's fantasy about my morning at Mass with the actual experience, and thought with a sinking heart that I had just tasted the true flavor of adulthood and found it sour where I had expected it to be sweet.

THE HOUSEHOLD was subdued for days, Mother in her room, Father and my brother John avoiding any mention of Sunday's events, and on the next Sunday Master Janyn was not at St. Antonin's. Again after Mass families with unmarried sons and a few widowers approached us for introductions. Father was friendly, Mother brusque, and they invited no guests to dinner that day.

Over the next few weeks Mother behaved for the most part as if I'd ceased to exist, casting a powerful spell over me. What was worse, I had been withdrawn from school just as she'd said, which deprived me of absorbing occupation. I lost all appetite and kept to myself more and more. I had no place, being neither a child nor a bride-to-be, caught in the void in between.

Then at last one spring day Father asked me to join him in the undercroft after dinner. He said he would be entertaining some important customers and would like me to look my best. I felt as if someone had lit a candle inside me, the warmth and light filling me and inviting me back to life. I had been weeding the kitchen garden and was suddenly acutely aware of how soiled were my hands and even my face. I asked my little brother, Will, to look after Mary for a while so that Nan might help me clean myself and put on my azure gown and green surcoat.

My old nurse shook her head over how loosely the gown now fit, and how pale I looked despite the sunny weather we had been enjoying.

"You are too much in church, child."

"Or I have finally spent enough time there, Nan, for my prayers have been answered. Father has forgiven me."

"For what?"

I shrugged. "It no longer matters."

By her muttering and jerky movements I understood that it still mattered to her, a great deal. She had been quietly fuming about my parents' treatment of me for a long while.

I T WAS cool in the undercroft, and I held my cupped hands close to an oil lamp as I waited for Father to finish instructing his clerk about how to display the cloth and ornaments he wished to show the customers. I had offered to arrange for wine and a little food for the guests, but the clerk had told me that he would see to that, as he always did.

"You will be surprised, I think," Father said to me as the clerk greeted the customers, "and I very much hope delighted to see who is here." His face was bright with anticipation.

There were stacks of barrels between the doorway and the area in which Father showed his merchandise, so I recognized his voice before I saw him. My heartbeat quickened, and I had an urge to flee, though not to avoid him, but rather because I felt as if I were being swept up into a great wave that would carry me far from the familiar earth, an inexorable wave over which I had no control.

"Father, is it Master Janyn Perrers?"

"So you remember his voice. That is a good sign, I think. You did say you liked him."

He *had* heard me that day.

"*Are* you pleased?"

"I do not know what to think," I admitted. This was no way to win Mother's affection, I thought.

But it was too late to say more. The small space was suddenly filled by Master Janyn and his father. I was glad of the shadows the men cast in the lamp-lit chamber, because I could take advantage of my familiarity with the room and feel less exposed, less readable. I did not want Master Janyn to see how I blushed beneath his direct gaze, nor how difficult I found it to look away from him.

In truth, I was his even before he asked for my hand.

Janyn's father, Master Martin, bowed to Father and me and asked after my health.

Again I felt myself blush as I replied that I was very well. His question embarrassed me. I assumed he had noticed how my clothes hung on my diminished frame. I wished I did not look so gaunt that it was the first thing on which he commented. It would not recommend me as a future wife to his son.

"I thank God that you have fully recovered," he said. "Dame Tommasa will also be gladdened by this news."

I must have looked as confused as I felt, for Father coughed and shook his head at me, a sign for me to let it pass. He then drew both men over to the display of cloth.

I did not join them right away, trying to think why Master Martin thought that I had been ill if it were not for my present appearance— for he implied that his wife had also been worried for my health. I could find nothing that made more sense than that Father had lied to them about my health, easily done since they were not in our parish and, in truth, I did look as if I'd been ill. The only reason I could think he would do that was as an excuse for having avoided them and in such wise appeasing Mother, who so disliked Master Janyn.

Yet here they were today, in our undercroft, invited by Father. I prayed this meant that Mother had agreed to look on Master Janyn with charity. It was hardly something she would confide to me. My spirits lifted once more as I considered the possibility of being betrothed to Janyn Perrers. I would want for nothing and have the most handsome, elegant husband. Noticing Father glancing my way I joined him and his guests. They were discussing the cloth Father had displayed, and some others that the clerk had fetched. One fabric looked as if it had been painted, gold stars and silver crescent moons against a dark color, almost black.

I ran my hand over it to feel whether the gold-and-silver pattern stood out, but it seemed part of the fabric.

"Is this not a fantastical cloth?" Father said to me.

I nodded. No more fantastical than the thought of my being Janyn Perrers's wife, I thought.

"I do not know why I purchased this," Father said, "for it is so strange. But I found it beautiful, and willfully ignored my misgivings."

Master Martin brushed beringed fingers across the fabric, then lifted it, feeling its weight. As he set it back down he said, "It is very fine, John. My wife would tell me to buy it."

Janyn chuckled. "Yes, she would."

Father shook his head. "Where might she wear such cloth without censure from all in the parish?"

"Here in London she would wear it only in our home," said Master

Martin with a little shrug, tapping the cloth lightly with one finger. "But in Lombardy she might wear a gown of such stuff at market, at feasts. Or line a cloak with it."

I lifted a corner of the cloth and gently rubbed it between my fingers. It was silky and had a rich heft. I could imagine it as a surcoat over a dark, or perhaps a gold, gown. "Dame Tommasa must miss her homeland very much then," I said. "I should like to see a city where one could wear such a beautiful robe to market."

Master Martin grinned broadly. "Perhaps you *shall* see such a city, Mistress Alice. What do you think—shall I buy enough for the lining of a cloak? Or a gown?"

"Or a surcoat," I said, feeling quite bold in revealing that I had considered what use I would make of it.

"Ah." He nodded. "With what color gown beneath?"

I hesitated, looking to Father for permission to continue. He nodded his encouragement. Indeed, he appeared pleased with me.

"A dark gold?" I suggested. "Or something even darker."

"You have a talent for this," said Master Martin. "That is good. Very good." I was grateful for the thorough education Father had provided me in the cloth trade.

Master Martin glanced at his son, who was watching me with his usual intensity.

"Which of these would you choose for my mother?" he asked me. He held up two gold cloths, one a much deeper shade than the other, almost a brown yet with the whisper of gold, the promise of light.

I pointed to that one. He turned to Father. "Mistress Alice has inspired me to make a gift of her choices to Mother. Let us discuss the measures later."

"Perhaps it is time that we sat and discussed the true purpose of your visit," said Father. "Alice," he took my arm, "come sit beside me." He gave me a little tug and at last I looked away from Master Janyn.

My heart raced as we took our seats, and I felt a new sensation along my skin as if my body were awakening from a deep slumber. If this was love, I had never loved Geoffrey.

"Alice, Master Janyn Perrers has approached me about taking you to be his wife," Father began, though it felt as if it were the end of his speech.

So here it was, the moment I'd dreamed of. Yet now that it was here I was frightened. I was not ready. Why was Mother not here? I did not dare ask, though the question burned in my throat.

"He is a good man with everything to recommend him, but a betrothal is not blessed by the Church unless both the man and woman agree to it. What say you, Alice? Would you be the wife of this man?"

I felt ill prepared. Though they had made much of finding me a good husband they had said little of what marriage entailed, and my still-unanswered questions as well as freshly inspired ones crowded my mind. *Might I have time to think about this, Father? Will loving someone in the way I believe I love him rob me of my soul? Has he said that he loves me? What happens between a man and a woman?*

"Daughter, I am owed an answer." Father's voice held a note of irritation, though he forced a smile, patting my hand. "Were you not aware that Master Janyn was honoring you with his interest?"

I looked at each man in turn. Janyn's eyes were quiet now, not drawing me in, but observing. He did not seem overly concerned about the outcome. Master Martin looked puzzled. Father looked worried and annoyed. I had no counsel, no confidant in the chamber. And it was clear that I was expected to choose now. I fell back on my obedience as a daughter.

"If you so wish it, I should be honored to be Master Janyn's wife, Father," I said.

I felt everyone at the table take a deep breath and the tension recede.

"God has blessed me this day," said Janyn in a voice taut with emotion.

"Dame Tommasa will be so happy," said Master Martin. "May God grant the two of you a blessed and fruitful life together."

"I pray that I please you in all ways," I murmured.

Father smiled. I noticed a slight tremor in his hands as he raised his cup to toast the betrothal.

I was to be Alice *Perrers,* beloved of the beautiful man who sat across from me; *Dame* Alice, mistress of his household.

"Might I kiss my betrothed?" Janyn asked.

Oh sweet heaven, I was suddenly overwhelmed by shyness and prayed Father would deny him.

Master Martin clapped his hands together. "But of course you may, eh, my friend?" He winked at Father.

I clutched Father's hand. He patted mine.

"A most appropriate seal," he said.

Janyn was rising, his lithe body moving away from his side of the table. He held out a hand to me. A large, elegant hand. I rose, stumbling a little, and he gently held me steady as we moved toward each other. He was tall, so tall. I stood on tiptoe; he bowed his head and gathered me to him, lifting me off my feet. His lips—wine and figs, I tasted. Oh dear God what sin was in that kiss. I rested my hands on his shoulders, savoring the sensations. When he set me gently on the floor again I thought I would faint. I could not imagine ever moving of my own volition again. But I steadied myself and stood, and hand in hand we faced our fathers. Looking at mine, I had a moment of misgiving. He looked lost, frightened. Meeting my gaze, he quickly forced a smile. But I had seen, I had seen.

"May all joy be yours, dear Alice, dear Janyn," he said.

"I pray God that I deserve such joy as I feel at this moment," said Janyn. "I pledge my troth to this most beautiful woman, Alice Salisbury."

Father nodded to me. "And you, daughter, you must pledge as well."

"I pledge my troth to Master Janyn Perrers," I said, embarrassed by how breathless I sounded.

Janyn squeezed my hand. "Not Master, sweet Alice. I am Janyn to you now."

WHEN WE were alone again, even the clerk having departed, Father and I sat quietly lost in our own thoughts. I bowed my head over my hands and inhaled the scent of my betrothed. Heaven must smell so.

"Look now, Alice, we must proceed with care."

I was pulled from my happy reverie by Father's serious tone, such a dramatic shift from moments ago. He frowned down at the table, playing with his mazer of wine, pushing it back and forth between his hands.

"Why, Father?"

"Your mother . . ."

I dared to ask, "Why was she not here?" When he did not answer at once, I guessed, "She does not know of this."

He shook his head.

"She will not be happy about it."

"No."

"The Perrers are respected, wealthy—why would she disapprove?"

He sighed and wiped his brow. "You are too young to understand."

I could not hide my feeling of frustration with his refusal to be honest with me. "Not so young as to have missed her words in church the day I first wore this robe. She said she would strangle me before she'd see me wed Janyn. What enmity is there between them?"

He looked stunned for a moment, then angry. "You heard that?"

"I did. She spoke it so that I would hear. Why would she threaten such violence, Father?"

"You never said a word."

"Nor did you." I held his gaze, imploring him to explain his silence, to apologize, to reassure me.

"Your mother says much that she does not mean, Alice."

"What does she hold against Janyn? I deserve to know, Father."

He opened his mouth as if to speak, then closed it and shook his head, dropping his gaze, as if in shame or confusion. "You know that he is a widower. She did not like his wife. That is all."

I did not believe him. "Father, tell me what Mother dislikes about Janyn."

"She dislikes nothing about him. I swear to you, daughter. And that is all that I can say about the matter."

"Why do you still push us together?"

"I will not have your mother ruin your happiness."

"He is not the only marriageable man in London. Though I do like him above all other men, I could find happiness with another." I did not believe that, but Father's behavior frightened me. "Someone who will not turn my own mother against me." Not that I had ever enjoyed her favor. But suddenly the thought of her hating me was too awful, too final. "I beg you, Father."

Now he looked me in the eye with a temper I had rarely witnessed. "I will *not* bend to her will," he growled. "You have pledged your troth to Janyn Perrers, made a binding contract, and you *shall* wed him. I'll hear no more argument."

Never had my father spoken so to me. I was dumbstruck. I had already felt depleted by the emotions I'd experienced while Janyn and his father were present, and this took away what little spirit I'd had left.

"Such dissembling. . . . It frightens me, Father. Why are you so desperate that I marry Janyn Perrers?"

"Desperate?" He shook his head. "You are wrong in judging me so, Alice. Janyn will be good to you. He is a kind, gentle man, as is his father. You will thank me for insisting on this union."

He did not hug me. He did not ask whether he had reassured me. He merely instructed me to remain silent about this meeting until he had told Mother of my betrothal.

When I left the undercroft I was surprised to feel the heat of the afternoon after the dim, chilly interior. I took Mary for a long walk. Listening to her happy chatter was a soothing balm.

I slept little that night, lying awake for what seemed hours, keenly aware of how suddenly precious my siblings and Nan were to me, how I would miss them. Yet I thrilled at the mere thought of Janyn, of our kiss. When I finally slept my dreams woke me with a yearning for him that I did not understand.

WITHIN A few days I received an invitation to dine at the home of Martin and Tommasa Perrers. It was most welcome, for the secrecy surrounding my betrothal had been so complete that sometimes I feared I'd merely dreamt the meeting in the undercroft. For his part, Father looked almost faint with relief that only he and I had been in the hall when the messenger arrived, though he assured me that he was ready to tell Mother of my betrothal. I dreaded that moment, and yet I also yearned to have it behind me.

The next day Father presented Mother with a cloak of pers as blue as her eyes, lined with miniver, a cloak so warm and soft that she chirped with delight when she tried it on and declared that now she could not wait for the first snow. The cloak fastened with a silver clasp made to look like delicate wings. I had never seen one so beautiful, and Mother only added to its beauty. My father watched her with a yearning that seemed almost sorrowful as she proceeded around the hall, spinning every few steps to reveal the full cut and the pretty lining. She was sweet to all of us at the table that afternoon. Seeing Mary's and Will's joy in her mood, I lost what little appetite I'd had, for I guessed that Father's announcement at the end of the meal would bring on a storm.

But at the moment I had expected him to call for a toast and announce my betrothal to the whole family, Father rose from the table and, bowing to Mother, held out his hand to her. "My love, will you step out into the garden with me?"

She smiled at his grand gesture and rose, accepting his hand, and they swept out the garden door.

Nan gathered the little ones and took them to the kitchen. The previous night, needing to tell someone before I burst, I shared with her what had transpired in the undercroft and about the invitation to dine at the Perrers' home. She, too, expected a storm.

Both John and I paced the hall awaiting the next act. When at last our parents returned, Mother's face was as white as alabaster and Father's blotched with temper. As she fled past me to the door leading to the solar stairs she glanced at me and I saw tears just starting to spill down her cheeks. She opened her eyes wide and appeared to be about to say something, but then pressed a hand to her mouth and hurried out.

"I did not think her good spirits would last," John said with a smirk.

Father turned on him. "Be quiet, you young fool!"

Later that day Father went out and returned after a while with Janyn, who presented me with a beautiful piece of escarlatte, a deep gold, he said, to match my eyes. Our hands touched as I took the gift, and I felt a jolt as if I had been struck by lightning.

"You honor me with this gift," I said, blushing as I bowed to him.

"As I am honored to have you accept my love, Alice," he said. Leaning close, he whispered, "I have not forgotten our kiss."

"Nor have I . . . Janyn," I whispered, my heart pounding.

We stood for a moment, smiling into each other's eyes.

John and Mother were called to toast us. Mother obeyed, looking hideously white and without spirit. My brother beamed and seemed genuinely happy for me. Father found it difficult to sustain a cheerful mien, losing all light from his face with each glance at Mother.

And so was my betrothal made known.

2

"And I to ben youre—verray, humble, trewe,
Secret, and in my paynes pacient,
And evere mo desiren fresshly newe
To serve, and ben ylike diligent,
And with good herte al holly youre talent
Receyven wel, how sore that me smerte;
Lo, this mene I, myn owen swete herte."

—Troilus to Criseyde, GEOFFREY CHAUCER,
Troilus and Criseyde, III, 141–47

• 1356 •

I HAD WICKEDLY prayed that Mother would refuse to accept the
Perrers' invitation to dine, but she was dressed in her finest gown
and cloak and waiting in the hall for me when I emerged from
Nan's ministrations. My best gown, now so loose fitting, did not feel
very special compared with Mother's.

Although I did not expect an answer, I asked her how old she had
been when she wed Father. I would turn fourteen in September.

"I was too young," she said in a low voice, without emotion. Although she had obviously taken great pains with her dressing, she was
not restless with excitement as usual when about to dine at someone's
home. For the first time in a long while she looked me in the eye. "Do
you think you are ready to be a wife, Alice?"

"How would I know, Mother?"

But she was gazing past me, and I realized that Father had joined us.

"She is ready, Margery," he said.

Mother's expression was cold. "What would a man know of that?"

Father put a hand beneath my elbow and smiled encouragement
as he led me to the door. "Come, Alice. I cannot wait to see your face
when you see how grand a home you shall have when you are wed."

When you are wed. Those words thrilled me far more than the
thought of having a grand home. I had seldom been in the abodes of

any but my own kin, and they were all much alike, suggesting prosperity without peacockery, their owners mindful of their good names,
aspiring to hold civic offices such as guild master, bailiff, alderman,
mayor. Even the Chaucer household was similar to ours. I was unpre-
pared for the home of Martin and Tommasa Perrers.

It was in a wealthier neighborhood than ours, closer to London
Bridge, all the houses larger. Dame Tommasa welcomed us at the door,
something Mother never did as she deemed it more seemly to have a
servant show guests into the hall. With a cry of pleasure Dame Tommasa folded me to her bosom, then held me at arm's length and said,
"Welcome to our family, Alice. You will be as a daughter to me." She
kissed me on the forehead, and then stepped aside to allow me to pass,
the gesture stirring the sleeve of her overdress. As it caught the light, I
saw with delight the gold stars and silver moons.

I felt as if I were stepping into a dream. The colors dazzled my
eyes as did the brightness of the hall, lit by so many lamps and wall
sconces that it was almost like daylight. Tapestries and painted cloths
festooned the walls, patterned and embroidered fabrics covered all the
furnishings. My eyes were drawn from one beautiful item to another
until I was dizzy.

Master Martin, his kind face alight with welcome, took my hand.
"My dear Alice, you are a vision of beauty."

I must have responded, but I cannot recall what I said for all my
attention was now on Janyn, who approached us with a welcoming
smile.

"My beloved Alice," Janyn said, taking my hands and kissing each
one, then looking deep into my eyes. I wished he would enfold me in
his arms as his mother had. But of course he continued on to greet my
parents.

I was not so absorbed in him that I forgot to watch how he and
Mother greeted each other. My parents stood just inside the door,
Father holding Mother's hand, his wide, beautifully draping sleeves
revealing a slight tremor. I guessed that he was tightly clutching her
hand to prevent her from making any ill-advised movement.

Janyn stopped a few strides from them, crossed his hands over his
heart, and bowed to Mother. "Dame Margery," he said. "Welcome."

She blushed, her blood providing the hint of color she so desperately needed, and bowed her head. "Master Janyn."

She tried to meet his gaze, but he avoided hers, having already turned to greet Father. I had never seen my mother look so vulnerable, so uncertain.

Janyn reached out with both hands to Father, and they clasped each other's forearms, bowing and then exchanging friendly greetings. They appeared to be quite comfortable together.

Mother struck up a stiff but cordial conversation with Master Martin.

Before the round of greetings could lag, Dame Tommasa swept us all over to a table laden with food. It sat in front of double doors that stood open to a courtyard crossed and criss-crossed with beds brimming with blossoming plants. Roses and flowering vines, many of varieties I did not recognize, climbed and twisted over small arbors and low walls, creating a display as colorful as that in the hall.

I sensed Janyn beside me. "Shall we walk in the garden a moment?" he suggested.

"Oh yes, please! But your mother—"

"The others will not begrudge us a moment of peace." He offered his arm, and I put my hand on it. My heart pounding wildly, I stepped onto the gravel path with my betrothed.

"You must love this house," I said, "so full of light and color. So beautiful."

"I have happy memories of this home," he said. "And I still often dine here with my parents. But you must know that I no longer live here."

I had forgotten, but I did not like to admit that, so I asked, "Do you live nearby?"

"My house is farther down toward the river, between the grand Coldharbour and London Bridge." A very fine location. "I shall ask your father to bring you there, so that you might see it. After all, it will soon be your home as well." He had led me to a far corner, to a bench beneath an apple tree in bloom.

As I sat, I withdrew my hand to spread my skirts but also to hide the cold that I had felt seep into me, thinking of living in Janyn's home with him. I had become part stranger to myself, one moment wanting to cling to him, the next my stomach fluttering at the thought of leaving my family home and living with him. I took a deep breath and looked around, distracting myself by trying to name the plants I knew.

Janyn had settled slightly sideways, so that he could face me. "I am as ill at ease as you are, Alice. Would it not be more pleasant if we had found one another by chance? It is difficult to feel comfortable when there are such expectations."

I liked that he had noticed my unease and did not pretend he had not. "Yes. I feel as if the others are holding their breath and watching us while pretending to ignore us."

We both laughed, then averted our eyes as if we had become too familiar too quickly.

"You do know that I am a widower?" he asked. "That I was married before, and that my wife died?"

"Yes, I do."

Daring to look at him, I found him watching me with furrowed brow as if trying to understand what I felt. I wanted to reassure him, but I could not think what to say.

He took my hand, putting his other over it in a protective gesture.

"I begin life anew with you, Alice. Whatever you wish to change in our homes so that they are more to your taste and more comfortable for you, you must do so. I want only your happiness."

I knew nothing of how to choose furnishings for a home, even less how to make one look like this beautiful place in which he'd been raised. Nor had I ever planned a garden such as this. But I did not want to disappoint him by expressing my doubts.

"Did you say 'homes'?" I asked. It was the first safe, practical question that came to mind, and I did so want to keep him talking. "You have more than one?"

He grinned, his eyes lighting up. I did so like to make them do that. "Yes. I have one in the city and one in the country less than half a day's ride away. Do you like the country?"

"I do not recall ever having been beyond Smithfield. I have always lived in the city." I studied a spider spinning a web on the corner of the arbor, not wishing to see Janyn begin to understand how young and dull I was.

"Then this shall be an adventure for you," he said. "Do you like riding? Have you a favorite place to ride?"

I wished he would stop asking so many questions. "I have never ridden a horse, or even a pony." The spider had caught a breeze and was swinging out to catch a tiny flying insect, but he missed.

"You shall have a gentle mare to begin, and you shall have lessons as soon as possible. Unless you do not wish to learn?"

I glanced up to see if he was serious. He certainly looked as if he was. "Oh, but I *do* want to learn to ride. Horses are so beautiful, so powerful. My brother John rode with Father on several journeys this past year. He looked so grand on horseback. He said that outside the city there were fields on every side, as far as he could see, and then dense woodland that could be dark as night in the middle of the day."

Janyn was smiling, but not in such a way as to make me feel foolish to have prattled on. "I thought you would like animals, and the country," he said. "I look forward to riding out to the manor by your side, watching you see the land and the house for the first time."

"I had not imagined we would live both in the city and the country," I said, trying out the *we would live* to see how it sounded aloud. It sounded very fine. Indeed, marriage promised to be more of an adventure than I had ever hoped to experience, being a girl. I was framing a question about what other animals Janyn had when his father stepped into the courtyard.

"Janyn, Mistress Alice, Dame Tommasa understands how pleasant it is to sit and talk in the garden, but she has prepared a feast and will be disappointed if you do not join us at once." Master Martin's broad grin and wink underscored the humor and lightness of his message, and I felt an upwelling of gratitude that he was to be my father-in-law. He patted me on the back as Janyn and I proceeded with him to the laden table, and I felt welcomed into the family.

I learned that day that like many London families the Perrers had continued the tradition of mixing English and foreign blood and connections. Janyn had a younger brother who resided in a monastery in Lombardy and a sister wed to a Lombard merchant—she lived in Milan. I wondered whether Janyn and I would travel to Lombardy to visit his siblings. Perhaps I would see the splendid market where Dame Tommasa might wear her fabulous overdress of gold stars and silver moons.

The meal was as colorful as everything else in the Perrers household, and my appetite returned. Dame Tommasa saw to it that my wine was well watered. I was grateful, for with her help I enjoyed the occasion and did not make a fool of myself in any way. Mother picked at her food and said little, but Father was expansive, talking of a shipment of rare spices expected any day. Dame Tommasa asked me about myself in an easy way, already showing more warmth toward me and more interest than my own mother ever had. Janyn discussed with her a mare for me—she knew of someone who wished to sell a horse that might do very well. My brother John teased me, certain that I would

be timid approaching a horse as tall as myself for the first time, and
Master Martin Perrers swore that I would prove my brother wrong.

As I departed that evening, Janyn kissed my hands. I floated home
on winged feet.

IT WAS the beginning of a new, exciting life for me. The next morning I accompanied Janyn and my brother John to see the mare.
Janyn coaxed her to face me so that I might see how sweet she looked,
how she responded to a gentle touch. With him guiding me, I stroked
her face and then her neck, and suddenly I was being lifted up to sit
sideways on her. It was only for a moment. Lifting me down again,
he let his lips brush my cheek and forehead. Oh sweet Mary, Mother
of God, was this how it felt to be the beloved of God? I crossed myself, realizing the blasphemy of that thought, and my brother laughed,
thinking I protected myself against the mare.

Mother saw to it that I was brought back to earth as soon as I
returned home. She had said nothing to me after the dinner at the Perrers home. Nothing. And when John and I spoke of the mare at dinner she loudly embarked on a tale of her walk to the market that day,
and what she planned to change in the garden. When Father did not
rebuke her I ached, deep inside, and imagined my icy hands shattering
against the table as I pressed it in rising.

Several days later I learned that the mare was now mine, and,
though Janyn would be away for a while on business, my lessons would
begin as soon as my parents could take me to the stables near Smithfield. My heart sank at the news of Janyn's absence but soared when
Father added that the wedding was set for late October.

Mother said—to him, not to me, "Your mother has offered to help
Alice prepare. To do this with ease, she suggested that Alice stay with
her until the wedding. I told her that was quite suitable."

I almost choked on the ale in my mouth, and looked to Father for
an angry response.

But he nodded. "It will work very well for all concerned if Alice
lives with her until the wedding." He spoke in an oddly soft voice and
avoided looking my way.

Little Mary cried out, "I want to go with her!"

"Grandmother should come here," said Will, banging his fist on
the table.

I would have laughed at my little brother's imperious declaration

were I not in shock. To leave so soon! Even John asked why Grandmother or I could not walk from one house to the other, we lived so
close.

But Father said, "It is already decided." From the set of his jaw I
read that to be the last word on the subject.

I N THE morning I lay in bed hoping I had only dreamed of my exile,
but I had just pushed back the covers and touched my feet to the
floorboards when Nan bustled in.

"I'm relieved to see you already rising," she said. "I've left Will and
Mary in the hall while I help you gather your things. I dare not leave
them long."

"I'm to go at once? Before breaking my fast?" I cried, still too
sleepy to check my despair.

Nan looked up from the chest she had opened. "Oh, my sweet
Alice. No, of course you are not being sent away without food. The
master awaits you in the hall. I trow he hopes to assure you that he
thought you would *enjoy* spending this time with your grandmother.
He told me Dame Agnes wished to do this for you, to have pretty
gowns made for you and to provide a welcoming hall to which your
betrothed might come to be with you."

"Because he is not welcome here. Are you certain that you do not
know why Mother hates Janyn so?"

"To understand your mother"—Nan shook out my second best
gown with more force than necessary—"I do not wish to try that. I
imagine spiders in her mind." Realizing what she had said about her
mistress, she crossed herself and asked me to forget her comment. "I
am angry with her for frightening you and behaving as if she does not
love you. But she is beset by devils, Alice. You are the victim, not the
cause, of her poor mothering. How much happier you will be with
Dame Agnes, eh?"

"But I won't have you and Mary and Will, or even John or Father
there."

That won me a sympathetic embrace and kiss.

"No, we cannot all go with you, my sweet." The affection in Nan's
eyes calmed me a little.

"Will you visit?"

"I believe the master will visit you with your sister and brothers."

"And you?"

"You will see me, I promise, even if I come by myself."

I gave her a grateful hug.

It was not the prospect of biding with my Salisbury grandparents that pained me. Although we had spent little time alone together, I enjoyed Grandmother, and she seemed genuinely to enjoy my presence. She was a handsome woman, tall and strong, and I admired the way she dominated any room she entered. Mother was beautiful in a soft, pretty way, and people always wanted to make her smile and to fetch and carry for her; Grandmother was elegant rather than beautiful, and there was about her an authority and wisdom that inspired people to respect her and seek her advice. She could, however, be unexpectedly critical. Indeed, her sharp honesty often stung. Still, she was one of my favorite adults. And Grandfather Edmund as well, who was kind and gentle. I was grateful to be invited to bide with them.

But it hurt to be rushed off as if Mother could not rid herself of me quickly enough. And Father—a few days earlier he'd said that when I wed he would miss the easy companionship we enjoyed, yet now he, too, was pushing me out the door.

I resolved to make the best of it as I joined Father and my siblings in the hall for bread, cheese, and thick ale. But my fortitude was tested at once as Mary began to cry and Will declared he had no appetite. Only John expressed envy.

"Our grandparents will give you all you desire," he said. "I must work for my keep."

"I would not mind working," I said. "If you have no work, the day is too long."

John laughed. "You will soon be so busy at night you will be sleeping all the day," he said.

"John!" Father barked, his face flushed with irritation. "I will not have you speaking so at my table."

Though he dropped his head and muttered an apology to Father, me, and Nan, John was smirking. I was sitting at just the right angle to see that. I hated that he noticed my blush when he glanced my way and mimed a kiss.

But he was my brother, and I knew that this familiarity would fade once we were no longer together day in and day out. And I would miss it.

Too soon Father rose from the table and said that we must depart.

Mary burst into tears again and I held her so tightly she squirmed a little, but when I began to release her she clung to me.

"Don't go!" she wailed.

I lifted her and sat back down on the bench, blotting her tears with the hem of my gown.

"I love you, Mary, and I wish you could come with me. But you need Nan, and she cannot come bide there as well and abandon Will—don't you see? I would have been leaving in a few months anyway, this is just a little sooner." I was babbling, but she had stopped crying, and when she began to hiccup I managed to make her laugh about it. Will joined in our laughter. "You see? Nothing has changed, we are all still as silly as ever!"

Mary clapped her hands with glee. I gently slid her off my lap and rose, brushing my skirt. I felt strangely mature, having taken on the role of mediator. How quickly I was shedding my childhood. I had no time to panic, for Father nodded to me and we hurried out, a servant following with my belongings.

As we crossed the square I asked if I might stop in the church to say a prayer to the Blessed Virgin.

Father sighed with impatience. "I have customers to see today, Alice. We cannot linger. Perhaps my parents will accompany you to church later." He reached for my hand.

I moved beyond his reach and stopped, forcing him to turn back to see what had happened.

"You are eager to rid yourself of me," I said. I had intended to hold my tongue, but his refusal to pause at the church was too much. "I won Janyn, as you wished, and now I am punished. Why?"

He glanced around to see who might overhear. Apparently he saw no one significant, because he did not chide me or say he could not answer that. "I pray you, daughter, believe me that I do this to afford you more ease so that you might enjoy preparing for your wedding. I wish you nothing but joy, my child."

"This was not Mother's wish?"

Father lifted his open hands, palms up, and slumped a little, his expression a mixture of great weariness and sorrow. "You have asked why she is so angry. She is angry with life, Alice, not you. She needs your prayers."

I was young, I was in pain, I was frightened, and his answer sounded like dissimulation, not honesty. But I did not challenge him.

"Come," I said, "my grandparents await me." I resumed walking, and Father fell in beside me. I could almost taste his defeat, and loathed him for it. I was raw with emotions I only vaguely understood.

Grandfather greeted us, and then sent me out to the garden to find Grandmother while he spoke to Father.

I found Dame Agnes, as she liked me to call her, kneeling in the kitchen garden separating seedlings. She enjoyed seeing to her own garden. "Hands that know the earth in all its moods know God's wisdom," she liked to say, though she always wore costly gloves to protect her hands, and a coarse gown that she shed for her more elegant everyday attire before she crossed the threshold again, a wattle hut tucked behind a hedge reserved for the purpose.

"Talk to me while I finish my task," she said. "It will not take long. Then we shall begin to make our plans. But just talk about little things for now."

I told her about my mare.

She sat back on her heels, clapping the dirt off her gloves and nodding with a satisfied look on her broad face.

"I told your father that Janyn Perrers would know how to treat you, and I am pleased to hear I was right. You should have been riding long ago. Astride. It strengthens the legs and that will help you birth your babies without all the fuss your mother made about it."

Horses and childbirth? Perhaps I was more ignorant than I had realized. I had seen animals birthing, and I knew the babies came out between the hind legs, so I understood how there might be a connection. But strength?

"Women sit in birthing chairs, don't they? Why need my legs be strong?"

Dame Agnes frowned at me for a moment, and then began to gather her gardening tools as she said, "To carry the weight of the child, Alice. Now come, I would greet my son before he hurries away."

Later that evening, when Grandmother came to see if I was comfortable in the pretty little solar room she'd had prepared for me, I was feeling wretched. My grandparents had made it clear I was welcome and loved, but still I missed Mary, Will, John, and Nan, even Father. This pretty room was unfamiliar, the pillows smelled of other people, not me. That I had several pillows to choose from, covered in soft, pretty linen, was something for which I knew that I should be grateful, and I was. But despite how comfortable the bed was I felt far away from everything I knew.

"Might you stay awhile and talk, Dame Agnes?" I asked.

"On the morrow, child. You need your rest, and so do I. Tomorrow we shall look at cloth and decorations for your new gowns. Perhaps leather for shoes as well."

"My friend Geoffrey Chaucer is home for a little while. Might he visit me here?"

"Of course, my love. Send him a message on the morrow. Invite him to sup with us one day soon if you like."

"Thank you, Dame Agnes."

She smiled and kissed me on the forehead, tucking the covers up to my chin. "Sleep well, my beauty."

"May God bless you and keep you," I whispered. I could not risk speaking more loudly because I was close to tears and it was clear that she did not wish to be forced to linger at my bedside.

She gave me another hug. "May He bless you and keep you as well, dear Alice." As she straightened, she glanced around the little room. "Just think how much grander your bedchamber will be when you are wed. Janyn Perrers will make a fine husband." With a contented sigh she slipped out.

I flailed around for a while, finding it difficult to get comfortable. It was not that I was cold, I had all the covers I could want, but I felt exposed, unguarded. For such a long time I'd slept with Nan, and then Nan and Mary. Now I was all alone in a bed that was hardly smaller than the one the three of us had shared. It occurred to me to clasp a pillow. It helped, and I slept.

I woke to the sound of Grandmother singing a hymn to the Virgin in the next room. Her beautiful voice cheered me, and the pain and loneliness of the past day receded.

Only now did I think about what she had planned for today—*we shall look at cloth and some jewels for your new gowns*. It had not sunk in that I might have new gowns. My own gowns. While I lay there pondering this delightful prospect, a maidservant scratched on the tapestry that covered the doorway.

"I've brought you some warm cider and a small loaf of bread to break your fast, Mistress Alice," she called out.

I welcomed her in. "But you need not have carried it up here," I said. I had never been served food in bed unless I was quite ill.

She set the cup and loaf beside me, on a little stool, and then glanced around the room. "I am Gwen, Mistress Alice. I'm to serve you. Have you all you need?"

"I have no comb," I said. I'd realized it last night; I had never needed my own.

Her sweet face lit up. "I shall bring it when I come to dress you in a little while." With a bob, she withdrew.

I pulled the stool over to the little window and opened the shutters. The sun streamed in, and as I ate I watched a bird hop about on the neighbor's roof. I was happy, just simply happy.

In a while Gwen returned with a comb, the frame of oak, the teeth of bone. It was plain, but the teeth were remarkably even and complete.

"Shall I comb your hair for you, Mistress Alice?"

Even if she had not sounded eager to do so I would have said yes, for I have always loved having my hair combed. She was gentle and thorough, complimenting me on its curl and thickness.

"And such pretty colors—gold, red, and brown. It changes as you move."

I asked her how long she had worked for my grandmother.

"I do not work for Dame Agnes, Mistress Alice. I work for Master Janyn Perrers. I have been here only a few days, to help prepare this room for you and to begin the needlework on your smocks."

It had not occurred to me that she might be from outside the household. "How long have you worked for Master Janyn?"

"It will be two years this Michaelmas, mistress. I was a kitchen maid and he told me I could be a lady's maid if I kept myself clean and tidy, and if I learned to do fine needlework and paid heed to the way fine folk dress and how they like to be served."

I had turned to look up at her and caught an expression of such gratitude on her sweet though plain face that I quickly averted my eyes before she noticed I had intruded on her emotion. It had been a fine thing for Janyn to do, I thought.

"How old are you?"

"Seventeen, mistress."

Older than me, yet she was small and had no figure to speak of.

"How would you compare this household to that of Master Janyn?" I asked, eager to hear more of him.

"It is quiet here, and the mistress is so kind and patient," she said.

"She is, I know. Tell me more. Master Janyn keeps a noisy household?"

"Busy. We are always rushing to prepare food and chambers and space in the hall. He has many guests, merchants and sometimes even finer folk. And, of course, there is only Dame Gertrude who oversees us all."

She had finished combing my hair and now bent over my coffer of clothes, sorting through the shifts and gowns. Shaking out my azure gown, she asked, "Will you wear this today?"

I was not certain whether I should wear my only presentable gown for shopping. But Grandmother was not there to advise me. "Yes, I will wear this." I could change if Dame Agnes disapproved. "Now, who are these finer folk?" I asked, not wanting to drop the promising thread of our conversation. She looked uncertain, but I could not tell whether it was about my clothes or the wisdom of answering me. "I'm soon to be mistress in his home," I said.

She turned to me with a broad smile. "I know, and I'm to be your lady's maid, if you will have me."

"Will I be entertaining nobles?"

Her smile was quickly replaced by a worried frown. "I was told never to gossip about those who came to the house."

"Is it gossip to tell me? Is that not why you were sent here now to be my maid, to tell me of the household? I'm choosing fabrics and decorations for my clothes today—I should know how grandly I will need to dress." I almost took it back, I sounded so like my mother, assuming that Gwen was simpler than I was and using that to manipulate her.

But Gwen's face cleared and she leaned close to whisper, "Twice the king's mother, the old queen dined in the hall."

"The queen mother? Isabella of France?"

Gwen nodded, her eyes huge. "Beautiful, she was, no matter how old she may be."

"How did she come to dine with Master Janyn?"

"And his parents," said Gwen. "They all seemed old friends."

My stomach fluttered. I had never been in the presence of royalty. Nor many nobles, for that matter. To be the mistress of a house that entertained Isabella of France, the king's mother—was this the source of Mother's anger? Was she jealous of the life I would have as Janyn's wife?

"Was the queen mother gentle and kind?"

Gwen giggled. "Oh no, mistress. I would not say so. But she was once queen and her father was king of France, so she need not please anyone but herself."

"Does Master Janyn have other great folk as guests?"

"None so grand as she, Mistress Alice."

I grew quiet as she finished dressing me. She took care to arrange my hair just as Nan had, catching it away from my face and letting it flow down my back. I felt a twinge of sadness, thinking of Nan, wondering what she, Mary, and Will were doing.

I soon learned that I had been right to worry about coaxing information from Gwen.

I found Grandmother in her chamber surrounded by such a generous assortment of cloth it would have seemed more appropriate in Father's undercroft. Her own gown that morning, a pale, patterned wool with pearls swirled on the bodice and long fitted sleeves, seemed very fine to wear on a day given to planning her granddaughter's wardrobe. Yet I had seldom seen her in anything as plain as my everyday gowns.

She noticed me looking at her and the surrounding finery and made a face, crinkling her nose and pursing her lips. "Sinful, I know," she said. "I collect pieces that I like and save them until I find a use for them. I quiet my conscience with the thought of all this being given to the poor of the parish when I die."

"We shall have elegant beggars on the streets," I said.

With a little yelp of surprise Grandmother dissolved into laughter, and I could not help but join her. We both laughed so hard we wiped tears from our eyes. It was a happy beginning.

After we had looked at several pretty cloths that she thought suitable for everyday gowns, she showed me a most elegant brocade in a pale red.

"Perhaps it is too elegant for a merchant's wife," she said. "I have not found an occasion on which I thought this appropriate for myself, to be sure."

I loved the pattern and the color, and that it was soft and smooth, yet had substance. Dame Agnes held it up to me and commented on the way the color brought out my sanguine complexion.

"The clothes cut down from your mother's were pretty, but your complexion is so different from Margery's that the colors suitable for her are not bold enough for you. This suits you."

I smiled and curtsied.

"Fit for a queen," she murmured.

"Or for one dining with the king's mother?" I suggested.

She looked amused. "I did not know you were such a dreamer, Alice. The Lady Isabella? Now when would you dine with her?"

"Gwen said—" I bit my lip. "Might something so fine be suitable for my marriage feast?"

But Grandmother was not so easily distracted. "What else has Gwen said about Janyn's household?"

"She was not gossiping, Dame Agnes. In faith, she said she was not to speak of the master's guests. But I insisted that she tell me about the household so that I might know how to prepare for my role as its mistress."

Dame Agnes sighed as she nodded. "It is true you must know what will be expected of you, Alice. But a maidservant must be discreet. You must be able to trust her not to speak out of place of anything that happens in your home. Janyn would not be pleased to hear that she had mentioned a guest about whom he has chosen to be secretive."

"You did not know that the queen mother had been his guest?"

My grandmother shook her head, and I saw in her eyes an enigmatic expression, of concern bordering on fear.

"Have you met the queen mother?" I asked, hoping to glean more of her feelings.

"No. But when I was not long married I was with my father when he spoke to our lady Queen Philippa. She is a blessing to this realm, a graceful, kind lady loved by all who meet her." Her expression had sharpened. There was a glint in my grandmother's eyes and an edge to her voice, even as she smiled and said such sweet things of the queen. My puzzlement must have shown, because Grandmother shook her head. "Such things were never said of the former queen. You do know of her disgrace? That she made war against her husband, the holy, anointed king?"

I knew that the queen mother was sometimes called the she-wolf for her audacity in waging war against her husband and wresting his crown from him. Although her lover Roger Mortimer had been executed for his part in that and for arranging the secret and most horrible execution of her husband, the former king, Isabella had merely been sequestered in the castle at Berkhampstead for a few years and then in Castle Rising, a comfortable place in which she was now free to entertain. And obviously she was free to travel to London and dine with my future husband.

"But the people supported her in setting her son—*the king's* son on the throne," I said.

Grandmother pressed her lips together and shook her head. "I'll say no more of her. It will be for your husband to tell you of her, as he knows her."

I deemed it best to return to the matter that most concerned me rather than aggravate Grandmother with more questions about the former queen, a woman of whom she clearly did not approve.

"I like Gwen, Dame Agnes. I do not wish to make trouble for her. If she is to be my maid, she should answer all my questions, should she not?" It was not so much that I could not bear anyone else to be my maid, but that her indiscretion was my fault, my doing.

"Calm yourself, Alice. I must consider this." Dame Agnes stood for a long while gazing out the window.

I wanted to ask her how well she knew Janyn, but I could not think how to ask it without sounding disrespectful. I wanted no strain between us. I needed Dame Agnes's love and trust.

I fingered the red brocade. "It is so beautiful. Perhaps someday I shall have a red gown."

Dame Agnes suddenly spun around, all smiles once more. "And so you shall, my love. I have something quite wonderful to show you." She held up a finger for me to wait and hurried out of the solar. As I waited for her I fingered the various cloths we'd chosen, imagining the gowns they would make. In a little while Dame Agnes returned with Gwen, who carried a parcel wrapped in undyed linen. Setting it on the small table at which we had been sitting, Gwen bobbed to both of us—I noticed that her eyes were swollen, as if she had been crying—and left the room. I was certain she had been scolded.

"Open it," said Grandmother. "It is a gift from your betrothed."

"Another?" Upset about Gwen I fumbled with the cord, but finally loosened the knot and peeled back the wrapping. Within was a bolt of cloth dyed blood red, the color much darker and more saturated than the pretty brocade. "Oh, Dame Agnes, what a bold crimson! Is this dyed in graine?" That was a costly dye derived from an insect.

"It is, Alice."

I lifted a corner and touched it to my cheek. "So soft!"

"I confess I could not resist peeking. He has an eye for color, does he not?"

It was not as pretty as the brocade, but I could see that it would be more suitable for a merchant's wife. "Will this be a gown for me?"

"Who else? He said that it is a shade that most young women could not wear without looking as if they were dressed in their mothers' clothes, but that you already have the grace and bearing to wear it." She draped the brocade over it. "Perhaps we might make a headdress with this to wear beneath a thin veil." She stood back and considered it, finally nodding.

"Is red not a color for royalty?"

"There are those who say so. Do not wear it if the dowager queen Isabella visits your hall, eh?" Grandmother must have sensed my uncertainty, for she added, "Many women wear such colors, child, depending on the occasion, or the guest list. Janyn will be able to guide you—with guests such as Gwen described, he must know how to comport himself and rule his household."

Rule his household. That brought me back to the problem. "Did you reprimand Gwen?"

"I did. I told her that I trusted she would not betray her master again, and she vowed she would not."

"She will resent me now!"

"Her feelings are unimportant, Alice. A maidservant serves you. I did tell her that you did not mean to make trouble for her."

I was about to say that I hoped Gwen would forgive me, but held my tongue as Grandmother's advice sank in.

"I will not promise that I'll say nothing to Janyn," she said. "I shall consider it awhile longer. She is skilled in needlework, her stitches very fine. She would be difficult to replace. But that your betrothed said nothing to me about hosting the king's dam suggests that Gwen was trusted to remain silent about it, and he should know of her indiscretion."

I understood the seriousness of the situation, but my part in the matter was something that I could not ignore. "I will vouch for her. I shall be responsible for her conduct from this moment."

"It is a noble offer, Alice, but one that you are too young and innocent to make with full knowledge of what it might mean to you." Again I detected something like fear in my grandmother's voice. "The royal family expect absolute loyalty from those they patronize, and if your betrothed believes Gwen is not to be trusted, you would find your support of her impossible to sustain. Still, I have not said for certain that I will speak with Janyn. And if I do, I would suggest that he speak to Gwen and then give her another chance to prove her obedience."

"Thank you, Dame Agnes."

She set aside the red cloth and brought forward a deep green silk patterned with gold stripes no wider than a strand of hair, holding it up to my face. "Oh, that brightens your eyes. With pearls like these, perhaps?" She pointed to those on her own gown. Then, draping a lock of my hair over the green silk, she said, "You have won his heart, child. I have great hope for your marriage. He will provide for, protect, and cherish you."

I sat down and took a deep breath. It seemed a good time to address my confused emotions about Janyn.

"What is amiss, child?"

"How should I feel about my betrothed, Dame Agnes? When he is near, should I feel hot and as if I might faint?"

It was the first time I'd seen Grandmother blush. She averted her eyes. "Such questions, Alice."

"Why do I embarrass you? Did you never feel this way about Grandfather?"

Lifting the cloth, she stroked it with the back of her hand. "So long ago." She sighed and her face softened as she again brushed the silk, then held it to her cheek and closed her eyes. "Oh yes, Alice, I remember the sweetness. He was not so handsome as your Janyn, even then, but he was tall and strong and had a wicked laugh and a devilish glint in his eyes, and I adored him. As I still do."

"Did you choose each other?"

Dame Agnes chuckled. "Times have not changed so much as that. Of course we were not permitted to choose. But for us it did not matter, for we liked each other well enough from the start." She set aside the silk. "And it seems to me that it is much the same for you and Janyn." Now she met my gaze. "What you describe would be considered a sin by many, but I counted it a blessing that I felt so about your grandfather. Lovemaking can be a frightening thing for a woman who does not welcome her husband's touch."

I could think of many men I would not wish to touch me, and shivered at the thought. I could not imagine ever shrinking from Janyn's touch. Yet I feared there was much I did not understand.

"Is it— Does it hurt, Dame Agnes?"

She enfolded me in her arms, holding me close. "The first time, yes, my child. I will not lie to you. But after that first time," she stroked my hair, "it is quite another thing altogether. And, in truth, I remember the pleasure of that first night far better than I do the pain." She held me away from her and I was relieved to see that she was smiling. "He has been wed before. He will know how to be gentle. Imagine the comfort of being enfolded in the warmth of your beloved's arms." She kissed my cheek.

But I was not entirely reassured. "Is it like— I've seen the dogs—" My throat closed up and I could not go on, nor could I look my grandmother in the eye.

She took my hands. "Yes and no, Alice. God raised us above the animals and gave us souls. When a man is cruel to a woman, he denies his God-given soul, becoming a lowly animal. When he is gentle and loving, it is not at all a beastly act. And I am certain that your Janyn will be gentle and loving with you. Oh, my poor child, your hands are so cold!" She rubbed them, then lifted my chin. "Look at me, Alice."

I reluctantly obeyed. It had taken all my courage to ask what I had so far.

"What frightens you?"

"Am I a beast without a soul to desire him as I do? To dream of him holding me?"

Tears welled in Dame Agnes's eyes. She slowly shook her head. "Not at all, Alice. I still desire your grandfather and dream of him doing far more sinful things than simply holding me."

"Truly?" My voice came out in a squeak.

"Truly. Now sit down and take a deep breath."

I did so.

She rubbed my back in slow, calming circles. "Your silly mother should have told you some of this. Well, we'll not mention her again." She patted my back, then lifted my chin. "What we discussed—your desire for Janyn and mine for Edmund—is never to be shared with anyone else."

Her hazel eyes were lit from behind by fire—apprehension, I guessed, from the pinching around her mouth and a certain breathlessness in her speech.

"I will keep it to myself, Dame Agnes. But why? You said it was natural."

"There are those who would tuck such information away for a time when they could use it against us. A woman is to be virginal in public. Our virtue is our worth. Only our husbands may know of our passions."

"And we of each other's."

Grandmother smiled. "Yes, my sweet." She brushed my cheek and pressed her forehead against mine for a moment. "Yes, my sweet Alice."

When she could see that I was breathing more easily, she smiled. "It is good to have that behind us. Now we can enjoy ourselves."

For the rest of the morning we spoke of headdresses, veils, jewelry, gowns, cloaks, and household furnishings until I felt comfortable once more.

B Y EVENING I was exhausted both in body and spirit. I retired early to my chamber and was tucked into bed, enjoying the sensation of floating between waking and sleeping when I became aware of my grandparents' voices. At first they were merely a hum in the background, a comforting reminder of their nearness. But they gradually grew louder, until I could understand much of what they were saying.

"I intended to ask his leave to tell you, Agnes," said Grandfather, his tone placating.

"You have never kept anything from me." The hurt in Grandmother's voice startled me. I could not remember having heard that in her voice before.

"We speak of the former queen, Agnes. I did not think it prudent to mention her. I daresay she has spies everywhere."

"What is he about, Edmund? Why would Janyn Perrers have aught to do with her?"

"Her indiscretions were many years ago, my love. She is an old woman. It seems a small miracle that she yet lives."

"That was not my question." Now Grandmother sounded irritated. "What does she want from the Perrers family?"

"Or they from her?"

"No, no. She is the one in control, you can be sure of it."

"I swear to you I do not know. I have given it little thought. It is best we do not know."

"But our Alice is joining that family, Edmund. Our sweet Alice. What does this mean for her?"

"That she shall not live a dull life," said Grandfather with a chuckle.

"This is no laughing matter, husband."

I heard nothing for a moment and was about to rise and press my ear against the flimsy wall that separated us when I heard footsteps, one of them walking across the floorboards.

"After all, the girl has survived Margery's neglect and her unforgivable jealousy of late," said Grandfather.

Jealousy. So I had guessed right. My mother resented my marrying into a family of such wealth and connections.

"Edmund! She is but a child."

"She is strong and clever, Agnes. She will survive an encounter or two with the she-wolf."

Dame Agnes muttered something I could not understand, and then they both grew quiet.

But sleep eluded me for a long while, my mind afire with what I'd overheard. When at last I did sleep I dreamed of a beautiful golden wolf devouring all the blossoms in Dame Tommasa's inner courtyard, trampling the stalks and vines in her careless grazing. I stepped into the garden to call her away. Blood stained her muzzle and dripped from her lolling tongue, and in her eyes I saw that the destruction of the plants was a small thing compared to what she had consumed in the hall. She turned and trotted toward me. I could not move. I must have screamed in my sleep, for I woke enfolded in my grandmother's arms.

"Sweet Alice, you are safe. Whatever the dream, it cannot reach you here."

I was alert enough to stop myself from describing it, fearful that Dame Agnes would realize I'd overheard; I valued the opportunity to hear what she and Grandfather were not telling me. As to the wolf not reaching me in my waking world, I prayed that she was right.

I N THE next few days I was measured for boots by a boot maker who showed us leather in colors I could not believe were not painted and so soft that I imagined it would feel as if I were barefoot when I wore them. Dame Agnes, her maid Kate, and Gwen measured me over and over again, and we all began to work on my gowns, using an alcove near my bedchamber in which shutters could be opened to welcome north and south light. It was a good time of year for such an endeavor, with the weather warm enough to allow us to sit by the open windows, and the sun shining almost every day. While we worked, Dame Agnes talked about the duties of the lady of the household. She also bade me attend her when she was seeing to her routines in the house and garden so that I might learn by assisting her. At first the complexity of the household and the authority with which Dame Agnes addressed the servants overwhelmed me. I could not imagine mastering such details or taking command in such wise. But with repetition the tasks grew familiar and as I gained confidence I found my voice. Each day I felt a little less apprehensive about running Janyn's household.

Gwen had adopted what Dame Agnes referred to as a respectful silence, even when dressing me. At first I accepted it as the proper behavior, but as it continued I detected a tension between us and felt more and more strongly that hers was a wounded silence. That would not do, not if she was to be my maid for many years to come. It was too uncomfortable. I feared that her resentment could bloom into something more hostile and that I would then be unable to trust her. I did not choose to live that way.

On the fourth morning since she had grown silent, I spoke.

"Gwen, I regret having put you in such a difficult position, wanting to please me and yet having been warned by Master Janyn to refrain from gossip about his guests. I apologize."

I had not expected her to warm to me at once, but was surprised that her response was to stop combing my hair and to back away a few steps.

"Yes, mistress," she whispered.

"I've made you even less easy with me. What is it, Gwen? What is amiss?" I knew it was not the way I should address a servant, but I would not be waited on by a woman who held a grudge against me.

"I never imagined you would tell Dame Agnes, mistress." Her eyes were lowered, hands hanging limply at her sides.

It was a hard lesson for me. "I accept the blame, Gwen. In future I'll not repeat what we have discussed. But I expect you to be just as loyal to me. Do you accept that?" I turned to look at her, and felt quite bold and mature as I said, "In faith, you must look me in the eye and tell me your decision. Either we trust each other, or I find another lady's maid. You already know my preference. What say you?"

The eyes she lifted to mine were satisfyingly astonished.

"I—" She took a breath. "I pledge my loyalty, Mistress Alice. I beg your forgiveness. I have been disrespectful in my behavior. I am happy with you and Master Janyn. I pray you, believe me, I will be true in heart and speech."

"I believe you. We'll say no more about it. Now come, Gwen, comb my hair."

I was far more comfortable that day as we all sat with our needle-work, and though she did not ask what had transpired I could tell that Dame Agnes sensed a shift as well.

The following day our routine was happily interrupted when Geoffrey came to dine with us. I was so glad to see him. It had been a week since I had seen Nan or my brothers and sister, whom I sorely missed, and he was the next best thing—in some ways even better, because I could confide in him and ask his opinion, and I sorely needed a confidant.

While we dined Geoffrey entertained me and my grandparents with tales of his fellow pages and the embarrassing mistakes he was learning to avoid.

"I lacked education in the fine points of interpreting people's dress, you see. Suddenly I was expected to know a person's rank merely by looking at their clothing. I had thought to learn their faces, but there was no time for that." He glanced at my new green silk gown and said, "For example, I might guess you to be a propertied lady of the realm, or the daughter of a prosperous Italian or French merchant. Not a wife, for your hair is loose. Ah, you confuse me, my good friend, for I know you well enough to be sure I am wrong on all but your being a maiden."

"Not at all," Dame Agnes said with a teasing light in her eyes, "for she is the betrothed of a man who is Italian on his mother's side and trades extensively in Italy and France!"

"Ah, but of course, Janyn's mother!" Geoffrey bowed. "You have my eternal gratitude, Dame Agnes. You have redeemed me."

A lively argument ensued about how stringently dress codes were followed, and the meal continued with much merriment. Afterward, my grandparents suggested that Geoffrey and I might enjoy some time without them and welcomed us to retire to the garden, where they might see but not hear us. I was most grateful. There was so much I wished to tell him.

But he was even more anxious to tell me something he had learned the previous evening.

"Your parents have been summoned to Castle Rising. Summoned by the queen mother, the Lady Isabella."

I grew quite cold though the sun beat down on me.

"My parents at Castle Rising? Why? Where did you hear this?"

He'd been watching me as if curious how I would react. Now he slowly nodded. "I thought you would be puzzled by this, as was I. Why? I do not know, nor did the man who told me of this. He is aware we are friends, and plainly hoped to learn more from me. But he did say that your betrothed and his parents are frequent guests of the queen mother, and that your own father has been there on another occasion—shortly before your betrothal."

"I had forgotten about that visit. Father had said little more than that he'd been to Castle Rising. I had thought he meant the town. He'd certainly not mentioned the dowager queen." I felt uneasy about saying more to Geoffrey, and just as uneasy about not doing so.

I began to understand how much Father might gain by my marriage to Janyn—the royal connections would bring preferments. It was no wonder he had been willing to defy Mother. I pressed my icy hands to my hot cheeks. Geoffrey watched me with interest.

"Do you think this summons has something to do with Janyn?" I asked.

"There is gossip about his family, that they are retained by Isabella. But that does not surprise me—she has done much to promote Lombard art in London, and Janyn's dam is a Lombard."

"But I do not see how my family would be involved."

"Nor do I, Alice."

"Should I be worried?" I had always valued Geoffrey's opinion. He had seemed better able to comprehend the world at large than I was, and now he was part of a noble household and well traveled.

He raised his eyebrows and shook his head. "You now know as much as I do. I confess that I am disappointed you did not know this already, and more!" He chuckled, but in his eyes I saw concern.

"I have been cast out from my parents' house, no longer privy to their comings and goings. But I begin to think that I have never been knowledgeable about their lives." I told him of my parents' apparent rift over my betrothal.

"So it is because of Dame Margery that you are here?"

"I believe so. Or because Father insisted on my betrothal to Janyn even against Mother's wishes. I don't know which one to blame."

Geoffrey took my hands and squeezed them. "I see that you are hurt, and I am sorry."

"Bless you."

"Are you pleased by the prospect of being Janyn Perrers's wife?"

"For my own part, oh yes, Geoffrey. And yet I fear it as well. He is older, and knows so much more of the world. And I much fear that once I am wed I'll not see any of my family."

"As for the latter, that might be true no matter whom you wed. A woman joins her husband's family and is guarded by them against anything that might threaten her honor. But he seems a fascinating man to whom to be bound—handsome and so elegant that I would think him a noble. I see that your grandparents mean for you to dress as well as he does."

I smoothed my silk sleeve. "It is not all their choice. Janyn has made generous gifts and provided me with a maidservant who is accomplished in all the skills needed for a fashionable lady's maid."

"Indeed. That gown becomes you."

I twirled for him. "You, too, are dressed in costly garb," I noted, pleased by the admiration in his eyes.

His brown jacket was a fine, light wool; his boots were of beautiful red Cordoba leather. I had never seen him in such elegant dress. I did not think it livery.

He blushed. "I thought I might spend a little money to feel like a man of substance when I am about in the city."

"It seems that I am to dress in escarlatte, silk, velvet, and soft leathers, and be an ornament of my husband's household."

"Criseyde's cloak," Geoffrey said, looking bemused. His expressive eyes seemed to gaze at something vast and distant.

"Who?"

"A poem of ancient Troy that we listened to night after night in the hall while a gentleman who fancies himself a bard was a guest in the household. My lady particularly loved the part about Criseyde and her lovers. She is sent from Troy to the Greek camp, and dons a cloak redder than roses, whiter than lilies, and decorated with pictures of all the beasts and flowers on earth, fashioned from enchanted cloth and lined with the skin of a fabulous animal whose fur includes every color God has ever created. The trimming comes from the hide of a beast caught in the river of Paradise. It is fastened by the two richest and most beautiful rubies that have ever been seen. Beneath it she wears a silk tunic, embroidered with gold and trimmed with ermine."

The image captivated me. I could see an exquisite woman in fabulous dress illuminated by the campfire, dazzling the men who thought her a specter.

Geoffrey bowed to me, his mood quieter now. "I'll tease you no more."

I did not understand why his mention of this Criseyde led him to a more serious mood.

"Are you finding time to compose ballads?"

"There is always idle time in which to compose in my head."

"Are you composing one of Criseyde?"

"She deserves a better poet than me. Now tell me," he said, laughing again and confusing me even more, "has Janyn kissed you?"

The mere question made me blush with the memory of our kiss.

Geoffrey slapped his thigh. "Ah! I see by your confusion that he has, and that it was much to your liking." His eyes were very merry.

I laughed. "Yes, he has kissed me, and yes, it was very much to my liking. And you? Have you met a suitable lady?"

"No. But parents are in no hurry to marry off their sons, just their daughters. In faith, I've seen few women younger than my mother."

We shared a companionable laugh, and I felt more at ease than I had in a long while.

"When do you wed?"

"Before Michaelmas."

"So soon?" He looked disappointed. "Then I shall not be there to witness it. I return to my new household in two days and shall not be in London until Christmas."

"Oh, Geoffrey. I had so hoped you would be there."

"Perhaps I can be second godfather to your first son, eh?"

"Children. I have not even thought about them, let alone choosing godparents." Janyn would no doubt choose a man of some prestige for first godfather. "I've been occupied with preparing my clothing and household items. Yes, Geoffrey, I would like you to stand as a godfather to our first son—or daughter." I giggled about what came to mind. "Dame Agnes says that riding will strengthen my legs for carrying the weight of children."

Geoffrey smiled broadly and took my hands for a moment. "I am happy for you, Alice."

"I feel most fortunate except for my warring parents and the she-wolf casting a cloud over it all."

"I am sorry about your parents. But perhaps you need not worry about the queen mother. The gossips love their clever names for those they fear. It makes them feel superior and less afraid. The king's mother is often at court now that so much time has passed since her treasonous and immoral behavior. In the end, the people were glad of her rebellion. It was Mortimer's greed for power that soured them."

"I overheard my grandparents speaking of her one night and they sounded uneasy about my marrying a man who communed with the queen mother. They must not have known about my parents being summoned to Castle Rising."

"Perhaps as Janyn's patron, Isabella wished to make certain that your mother will not cause trouble. I have observed that nobles often look on commoners as well-to-do servants. She may feel she owns him in some way."

I paused and turned to him. "Have you any advice for me, my worldly Geoffrey?"

He grew serious. "I have seen good people seduced by wealth and finery to their ruin. Have a care, my friend."

"Geoffrey, you make me shiver."

He forced a laugh. "You asked! But do not mind me. You know that I delight in hearing my own voice. You have ever been more practical and clear-headed than me. You will fare well."

It grew late, and my friend reluctantly departed. But he swore that he would not be a stranger, and I believed him. As I lay abed that night I tried to recall his description of the enchanted cloak. Fabulous beasts, every color imaginable, great rubies . . .

IN THE morning, knowing that my parents were away, I coerced Dame Agnes into accompanying me to see Nan and the children. I might have slipped away at any time to see my siblings despite how busy we were preparing for my marriage, but I had dreaded an encounter with Mother. We sent a message that we would come the next day—I did not want Nan to feel that I was checking up on her with a surprise visit while she was in charge. I had recently made new hats for all three of my siblings from scraps of beautiful cloth, and I looked forward to presenting them. Gwen asked to accompany us so that the children might meet her.

"Then when they visit I'll not be a stranger to them."

I was glad that I had made my peace with her.

I had not anticipated how odd it would feel to return home after little more than a week away. Nan greeted us at the door looking far more than a week older, and although I recognized the gown she wore it seemed more frayed and patched than before. The furnishings were unchanged, yet they seemed unbalanced, as if the hall had grown and the furnishings had shrunk. Everything felt subtly unfamiliar, as if my spirit had been erased from my former home.

After a tearful reunion with Nan, Will, and Mary—John would try to stop in later if his master could spare him from the shop—I asked about their activities since I'd left.

Later, when the children were absorbed in trying on their hats with Gwen's and Dame Agnes's assistance and searching for a gift they had made for me, I asked Nan what she knew about my parents' journey.

When I'd arrived my first impression of my beloved nurse was that she was weary and heavy of heart, and now her words confirmed that at least in part.

"A messenger came—well dressed, thought highly of himself, insisted on waiting for the reply. Cook fed him while the master and mistress went above and spoke in hushed voices behind a closed door. I had handed them the note, but they had told me to leave the room while they spoke to the messenger, and then I was sent out with the children while they discussed it and I presume composed their response. As soon as the messenger departed I was ordered to look after the children while they prepared for a journey, and was told that Cook and I would be seeing to them for a week or more. Such a fuss, Alice. Your parents seemed excited and fearful at the same time. Cook says the messenger began to say something about a castle, but changed it to Norfolk. She said that he wore livery that had the royal fleur-de-lis on it. We thought of Castle Rising—the Lady Isabella, the king's mother, lives there. But why would she summon your parents?"

My experience with Gwen had taught me to pause and consider Nan's position in the household before I said anything. I judged it best not to tell her what I knew, for then she would not be burdened by keeping a secret from her employers.

"I wish I knew what it meant, Nan. It sounds exciting. Mother must have been delighted to have an excuse to travel and be seen in her pretty clothes. Do you think Father has found another partner for a ship? He so wanted to buy another ship."

As there was always much intrigue around large commercial investments, Nan seemed satisfied with that possibility.

"You are looking very fine, Alice. Dame Agnes is taking good care of you."

"Every day I work on such fantastic gowns and headdresses, Nan. I never dreamed I would be so finely dressed. But it does not fill the loneliness I feel being apart from all of you."

We held each other's hands and studied each other's face.

Nan broke the emotional silence as Dame Agnes approached. "Try to be content in the home of your loving grandparents, Alice," she said softly. In a normal tone she added, "I see how Dame Agnes and your maid treat you, and I am no longer worried for you."

Despite my initial feelings of strangeness, I enjoyed the day immensely and it was hard, very hard, to take my leave of Nan and my siblings. We were almost out the door when John rushed through it. My heart leaped with joy to see him, and to see how much he had wanted to catch me. We held each other tightly—it was the first time we had hugged each other in years.

He stepped back and looked at me, then pulled me out into the yard, away from the others. "You've gained back your color and some weight. I am more than glad to see you thriving, Alice. You are better off with Dame Agnes—I told Father that it would prove so."

"Father told you of his plans before I heard of them?"

"He told me to shut me up. I had asked him to do something about Mother's behavior. You would have laughed—I told him that I would not stand for her treating you so." He laughed at himself, a melancholy sound. "As if I had it in my power to do anything to protect you."

I was moved beyond words. "She has been even more spiteful toward me of late than is her custom."

"I am glad you came today, when she is well away from here."

"Please come to dine with us someday soon," I said.

"An apprentice lives at the mercy of his master's whims, Alice. But I will try." He took my hands. "You did not ask whether I knew where our parents have gone. That means that you do."

I shook my head. I did not care to speak a lie to my brother, who had been so good to me.

He looked disappointed, but not disbelieving. "The suddenness of their journey frightened Cook and Nan. I had hoped you would know who or what might inspire such haste."

"In faith, I was so glad to hear they were away and I might see you and Mary and Will that though I did wonder, I was too excited to care much."

Dame Agnes came out to urge us to complete our farewells, for it grew late. Mary and Will ran out to embrace me and deliver wet kisses one more time, and John and I clasped hands as he promised to try to dine with us soon.

I cried myself to sleep that night. I did not understand how I could be both happy and sad about the way my life was changing. Nan used to say that God always mixed the bitter with the sweet so that we did not forget that every pleasure has its cost.

3

"And shortly, deere herte and al my knyght,
Beth glad, and draweth yow to lustinesse,
And I shal trewely, with al my myght,
Youre bittre tornen al into swetenesse.
If I be she that may yow do gladnesse,
For every wo ye shal recovere a blisse—"

—Criseyde to Troilus, GEOFFREY CHAUCER,
Troilus and Criseyde, III, 176–81

• 1356 •

IN THE morning, noticing my still somber mood, Dame Agnes suggested I might accompany Grandfather to their parish church for some quiet prayer. She, Gwen, and Kate could spare me from the needlework for a while.

"You have worked hard of late and it will be good for you to walk about."

St. Mary Aldermary was another parish church for wealthy merchants, and as Grandfather and I stepped within, the murmurs of the chantry priests sounded reassuringly familiar.

"I shall kneel in my usual spot," said Grandfather. "Come and fetch me when you are finished with your devotions." He had brought with him a subtly embroidered cushion—I recognized Dame Agnes's stitching—and was soon settled near the main altar, his dark robes falling gracefully from his broad shoulders. His head, warmly wrapped in a hood that draped about his neck, bowed low over his folded hands.

I loved him so much in that moment. He had always been kind to me, a comfortable companion.

I went at once to the statue of the Blessed Virgin and knelt on the prie-dieu before it. Pouring out my fears and uncertainties to the gentle Mother of God calmed me.

On the walk back to the house we talked of my own father's wedding.

"He could not believe that God had blessed him with such a beautiful wife," said Grandfather. But there was no joy in his voice, and, glancing up, I saw that his high forehead was creased and his eyes sad.

"You need not hide his disappointment from me, Grandfather. I know that my mother has been difficult."

He gave a startled smile and squeezed my hand. "You are almost too good a listener. But that will serve you well." His dark clothing made him look somber, but his face was kind. "Why do we force our daughters to wed so young? That was their problem, I believe. Margery had dreamed about a life with my son that could never be, the sort of luxury and traveling that only nobles can afford, and even then the women seldom find exciting." Grandfather squeezed my hand again. "Forgive me, I pontificate."

"So she would have been dissatisfied with anyone of her own station?" I asked.

"In truth, that is precisely the problem," he said.

"Then her youth made no difference."

He grunted and stopped near the gate to the house, considering, his ruddy face crinkling and wrinkling as he thought. I loved the way his entire body took part in everything he did, even prayer.

"You are quite right, granddaughter. Quite right." His face rearranged itself into a smile in which his pale eyes and white whiskers participated. "You have released me from the burden of guilt I have borne for hastening your parents' betrothal and marriage. But you, Alice, you seem content to leave your family and embrace that of your betrothed."

"I've been pushed from the nest, Grandfather."

His smile grew uncertain. "Of course. How thoughtless of me."

"But I am well pleased with Janyn, and, for the moment, to be living with you and Dame Agnes."

He beamed. "It is delightful to have you in our home, Alice. And you have such a fine suitor. You shall have an exciting life with Janyn Perrers, I trow, if his gifts so far are any indication. And your grandmother told me that you know of his connection with the dowager Queen Isabella." He put a finger to his lips. "A family secret." Resuming his slow walk he added, "I am much relieved by this talk. Bless you, child."

We had reached the yard, and there, calmly eating an apple from Grandmother's hand, was my mare, accompanied by a man with the tanned leathery skin of one who spent little of his time inside.

"There you are!" Grandmother waved us over. "Alice, this is Master Thorne, your riding instructor, come to walk you about the yard so that you might become better acquainted with your mare while he judges how to begin your training."

"Master Thorne," I said, bobbing my head to him.

"Mistress," he nodded, his dark eyes frankly assessing me.

Dame Agnes ordered me into the house, where Gwen helped me change into a gown less full, of a cloth easier to clean.

Once I was back in the yard, Master Thorne brooked no delay. I was noting just how tall the mare was when I was ordered to step up onto a stool, and with Grandfather assisting me, I mounted. Sitting sideways on the platform felt awkward. I was glad of having changed— less skirt to manage. How far away the ground seemed, how close the sky.

"Her name is Maundy, but you might find a name that better suits the pair of you, mistress," said Master Thorne. He then made a little sound, and the mare began to walk, very slowly, very gently.

I felt as if I were a part of the mare and she of me, and the grace with which we moved together filled me with a strange mixture of peace and delight.

Master Thorne looked at the mare's face, then mine, and nodded. "God smiles on this match. It will bring me joy to train you, Mistress Alice." Too soon he asked Grandfather to assist me in dismounting.

"I must take Maundy away to the stables, and you will come to me there on the morrow, in the early morning," said Thorne. My grandparents boarded their horses a short walk away.

On impulse, I hugged the mare's head. She nuzzled my ear. "The name does not suit her," I said.

Master Thorne inclined his head. "Choose another, mistress, and we'll train her to it."

"A good beginning," said Grandfather as Master Thorne led the mare out of the yard.

"Have you any name in mind?" Dame Agnes asked as we returned to the hall.

"Serenity," I said. "That is what I feel in her presence."

"It is an odd name for a beast," Dame Agnes said with a chuckle, "but it has a beautiful sound."

THE NEXT few days flew by as I divided my time between riding lessons and the finishing touches to several gowns, surcoats, and shifts.

"Why are we rushing with the clothing?" I asked one morning. "There will be weeks of nothing to do before my wedding."

Grandmother laughed. "When Janyn returns he means to escort you through your future homes so that you might tell him what you wish to change and how you wish to change it. You will be too busy for needlework and by then I expect you'll be asking us to work on cushions and hangings for the bedchambers and halls. We will also be planning the wedding feast." Her color was high and her eyes bright with visions of social delights.

I said little, choked by all that seemed to be spinning out of control around me. But I was able to set aside my worries and be one with Serenity. Riding was not at all what I had imagined. I had not expected to feel such a bond with the horse, to be so aware of sitting on a living being. The power of Serenity moving beneath me, her response to my subtle movements—I became aware of my own body by the way I was able to sense hers.

That evening as Dame Agnes sat on the side of my bed wishing me sweet dreams I confessed, "I fear I take too much pleasure in riding."

"Oh, my sweet Alice," she murmured, brushing my hair from my cheek and bending to kiss me, "your feelings have been shared by many other young girls. God does not proscribe an innocent bond with your horse."

I believed that she loved me and was encouraging me to be happy.

But she also wanted to prevent anything that might create problems in the future. I saw that in her eyes, heard it in her voice.

"I pray for happiness, Dame Agnes," I said, "to follow your example in running a household with ease and grace, and to be a good wife to Janyn." And to be blessed with joy in my partner, as she was with Grandfather.

JANYN RETURNED to London half a week earlier than Dame Agnes had planned, throwing her into a panic. She insisted that all my clothing be ready when he made his first appearance—the very day she learned of his presence in London she had invited him to dine, and he had accepted for the following afternoon.

When I entered the hall, I felt a stranger to myself. I'd first worn my deep green silk gown when Geoffrey had paid a visit, but the gold surcoat, jeweled girdle, and pearl headdress were new. I felt bejeweled and untouchable, as I imagined a queen might feel, distanced from her subjects by gold and gems. It was a heady feeling.

The sun had darkened Janyn's complexion and he looked glorious, as I imagined a lion might look. As I approached I felt a great power as his expression of impatience metamorphosed into a look of sheer delight and then something darker, a hunger. As if he *were* a lion and meant to devour me. Yet I did not fear him. I felt I shone in his presence. I came alive.

"Sweet Mother in Heaven," he said when I reached him. "You are a vision, my beloved." He took my hand and kissed it, lingering over it. The caress of his breath robbed me of mine, but at the same time his firm grasp reassured me. He was real. Our betrothal was real. And he desired me.

"I have missed you, Janyn."

Now he looked up, into my eyes, and held my gaze for a moment, as if assessing my regard. I was surprised by how familiar he felt to me.

"Master Thorne tells me that you ride as if you have been doing so all your life."

"Master Thorne is most kind, but overstates my ability," I said. "I do enjoy riding, and Serenity is a most beloved companion."

Janyn's high forehead creased in thought. "You have named your mare Serenity? You are a delight." His eyes lit up and his tanned face crinkled into a teasing grin. "But you will not ride her for long.

She is slow and wanting in refinement. I chose her only while you learned."

In that moment the maturity the gorgeous clothing had loaned me collapsed and I felt young and silly. I could not bear to think of parting with Serenity. I loved her. I felt foolish for not having understood that she was not a grand horse. I turned away from him and prayed that I might regain my composure.

"Shall we be seated?" Dame Agnes said, motioning to Janyn to join Grandfather at the beautifully decorated table. With her hand beneath my elbow, she held me back. "He meant no harm by his smile, Alice," she whispered, "and I am certain that he will allow you to keep the mare at your country house. Take a deep breath and be of good cheer. You look beautiful and he adores you."

I had not thought about how difficult it would be to sustain the behavior now expected of me. But I reminded myself there was no returning to my parents' house, and I was most fortunate to be betrothed to a man so much to my taste. Securing this marriage was worth every effort on my part.

I took the deep breath Grandmother prescribed and followed her to the table. With each step I tried to grow a little taller and more graceful, and although I was not smiling by the time I took my seat, I was composed.

Dame Agnes gave me a smile that expressed her relief that I had not made a fuss.

"You have the nutty color of a man who has been at sea," Grandfather said to Janyn, who bowed his elegant head in response.

"The sun shone down on me as I crossed the Channel, it is true. Trade took me to France and Lombardy."

"Do you often cross the Channel, Master Janyn, or do your factors do more of the travel for you?" asked Dame Agnes.

"As a widower I had little to hold me here, so I often made the journey. But now"—he glanced at me— "I hope to make much greater use of my factors."

I blushed. "I am glad of that," I murmured, managing a tremulous smile.

It seemed to please all at the table. Conversation continued along pleasant avenues with stories of the journey and Grandfather's anecdotes about my riding lessons.

Janyn invited me and my grandparents to dine at his London home the following day.

"As we are to wed in less than a month, I am eager to show Alice her new home so that she may advise me on what I must do to ensure her comfort. I would be delighted if you would escort her to our home tomorrow, Master Edmund, Dame Agnes, so that we might confer and then discuss our plans over supper."

Our home. Janyn had taken my hand and squeezed it while he said that, and when he was finished he kissed it and looked into my eyes with such an affectionate expression that my heart fluttered.

Grandfather regretted that he must attend a guild event on the morrow. "But Dame Agnes and Alice are the ones you need there, and they will surely attend you."

M Y FUTURE home was much like Janyn's parents' house, the street façade matching that of its neighbors except that it was slightly larger, with more chimneys. And, like that of his parents, Janyn's hall door opened onto a fantastic world of color and light. Breathless I stood, letting my eyes feast on the wall hangings; the cushions; the delicately painted wood and embroidered cloth; statues; shelves and cabinets displaying pewter, wood, and silver dishes, and Italian glass goblets, pitchers, and flasks.

I could not imagine what I might add or change. A fit of shyness overtook me a few steps into the hall.

"Sweet Alice, this is to be your home," said Janyn. "I hoped you would be curious."

I needed little more coaxing, for I did so wish to explore. I found the cushions wondrously thick and comfortable and the fabrics more than pleasing to the touch. The pewter was as fine as I'd seen in churches.

"That is York pewter," said Janyn. "The finest."

"Everything is not only beautiful, but well cared for," I said. "My compliments to the housekeeper. Will I meet her today?"

The question apparently reminded Janyn of something troubling. "Gertrude is away at our country house today. And therein lies a difficulty. Angelo, the cook, encountered a problem earlier and became so intent on solving it that he is now very late in getting the food to the table."

Dame Agnes assured Janyn that she would find a way to save the day, and taking Gwen with her she retired to the kitchen.

Janyn's air of unease dissolved as soon as they disappeared. I wondered whether he had arranged for just such a crisis so that we might be alone.

"At last," he said with a conspiratorial grin. "We will be more comfortable discussing the decorations for the bedchamber without an audience, do you not agree?"

I liked that I had guessed correctly. He seemed more approachable now, less a cipher. It was the sort of thing Geoffrey and I might plot.

"What I have seen so far is beautiful, Janyn." I smiled up at him and put my hand in the crook of his arm. "I should like to see the bedchamber." My own boldness surprised me.

As we climbed the outer staircase to the upper story he said, "Before returning to London I spent a day at Castle Rising, the home of Isabella, the Queen Mother. She is eager to meet you, Alice."

I noticed a hint of concern in his voice. I had debated with myself whether or not to inform him that I already knew of his friendship with her, and had decided that I would act surprised, protecting my relationship with Gwen. I took his slight unease as a sign that I had judged correctly, that this relationship demanded discretion.

As we reached the upper landing, I turned to him. He touched my cheek with the back of his hand, a gentle, loving gesture that seemed effortless. I was learning that he was not a man who must needs struggle to express affection and I loved him all the more for that. I lightly pressed my face into his hand. Just a subtle gesture. I did not linger, staying just long enough to sense that he'd felt my response. I was discovering I enjoyed the repartee of touch.

"The king's dam, Janyn? In truth? How come you to be acquainted with her?" I had no need to feign breathlessness though it had little to do with Isabella.

"I know her by a long connection through my mother's family, who have negotiated Her Grace's purchases of fine artwork and jewelry from northern Italy. Her Grace has a keen appreciation for Italian design."

"I can imagine Dame Tommasa in her beautiful new surcoat with the celestial bodies, bowing to the dowager queen. You were teasing me, saying that she might wear such elegant clothing in Italy. She might wear it to entertain the queen mother!"

I could see in his eyes that my excitement delighted him. But there was still a hint of something as he said, "No, I was not teasing. She might wear such a robe in Milan." He smiled and pulled me close. But we were interrupted by a servant opening the outside door to us. We exchanged rueful glances and then stepped into a passageway. It seemed like a screens passage, off which doors opened. I'd never seen one in an upper story. The house was larger than I had guessed. The servant opened another door farther down the passage and stepped aside.

"Mistress, Master," she said with a little bow and a gesture toward the room.

The bedchamber was at least twice the size of Dame Agnes's and filled with light from several glazed windows on the south wall. Glazed windows in a bedchamber seemed an indulgence only the very wealthy might even consider. It was more simply furnished than the hall below, but everything was beautifully made and costly. I immediately moved about, touching surfaces, feeling fabrics.

When the servant had stepped back into the screens passage and closed the door behind her, Janyn spoke. "You will never guess who I found to be Her Grace's guests."

At last we came to the news that Geoffrey had first brought me. I had wondered how long it would take for Janyn to confide in me. "The king and queen?" I played at guessing. Fortunately my activity made it easy for me to hide my face.

"Your parents."

I was standing by the great bed, running my hands over the silken bed curtains. "What wonder is this? The dowager Queen Isabella and my parents?" Now I turned, and my expression must have been sufficiently amazed. "Janyn, you tease me."

He broke into a glorious smile and laughed, a deep-throated laugh. "I speak the truth. Your father did think it a wonder when he was first invited. You see, I bring him opportunities by our marriage."

"And great honor," I said.

Janyn nodded. "Honor and preference. Your family will want for nothing."

I swept around, looking at the glorious furnishings, the spacious chamber. "Nor shall I! Oh, Janyn, I am happy for all of us." And I was, especially for myself, Mary, Will, and John.

Janyn sat down on the edge of the bed and took both my hands as I stood before him. "But this connection is not to be discussed in public." His voice was suddenly quiet and he studied my face until I looked him in the eye. He was now grimly serious.

"I shall obey you in this, of course, Janyn," I said. "But might I ask why it is to be a secret?"

"You know the dowager queen's history?"

I nodded.

"There are those who still see her as a traitor, who believe she wanted the throne for herself, not her son."

"But that was long ago. And her son King Edward is so loved by his people."

"It was, and he is. But there are those with long memories who hold their anger and resentment close to them, nursing their pain, eager to strike out."

I did not want to know these things. I wanted to explore what was to be my new home. I wanted to kiss Janyn. But he obviously wished to discuss this now. I was disappointed that this was why he'd brought me to the bedchamber.

"I understand, my love," I said, working to keep the disappointment out of my voice. "But how came my parents to Castle Rising?"

"By Her Grace's invitation. She wished to meet the parents of my betrothed."

If he'd meant to cool my ardor he had succeeded. I remembered Geoffrey's suggestion that Isabella might feel she owned Janyn in some way. "Why would she care about my parents? What could they possibly be to her?"

"Are you not pleased by this attention from the king's mother?"

"Of course I am," I said quickly. "It is beyond anything I ever dreamed."

"It is an honor, and she is a noble and gracious woman. But I see that you are troubled, Alice. What is it?"

"This summons to Castle Rising, was it to appease Mother? To show her that she will share in some of my good fortune?"

"I had confided in Her Grace my suspicion about why our betrothal was delayed, and it would be her way of helping, to flatter Dame Margery with her attention."

"That was kind of Her Grace."

"She is a kind and loving woman. A great lady."

"She must value your friendship."

Janyn nodded. "Even the powerful have need of trusted companions."

He chose his words with great care when he spoke of Isabella of France, pausing longer before responding then than at any other time.

I had expected a simpler life than the one he was painting for me. This was overwhelming. Yet it *was* thrilling to be marrying a man who walked with royals, to imagine entertaining them, dining with them.

"You still look troubled," he said.

"I pray that my parents can be trusted to be silent."

"Is that all?" He looked relieved. "Then I can assure you, be at ease, my love. Her Grace will have made it clear to them that they must be discreet if they wish to remain in her favor. You need not worry."

"But surely in the very need for secrecy you have suggested a certain danger to us all?" I did not intend to play the fool.

He nodded. "I meant that you need not worry about your parents' discretion. Yes, the secrecy is for our protection."

"I am glad that you do not seek to protect me from the truth."

Janyn crossed his hands over his heart. "Never, my love." Then he gestured toward the curtains, the other furnishings of the room, the great bed on which he sat. "Does it please you?"

"I am delighted by all I have seen, Janyn. Glazing on the windows of our bedchamber? I would never have dared suggest it. And the silk hangings, the immense bed. I never thought to live in such comfort. It is as I've imagined palaces in Paris or Venice."

"It is perhaps more the fashion for wealthy merchants in those great cities. But my mother has always believed that God does not begrudge us comfort and beauty as long as we give Him thanks and make certain that all in our households share it."

"I shall learn to be at ease with it, then," I said.

"You need to learn?"

"It does seem sinful." I fought a smile.

"And yet bishops and popes live in far greater splendor."

I laughed. "Oh, Janyn, I have no experience of such exalted men of the Church. I spoke but in jest." I moved away from him as I heard footsteps on the stairway.

Janyn reached for me and pulled me back. His smile was teasing, but in his eyes there was something more. Suddenly I feared him.

"Why do you move away from me when you hear a servant on the stairway?" he asked, his voice soft, coaxing. "We are betrothed. We might do what we will in our bedchamber." Slipping his arms around me he pulled me so close that my chest was pressed against his.

"But, Janyn—"

He silenced me with a kiss. More than a kiss. His tongue searched my lips. I had begun to fight him, but thought suddenly what a fool I was being. This is what I wanted and there was no one, not even God Himself, who would condemn me for giving in to Janyn, my betrothed. I melted into his arms and as I opened my lips to his he pressed me to him so tightly that I could feel his excitement.

I boldly touched him there. He moaned, and then released me from his embrace.

"My sweet Alice. I think we will be more than fond of this bed." His eyes were strange, darker and softer than I'd seen them before. "But let us save our passion for our wedding night."

"Why? You said yourself that we might do what we will."

"I promised your father, my vixen, that is why."

I took a deep breath, feeling confused and a little angry. For reasons I did not understand at the time—what fourteen-year-old girl understands frustrated desire?—I wanted to punish him.

"Why is my mother so against our betrothal? What is between you?"

"Your mother?" Janyn frowned in puzzlement, but as I watched he rose and stood at a little distance, his expression changing to one of unease. "Let us not speak of your mother."

"No one wishes to speak of my mother, and yet she is at the center of everything that is happening to me. Even the Lady Isabella perceives that. I am sent from my own home because of Mother's response to our betrothal. Do you think this has been as nothing to me?"

"It is your parents who should explain."

"And if they will not? It colors everything for me, Janyn. I yearn to be happy, but I fear that there is some hidden threat to our joy."

He took off his hat and raked a hand through his hair, a gesture of discomfort that I had not witnessed in him before. Perhaps my seeming unkindness was in truth a way to evoke a response from him.

"I had thought to speak of this after we were wed." He'd sat back down on the bed, his hands limp on his thighs, head lowered. "I was selfish. Fearful lest you choose your mother over me."

I thought I would be a great fool to do so. But I said nothing. I needed to hear what he had to say.

"Your mother is an unhappy woman, Alice, and she blames others, never herself, for her unhappiness. She expected your father to lift her out of her darksome moods, and when he did not, she began to resent him. She punished him by telling him that another husband would have been able to save her."

"Yes, she could speak in such wise to my father. And being the good man that he is, he would suffer it without complaint to others."

"He is a good man and a kind friend," said Janyn, "but Dame Margery does not see beyond her own hunger. She does not see that she has been blessed with a loving husband and a good life. She has instead poisoned her life. She has taunted your father by favoring his friends in ways meant to embarrass him and inflict pain."

"And you were one of those men?" I guessed it by the sting of his words, the pain in his voice.

"To my great discomfort, yes."

"I overheard my grandparents say she is jealous of me. Did she love you?"

"Perhaps she told herself that she loved me, but she knows nothing of my heart or soul, Alice. I think it far more likely that she envies you the life she imagines you leading in my household, more exciting than hers, more gowns, more jewels."

I could not argue with his depiction of my mother, but sensed him holding his breath, hoping he'd said enough to satisfy me.

"That is why you avoided our home?"

He grasped my hand and pressed it to his cheek. "Yes. Margery desired me, Alice, and she assumed that I desired her."

"Did you ever love her, Janyn?"

To his credit and my immense relief he did not rush to respond, but looked inward, remembering. He slowly, sadly shook his head.

"She is a beautiful woman, and she knows how to give a man her full attention so that his heart warms to her. I have no doubt that I made a fool of myself praising her when I first beheld her. But it took little time for me to understand that she has nothing to give—she sucks the life from all who love her, and hoards that love, giving nothing in return. I thank God that I was never such a fool as to fall in love with her." He looked into my eyes. "You need have nothing more to do with her, my love. No one would expect you to do so after her unnatural behavior toward you." He reached out and pulled me close, holding me in what felt to me a fiercely protective embrace. "I pray that you believe me."

It explained all the secrets my parents had kept from me regarding our betrothal. "Now that I know why they behaved so, I am no longer afraid."

"Do you regret pledging yourself to me, Alice?"

"No. You need never doubt me."

He held me close for a moment, and I felt his heart pounding. When he released me I stepped back and took a deep breath.

"Will I meet the dowager queen?" I asked.

Janyn seemed relieved by the shift in subject. "You shall, and very soon. She will be on progress to London shortly after we are wed, and as she is most eager to meet you she will pause for the night at our home north of the city. We shall, of course, be there to greet her."

My heart fluttered. It did sound exciting. And perhaps once I had met her, observed Janyn's behavior with her, I might be reassured. I prayed it would be so.

"What of my grandparents? Will you tell them about my parents being guests at Castle Rising, and your friendship with the queen mother? It will be difficult to say nothing, and surely Father will wish to speak of it with them."

Again Janyn hesitated. I feared that his friendship with the dowager queen was not merely a matter of privacy, but one of secrecy and loyalty, and that he meant to guard the secret with his life. In the next breath he assured me that he had intended all along to tell Dame Agnes that very day, while we dined. He said that Grandfather already knew, but had sworn to keep it a secret, even from his wife.

"There *is* danger, Alice."

I crossed myself. Grandmother, too, would be sworn to secrecy, I thought.

It was precisely so. Dame Agnes bristled when Janyn spoke of the importance of secrecy, insulted that he would consider her so simple as not to understand.

"Befriending the she-wolf," she tsked as we walked home afterward. "I question his judgment, Alice, and that of Dame Tommasa's kin. The dowager queen has been trouble since the day she landed on this island. He is your betrothed, so I shall say no more against him. But be careful around that woman, Alice. Have all your wits about you when in her presence."

"Do you think I will be easily influenced by her?"

Dame Agnes glanced at me and her expression softened. "No, not you, dear Alice. And it is plain Janyn loves you. That is all that matters."

Her reassurance was affectionately meant but sounded insincere. The rich food curdled in my stomach, and I went to bed with a terrible ache in my belly that night. But as my thoughts turned to Janyn himself, his kisses, his willingness to answer my questions about Mother, I felt better. I fell asleep imagining lying beside him in that great bed.

SHORTLY AFTER dining at my future home in the city, Janyn, Gwen, Grandfather, and I rode out to the country house, Fair Meadow. The house nestled in a gentle valley, surrounded by woodland. The undercroft was built of stone, the upper stories of wood. What it lacked in elegance it made up for in spaciousness and such pretty views I wished the window openings were larger. Janyn teased me when I said so, swearing that I hoped to freeze us in winter so that we would never step out of bed. His eyes caressed me and I laughed and kissed his hands. I was very happy.

My parents dined with me at the home of my grandparents several times over the course of the summer. Mother was subdued, Father loquacious. Janyn was always otherwise engaged. Her presentation to the dowager queen had apparently inspired Mother to resume speaking to me. She admired my gowns and asked about the horse and the house in the country, going out of her way to avoid Janyn's name. When Father spoke of the honor of being guests at Castle Rising, Mother said little, but her eyes shone. I noticed that she had several new gowns as well, one of a silk that looked like the reflective surface of a lake, and I guessed it to be costlier than anything she had ever owned. Father must be bribing her to behave.

I saw Mother in a different light now, as my equal rather than my elder, as the competitor who had lost. But when my grandparents stole worried glances my way, I wondered whether I would someday regret my victory.

4

Resoun wol nought that I speke of slep,
For it acordeth nought to my matere.
God woot, they took of that ful litel kep!
But lest this nyght, that was to hem so deere,

Ne sholde in veyn escape in no manere,
It was byset in joie and bisynesse
Of al that souneth into gentilesse.

—GEOFFREY CHAUCER, *Troilus and Criseyde,* III, 1408–14

• 1356 •

MY WEDDING day dawned sunny and cooler than it had been so far that season. I had slept little and could not eat for the roiling of my stomach at the thought of lying with Janyn that night—so I would have been shivering with chills no matter what the weather.

Gwen, Nan, Dame Agnes, and her maidservant, Kate, dressed me. The red escarlatte gown had been so well fitted that I could freely move about, dance a jig, reach and bend, despite how it hugged my body like a second skin. The color brought a blush to my cheeks on a day when I might otherwise have lacked it. I wore a delicate circlet of gold and pearls, a gift from Dame Tommasa. My slippers were of red satin and a leather that had been tanned to match the dark gold of my surcoat, made from Janyn's betrothal gift to me.

"You are a vision of beauty," said Dame Agnes, almost choking on the words as her eyes filled with tears.

Gwen held a small mirror so that I might see myself. I turned back and forth, twisting and bending, standing on tiptoes and crouching. I could see only tantalizingly small parts of the costume at one time.

"Would that we had a larger mirror!" I said.

When someone knocked on the door, Kate went to see who it was while the other three hid me from sight with their bodies.

"Dame Margery," the maid said, stepping to one side.

My stomach fluttered. I had wondered when Mother would appear, for I knew that no matter how she felt about this marriage she would not forgo an opportunity to be, if not the center of attention, then very nearly so.

The others moved away, as if unveiling me. Mother stood in the doorway, uncertain of her welcome. In her finest silk gown and a crespinette sprinkled with pearls she looked as much a bride as I did, except that her fair hair did not fall free.

I stretched out my hands to her. "Mother. I am glad you are here."

As if distrusting my gesture, she tucked her arms behind her. Taking a few steps closer, her pretty pale gray slippers peeping from beneath her hem, she gave me a little bow, then turned to Dame Agnes and did the same.

"I shall leave you with your daughter while Kate dresses me," said Dame Agnes. "Would you like Gwen to leave as well?"

Mother shook her head. "I should like her to stay as witness that I have come in peace." Her voice held a sharp edge with which I was familiar. She felt ordered about, unappreciated, and would soon lash out at someone in retaliation. Probably me, the person she apparently blamed at present for her unhappiness.

"Peace?" I softly repeated. "We are not at war, Mother."

"Your father thinks otherwise, Alice. Come now." She moved over to the window, her silk gown richly rustling as she walked. "There are things I must tell you."

Dame Agnes bowed out of the room with her serving maid. Gwen busied herself with tidying the chamber.

Now Mother reached out to examine my surcoat, feeling the two layers, then lifting my skirts a little to see my shoes.

"You've done well for yourself, Alice. Such rich cloth, fine leather, silver and gold. And pearls in your hair." She frowned as she touched her own headdress. "You have studied me."

I'd had no part in choosing the pearls, but there seemed little point in correcting her. "I do not think it unnatural for a daughter to emulate her mother," I said, working to keep my voice soft, calm.

She waved away the comment. Her eyes bored into me, hard and cruel, as she said, "I must tell you what to expect tonight."

Had I not already been apprehensive about the bridal bed, her look and tone would have made me so. "There is no need. Dame Agnes has told me all that I need to know."

Mother raised an eyebrow. "So she said. But she does not know your betrothed as I do."

"What has that—" I realized what she was implying and my hand flew up toward her face.

She caught it and laughed. "Were you unaware that I knew Janyn? How could you think your parents would agree to your betrothal to someone they did not know?"

I thought for a moment she had not meant to imply what I'd thought she had, that Janyn had wooed her and possibly even bedded her, but she glanced over at Gwen to see if she was listening and then I remembered her wishing my maidservant to witness our conversation. She was teasing me while cleverly choosing her words so that to Gwen she would sound almost loving. Mother was a skilled performer.

"You want only to ruin my wedding day by sowing doubt, Mother. I'll hear no more."

"But you must! You must know what your father made Janyn promise. From what Dame Agnes has told me about your feelings for your betrothed, I fear you will be disappointed. There will be no love-making until you are sixteen. That is what I meant— Dame Agnes did not know of it, so she could hardly tell you—prepare you."

No lovemaking for two years? "Then why are we to be wed now?"

Mother tilted her head and fussed with the front of my robe. "Business, Alice. Your marriage is all about the guild and trade connections. But your father has ensured your protection—see how he loves you? If Janyn breaks his vow by bedding you tonight, he forfeits your dowry."

I refused to address her attempt to twist my heart about Father. She had always resented our closeness. "Janyn is so wealthy he does not need my dowry," I said.

"Do you think yourself such a prize?"

I did not flinch from her cutting remark, though it did sting. But surely Janyn did have all the wealth he could want. I was confused. I had been apprehensive about lovemaking, but now that I might be forbidden it, I felt as if I'd lost something most precious to me. She had robbed me of my excitement about the coming ceremony and feast. Could it possibly be so? Janyn had said he'd promised Father to wait only until tonight.

"You've little to say for yourself today." Mother used her veil to hide her smile, but I saw it in her eyes.

"What is there for me to say?"

"Well, come, then." She held her hand out to me. "Let us go down to the hall."

I shook my head. "I would be alone for a while."

Mother loudly sighed and reached for my hand. I pulled away from her.

"Leave me," I said, with no shadow of respect in my voice, my eyes, my posture.

She laughed, but I knew by her blush that my response was not what she had expected. "Come, daughter. Be grateful. Your doting father means to protect you. You are so young. If you were to conceive at once, you would suffer carrying a child."

"Women my age bear children every day. Leave me, Dame Margery." I could not call her "Mother." "I'll not walk out with you."

With another great sigh, she left the room. As soon as I heard her on the stairway, I turned to Gwen, who had finished tidying and resorted to rearranging items in order to look busy.

"Ask Dame Agnes to come to me here," I said.

I sat down on the bed to wait, fighting tears.

Gwen returned. "She has gone down to the hall, mistress."

"Fetch her."

I hugged myself, chilled by Mother's final blow. I vowed that I would hear nothing more from her lips.

When Grandmother sailed into the room, her green silk gown rippling behind her and her kindly face crinkled in concern, I fell into her embrace.

She pressed me to her bosom, then released me and stepped back to get a look at me. "What is amiss? Gwen looked so pale I feared I would find you lying on the floor bleeding. God be praised, you look unharmed." She stepped closer. "It was Margery, I trow. What did she say to you?"

I told her, and although she expressed indignation that her son would demand such a thing, or that he would deem me so fragile, she admitted that she did not know for certain whether or not it was so.

"But, my sweet child, I cannot believe Janyn would agree to it. I have seen you together. And he is rich as Croesus." She sank down onto a bench and fanned herself as she thought. "But of course!" she suddenly said. "Gwen, what are your orders regarding the bridal chamber?"

Gwen's face brightened. "I am to prepare the bridal chamber this evening for all to toast you when you are abed. Together." She looked at me, then Dame Agnes. "Would Master Janyn observe this ritual if he had promised what Dame Margery suggested?"

"It is the custom, is it not?" I asked.

"Only a fool would challenge his vow in such wise," said Grandmother. "So be of good cheer, Alice!" She lifted my chin and with a linen cloth dabbed at my eyes.

I had not been aware that I'd been weeping. "Do I look horrible now?"

Gwen lifted a mirror so that I might see I looked no worse than before.

"I am sorry that I doubted my son's complaints about Margery for so long," said Dame Agnes. "She is every bit the venomous lamia he described."

The rest of the day was a blur but for brief encounters with Janyn, who watched me with such hunger and kissed me with such enthusiasm that I thought we would both go mad if Mother's story were true. For Dame Agnes's argument had not convinced me that it was not.

As I stood on the church porch repeating my vows my heart constricted at each promise of obedience, thinking of my father's command. But when Janyn caught my gaze, looking on me with excitement and love, I momentarily took heart.

Upon leaving the church, Janyn—my husband!—took my hand to escort me to the guild hall in which we would have the wedding feast, and I was seldom out of his reach for the rest of the day despite the crowd of more than fifty guests jostling for our individual attention. I diligently avoided looking at Mother at the high table and must have succeeded in shutting out her voice as well, for I remember nothing of her after she'd left my bedchamber in Grandmother's house. As we quit the table Father kissed me and held me close for a moment, saying that he prayed we would be happy and that life would treat me gently. I hesitated to ask him about the vow, knowing that if Mother had lied my question might widen the rift between them, but I could not help myself.

The hall was crowded and smoky, and Father's hat was at just the right angle to cast shadow over his face, so I could not be certain of his expression. But his words rang false as he said he had considered asking it of Janyn. "Perhaps I spoke of it to your mother. But, in the end, I decided against it."

So Mother had concocted a hurtful lie, and Father had corroborated it. I need not have worried about widening the rift between my parents. It was the rift between my parents and me that had grown.

When the time came for Janyn and me to progress to our London home, my parents made their apologies and withdrew to their own. But half the inebriated crowd accompanied us. I had drunk little, but as Gwen and Dame Agnes undressed me they coaxed me to have some brandywine.

"To calm your shivering," said Grandmother.

In truth, I could not speak because my teeth chattered so. The brandywine was welcome. My night shift was too thin to provide any warmth, and though the bed was piled with wonderfully thick blankets my feet felt as if they were encased in ice. I sat propped against an extravagant pile of cushions all covered in softest linen, embroidered with our initials, *AS* and *JP*.

Janyn arrived through a side door, wearing a shift shorter and of a more substantial linen than mine. As he sat on the bed and swung his legs up, I kept my eyes on the straight, silky black hair on his calves, the surprisingly graceful shape of his ankles and feet. He kissed me on the forehead and lifted the covers to slip his legs beneath. His warmth was so sweet and comforting, until the fuss at the main door of the room reminded me of what this was all about. As Grandmother opened the door to the celebrants, Janyn slipped an arm behind me, resting it on the pillows, his hand gently cupping my trembling shoulder.

"I love you with all my being, Alice," he whispered. "When they are gone we can talk into the night. I'll not force myself on you."

It helped. I was able to turn to look at him, and we kissed for all the guests to see, a gentle kiss.

It was received with cheers, jeers, and the demand for a more passionate kiss.

We embraced, and now the kiss was hard and lingering, and I was no longer cold, no longer frightened.

I remember nothing of the toasts to our health and my fecundity. I was living for the moment we were alone.

And when at last our guests had departed and we were alone in our great bed, we turned to each other and embraced. There was no speech between us. I twined my legs around him as he cupped my breasts in his hands. When he penetrated me, I cried out in hunger and held him tightly, wanting to devour him. His deep, surprised laughter, his groans and cries, his final, violent thrusts, were all beautiful to me, and I thanked God for such a gift as our love, our passion.

Later, the memory of the momentary pain surprised me, and the evidence of the bloodstains. I wondered at the power of passion to numb all other senses.

We talked, drowsed, kissed, and began all over again. In the morning Gwen and the chambermaid exchanged smiles over the bloody sheets and gently bathed me. I was pampered and petted for several days, dozing in the afternoons, for our nights were far too active to be

restful. I had never been happier. The only shadow on those days was
the memory of Mother's malicious lie, and Father's cowardly corroboration. But she could hurt me no more.

A s WE settled into our domestic routine, my passion for Janyn ex-
panded into an all-encompassing love, for he behaved toward me
with a level of consideration I had never experienced. Father had told
him how he had taught me his own trade practices and encouraged me
to make suggestions; he said I'd become a valuable partner. Janyn was
delighted to benefit from this. He sought out my opinion on all manner of issues—household purchases, social engagements, trade negotiations. Dame Gertrude, who had served Janyn as housekeeper while
he remained a widower, had been instructed to hand over the keys and
all governance of the household to me at once. But as women do, we
found a comfortable compromise, one that allowed me to learn all that
she might teach me while testing my own abilities. I was only fourteen,
and everything was new to me.

I discovered that my strengths lay in ascertaining the quantities
required and judging the qualities of goods and furnishings, while
Gertrude was far better than I could yet be at supervising the servants. I loved the heft of the keys hanging from my girdle; it was a
relief to me that Gertrude seemed to have no misgivings about handing them over.

Though my days brimmed with new experiences I missed John,
Mary, Nan, and Will, saving up stories to share with them. Two weeks
after our wedding Janyn suggested we invite my family to dine with
us. My Salisbury grandparents, Father, Nan, and my siblings came;
Mother claimed to be ill. Mary and Will were stiff with shyness at
first, but Gwen soon engaged them in games of tag in the garden
and around the hall, and thanks to her that day was filled with their
laughter. Father seemed more comfortable with Janyn than he had
been on our wedding day, which suggested to me that they had met
since then over business. I caught him watching me several times with
a bemused expression, as if surprised to see me in charge of my own
home, affectionately teasing my husband, laughing with Nan over
mistakes I'd made in my first attempts to perform tasks she'd always
done for me. The day was one I would cherish in my heart for a long
while.

After our guests departed, Janyn asked whether there had been anything lacking in the day, anything I might have wished to have happened that had not.

"No, my love, nothing. All my loved ones were merry and well fed, and happy to see our contentment."

He pulled me close and whispered, "Will and Mary inspired me to wonder what it will be like when our little ones are dashing about the hall and gardens, squealing, shouting, laughing."

Knowing of the pain he'd suffered with the loss of his wife in childbirth as well as the baby they had anticipated with such joy, I always tried to keep my tone light when I spoke of our own hope for children. Now I asked with a teasing smile, "Do you dread it?"

"Dread it? I think it will be the most joyous place with such noise and activity." He slipped his hand inside the low neck of my undergown and pressed my breast.

I bit his lip. "Let us go to bed, my lord, and make a baby for your pleasure."

His voice suddenly husky, he ordered the servants to put the hall to rights and told Gwen to prepare me for bed, for I was uncommonly weary after the long day.

A S THE time grew near for our move to Fair Meadow I tried to learn more about Isabella of France to prepare myself for meeting her. I had lately learned from Gertrude that the woodland beyond Fair Meadow was Epping Forest, and that Isabella would be hunting there the morning before she dined with us. Janyn would hunt with her. The housekeeper much admired the dowager queen and her good health—she was said to be at least sixty years of age!

"You must study her preferences, mistress, and follow her diet in all things. Then you shall enjoy a long and active life and retain your beauty."

I asked Janyn, "Should we hire minstrels and musicians? If she hunts, she surely dances."

"Indeed she does, and her own minstrels and musicians accompany her wherever she travels."

I clapped my hands and hopped about in a merry jig.

"I am sure she will adore you, Alice, my love."

"Might I join the hunt, Janyn?"

"When you have hunted with me a dozen times, then you shall be included in the dowager queen's party. She has no patience with those who fall behind. Which reminds me . . . although I have promised not to separate you from your beloved Serenity, you do require a hunting horse. I must see to that while we are in the country."

I was to hunt. The anticipation kept me humming through all the preparations for our journey. Janyn's parents would accompany us, and for several days beforehand we stayed in their home while ours was being packed. The room in which we slept was separated from his parents' chamber by a wooden wall that was little more than a screen. I was upset to see it, for it seemed a certainty that we would have no lovemaking while there, our passion being no quiet engagement.

"The room is not to your taste?" Janyn asked, seeing my face.

"Your parents will hear us," I whispered, touching the flimsy wall.

He grabbed me up and tossed me onto the bed. We were not altogether silent. I mentioned this afterward as we lay side by side.

"Do you think they would not expect such noises from our bedchamber, Alice? My mother will make offerings of thanks in church, she so yearns for grandchildren near at hand to fuss over. My sister's children are so far away."

WE WERE a large and merry train of wagons and riders as we wove out of London and into the country on a gray but dry morning. A storm had blown through the previous day, ripping many of the beautifully colored autumn leaves from the trees, and the road was slippery with their sodden remains, but there was still enough color to be magical, and as the day warmed, a mist hung over the valleys and woodland.

Arriving at Fair Meadow as the lady of the manor was a very different experience from my earlier visit. Now it was a homecoming, and the servants warmly welcomed me. I could not imagine being happier.

JANYN DEPARTED before dawn on the day he was to hunt with the former queen. I rolled over to enjoy what lingered of his warmth and scent, but as his side of the bed cooled I grew restive, my feet too cold despite the bedclothes, the curtains around the bed shielding me from drafts, and the brazier I could hear simmering out in the chamber, close enough to keep the chill from the bed. My feet being cold usually bespoke fear, and though I lay there trying to convince myself that I was not anxious about meeting the queen mother, I had been praying for days that I would please her, and in so doing please Janyn.

It would be midafternoon before the hunting party returned, and the house was ready. We had worked hard for two days arranging all that we'd brought from London, planning the meals, the sleeping arrangements. Janyn, Dame Tommasa, and Gertrude had, in truth, had little need of me, but I had watched with care, asking questions and committing it all to memory for the next time. I meant to take my responsibilities seriously. Yesterday a company of the dowager queen's servants, including a lady-in-waiting and a priest, had arrived with many chests and some furniture.

I was confident that Gertrude was already up and reviewing the plans with the household. Gwen would be there as my eyes and ears. So why could I not drift back into a calming and renewing sleep? Beyond my anxiety about pleasing her, I feared Isabella of France. It appeared most people walked softly in her presence.

The daughter of the King of France and the Queen of Navarre, she had been bred to be a queen. Her betrothal to the young Edward of Caernarvon had been urged by the Pope as the best hope for peace between England and France. Beautiful, educated, and fabulously robed, according to my grandmother, she had arrived in England to discover that her handsome young husband had already lost his heart and pledged his undying devotion to his comrade-in-arms, Piers Gaveston. Not one to concede defeat Isabella had quietly encouraged the barons' natural animosity toward Gaveston, and devoted herself to the young king, her husband, making herself his indispensable partner.

Years after Gaveston's execution another handsome knight, Hugh Despenser, usurped Isabella's role as Edward's partner. Despenser was not satisfied with fortune and favor like Gaveston, but thirsty for power and ruthless in taking it. Isabella sailed to France, arranged for her son, Edward's heir, to join her there, and allied herself with Roger Mortimer, an English baron whom Edward had exiled and stripped of lands and titles. She shared Mortimer's bed and with him planned and executed an invasion that led to Despenser's long, painful, and very public execution and eventually the murder of King Edward, her husband

and father of the present king. Even in her waning years Isabella was a powerful woman, entertaining the ruling families of Europe in her elegant palace at Castle Rising or one of the other royal residences.

I had not known a woman could hold so much power. And even if she had wielded it while queen, to have retained some of it after her lover arranged for the murder of her husband, an anointed king, went against everything I'd ever been taught about the role of women, or our abilities. I imagined her having male genitals hidden beneath her elegant skirts and a demon for a familiar on her left shoulder. But everyone in the household spoke of her as beautiful, profoundly feminine, graceful, and just, if not overly merciful.

Thinking of Isabella was not calming me. I rose and sent for Gwen, intending to go riding before I dressed for the dowager queen's arrival. Serenity was saddled and ready for me when I stepped out into the yard. Janyn's father stood beside his own horse.

"I welcome your company, Father," I said as I kissed him on the cheeks, "but a groom would have sufficed as my companion."

"Not today, my dear daughter," he said. His eyes were merry, and in them I read that he had leaped at the chance to escape the last-minute flurry of preparations.

The morning was beautiful, a beneficence of warmth—for late October—and sunshine after a stormy night. My father-in-law was loquacious, recounting past feasts in the company of Queen Mother Isabella. Hearing the temerity in my questions, he cast all his stories in the light of the dowager queen's affection for our family.

But I returned home only slightly less frightened than when I had departed.

Gwen and Dame Tommasa hurried me to my chamber to bathe and dress so that I might be present in the hall the moment the herald announced the royal visitor approaching. Despite Dame Agnes's warning that I should not wear red when entertaining the dowager queen, my mother-in-law had insisted on it, brushing aside the well-meant advice with assurances that the Lady Isabella would approve of my wearing it. I was to wear my wedding garb, but of course this time my hair was gathered up off my neck and partially covered by the beautiful red brocade headdress. I was now a married woman, welcoming a great lady and her company to my home—someone I had never met and already feared and distrusted.

Dame Tommasa kept up a flow of chatter as she assisted Gwen, determined to see me smile.

"It is proper that you are fearful lest anything should go amiss, Alice, but rest assured that you have the best help, and the household knows what is expected of them."

"Not to mention the ten servants, a cook, and a lady of the chamber," Gwen murmured, her eyes amused.

But I found it impossible to be lighthearted. "I have never been in the presence of royalty, yet now I am about to welcome the mother of my king into my home and converse with her. I am frightened, Dame Tommasa." There. I had said it, though it embarrassed me to admit it.

My mother-in-law's response made me regret having so spoken. She shook her head at me and with a half smile said, "You *would* ride out this morning. Now you are weary and making much ado about nothing. Her Grace is your guest, Alice, and you shall be a most gracious hostess." She gave my hands a vigorous rub, then chucked me beneath the chin. "Now I must finish my own dressing." With a last hug that seemed intended to shake me to my senses, she sailed out of the room.

"Would you like to see the chamber we have prepared for Her Grace, and how we have decorated the hall?" Gwen suggested.

I gathered myself and resolved to enjoy myself. "Of course! The chamber first, then the hall."

We descended to the lower level, where a beautiful chamber that Janyn used for his meetings with merchants or his steward when he wanted more privacy than the hall might afford had been transformed into a bedchamber for the dowager queen. A large, grand bed had arrived two days earlier, together with chests bursting with wall hangings, bedclothes, and cushions. I had at first been offended by the implication that we had nothing fine enough for Her Grace, but Janyn assured me that Isabella always provided her own bed and bedding if possible. It was the custom of nobles.

"But what could possibly be more beautiful than what we might provide?" I had asked.

Janyn's laughter left me feeling naïve. It was a jolly, full-throated laugh, as if I had said something very funny. "I forget that you have never seen a royal residence, my sweet, innocent Alice." He looked at me, then hugged me to him. "Forgive my laughter, my love. God knows I would not insult you. I delight in your innocence. I will be sorry when you have seen all that I have seen, when I've nothing new to show you."

Now I looked at the gold and silver thread, the lapis lazuli pigments on the tapestries, the bed curtains, the coverlets, and saw that it was true; we had nothing so fine. On the window ledges cushions of indigo embroidered in gold and silver thread welcomed one to sit and gaze out at the fields and woodland. Several maidservants sat sewing near the south window, and one was stirring something over the brazier. Lady Jane, Isabella's lady-in-waiting who had been sent ahead to ensure that all was ready for Her Grace, kept them well in hand. At dinner the previous evening she had been sweet company, making up for the priest who was a dour Frenchman, too rude and dismissive for my taste.

A great wooden bath stood in one corner, by the brazier, and an intricately carved wooden screen nearby, ready to shield Her Grace from drafts.

"All seems ready," I said. "Let us move on."

Down in the hall there was little evidence of the frantic rushing about of the past few days except for the transformation of the great chamber. Unlike our home in London, the hall at Fair Meadow was not tiled but stone-flagged, and softened with rushes, a true country house. The fresh rushes were strewn with fragrant herbs to sweeten the room, and a fire merrily burned in the fire circle. No dogs lounged about, and the great trestle table was set up, covered with a brightly painted cloth, the benches piled with colorful cushions.

Gertrude appeared, trailed by a serving boy carrying more cushions, so many that he looked ready to topple over with them. I wondered where she meant to put them, and then I saw—there were more benches ranged along the wall.

"How many will be in Her Grace's company?" I asked Gwen.

"Thirty at least," she said, "but that includes the twelve who arrived last evening. She has been known to bring as many as fifty."

"I should think she'd seldom travel if it requires such a party!"

Gertrude sent off the serving boy and joined us. "Mistress, how beautiful you look today." Her smile was sweet and she gave me a little bow.

"I am pleased with all you have done," I said. And so grateful that she had experience of such events.

We all turned toward the yard as a horn sounded.

"That will be her herald," said Gertrude. She gathered her skirts and hurried from the hall.

Once more my hands turned to ice. "Where shall I stand?" I asked Gwen.

But it was Dame Tommasa who answered, sweeping into the hall, "You shall stand at the hall door when all the party has dismounted, Alice. Until then, let us sit by the window and enjoy the breeze." She guided me by my elbow to one side of the hall, beneath a long window.

We were soon joined by Lady Jane. "Oh, Dame Alice, what a vision you are!" she exclaimed as she gracefully perched beside us and gazed at me, then the room. "It is no wonder my lady loves this place. I have been walking in the gardens, and cannot remember so peaceful and beautiful a morning."

"Have you seen Dame Tommasa's garden in the city?" I asked. "It is a wonder of peace and beauty in the middle of noisy, crowded London."

"I should love to see it someday."

"You would be most welcome," said Dame Tommasa with a beatific smile. She gave me a little bow in thanks.

My heart leaped at the sound of the hunting party's arrival, but when I began to rise Lady Jane stopped me, gently resting a hand on my shoulder.

"They will not dismount at once. I pray you, be at ease awhile longer."

Though I sat still I was anything but at ease. When I was finally guided to the hall door my knees wanted to lock with every step. The yard, so peaceful when last I'd walked through it, was now roiling with people and beasts moving in all directions. And then I spied Janyn, resplendent in hunting green. He was speaking to a woman who must be Isabella of France, the quiet center of the pack. She stood beside a black horse unlike any I had ever seen before, so sleek, so graceful, yet large, and with a hint of wildness in his eyes. Isabella wore widow's weeds of style and elegance. Over a black gown she wore a black leather surcoat, with matching long gloves and hat. I imagined that the leather had been chosen to protect her clothing from the horse's sweat. It created a dramatic contrast, the black against her pale hair and skin. She knew the effect she had, I was certain.

I wondered for whom she wore the weeds, for whom she mourned— her late husband or Roger Mortimer? Or if she simply mourned her own lost queenship.

As if she had sensed my regard she swept around to face me, looking right into my eyes. Though we were at least twenty strides apart, I
felt that her gaze penetrated to my heart and she saw my fear. She gave
me a cold smile, then turned back to Janyn.

He and all the others bowed to Isabella and moved to one side
as she proceeded through the crowd, everyone allowing her to pass.
Did they, too, watch her in awe beneath their lashes? I wondered. She
glided, as if her feet merely skimmed the ground. She looked neither
to right nor left, but neither did she watch where she walked, which I
certainly would have done in an unfamiliar yard, with horse and dog
droppings likely to be all about. But her eyes seemed fixed on the
lintel of our great door. What confidence she had that no one would
allow her path to be befouled. As she drew close, she lowered her gaze
to note our little gathering in the doorway—Dame Tommasa, Master
Martin, and Lady Jane standing behind me.

I bowed low and managed to welcome her to Fair Meadow as my
mother-in-law had rehearsed me. When she was within a few arm's
lengths of me I realized with surprise that Isabella was shorter than
I was—from afar she had seemed to tower over the others. Her eyes
were hazel, like mine, her expression one of impatience barely masked
by a polite smile.

"The hunt was glorious and we are weary, Dame Alice."

Only then did I notice the shadows beneath her eyes, how shallow
was her breathing.

Lady Jane stepped forward, offering to lead her mistress directly to
her chamber.

As they progressed through the hall the line of servants bowed,
and then several scurried off to fetch the heated water for Her Grace's
bath.

Now a wry-faced nobleman, dressed almost as elegantly as Isabella,
stepped up to me.

Janyn introduced him as a count; I no longer remember of where
or what his Christian name was. I do recall him bowing to me and declaring himself heartsick that his friend had found me before he had a
chance to woo me himself. I fear it turned my head a bit, and I floated
away with him and his younger, English companion, Sir David, to sit
with them while they enjoyed some wine and cold refreshment. Janyn
went off to dress for the feast. Lady Jane had informed me that Sir

David often acted as the dowager queen's courier between her and Janyn, and that I would see him often. The count was a distant relation of Isabella, no one I need remember.

Sir David brought news of my good friend Geoffrey, whom he'd met at a tournament. My friend had made a point of toasting Janyn and me by name, as it had been the day of our wedding.

"He is to join the household of Prince Lionel and his wife, the Countess of Ulster. Lionel is the king's second-born son, and the countess of almost equally noble blood. It is quite an honor."

I was happy for Geoffrey, and amused to hear that he already had a reputation for witty banter.

"Indeed he is very well liked," said Sir David, "and will continue to rise in the noble households. Since you are favored by Her Grace, you will have opportunity to see your friend often, I should think."

"I am grateful for such gladsome tidings," I said. I had not thought to see much of Geoffrey now that our paths had so diverged.

The musicians had set up in a corner of the hall and began to play a merry tune. I felt as if I were dreaming, the hall so beautiful, the company so elegant—including myself—and the food and music promising a most delightful afternoon and evening.

MY DELIGHT dimmed as soon as the dowager queen joined us in the hall. I could not imagine any queen more resplendent than Isabella—I was certain that her daughter-in-law the present Queen of England must feel lacking beside her. I certainly did. I had felt guilty about the splendor of my robes, jewels, shoes, veils, but saw now that they were modest in comparison with royalty's—or at least with Isabella's. The jet and obsidian adorning her dark silk-velvet gown caught the light with such a shimmer it seemed as if they were alive, as if she had gathered thousands of butterflies and commanded them to flutter their wings and cover her as she moved. Her robe scintillated so that when she was in the room the eye was drawn continually to her. And she wore it with ease and grace, absolutely accustomed to her own splendor.

To my great relief, Her Grace seemed to warm to me as the meal proceeded. Janyn had been speaking of how quickly I had learned to ride and teased me about my fondness for my slow-gaited mare, saying I had named her Serenity.

"But that is a very fitting name for a beloved mount," Her Grace declared, and turned, tilting her head to one side, seeming to look at me for the first time. "She blesses you with serenity?"

"She does, Your Grace." I searched for something to add. "The noise around me seems to recede when I ride her, and the air softens."

She graced me with a breathtakingly beautiful smile. Her eyes lit up, her ivory skin gathered at her temples, and a dimple appeared to the left of her wide mouth. How her king could have looked at another when she was near, I could not imagine.

"Your husband tells me that you wish to hunt. You shall join me when you have had some experience. I like a woman who feels at one with her horse. I should think you might also enjoy hunting with a hawk."

A while later I heard her comment to Janyn, "It is a pity her parents did not have her riding and hawking, but they did seem of simple stock. How fortunate that you plucked their swan from the nest before she sank to their level."

Later, as she sat listening to the minstrels in the hall, Isabella fell asleep, her face slack, a thread of spittle slipping from one corner of her mouth. Both Janyn and his mother looked exceedingly uncomfortable, not disgusted but fearful. I did not understand their distress. Isabella was an old woman who put on a good display of vigor but could not sustain it. I had found it comforting to see this human side of her. Their unease troubled me.

In bed that night Janyn was fulsome in his praise of both Isabella and myself, almost too much so, as though desperate to believe that all was well. But perhaps I was being too sensitive. He was wild in his lovemaking, which must be a good sign. I did not speak of my anxieties and uncertainties.

THE NEXT day Janyn and Dame Tommasa conferred with Her Grace in her chamber for several hours while I enjoyed a ride around the estate with Master Martin, the count, and Sir David.

At the feast afterward I caught snippets of exchanges between Janyn and his father about a journey to Lombardy in late winter. I sensed a tension between them, and prayed I was mistaken in this. The minstrels were singing, there were many conversations in progress, and it was possible I was mixing up the words of one group with another's.

Isabella had been with us several days before she again turned her attention to me. After instructing me on a point of etiquette regarding the way I addressed Gertrude, about which I was mortified despite having been warned she might say such things, she declared herself very glad that she had made certain our marriage would take place.

"I am as delighted with you as Janyn said I would be," she said. "The effort to guarantee your union was not wasted." She had leaned closer to say in a conspiratorial voice, "I see by the way your husband looks on you that your bed sport is everything he had hoped."

That he had spoken to her of his taste in lovemaking seemed to suggest a relationship inappropriate to his station—as had been her relationship with Roger Mortimer. I studied her, wondering with dismay whether this exquisite bird of paradise had been my husband's lover. How else would she understand his looks?

"Your Grace," I said, "I am the happiest of brides, and deeply honored by your interest." I managed to say it without choking on my sudden suspicion.

In bed that night, I was tense with questions and close to tears. Janyn noticed at once.

"My sweet Alice, my love," he murmured, stroking my hair. "What troubles you?"

"What had Her Grace to do with our betrothal? How can she guess from your eyes that we enjoy our lovemaking?"

He said nothing for a while, lying back on the cushions, folding his arms behind his head. The soft black hair on his chest attracted my hand, but I resisted. I wanted an answer, and the moment I touched him I would doubtless lose my chance.

"She values my services, and knows that an unhappy man is a reckless man. Therefore she wanted me happily married once more, with a beloved wife and children to inspire caution in my travels, and she knew that you were my heart's desire. As for my eyes, I cannot say." He chuckled at the ceiling. "How strange that she spoke of that to you." Then he turned on his side, his eyes caressing me as his hand idly skimmed my belly.

"Were you lovers?" I demanded.

"You are jealous? How delicious! But Isabella of France and Janyn Perrers, merchant? No, my beautiful Alice."

He began to kiss me with an ardor I could not find it in myself to resist. Such was the pattern of our nighttime discussions.

I did not see at the time how he used our lovemaking to silence my questions, subtly suggesting to me that in wanting to know more than the little he told me I risked my happiness. I was only fourteen and so much in love.

5

> *But right as when the sonne shyneth brighte*
> *In March, that chaungeth ofte tyme his face,*
> *And that a cloude is put with wynd to flighte,*
> *Which oversprat the sonne as for a space,*
> *A cloudy thought gan thorugh hire soule pace,*
> *That overspradde hire brighte thoughtes alle,*
> *So that for feere almost she gan to falle.*

—GEOFFREY CHAUCER, *Troilus and Criseyde*, II, 764–70

• 1356 •

ON THE day the dowager queen was to depart, I awoke feeling sick to my stomach. Gwen suggested I ask Dame Tommasa to take my place in the hall, but I feared I might insult the dowager queen should I fail to bid her farewell. As it turned out, I need not have bothered. The Lady Isabella broke her fast in her chamber and remained there until the company was ready to depart.

As we awaited the dowager queen's appearance, I asked my mother-in-law whether we had offended Her Grace that she should so sequester herself on this last morning of her visit.

"Her Grace is indisposed this morning. When she drinks too much brandywine she is beset with nightmares that shatter her sleep."

I wondered whether she dreamed of her late husband's execution, but before I could pursue the topic a flurry of activity heralded Isabella's departure. She did indeed look pale and exhausted, yet dressed for riding. An indomitable spirit.

. . .

O NCE WE bid our guests farewell I permitted myself to contemplate the wonderful possibility that I was with child. My flowers, as Dame Agnes had taught me to call my monthly flux, had been
unreliable since my wedding night, so I had not dared to hope. But
after five queasy mornings . . . I enumerated my symptoms to Dame
Tommasa.

With a joyful sigh she enfolded me in her arms. "My precious
daughter, you must tell Janyn at once!"

It is impossible for me to describe the joy with which my husband
received the news. His eyes, always so expressive, seemed to melt with
love for me. He reached out for me, then seemed uncertain.

"I will not break under your touch, my love," I assured him. "In
truth, I need you to hold me."

I slept in his arms that night, and it did not matter that when I
woke I felt ill again. I felt cocooned in a nest of such love that I regretted nothing, not even the nausea. Indeed, though I'd already felt as
if nothing were denied me, it had been nothing in comparison with
the way Janyn and his parents and all the household now indulged my
every whim.

I had only two regrets, that I could no longer ride Serenity and
that we departed for London within a fortnight of Isabella's departure.
Master Martin could stay away from his trade no longer and Dame
Tommasa felt that she should accompany him, and yet she did not wish
to leave me at Fair Meadow with only the servants and Janyn to help
me adjust to my first pregnancy.

Despite the regrets, I quickly cheered up, thinking of sharing my
happy news with Nan, Mary, Will, and John. I returned to London in
a cart well cushioned by bedding and covered in sailcloth.

We resumed a comfortable rhythm of domestic routine, church,
and entertaining. Janyn made no delay in introducing me to his circle.
He had only one concern.

"Make no mention of the royal guest we entertained while at Fair
Meadow," he warned.

"But surely folk know that you trade in her name."

"Of course. But it is never discussed. And as for her favor, it is
unusually personal, Alice, and might therefore inspire jealousy or
suspicion."

"Suspicion of what, my love?"

"The royal family are ever in need of money to fill their coffers, and those merchants and bankers—especially the bankers—who make them loans are most favored."

"You have loaned money to Her Grace?"

"A little. But others would surmise that I have loaned her far more, and then, thinking I must have money to spare, would wish to borrow from me as well. I have none to give!"

"You spend it all on me."

He laughed. "It is well spent, my love." He quickly grew serious again. "Favor brings preference, and there are guild rules, though the royal family and the great barons are not bound by such constraints. So we do not speak of such things."

"What of the servants? Surely some of them gossip; they are only human."

"What matters is that we say nothing, my love, so there is nothing but the gossip of servants, which is hardly proof. Do you understand?"

"I shall not refer in public to Her Grace."

He was well pleased. In truth, to say nothing of Her Grace's visit was so simple that I found it no burden; but the prohibition chilled me. I worried that such a secret presaged trouble, and feared what might happen. The not knowing cast a shadow over my happiness.

Despite my condition, I was soon busy with the household. I shopped, sewed, and even hired additional servants, being certain to consult Gertrude, Angelo the cook, and Gwen beforehand. I enjoyed bargaining with merchants, choosing new materials to brighten up the house—Dame Tommasa had inspired me. In general I found my duties immensely satisfying.

But my moods were increasingly mercurial, and I was glad of the daily round of prayers at my new parish church, especially once I had found a confessor who put me at ease. John de Hanneye was a young priest assisting the elderly pastor, in preparation for his first preferment to a parish of his own. He knew Janyn and liked the Perrers family, but that was not why I was drawn to him. From the first I felt a strong connection to him, a familiarity I could not explain. Gwen liked him as well, and was good about wandering away to entertain herself while I spoke to him. I took the risk of confiding in him my anxiety concerning Her Grace's influence over my marriage, my husband, and his mother—I'd taken the precaution of doing so in the protection of confession. I appreciated that he listened with sympathy, but without offering empty reassurances. Together we prayed that God would protect my family.

I met a great many of Janyn's guild fellows and their wives, and made some new friends. But there was one occasional dinner guest I disliked and distrusted from the start, a Fleming by the name of Richard Lyons. By his rough manner and the coarseness of his speech he was clearly of low birth, yet Janyn's fellow merchants tolerated his unpleasantness because he was wealthy and very influential, particularly in the lucrative court circle. He leered when he first met me, with his bold gaze unclothing and ravishing me. I yearned to slap him.

But Janyn squeezed my hand and whispered, "Pay his manners no heed, speak to him as if he had all the courtesy of a knight in the court of love, Alice. I need him. He has an uncanny ability to be in the right place at the right time. He has ingratiated himself with much of the royal family and other noble houses by being the first to offer loans when they are embarrassed for coin."

I was also wary of the Lombard financiers and traders with whom Janyn associated. He was not considered a member of the group, whom Londoners referred to as the Society of Lucca, but he knew them through Dame Tommasa's family. He explained that as he traded in their territory he needed to assure himself of their friendship. Although they were elegant, courteous, full of exciting tales, and all in all delightful companions, I could not help but consider them dangerous to know.

The problem was that the London merchants considered them rivals, and indeed the Lombards enjoyed advantages—such as lower taxes and other favors from the king, in exchange for loans—that the London merchants did not share. The men of the Society of Lucca were also notorious smugglers, and it was understandable that merchants who foreswore potential sources of wealth in order to obey the law of the land and the rules of their guilds resented smugglers above all other folk. I feared that our association with them might jeopardize our reputation, but Janyn said much the same of them as he did of Richard Lyons, that he needed them. As was not the case with Lyons, however, he also enjoyed their company.

At Christmas we entertained Janyn's parents, but not mine. Father told me that my husband's connection with the Society of Lucca, of which he'd been unaware before my marriage, was unacceptable to his

guild of grocers. There was doubtless some truth to this, but I knew
that he and Janyn still did business, so it was plainly Mother's decision
to avoid my hospitality. It was enough for me that Father did not prevent Nan from bringing Will and Mary round for weekly afternoons of
games and jollity; nor did my brother John's master suggest he should
not sup with us on Sundays.

IN LATE winter came a blow for which I should have been prepared,
but when Janyn announced that he would depart on a journey in a
few weeks I felt sick at heart.

We were sitting before the fire after dinner when he said, "Alice, I
must leave in a fortnight for Lombardy. I wanted to tell you before you
heard it from my parents or my factor."

It was the news I'd dreaded. All I could think to say was, "So
soon!" I reached for his hand.

He pressed mine. "You knew that this day would come. I have
never hidden it from you."

"But it is not yet spring," I moaned. "Should you not wait until
the spring?"

"What if I should be delayed and not return in time for the birth
of our first child?" he asked.

"But traveling in winter!"

He cupped my face in both his hands and looked long into my
eyes, then kissed me and held me close.

"My love, I must go now. I have made the journey at this season before, and was home well before midsummer," which was when
Dame Tommasa believed I would be brought to childbed. "You must
trust in God. Pray that He watches over me."

"Is it the dowager queen who sends you and puts you at such
risk?" I asked.

"In part. But we have agreed not to speak of her."

"In the company of others, but surely we may discuss her here, in
our home, with none to hear?"

"The less you know, the easier it will be for you to say nothing."

As I moved to protest he silenced me with another kiss.

"You are not a fair player," I pouted.

"What say you of this? To compensate for my silence on my travels
for Her Grace, I shall include you even more in my work. I'll discuss
with you all my business affairs not related to Isabella and take your

suggestions into consideration. I'll ensure that you meet all with whom I trade, so that you may make informed decisions." He cocked an eyebrow. "Well?"

I may have been young and inexperienced, but I saw in his proposal a way to be part of his life, not just a pretty pet.

"Yes. It is a fair trade. But you forfeit all peace between us should you go back on it."

Our new agreement did nothing to ease my fears about his journey, but Janyn immediately began to fulfill his promise, introducing me to yet more men with whom he traded, and showing me through the storerooms where he explained the value of the spices, jewels, cloth, statues, and sundry other merchandise. He even showed me the lists he kept of his contacts and what he judged to be their strongest points. There was little time to teach me more, but I took heart from his obvious approval of my questions and suggestions. I was grateful for his tutoring. It was to prove an invaluable gift.

And then he was gone.

DURING THIS first separation I did not lie abed nursing darksome thoughts, though part of me was often inattentive to my companions. Gertrude had suffered a fall and would be confined to a chair throughout the spring, so I was learning to deal directly with the lower servants. Janyn had instructed his factor to consult me on accounts, Dom Hanneye listened with calm and sympathetic attention to all my fears and hopes, and the wives of the guild included me in gatherings spent embroidering cushions for the benches in the guild hall and church. I was particularly honored to be asked to stand as second godmother to the infant daughters of several guild members, an important bonding ritual among the families.

Members of the guild and many of the Society of Lucca kept me informed of news along the route Janyn was taking, even occasionally bringing word of him from conversations with merchants newly arrived from the Continent who had encountered his party. Master Martin and Dame Tommasa dined with me almost every day, and Dame Agnes and Master Edmund often joined us as well. Nan continued to bring Will and Mary to spend the afternoon at least once a week.

IN LATE spring my love returned. He had written that he expected to sail up the Thames in early June, but God blessed his travels and he arrived a week earlier than I'd had any hope of seeing him. Heavy with child as I was by then, I lacked all grace and feared that Janyn would greet me with cold indifference. But he did not do so. Although our kisses required some careful positioning, they were long and passionate. We agreed to disregard the suggestions that we sleep apart for my last month.

On the first evening we left the lamps burning longer than usual so that we might gaze on each other. He was stroking my stomach when the baby kicked. Startled, he withdrew his hand and stared as my belly moved seemingly by itself. I reached for his hand and guided it back.

"Is it not a wonder?" I whispered. "Our child is alive within me, kicking and stretching and letting me know that soon it will be bored and choose to come out into the light."

Janyn's dark eyes were wide and moist as he moved his hands over my belly, seeking more contact with our child.

"A miracle. A blessed miracle," he said. "But is it not painful?"

I shook my head. "The weight is painful, and the stretching of my hips, but from the moment our child moved, I have felt"—I searched for a word to describe the companionship—"I have felt a part of life, not simply an observer."

"You are most precious, my love," said Janyn. "I pray that you may never suffer, that God will guide and protect you in all ways."

When I woke in the night I was in Janyn's arms, safe and warm, and my heart swelled with love.

SIR DAVID, who had been so charming when he was our guest at Fair Meadow in Isabella's company, arrived a few days after Janyn's return. I thought it a coincidence, but soon learned from his conversation that the queen mother had been even better informed than we had about the timing of my husband's return. As we dined, Sir David expressed his hope that my lying in would occur while he was yet in London, so that he might be the one to give Her Grace a firsthand account of her godchild.

"Godchild?" I looked at his smiling face, then at Janyn, whose expression was guarded. He was closely watching my reaction. "Oh, yes, I pray that my time is near," I said.

Looking relieved, Janyn reached to squeeze my hand. I did my best to hide my unease, but found it difficult. He might have warned me. I did not welcome this news, and especially not coming from someone other than my husband. I hated my growing sense of being owned by the dowager queen, of being controlled by her in every aspect of my marriage, to some dangerous purpose. Perhaps pregnancy exaggerated my reaction, but I felt suffocated by her patronage.

Fortunately the talk moved on to other matters, and after the meal Janyn and Sir David retired to the parlor used for such meetings. It was a fine afternoon, warm and sunny, and Dame Tommasa had sent word that she would meet me in the garden with a surprise. I took my needlework there, determined to set aside my fears for the sake of the child in my womb. I managed to fall asleep leaning against a lattice with the sun warming my feet. Gwen woke me when my mother-in-law arrived.

"She has come with a cart filled with seedlings of your favorite plants from her garden."

For the rest of the afternoon I fell into the excitement of planning. Though in my condition I could not work the soil, I enjoyed consulting Dame Tommasa on the placement of the plants and imagining how the garden would look the following summer. It was a testament of faith in the future, much like the child growing in my womb.

My delight distracted me from Sir David's surprise comment until Gwen and my mother-in-law had helped me up to my chamber. Remembering, I told Dame Tommasa. Her eyes filled with tears.

"Such gladsome news! Son or daughter, they will be helped along in life by a connection to the royal family. I cannot wait to tell Martin." But, despite my efforts to hide my doubts, my perceptive mother-in-law noticed that I was not so sanguine. "Are you not pleased?"

"I am aware of the great honor she does us," I said, hanging my head more than was necessary for Gwen to comb out my hair.

"And so you should be, my child."

I could not stay bent over for long. Straightening, I asked, "But if her favor is to remain a secret, how do we explain such a godmother? And are we to name our child Isabella if it is a girl?"

Tommasa opened her mouth as if to respond, then shut it, her large, beautiful eyes sweeping the room as if she might find inspiration in the fabrics or furnishings.

"That is a difficulty I had not considered," she murmured as if speaking to herself.

I refrained from voicing my deeper concern. She was subdued and distracted after that, and I was relieved when she departed. I was weary to the bone and fell asleep almost at once.

It was late when Janyn came to bed, waking me with the cough he had brought with him from his travels.

"Is Sir David gone?" I sleepily asked.

"Yes, he is biding with his wife's family nearby."

"Did your meeting go well?"

"Yes. He is a most courteous and agreeable man. I stepped into the hall and saw Mother working in the garden. Are you pleased with all the plants she's begun for you?"

"You know that I am, and grateful for all that she is teaching me about their care." I stuffed another pillow behind my head so that I might see him better as I asked, "Why did you not tell me of Her Grace's offer to be godmother to our child?" I fought to keep my tone light.

"Because I did not know of it until Sir David mentioned it."

"When do you imagine she intends to inform us?" My tone was sharper than I'd intended.

He placed his hand on my stomach. "Had I known of this I would have prepared you, my love. I pray you believe me."

I patted his hand, the now-familiar fear choking me. In all other things Janyn was confident, assured, but regarding the queen mother he seemed to walk on shifting sand, aware that though he had so far managed to stay upright he was ever in danger of sinking.

"I told your mother that Isabella intended to stand as godmother," I managed to say.

"Of course you did," Janyn said. "I would wonder had you not." His confidence was shaken. I heard it in the way he forced his words.

"We wondered how we are to keep it secret."

"I wonder as well, my love."

"If we have a daughter, will she be named Isabella?"

"That would follow by custom, a child taking the first godparent's name, but Her Grace may choose, as many do, to suggest another."

"I am frightened, Janyn. She has such a hold over you. Over us."

He paused for a moment, his hand on my stomach moving slightly, as if he'd begun to clench it and remembered he must not. When he spoke, he sounded weary. "She was queen of this realm, Alice, and she is the mother of our king. We are her subjects, and if she singles us out for preference we are honored, and are bound to honor her in all ways."

"You sound as if you are repeating something your mother told you many times."

He forced a laugh. "Already you know me so well."

"You have in the past chafed at your responsibility to Isabella?"

"She did not favor Janet." His first wife. "She summoned me to Castle Rising a week after my wedding and made it clear that I was to come alone. I wanted to refuse, but Janet and my parents convinced me that I was being childish, that I would jeopardize our comfort, our future, by disobeying the queen mother." He took a deep breath. "Let us not dwell on old sorrows. The baby will hear and have a bad night." He kissed my hand.

I wondered whether Janet had also been afraid. I pushed away that question as Janyn turned down the lamp and snuggled up against my back, easing my backache and quieting the baby. We slept through the dawn. That was the blessing of being with child—until the last few weeks I slept well, no matter what the chaos in my life.

When my grandparents supped with us in that time between Janyn's homecoming and my lying in, I asked Dame Agnes to be with me when I gave birth.

"Me?"

"I would like someone from my family to be with me."

"I should be honored, sweet Alice. Of course."

"Bless you, Dame Agnes," said Janyn. "You make us both very happy."

It was less than a fortnight before my lying in that the queen mother finally sent a messenger formally stating her intention of standing godmother to our child. If it was a girl she would of course be first godmother, and our daughter would be named Isabella.

MY SWEET Isabella was born at the end of June after a long labor that I later learned frightened Janyn. Dame Agnes and Dame Tommasa were lovingly present throughout my ordeal, as well as my dear Nan, Gwen, and Felice, a midwife I liked very much.

My first daughter was rosy cheeked and dark haired, with wonderfully long fingers and toes and the appetite of a ploughman. From the moment I beheld her, and especially once she found my heavy breast and gave suck, I adored her. Of course I still loved Janyn above all men, but from the moment she was born Bella was the center of my life. She was always "Bella" to Janyn and me and all the family.

Dame Tommasa stood in for the dowager queen at Bella's baptism, with the wife of Janyn's guild master as second godmother, and

Geoffrey as godfather. My Salisbury grandparents and my parents attended the christening, the latter, I presume, because it was quite a social affair, though of course I was still sequestered in my lying-in chamber. Mother did not bother to slip in to see me, though most of the other women attending did so.

I wept as I nursed Bella that night. Of course my emotions were raw so soon after childbirth, but I believed that Mother's slight was intentional. Fortunately, this sorrow did not, could not, consume me, for something far stronger lifted me up—I loved motherhood. I refused a wet nurse because I wanted to enjoy everything about this time, and Janyn did not try to overrule me, for he, too, shared my absorption in Bella. He often sat with me as I nursed her, his face alight with love.

In July the Perrers and my grandparents, my brothers and sister, Nan, and many friends attended my churching, the ceremony in which I lit candles on the lady altar in thanks for my safe delivery. It was an elegant, merry occasion, made more exciting by signaling my readiness to resume lovemaking. Janyn brooked no further delays.

A month later we were informed that Isabella the queen mother was on progress to London and would grace us with a two-day visit to Fair Meadow in a fortnight. She expected, of course, to meet her goddaughter and namesake. I told myself it was a great honor and averted my mind from the familiar worry with the frenzy of activity preparing for the move.

Only then did Janyn insist I engage a wet nurse. "It is important that you begin to trust Bella to others, Alice. As my wife you have responsibilities. I need you by my side, with the queen mother and whenever we entertain. There may come a time—" He stopped himself and looked away. "I see you have begun packing."

I reached up and took him by the shoulders to turn him back to me. He looked down with an apologetic smile.

"You were saying there may come a time?"

"Alice, come." He drew me over to a bench and sank down with a sigh, patting the space beside him. "I am your elder by many years. One day, God willing not too soon, you will be fully in charge of our daughter and all our children. That is why I've been so keen for you to learn my business and the customs of our circle, so that you may move forward without fear. I do not mean to be harsh in insisting on the wet nurse." He put his arm around me.

I rested my head against him, feeling the pounding of his strong heart. I willed myself to believe there was nothing more to his comment than he'd said.

We rode side by side to Fair Meadow, and my precious Bella was none the worse for being hours without me, riding in the cart with her wet nurse. In fact, it was lovely to see her face light up as I approached her in the yard of our home and to hear her gurgling laughter as she grasped my nose.

Once there we had two days to prepare for the queen mother. Gwen and Dame Tommasa fussed over my gowns, making tucks— I seemed to have lost more weight in the past few days—and adding jewels. My hair was washed in a complicated mixture of oils and lotions, requiring me to sit outside in a wide-brimmed hat with a gap in the crown through which my hair was pulled to allow the sun to brighten it. At the same time my face was subjected to a disgusting paste that hardened painfully—it was to erase the freckles that I'd collected working in the garden the past fortnight.

"I am not wooing the queen mother," I protested, but my tormentors did not even pause in their endeavors.

I complained to baby Bella and her wet nurse as they sat in the shade nearby.

"I can think of little more delightful than having such a fuss made over me," said Mary, the nurse. "Do you not feel like the queen herself?"

Peering at her through the strands of hair that drooped from the hat, I burst out laughing. Soon she was laughing as well, and Bella gurgled and kicked.

That is how Janyn found us, and he gamely teased me about my frightening appearance.

Our time at Fair Meadow was everything I'd hoped for. The long, late-summer days, the slow, languorous lovemaking, the hours spent admiring our daughter and planning for more children. How I loved Janyn and Bella, how happy we were. I see our country home as always in sunshine. I was determined that it be so.

But before we could relax together there we faced a day and a night of entertaining the queen mother and her retinue. We received word shortly before her arrival that she would have in her company her grandson John of Gaunt, the king's third son. He would not stay the night, but after feasting move on to a royal lodge.

"It is a great honor to welcome the young Earl of Richmond," said

Janyn. "He will fall in love with you. He is but a few years older than you are, and very handsome. I think I shall be jealous."

The difference in our ages seemed much on Janyn's mind of late. "I see no man but you in my dreams, my love," I assured him.

Albeit as fabulously dressed as she had been on her last visit to Fair Meadow, Isabella seemed subdued. Even with the assistance of her groom she stumbled on dismounting and for a moment seemed shaky and confused. I crossed myself as the elegant John of Gaunt, Earl of Richmond, and Sir David rushed to support her on either side. It was as if her years had suddenly caught up with her.

"*Deus juva me,*" Dame Tommasa murmured beside me. She had turned quite pale.

But the queen mother gently waved away Sir David and lightly rebalanced herself against her grandson's proffered hand. Although her steps were stiff rather than fluid as in the past, she did not falter as she approached us. Janyn ran forward to bow to her and welcome her to our home, and I followed close behind.

Her smile was radiant and her eyes clear as she regarded us with affection. After compliments all round we entered the hall, and when Isabella was handed her namesake, Janyn beaming beside her, Gaunt presented my daughter with a silk-clad cushion alive with embroidered unicorns and other fanciful, merry little creatures.

"And when she is ready, a pony shall be added to your stables for my namesake," said Isabella, kissing my daughter's forehead.

Then Gaunt touched my arm and asked if I would return to the yard with him.

His eyes were blue gray, with dark brown lashes and arched brows; his hair was blond; his jaw, square and strong. He was a tall man, with wide shoulders, and so handsome he seemed more a god than a man. I followed him out the door—for how to refuse him?—with apprehension, wondering what was amiss.

Isabella's groom stood in the center of the yard holding the reins of a magnificent mare, muscled and sleek, coat dark and glistening. She pawed the packed earth and shook her head with a throaty whinny as we approached.

"The Lady Isabella says she promised you a hunter," said Gaunt, "and she has kept her word."

I stopped, staring at the beautiful creature now regarding me with cautious interest. "Mine?" I asked in a choked whisper. I could not possibly control such a horse.

"Would you care to give Melisende an apple, Dame Alice?" the groom asked. He nodded to a young servant who stood at a little distance, and the lad ran to me and proffered several apples.

Of course I stepped forward, took one of the apples, and held it behind me as I gently stroked the horse's side. Melisende nudged my shoulder, searching for the fruit. Her careful training was evident in the way she took the treat from my open hand.

"You have made the Lady Isabella very happy with a namesake, Dame Alice. I thank you."

I said something sufficiently courteous and grateful, all the while wondering how these royals were schooled to express themselves so calmly and naturally while offering such obvious untruths. Once Isabella had decided to stand as godmother for our child I'd had no choice in the matter.

My hunter was to be curried and rested. I was eager to ride her, yet felt disloyal toward Serenity and reluctant to be even more in Isabella's debt. I was also discomfited by the direction of the earl's gaze—to the point at which my necklace disappeared between my breasts. However, I expressed my thanks to him as fulsomely as Janyn would wish me to.

The meal was lively with banter and descriptions of the latest tournaments and feasts at court. I learned that our king reveled in lavish and elaborate displays, particularly enjoying dressing up as legendary heroes. Isabella was proud of him, and Richmond seemed painfully aware of walking in a great man's shadow. I wondered how it would be to meet the king, and whether I ever might. I closely studied how Janyn and his parents interacted with the royals, in order to follow their example. They seemed at ease, except that they took care not to contradict or fail to respond to either the dowager queen or her grandson. I was proud of being a Perrers at that moment, and grateful for all that my marriage had brought me.

After the meal everyone dispersed to rest for a while. Gwen had piled the cushions on my bed so that I might recline without needing my hair redone. I had dozed just a little while when she woke me.

"The queen mother is asking for you. She says she has something to show you in the stables."

But I had already seen Melisende. Surely she knew that. Gwen hurriedly dressed me in a riding outfit, and I found Isabella in the hall. She was dressed much as she had been when I'd first seen her, in her dark hunting garb, and seemed revived by her rest.

"At last," she breathed as I appeared. "Proceed!"

Out in the stables, my new hunter had been saddled, as had Isabella's beautiful horse, Janyn's, Master Martin's, and Sir David's—the Earl of Richmond had already departed for the royal hunting lodge. We walked out of the stables, the grooms guiding the ladies' horses and the men walking their own, and moved toward the mews. The falconer appeared with a hooded merlin on his wrist, her tiny bells jingling as she fluttered a little. He carried a glove.

"In thanks for permitting me the great joy of standing as godmother to your daughter, and of giving her my name, I present to you this merlin," said Isabella, her beautiful face lit with the pleasure of presenting a fabulous gift. The small, costly hawks were favored by nobles. "May Dido hunt well for you."

"My lady," I said, trying not to gasp, "you honor my family. May God watch over you and bless you in all ways."

The falconer handed me the glove and requested that I slip it on. As soon as I did so, he secured the merlin's claws with the jesses on my glove and said, "Once her hood is removed, do not blink or she might attack. If you hold her too far from you she will flap her wings as a sign to bring her in closer." With that he disappeared, returning with the others' hunting birds as I was wondering what on earth I might do to prevent myself from blinking.

As the merlin moved, her bells sounding so sweetly, I turned to her, this beautiful and powerful creature on my arm. Her tiny hood was fashioned from what looked like buttery soft leather tanned a pale gold, with a perky plume of red and gold feathers. With the bells and the fashionable hood she might have seemed a pampered pet—but her fierce beak and claws and powerful wings were a reminder of her true character. I loved her from that very first moment.

"My lady Dido," I whispered, "I am Alice, your companion in the hunt."

Sir David, the only one close enough to overhear me, chuckled. "Well done, Dame Alice. You hold her as if you'd had many such falcons, and you address her with the respect she deserves."

His compliments helped me relax, though I still worried that my arm was not sufficiently strong for me to carry the merlin and ride on horseback, especially on an unfamiliar mount. But this last worry was banished—once the others had their birds the falconer returned and took mine from me, saying, "I'll hand her back when we've ridden into the fields, mistress."

Janyn had joined me.

I was speechless with excitement and also fear, not so much of the horse and merlin, but of making a fool of myself with so many firsts in such august company.

"Come." He'd brought a mounting stool and held out a hand to me.

I accepted his help with immense gratitude, and soon I sat high up on my beautiful hunter. Melisende was well trained, and though she was a challenge, and therefore a little frightening, that seemed as it should be. She was a large, powerful animal, her training but a cloak that might be shed at any time. I wondered whether this was why powerful people so enjoyed hunting and hawking, the danger inherent in riding a powerful animal, handling a wild bird, letting loose the tracking dogs. Certainly Isabella glowed with life astride her hunter and Janyn moved as one with his powerful steed as we rode to the meadow in which we were to hawk.

After dismounting, with my merlin now on my glove, I followed the falconer's careful instructions and removed Dido's hood. Her eyes were wild and cunning, and for a moment I could not breathe, as if she had ordered me to stop all motion while she considered me. And consider me she did. God watched over me, for I did not blink during the long examination. When the queen mother called out that we were ready, I must have moved a little, holding Dido farther from me. She flapped her wings with annoyance, but calmed the moment I drew her closer.

"Forgive me," I said to her. "I am new to this."

The falconer showed me how to loosen the jesses for the hunt. I had hardly completed the task when Dido took off after a bird. I remember it as a crane, but the prey does not matter. What mattered was the beauty of my merlin's flight, her fierce attack and, the best part of all, her return to my glove when I tapped it as the falconer had shown me, dangling a gobbet of meat from my gloved fingers as a lure.

Both Janyn and Isabella nodded their approval. That, too, warmed my heart.

. . .

W E SPENT a quiet evening in the hall, everyone pleasantly tired, and withdrew early to bed. As it was warm, the glazed windows in the house stood open, and in the quiet hours I was awakened by voices in the garden below. I thought I recognized them as Isabella's and Lady Jane's. When I began to rise to attend them, Janyn held me back.

"Her women will see to her, Alice. She is often restless at night. Let her be." His tone was stern though his voice was hoarse with sleep.

I lay back on the cushions, though I was now wide awake. "Do you think that she knew her lover had ordered her husband murdered? Do you think that is why she wakes in the night?"

"We do not speak of that, my love."

I raised myself up on one arm and touched his shoulder. "But we are so bound to her. Is it not natural to want the truth about someone we serve?"

"She is generous with our family, Alice. Why should we question her?"

"Are you so worried about losing her custom?"

Janyn sat up, brushing his hair from his forehead and rubbing his eyes. "God's blood, Alice, leave that to the past. She is the daughter, sister, widow, and mother of kings and we are common folk. Though we might wish to know the truth about what happened to our former king, and though we might rightly feel it is in the interest of our own safety to know more clearly the woman who so favors us, we must let it be. It is too dangerous to challenge the king's family. There is far more at stake than the loss of some trade." He tousled my hair. "I would have thought you would be happily dreaming of merlins and beautiful hunters."

"I was." I tried to calm myself, but it was no use. "Why does she so favor us, Janyn? Godmother to our child, the bird, the horse, her assistance in convincing my parents to allow us to wed. What are we giving her in return? It must be more than your services as a trader."

To my surprise, he began to laugh. "I do not know how I thought to quiet you on this. For all the reasons I love you and value your counsel I should have expected your impatience with mystery."

"You do know more than you've told me."

He turned up the wick on the oil lamp, allowing more light. "Is there any wine left in the mazer beside you?"

I lifted it from the shelf beside me and passed it to him. He seemed intent on draining it.

"You'll be too drowsy to talk," I teased.

He lowered the mazer, but did not hand it back.

"The Lady Isabella led a successful revolt. She had gathered a formidable force, a huge force, and most of them were the king's subjects. When her own son seized her lover, the commander of her troops, she feared for others among her supporters who might also be taken. Some of those men escaped to the Continent. A few important ones settled near my mother's birthplace. Isabella writes to them, and they write to her. My mother's family are her couriers."

"You?"

He nodded. "At present I am the most active from here."

I crossed myself. "But that was so long ago. Thirty years. How many are still alive? Why would they yet fear the king?"

"Many yet live. As to why they have not returned, I do not ask." His voice had grown tense. "I am merely a courier. And the queen mother is very grateful for our service, and especially our discretion. Now, let us sleep." He lay down with a weary sigh, his back to me.

"Thank you for confiding in me, my love," I whispered as I snuggled against him.

But sleep would not come for me. If the soldiers stayed in Italy out of fear of the king's wrath, or of others who had supported Isabella's husband, Janyn took a terrible risk in playing courier between those men and Isabella. No wonder we were so favored, and so secretive. I shivered as I prayed that when she died we might be released from this burden and live peacefully.

I SABELLA ROSE early the following morning and asked to see her namesake once more. As she bent over my Bella, remarking on her beauty and gentle demeanor, I was a proud and happy mother. But as the dowager queen lingered, poised above my beloved baby, her gorgeous dark clothing glittering in the morning light, I had a passing unease, a moment in which I saw her as a figure of Death.

I was much relieved when her party rode out of the yard.

O N OUR return to London, Janyn informed me that he had acquired property in Oxford in my name "to provide you a comfortable income in rents should anything happen to my fortune."

"Are you in danger, my love?" I could not think why else he would couch it in such words.

"Each day we wake to uncertainty, Alice. I can no more predict how long I shall live, or whether I shall remain in favor with the queen mother and my guild, than I can predict when you shall bear another child and what sex it will be."

An incident shortly suggested what Janyn had to fear. I noted it because suddenly a tutor appeared who was to improve my French and Latin speaking, reading, and writing.

"Have I displeased you?" I asked. Who would not?

Janyn assured me that he meant my education as a gift that would support me through life, the most precious gift he could think to give.

It was as I sat with the tutor one morning in the hall that Dame Tommasa hurried in, her beautiful eyes wide with alarm and fear. She took Janyn by the arm and drew him off to a quiet room. In a little while my mother-in-law departed, without having said a word to me. Never before had she ignored me. Janyn looked grave as we supped, but said nothing. Even in bed that night he would not say what had so upset his mother.

"It is worse for me not to know," I said, kissing his neck and shoulders, "for my imagination conjures terrifying things when I worry."

"Later, my love. I would rather not talk of it until I know what truly happened."

I had wild dreams that night—floods, imprisonments, fires, my sweet Bella burning with fever, Janyn injured by a runaway cart in a narrow street.

My younger brother and sister came with Nan the following morning, and at midday my brother John joined us for a festive meal. Janyn had left early on business. Now I learned that two of our acquaintances among the Lombard traders claimed they had been attacked by a group of mercers the previous day, and that accusations were flying between the Society of Lucca and members of the mercers' guild.

"Were they badly hurt?" I asked.

"Do you know them?" John asked, looking ill at ease.

"They have been guests in our home," I said, "though I do not know them well."

"Dangerous friends," he said.

"Are they?" Nan asked. "I heard that the attack was unprovoked. Why would a group of mercers attack a group of merchants who had done nothing to them? The mercers broke the king's peace—does he not hold the Lombards in his protection?"

"The king's protection makes the Lombards bold. Many of them are smugglers on such a scale as a London merchant would never attempt," said John.

I could not argue with that, for it was true of some of them, and though I might correct John on the *many*, I chose not to, for I did not wish to silence him. I wondered whether the society was connected to Isabella's men who hid in Italy.

"The two Lombards have made loans to the king," I said. "They all have. That is why he protects them."

"If they enjoy the king's favor, what could the London mercers hope to gain by allowing these attacks? That is what I wonder," said Nan. "Master Martin said that the guild has done nothing to punish the men accused."

"They do not know who took part in the attack," said John.

I could see by Nan's expression that she had heard otherwise. This was nothing I wished to know, balancing as I was on the fence between the factions.

After my family departed I was overwhelmed with a sense of divided loyalties. Janyn and Bella and all I held so dear were threatened by an ugliness we could hardly escape. I went to church and confided in Dom Hanneye about my fear that Janyn's sudden rush to educate me had something to do with the growing enmity between the London guilds and the Lombards, and that we might find ourselves alienated from the guilds. He tried to reassure me with the news that some mercers had gone to the mayor in support of the victims.

"It is not as simple as the Londoners against the Lombards," he said. "I suggest that you set aside your worry and accept with love and gratitude your husband's gifts of knowledge. Seize the opportunity he is giving you. Few women—indeed, few men—are granted such riches. I do not mean to deny the enmity between foreigners and London merchants, Dame Alice, but your family is respected in this community, and your husband and his father are Londoners by birth and guildsmen—they are not the enemy."

I was grateful for his advice. That evening Janyn told me of the attack and I was able to respond with a calm maturity that I could see relieved him. He told me little that I did not already know, but it was significant that he told me as soon as he felt he had all the facts. I took it as his being forthright with me. I was not yet at ease, but immensely comforted by his candor.

. . .

A FEW EVENINGS later Janyn joined me in the hall while I was working on some embroidery in the fading light.

"You should rest," he said, squeezing my shoulder. "You have much to do in the next few days."

"Nothing out of the ordinary."

He chuckled. "Indeed? Is it every day we are invited to a hunt at Hertford Castle, where the queen mother is in residence?"

I dropped my work. "We? Invited to the Lady Isabella's palace? To hunt?" With each question my voice rose in excitement.

"Is that delight or dismay?"

I was to travel with my love. I rose to throw my arms around Janyn, kissing him on the neck, on each cheek, and then on the mouth, a much longer kiss.

"Ah, delight," he said, his eyes merry. "You are so beautiful, my Alice. You bring me such joy."

6

> But al to litel, weylaway the whyle,
> Lasteth swich joie, ythonked be Fortune,
> That semeth trewest whan she wol bygyle
> And kan to fooles so hire song entune
> That she hem hent and blent, traitour comune!
> And whan a wight is from hire whiel ythrowe,
> Than laugheth she, and maketh him the mowe.

—GEOFFREY CHAUCER, *Troilus and Criseyde*, IV, 1–7

• 1357 •

E VEN SO long after the event I recall my excitement as we departed for Hertford Castle. We had been married for a year, one filled with many new experiences for me, but this would be my first visit to a royal household. I was to meet the king! The previous night my excitement had been dampened with worry about how my sweet Bella would fare without me even for just short of a week. In truth, it was equally about how *I* might fare without *her*.

But once seated on Melisende in the brisk morning air, Janyn riding beside me so handsome and full of life, I asked God to help me shrug off the futile worry. He answered my prayers, for I was soon caught up in the bustle of the London streets, absorbing it with eyes, ears, and nose. And then, as we rode out of the city into the countryside, the sudden quiet soothed me. I enjoyed the journey until I beheld the grim outer walls of the castle.

Until that moment I had not wondered who else might be in residence, or visiting, in addition to the king. I was terrified enough to be meeting *him*, though of course I was equally thrilled. I wondered whether he would *look* like a king—more than a mere mortal man, wise, powerful. As we passed through the outer gate and rode into the bailey, I stared up at the elaborate façade of the keep, an elegant ashlar paint with soft red accents. Stationed at regular intervals outside were elegantly dressed guardsmen. I was overcome by a sense of my own insignificance, my common background. This was so obviously a royal residence, and I was but a merchant's wife. In my excitement I had not really considered that.

As Janyn helped me from my horse I clung to him and whispered, "What in heaven's name are we doing here? This is not our place. We are merchants, not courtiers."

He kissed my cheek and gently stepped back from my clinging embrace.

"You are an invited guest, Alice. It may be a royal residence, but you are welcome here. Be at ease." He lowered my traveling hood and kissed my forehead. "You are weary from the journey, that is whence comes your distress."

As we climbed the steps to the hall, my sudden painful awareness of the gulf between my status and that of the dowager queen added a terrible weight to my legs.

The size and magnificence of the palace interior awed me. We entered by a short corridor lined with beautiful hangings, gold and silver torches and lamps, then stepped into the echoing expanse of the great hall, where we walked on tiles such as I had seen only in the grandest churches. Servants better dressed than most Londoners were stationed behind intricately carved screens or against the walls as if guarding the immense chests and cupboards. They moved quietly, spoke softly.

On a dais at the far end sat two men deep in conversation. A servant led us very close to them. I tried not to look, but my eyes seemed to have a will of their own, and I found myself staring into very blue eyes, wide and penetrating. They belonged to a man with high, prominent cheekbones, a long, elegant nose, and although a trimmed white beard hid it, I detected a strong chin. His handsome, well-proportioned face was framed by white hair that was luxuriant, wavy, and adorned with a crown.

It was the king. Sweet heaven, he was everything I'd ever imagined a king would be. From broad, straight shoulders hung a most exquisite blue silk robe powdered with gold-and-silver fleur-de-lis. He seemed to consider me for a few breaths, and then, with a nod, he turned away. I tried to hide my gasp as I sucked in air, for I had held my breath while King Edward's gaze touched me. My steps faltered and Janyn put an arm around me.

"You are so weary, my love?"

With tender concern he assisted me as we followed the servant into another corridor just as beautifully decorated as the entry, and were shown into the queen mother's parlor—a jewel of a room. The stone walls were three feet thick and therefore let in only muted light, but they were whitewashed and decorated with painted flowers and hung with rich tapestries. Woven mats and cushions in brilliant colors softened the imposing furniture and the tiled floor.

Isabella the queen mother rose from a small bed on which she had been lounging and greeted us warmly.

"You will rest awhile, and then meet our other guests at the feast in the hall. Tomorrow we rise early to hunt."

I had managed to speak only a few words to her, dumbstruck by all the magnificence. We were shown to a small but luxuriously decorated chamber tucked into a corner of the upper story. Gwen undressed me, and I fell at once into a deep sleep. When she woke me later I was confused by my surroundings.

"Where is my baby? Where is Bella?" I cried.

Janyn and Gwen reassured me that all was well, and reminded me where I was. My confusion frightened me, but they both believed it was caused by the long journey, my first experience of traveling so far.

I wanted to believe them, but just in case my fear had been a premoni-
tion I asked if I might slip into the chapel to pray.

"First let Gwen dress you for the feast, and then I shall escort you
there for a brief prayer. But we must not dally." Janyn bowed to me and
withdrew to a cushioned chair by the door.

Behind a tall carved screen that seemed to be writhing with fantastical winged creatures, Gwen had laid out a new gown of red silk
shot with gold and a silk undergown in a blue as rich as lapis lazuli. My
crespinette was gold. For the first anniversary of our marriage Janyn
had given me a ring of silver, gold, and lapis. My shoes were a deep
blue as well.

In the mirror I could see my dazzling self. I did so love to dress
in exquisite clothes. Yet I stared back with frightened eyes. I did not
belong in a royal household. I did not know how to behave.

Janyn's expression when I stepped out from behind the screen reassured me. "What a beauty you are, my Alice," he murmured, kissing
my hand, my wrist, my neck. . . .

Gwen reminded us that we had little time to spare for the chapel.
With a bow, Janyn escorted me from the chamber. We glided through
corridors made quiet with wall hangings—I wondered how much of
her fortune Isabella had spent on these trappings, for surely they had
not been here when she arrived. They seemed to me to reflect a woman's taste, stories from myth and romance, no battle scenes or even religious motifs. It was as if I were walking through a fabulous romance.

The chapel was a stark contrast, with a dance of Death painted on
one wall, the skeleton figure at its center a terrifying reminder of our
mortal existence. I crossed myself for protection. Yet the stained-glass
casement behind the altar was quite peaceful, depicting the Blessed
Mother and Christ child. I knelt at a prie-dieu before a statue of the
Virgin Mary and bowed to my prayers. I prayed for my Bella, that she
was safe and at ease with her nurse. I prayed for Janyn, that he would
always enjoy God's protection in his travels. I prayed that I might be
a good wife, all that Janyn wished me to be. I prayed that I might not
embarrass or disappoint him here at the court of Isabella of France,
once queen and now mother of the king. I prayed that the king might
not judge me to be a common, inelegant woman, and then quickly
took back that prayer, embarrassed by my pride.

While I had knelt there someone had joined us in the chapel. I had
smelled a sensual perfume from his clothing as he passed me and then

heard the prie-dieu creak as he knelt near the altar. He had paused near me but I had not glanced up, feeling safe in Janyn's presence.

My husband, who had knelt behind me, whispered that we must go. As I rose, I turned toward the altar. It was King Edward who knelt there, head bowed and resting in his hands. I took Janyn's arm and let him draw me from the chapel, my heart pounding. I had prayed in the presence of the king! Was that why I had prayed that he would not look down on me?

"We were in good company," Janyn commented as we checked the condition of each other's clothing. "That was King Edward himself."

"I know," I said. "The crown."

We shared a nervous laugh and then continued to the great hall.

It was a grand company in which we dined that day, Isabella the queen mother, King Edward and his plump and vivacious queen, Philippa—I liked her at once; John, Earl of Richmond, whom I'd already met; Lionel, Earl of Ulster, the king's second son, and his wife, Elizabeth, Countess of Ulster; and several foreign noblemen whose names Janyn did not yet know. Arriving just before us was someone I had not expected to see in such august company, Richard Lyons.

"What is he doing here?" I asked Janyn.

"I should think he is ever welcome, considering the loans he has made to both the queen mother and the present queen," he said. "They both spend far more than they can afford. That is his wife, seated at the far end of the second table, Isabella Pledour."

She was not a pretty woman, heavyset and sour of face, but tastefully and expensively gowned.

I was relieved that we, too, were seated at the second highest table with the less important folk—a merchant and his wife from St. Albans, two Grey Friars and another merchant couple from London, and best of all, my good friend Geoffrey.

"Alice! You look more beautiful each time I see you," he exclaimed.

I noted how he had grown into his grand clothes, his bearing, speech, and gestures more refined and confident than before.

"The countess's household suits you, Geoffrey?" I asked as I settled beside him.

"It would suit me better if I were better suited for it," he said, then burst out laughing as I applauded his wit.

Reversed sentiments were an old game with us, and his playing it at once put me completely at ease. I'd begun to feel that, now I was

Janyn's wife and Bella's mother I had ceased to be fully Alice. As we talked I felt that older part of me awaken.

Janyn and Geoffrey exchanged a few words. Then, apparently relieved that I had someone to talk to, Janyn left us to catch up with each other and turned to the merchant from St. Albans.

"He is a handsome man," said Geoffrey, "and courteous, well spoken, wealthy, successful. Has he a fault?"

"I'm searching for it, but I fear I search in all the wrong places, for I've yet to find one." I blushed.

Geoffrey laughed. "No doubt you have yet to find a fault in my godchild, either." He cocked his head and lifted a brow in query. "The Earl of Richmond is very open about his grand dam being your daughter's godmother." He sighed and shook his head. "My parents were wrong about your limited prospects, eh?"

I smiled but did not reply at once, adjusting to the news that our efforts to conceal the queen mother's favor toward our family had been undermined by Richmond.

"Are you not pleased that he does not seek to hide your favor?" Geoffrey asked.

"I am puzzled why the earl would mention it to anyone. We are unimportant folk, so surely he was not bragging."

"Perhaps he was. He is fond of his grandmother and fiercely defends her when the old rumors are repeated."

"Is his brother Lionel also fond of her?" That was the brother Geoffrey would know best, being in his household.

"Less than John, more than Edward," said Geoffrey. "Perhaps she has grown more affectionate with each grandchild."

Leaning close, I confided, "In truth, I am uneasy about even our slight intercourse with the royal family. I do not think crowns bring peace and contentment."

"That is not their purpose."

"Nor does the royal family seem warm and loving."

"Because they all want the crown!"

We laughed. My old friend was a most reassuring presence in this setting.

I was glad that Lyons was at the far end. Except for a few words overheard in lulls in the conversation, I was able to ignore him, though Geoffrey did find fault with the Fleming's bright hat and mispronunciations.

"Surely he might better learn the language in which he trades day to day," he muttered. "You see how even his wife winces when he speaks."

"He is more fluent in French," I said.

"But he lives in London, my friend, and please do not play the innocent with me. You despise him. I feel you bristle when he glances your way, or you his."

"You know me far too well," I said.

He shook his head. "I know you not at all these days, Alice. A guest of Isabella of France, mother of her most beautiful goddaughter, passionately in love with your husband, a Lombard merchant, your home filled with luxurious items I shall never afford."

"He is not a Lombard but a Londoner born, Geoffrey."

"I did not intend it in the derogatory sense, my friend. His mother is Milanese, is she not?"

"Yes, and his father and his father before him and his father before him were all born in London, as was Janyn."

Geoffrey smiled and bowed to me.

"You are different as well," I said. "Serving in the household of an earl, supping with the queen mother and the king and queen. . . ." I smiled and bowed to him. "We have both come far in a short while."

Janyn suddenly leaned into our discussion. "We must find a suitable wife for you, eh, Geoffrey?"

"Do you have a handsome sister?" Geoffrey asked, his eyes alight. "I should like a pretty wife."

"I've no unmarried sister, but cousins. . . ." Janyn's eyebrows danced and his eyes twinkled.

I loved him so in that moment. I believed he had noticed the tension between me and Geoffrey and had come to my aid, lightening the mood. It was a loving gesture.

Later, as I walked in the garden with two of the merchant wives and one of the Grey Friars, one of the women said, "Is that not your husband speaking with Queen Philippa, Dame Alice?"

It was. My heart burst with pride to see how comfortable Janyn looked in such company.

"Yes, it is Janyn. Is he not the most handsome man?"

The women, both older than I was, teased me about being so in love with my husband.

"God is smiling down upon you," the friar said. "May your union continue to be so blessed."

We moved on to other matters—there was much gossip about King Jean of France being in London, held for ransom since his capture in battle in France. It was said that he felt honor-bound to live in exile himself rather than substitute one of his sons, and had proved to be a most gentle, courteous "prisoner"—as a king he of course lived in great comfort.

"The folk of London so adore him, it is as if they would prefer him to be their king," one of the women said with clear disapproval.

The other woman quite obviously loved collecting details of the elegant life the French king led even in captivity. "Lady Isabella the queen mother has loaned him several of the romances of Arthur and Charlemagne she so enjoys," she said. "And Queen Philippa herself has sent him household furnishings and rich foods. The king visits him. They play chess!"

I had heard much of this, of course, as many guild members were supplying King Jean's household, but I was ill at ease discussing it in the garden of a royal residence. It smacked of disapproval of the king's decision to ease King Jean's distress. Yet all spoke of the French monarch as a kind, pious man.

"I think it most Christian of the king to treat his peer with such respect and grace," I said. "And most courteous of Queen Philippa to ensure King Jean's comfort."

My companions did not respond, but gazed seemingly aghast at something or someone behind me.

"I am indebted to you for your kind support, Dame Alice," said a woman behind me.

I turned and beheld Queen Philippa. Though she was smiling at me I dropped at once into the humblest bow I could manage, and stayed there until Janyn put a hand beneath my elbow and guided me upright.

"Your Grace," I said for at least the second time. I could think of nothing else to say.

Janyn suggested that we walk, and the three of us, my husband, the queen, and I, drew away from the others.

"The queen mother speaks with such delight of her goddaughter," said Philippa.

I was dumbfounded that she even knew of my sweet Bella. "I pray each day that God shower Lady Isabella the Queen Mother with blessings for her kindness to my family, Your Grace."

"As I am certain she prays for you and your little family, Dame Alice. Your husband has been telling me of the garden you are creating at your home in London. I have heard that my husband's father found great satisfaction in digging in the earth, shifting soil. He said that it helped him find his feet and legs. Does it do so for you?"

It was such an unexpected topic that I hesitated, needing to think. I felt her eyes on me, deep green eyes that held both kindness and something much more calculating. I almost stammered some foolishness, but then remembered how proud I had been just moments ago of Janyn's ease with the queen. I took a deep breath.

"When I've spent hours on my knees with my hands in the soil I am reminded of the miracle of life, Your Grace, and I thank God for the gift of waking with each new day. The king's father must have been a wise man."

The green eyes clouded over for a moment. "In some things he was said to be surpassingly wise."

She studied the tips of her embroidered shoes for a moment. When she raised her head, her mood had shifted and she beamed as if life delighted her. I noticed that her skin was as translucent as the pearls on her headdress and collar. I'd thought her plain, though elegant of dress and manner, but saw now that she had a beauty that shone when she smiled.

"Your husband tells me that he consults you in financial matters and that you have proven an excellent adviser. Do you enjoy such occupation?"

"I do, Your Grace, and am honored that my husband finds my advice worth considering."

"The king chides me about my lack of interest in such matters. I could use a woman near me who might engage me in such issues, or at least suggest what I might say to the king to satisfy him." She smiled at me, gave Janyn a teasing glance, and then turned the conversation to Milan and other favorite cities.

I was left to wonder over that last little exchange, but perked up once more when I was included in a brief discussion about children. Then the queen nodded and left. Janyn complimented me on my conversation and courtesy.

We were soon interrupted by the merchant from St. Albans, who wished a word with Janyn. I needed a respite from the heady company and sought out Gwen, wishing for her solid, familiar presence. As we were strolling past the chapel we came face-to-face with the king and dropped at once into deep bows.

"Do rise, my ladies. I do not care to be an object of worship in my mother's home, among her friends." His blue eyes were teasing. "Janyn Perrers's wife, I think?"

"Yes, Your Grace. Alice."

"I am told you are a clever young woman, with a mind for business. So I ask you, would I do better to invest in fine furnishings to decorate my palaces or in spices?"

At that moment I wanted to be known for my beauty, not my cleverness in business. There was something in his voice, his eyes, the scent of him. I wanted him to look on me with desire. The thought made me blush. Only Janyn had ever had such an effect on me.

"Your Grace," I murmured, bowing my head for a moment to compose myself. "I would advise you that spices would bring you more coin, but beautiful possessions would enrich your soul. It is similar to the choice between cloth of gold and escarlatte—the cloth of gold enhances your image as a mighty king, but chafes the flesh, whereas the fine wool impresses only those who know its value and recognize it by how it drapes, yet is most pleasing against the skin. . . ." I realized I was babbling, but even worse that my mention of flesh had invited him to look on me in a way that made me feel like his prey. A far-from-unpleasant sensation, but I prayed he did not suspect me of flirting with him. "Forgive me, Your Grace."

"For what, Dame Alice? I see that you are clever indeed. And pretty enough." He averted his eyes from my low-cut bodice and said in a hearty tone, "Can you hunt? Can you ride? On the morrow we shall see if you possess all the graces, eh?" With a nod and a chuckle, he continued into the chapel, his man hurrying afterward, finding it difficult to match the king's long stride.

"Pretty enough," I whispered.

"He is magnificent, just as they said," Gwen murmured.

I had little to say for myself the rest of the evening, stunned into silence by the encounter with King Edward. I had never experienced a presence such as his. While he spoke to me his blue eyes had held mine captive and his voice had resonated in my head, my heart, my belly, and down my bones to my extremities. I had no words for the sensation at the time, but now I might call it enthralling. I felt as if I had actually been unfaithful to Janyn, and made it up to him with passion that night, though I caught myself fantasizing that it was the king who groaned with pleasure.

On the following morning I was uncomfortably aware of the king's eyes on me, but as soon as I accepted a merlin from the falconer I focused only on her. She was not as large as my own, and of course she did not know me. Before I removed her hood I spoke to her for a while so that she might hear that I meant her no harm. The falconer nodded his approval; King Edward did so as well, which momentarily unsettled me. But once the merlin took flight it was no struggle to lose myself in her, to see nothing but her. We had some success, the bird and I, that morning, and I was in high spirits as we returned to the castle.

Geoffrey had not participated in the hunt, but as I took my seat beside him in the hall for the day's feast he congratulated me on my prowess and on attracting the interest of the king.

I glanced at Janyn, fearing he had heard, but he was engrossed in conversation with a friar. Turning back to Geoffrey I found him grinning, but his eyes were more searching than amused.

"What think you of the most admirable of kings?" he asked.

"He is my king. I hold him in great respect and pray that God blesses him and keeps him safe from all harm."

Geoffrey waved all that aside. "But as a man?"

I considered. If I refused to play his game, Geoffrey would guess that I was delighted by the king's attention. If I played the game, he would guess I simply enjoyed being admired. I did particularly enjoy the latter, having spent so much of my life in my mother's shadow.

"I have never felt such a presence as his, nor have I ever seen such blue eyes. Why did you not hawk with us?"

He raised his brows in comic surprise. "Me? Have you seen me astride? I am the clumsiest of riders, and all birds dislike me. I swear it is true! They chide and criticize me until I want to pluck them." He laughed with me. "You would have disclaimed me had you seen me among the others this morning. But animals have always found you calming and worthy of their trust. I am glad for you that the Lady Isabella saw to it that you have a hunter and a merlin."

I turned the conversation to questions about Geoffrey's travels with Lionel, Earl of Ulster.

Janyn eventually joined us, and Geoffrey told him tales of how as a child I'd collected kittens that my mother refused to allow me to keep and then worked hard at finding them good homes, coaxing and cajoling neighbors to adopt the sweet creatures. Janyn enjoyed the tales.

Lady Isabella saw us briefly before we departed for home.

"My daughter-in-law finds you most pleasant," she remarked.

"The queen is most kind."

"My son admires the way you leave your body and soar with your hawk."

I blushed under Isabella's keen regard.

"His Grace is most perceptive," said Janyn.

We returned to London in a merry mood.

IN NOVEMBER I found myself again with child, a cause of celebration for Janyn and me. I thought it would be a perfect time to encourage my siblings Mary and Will to participate more in Bella's life, assisting me with her care both before the baby was born and afterward. But Mother managed one more cruelty, suddenly forbidding Nan to bring Mary and Will to my home, and forbidding me to see them in their home either.

I went to Dame Agnes, hoping to learn how Mary and Will were faring.

"Dame Margery has no gift for mothering," said Grandmother, "and no room in her small heart to love anyone other than herself. I wish it were otherwise, for your children and for my son." She embraced me. "Do not worry about Mary and Will. I will arrange for them to meet you here. Margery will not dare defy me. Bring my great-granddaughter next time you come, I pray you. She brightens my day."

She asked about our time at Hertford Castle, making an effort I much appreciated to be curious and neutral about the dowager queen. I returned home in much better spirits.

It was a more difficult pregnancy than my last. When I grew restless with enforced rest, missing the release I found in riding, Janyn encouraged me to apply myself to the studies he had set me. I did enjoy them, particularly languages and composition. I appreciated the way they brightened my thoughts and set me puzzling over ideas far removed from my unhappy parents.

And there was always Bella to amaze and delight me.

. . .

B UT CLOUDS gathered on the horizon. In February we heard that the queen mother was very ill at Hertford. Dame Tommasa and I spent many hours praying for her. I was alarmed by my mother-in-law's obsessive piety. But it seemed our prayers were heard, for in a few weeks Isabella recovered and resumed her usual activities. But Janyn remained convinced that the dowager queen would be dead within the year, and the prospect seemed to suck the life from him. I could not understand. Of course she had been most generous to us, and his journeys on her behalf had been most lucrative, but the accounts that I reviewed with him were all in excellent health, his trade encompassing much more than what he did on her behalf. His reputation in London was growing, and his guild master referred to him as a future mayor. Yet Janyn grew fearful, overly protective, cautious to a degree that frightened me.

Often now he turned his back to me once we were abed, denying even this comfort to both of us.

"Do you no longer love me?" I finally summoned the courage to ask when he turned away once again.

He turned back. "My sweet Alice, I love you more than words can say." He pulled me close and held me for a moment. "I pray you, forgive me if I have caused you pain. My mind and heart are overburdened. I am searching for a way to protect you and our daughter."

"Protect us from what?"

"The uncertain future."

"You and God will protect us, Janyn, my beloved."

"You are so young and innocent, Alice. So loving and trusting." He looked away as his voice filled with tears.

I sensed more and more that he was weaning me from him, from my need of him. I faltered in my resolve to be strong and to trust in God's guidance. I spent hours in church, praying and pouring out my heart to Dom Hanneye. Neither God nor my confessor offered any comfort beyond reminding me that Janyn loved me, and I loved him.

I felt almost relieved when Janyn departed in late March on "one last trip" to Milan for the queen mother, for then I might at least regain some calm.

"If anyone should inquire, I am in France," he instructed me. "You must not mention Milan or Lombardy."

"Why must we lie about this journey?" I asked.

"For our safety."

"Do your parents know where you will be?"

He nodded. There were shadows beneath his eyes and his breath smelled sour. He had not been eating well, but had been drinking far more than was his custom, late into the night.

IN APRIL there was much talk in the city of an extravagant St. George's Day celebration at Windsor. It was said that our king and queen, the queen mother, King Jean of France, and his son Phillip were all in attendance, and that knights from all over Christendom were taking part in the tournament. I looked forward to reassuring Janyn on his return that all was well with Isabella.

It was at that time, on a day like any other, when a sudden pain in my stomach brought me to my knees in the hall. Within moments I was kneeling in a pool of blood. I am told that my screams were so loud that neighbors came running with weapons drawn, certain that I was being attacked. Dame Tommasa and Gwen were at my side at once, but I wept for Janyn; I wanted only Janyn. Unfortunately he was at sea, headed for Milan, believing that when he returned I would be big and fat with child.

But it was not to be. And with the change in him I feared it might be some time before I conceived again. I mourned that child as I had never mourned for anything in my life. I so wanted a sibling for my little Bella, a brother or sister she might love and with whom she would share secrets and treasures.

"You shall have many more children, Alice," Tommasa assured me.

Felice the midwife agreed. "What happened is as common as a cough in winter, and has no influence on your next pregnancy."

Dame Agnes arrived with gifts of food, new bed curtains, a tisane she said had helped her after she lost a child. She sat by me, talking of happy things or sitting quietly fingering her paternoster beads. Yet I drew no comfort from her or anyone else for many a day. Janyn's drawing away from me, his dread of the future, and now this loss—it all seemed more than I could bear.

Until one morning I heard my sweet Bella shrieking and calling for me. My daughter's fear lifted me from my bed and into life once more. When I knelt to her where she sat in the hall, kicking her heels and refusing to be comforted by her nurse or her grandmother Dame Tommasa, her tears dried up and a smile lit her swollen face. She reached out for me and in a heartbeat I'd gathered her in my arms. She rested her hot little head on my chest and gave a great, trembling sigh. I had never held anything more precious.

For weeks I kept her near me, whether I was gardening, reviewing the accounts, studying, or doing needlework.

I had hoped to find some calm in Janyn's absence, but my sense of underlying disquiet was hardly dispelled. Our acquaintances did not include me in gatherings as often as they had the previous year, nor did they seem as friendly when I was among them. I noticed uneasy pauses in conversations when I approached, and I stood as godmother to none of the newborns—I thought this might have been because of my own loss, but would later learn that was in truth only a very small part of it.

The culmination of this dread took human shape one day in mid-May. I was at market with Gwen and a manservant when a stranger approached us, asking after Janyn. He was elegantly dressed and had a soldierly bearing. This was no merchant asking after a peer.

"I pray that his business in Lombardy is quickly resolved," he said.

"You are mistaken, sir. My husband is in Rouen," I said.

He had the gall to finger my gris-lined cloak. "Royal patronage brings many privileges. And dangers."

"Unhand my mistress!" my manservant demanded in a loud voice.

"You are obviously a madman," I hissed, and quickly took my leave, my companions staying close to me on either side. I do not know how I managed to reach home, my legs shook so.

Janyn's parents tried to hide their distress on hearing of the incident, but I judged it no coincidence that they suddenly decided we must attend to some improvements at Fair Meadow. When we departed for the country in late May I was glad to leave the city and the shadows that haunted me there. Once settled at Fair Meadow I took every opportunity to ride and hawk. Bella grew brown and chubby, more beautiful than ever.

But I had a recurring dream from which I woke with a frightening sense of foreboding that carried through the day. In the dream I stepped into a puddle on my way to the market and slipped into a dark, fathomless sea, sinking, sinking. I woke in a bed that looked like my bed, but when I rose the household staff and the family abiding in the home were all strangers—and they could not see me. I did everything I could think of to get their attention, but to them I was not there.

Janyn's return in late June did little to reassure me, though I was relieved that he looked healthier than when he'd departed and had lost the haunted look. He'd not received the letter I'd written to him about losing the child until he was on his journey home, so that was a fresh grief. He held me close and murmured sweet and loving things. Yet I did not sense in him the same intense pain I still held within my heart. Perhaps it was different for a man, not being the one who bore the child. Yet, remembering his delight in Bella, I found myself worrying about the quiet resignation with which he accepted our loss.

Something troubled him. He seemed unable to settle to anything or to relax with Bella and me. He was impatient with the slow pace in the country and wondered aloud often whether he ought to return to London.

"But you have only just arrived, my love. I'd hoped we would enjoy riding, hawking, being together again. Perhaps planting a new seed." I pressed my flat belly.

He kissed me absently. "There is much to resolve, much to plan." He still believed the queen mother would be dead before Christmas. He had seen Isabella at Leeds Castle, where she had taken ill once more as she was resting before returning home from a pilgrimage to Canterbury. "They say she is suffering from an unfortunate mistake in the strength of a medicine, but in truth I believe that medicines are failing her."

"Your devotion to Isabella is proper and commendable, Janyn, and I am sorry that she is so ill, but we have so much to be grateful for beyond her patronage. Our daughter thrives, and with some pleasurable effort and God's grace we shall have more children. Your guild master sees much success ahead for you. And we have our love, Janyn. Your sorrow over the queen mother will pass. Your life is ahead, not behind."

"I should meet with the guild master."

His coolness stung. "Of course. But would you not like to rest here in the country for a while? You have been traveling since early spring."

"It is difficult to rest when there is so much to do."

But there had always been much to do. I could not understand why he viewed all with such urgency now. Nor why he avoided speaking of our family and our future.

"How fared you in Milan, my love?"

"I cannot talk of it, Alice."

"Can you at least tell me whether you accomplished what you had hoped?"

"For the most part, yes. But we must not speak of it."

And all these discussions ended with him saying, "The man who accosted you at the market. Tell me all you remember."

Perhaps that was why he wished to head to London, to find out more about the stranger. Over and over I told him all I could remember. Each time I described the stranger Janyn would shake his head, say he knew no one who fit that description, and commend me for remembering not to acknowledge that he had been in Milan.

"But the man knew. Or guessed. And he let me know that he guessed you were on royal business. What does that mean, Janyn?"

Each time we reached that question he would assure me that it was nothing and walk away with a deep scowl.

He was home no more than a month when we received word that the queen mother and her daughter, Joan, Queen of Scotland, would be passing through on their way to Hertford Castle and we were to attend them at the royal hunting lodge in a few days.

"Why is she not staying here?" I asked Janyn.

"Her party is too large for this house."

I dreaded it. "Do we stay the night?"

"Of course."

"Does she want us to bring her goddaughter?"

"No, my love, this is an official visit, not a social one."

"I do not like the sound of that."

"We are commanded to attend the queen mother, Alice. You know that we have no choice."

THE HUNTING lodge was a handsome stone-and-timber home, at least thrice the size of Fair Meadow, set in beautiful parkland groomed with care to seem tamely wild. Perhaps it would be pleasant to spend a few days in such a pretty place. For Janyn's sake as well as my own I set my mind to enjoying myself.

But my calm was tested immediately upon our arrival when we found that we were to be escorted to Queen Philippa in the hall of the lodge. Apparently Isabella was exhausted by the journey and would see us in the morning, after she had rested.

I looked at Janyn. "The queen?" I mouthed, startled.

"I was not told that Queen Philippa would be here."

Something in his posture said that although he'd not been told he was not surprised, and that frightened me more than simply meeting the queen unexpectedly.

Resplendent in green silk trimmed in gold and decorated with pearls and gold filigree buttons, Queen Philippa cut an imposing figure. Yet she greeted us with friendly words and a kind smile, asking about our ride, about baby Bella, and expressing her sympathy for my miscarriage. Isabella must have told her about the latter, for I had not been with child when I had met Philippa at Hertford.

"I should like you to come to my chamber for a light meal at sunset," the queen said to me. "Your husband will dine with the others. It will be pleasant to have a quiet meal with you and Joan."

"Your Grace," I managed to say as I bowed.

THE BEDCHAMBER in which I dined with the two queens looked out on the park and had sufficient windows that it was wonderfully airy and filled with the delicate scents of summer. A table had been placed near the window, and a brazier glowed nearby to ward off any chill as the sun set. Queen Joan was pretty in a brittle sort of way—she reminded me of my mother, which did not endear her to me. Her personality was likewise brittle. But she was courteous to me, and pleasant enough. We spoke of children, households, the price of silk and leather, the sorts of things women talk about when relaxing together. It was not until the food had been cleared that Philippa came to the point.

"The queen mother has spoken so often of you," she said to me. "She tells me that I would benefit by having you in my household."

"Your household, Your Grace?"

"As a damsel of the chamber, assisting me in dressing, and, I hope, teaching me the value of money."

As she spoke I recalled our conversation in the garden of Hertford Castle, the puzzling comment about someone like me being useful to her. But dressing the queen? She plainly considered it a great honor, but in my experience servants dressed adults. Servants. "Your Grace, I have never imagined such an honor," I said.

But Janyn had, I was suddenly certain of that.

"In Hainault, my homeland, it was the custom for nobles and merchants to feast and celebrate together. We believed it important to understand one another. Edward and I wish to have a deeper connection with the merchant class of London. We need to understand how you view the world. Your husband agrees."

With those words she erased any possible doubt about Janyn's collusion. "Your Grace, I have a family, two houses, a daughter—" I began, grasping for a lifeline.

"You shall see them often, I promise you." She rose and held out her hand for me to kiss. I did so.

"My husband was likewise delighted with you. I think we shall all benefit from this arrangement." She nodded to a servant to show me out.

I managed to withdraw without mishap, though I found it difficult to breathe.

"Dame Alice, what is amiss?" Gwen said when I rushed into the bedchamber.

Janyn rose from a table near the fire, his head tilted in the way he had when he was trying to understand what he was seeing. "You are unhappy, my love?"

"I am summoned to the royal court. To live at court. Away from you, away from Bella. I'm to be a servant to Her Grace. You knew! You knew and you did not warn me. How could you let me find out in such wise? Why are you doing this to me?" I fell onto the bed, facedown, burying my face in my forearms and letting the tears come.

I felt Janyn sit down on the edge of the bed, but he did not touch me. In a little while, when I turned my head to one side to breathe, Gwen gently touched my shoulder and asked if she might help me disrobe.

I turned, sat up, and without speaking submitted to dear Gwen's ministrations. Only when she had withdrawn did I turn to Janyn again.

"Is this what you want for us?"

He looked weary, and as if he'd suddenly aged.

"If the world were a safer place, no." He held up a hand to silence me when I began to speak. "This is a great honor, Alice. Your position will be much like your friend Geoffrey's, but even closer to the king and queen. My love, it is a wonderful thing."

"Why did you not prepare me for this? Discuss it?"

"Look at you now, Alice, how you resist this. Would you have come had you known?"

"Listen to yourself! You resorted to trickery. I have trusted you, Janyn. I have obeyed you in all things, and this is my reward? You deceive me?"

He raked his hands through his hair, his breath ragged. "It is best this way, my love."

"Best for you. So tell me now, did you ask the queen mother to arrange this?"

"I did."

I turned away from him, my mind connecting all things mysterious in the past months. "My tutor? All that was in preparation?"

"Yes."

"Why, Janyn? Have you tired of me?"

"Oh, my love." He pulled me into his arms. I felt his heart pounding. "Oh, my love. I've done this for you. And for Bella."

I tried to free myself but he held me tighter, then began covering me with kisses. He knew where to kiss me, he knew my vulnerable places and made it impossible for me to resist him. I was afire. I needed to satisfy the desire that overwhelmed me. Afterward I was angry with myself for succumbing to my passion, for seeming to accept Janyn's betrayal. But perhaps there was hope. I prayed that I had conceived. Surely if I were with child I might be passed over for the honor of dressing the queen.

AN EARLY-MORNING hunt raised my spirits a little. The woodland was beautiful. But later, in our conversation with Isabella, the Queen Mother, I clearly saw that anything but gratitude for my position in her daughter-in-law's household would be met with regal anger.

Ever obedient, I held my tongue. I suffered in lonely, desperate silence. Most painful was Janyn's deception. I saw I was always to be at the mercy of others' decisions. How I would keep my faith, how I would nurture my own child when I felt so powerless, I could not see.

MY COURSES came shortly after we returned from our visit to the queens. I wept most bitterly and refused to rise from bed for a day, my hope for a reprieve from court dashed. Dame Agnes held me close, and when I babbled about why I was so desperate to conceive she murmured prayers.

I SOUGHT GEOFFREY'S advice. He listened with a grave expression. "The only possibility that makes sense to me is that some danger to your family lies behind this, Alice. It is not necessarily a good thing to be close to Isabella of France, the Queen Mother. There is much blood in her past."

"You assured me I need not worry about her when last we spoke of this."

"I know. But your situation suggests I was wrong."

We bowed our heads, momentarily silenced.

But I had too many questions to be so for long. "In your experience, do couples at court see much of one another?"

Geoffrey did not answer at once, apparently gathering his thoughts. "If they so desire, yes. The royal family would prefer fewer illicit liaisons at court—unless, of course, the affairs are their own."

I crossed myself.

"I do understand your unhappiness, Alice. Janyn has chosen a perilous path. But perhaps the court is the only safe harbor for you."

"And what of my daughter? Do you think I will be permitted to see Bella frequently?"

"That will be more difficult. I think you must resign yourself to seeing her only on occasion."

My heart hurt. "Why is obedience so painful?"

"If it were not, there would be no need to insist upon it." And then Geoffrey did something unexpected. He took me in his arms and hugged me, then kissed my cheek. "You have been sorely tested these past few years. Always know that you have a friend in me. If you send for me, I will come if I am able."

"If you are able. That is the sad truth of our stations, is it not? We are servants, though all see us as blessed with great fortune. We are bound body and soul to our lords or ladies. As is Janyn, and as indeed were his parents before him."

BOOK

II

THE QUEEN'S
HANDMAID

7

How myghte it evere yred ben or ysonge,
The pleynte that she made in hire destresse?
I not; but, as for me, my litel tonge,
If I discryven wolde hire hevynesse,
It sholde make hire sorwe seme lesse
Than that it was, and childisshly deface
Hire heigh compleynte, and therfore ich it pace.

—GEOFFREY CHAUCER, *Troilus and Criseyde,* IV, 799–805

WHEN HAD I a choice to be other than I was? The queen mother and Janyn had decided I was to be a lady of the court, and short of running away I must accept their plan. They said it was for my good, for my daughter's good.

But what of my heart? Janyn promised me that he would visit me often, and we would have time together in our homes with Bella when the queen was nearby. My husband would visit—I wanted to live *with* him. I wanted to live with my daughter, to bring her up to be the woman I dreamed she could be.

I did not like that this separation must have been planned long ago, that it had led Janyn to insist on hiring a wet nurse, that the queen mother's being my baby's godmother had been the first step. I wondered why Janyn had pursued me, why he had wished to wed me at all. I hated the way such questions tainted my precious memories.

• 1358 •

ALL THAT summer I held my breath, as if thus I might be forgotten by the royal family. As the fields ripened for the harvest I dared to hope. And then Janyn and I were summoned to Hertford Castle. I was haunted once more by my nightmare of the golden wolf, my family's blood staining her muzzle, dripping from her lolling tongue, and rode toward Hertford with such evident dread that Janyn and Gwen both feared I was ill.

On our arrival the queen mother sent word that she would see me alone. Something in his face told me that Janyn had expected this request. I followed the page with feet of lead.

As I entered Isabella's bedchamber I could see at once how ill she was, how close to death. Her eyes had withdrawn into her skull, her once erect spine had crumpled. She sat propped up by a mound of cushions and her hand trembled as she extended it for me to kiss. All the fragrant oils burning in the chamber could not mask the stink of the sickroom. She patted the space beside her.

"I've little breath. Sit up here near me, Alice."

She ordered her servants to leave us alone.

"But what if you need assistance, Your Grace?" I was not comfortable being responsible for such a great lady.

"Then you shall call for them. I should like for just a moment to be free to talk to a friend without being overheard." She settled her sunken eyes on me. "I know that you are not happy about being summoned to serve in Philippa's household." She spoke slowly, summoning up breath with painful effort.

"It is an honor I did not desire," I admitted, having no reason to demur if she'd already guessed.

"I have arranged this for your safety, and your daughter's. Especially for hers."

I crossed myself for protection from evil, from the terrible golden wolf that haunted my sleep. "What danger threatens us?"

"I will not tell you all, for they would only rip it from you when I am gone."

Words that could not but chill me. "They? Who, Your Grace?"

She held up a hand for me to be patient as she caught her breath.

This was the moment I had both yearned for and dreaded. I was about to learn the truth from the queen mother herself. I pressed my hands together and fiercely prayed for her and for my family. When her breathing sounded less labored, I opened my eyes.

"Janyn's mother and her parents saved someone most precious to me," she began, "at great risk to themselves. The family continues to protect this person, still at great risk. In thanks for their service, I vowed to save you and my goddaughter. For your husband, who loves you as his life."

The words twisted my heart. "What of Janyn? Is he in danger?"

"Every moment." She reached toward my hands. I pried them apart and proffered one. She took it in hers. "Do not doubt his love." She was very weak, her hands dry and cold.

Though I shook with emotion and was desperate to hear all she knew, I forced myself to be patient. "Your Grace," I managed to say.

"You must take care and be guided by others." She pressed my hand. "Pray for my soul, Alice. Do not curse me."

I could not promise that. As I kissed her hand I felt anger pushing aside my anguish and fear. Anger about all the planning, the secret arrangements made behind my back.

"I must rest," said Isabella. "Call my servants. Go to your husband."

I was unsteady on my feet when I rose from the bed, but I managed to reach the corridor and summon Isabella's attendants. Janyn awaited me there, and I stumbled into his embrace, desperately in need of his strength. He led me out into a quiet part of the gardens where we walked for a while arm in arm, not speaking, just being together.

When I trusted myself to speak sensibly, I said, "I know little more except that we are ever in danger. She said that if I knew all, 'they would only rip it from' me when she is dead. *Who* would? And who are you protecting? Why would such desperate people believe that I know nothing? This is not a joust with polite rules, Janyn, this is my life, our marriage, our family." I gasped, suddenly so angry that I found it difficult to breathe. Who was it Janyn visited in Italy so regularly? Not the soldiers who had supported Isabella, as he had told me, but someone "precious" to her. I turned away from him. He could not comfort me, for it was he, his family, who had brought me to this moment of understanding that all I loved teetered on the edge of disaster.

Janyn drew me to him. "You will be protected in the queen's household."

I stiffly endured his embrace, refusing to yield. "What of our daughter? What of *you*?"

He released me. "The plan had been that our Bella was to stay here, with her godmother."

My anger softened at the distraught note in Janyn's voice, seeing how he clenched his hands. Perhaps Bella might be safe in the bosom of the Salisbury family if Isabella was gone. "What of having her own great-grandmother, Dame Agnes, care for her?"

Janyn took my hands. "Look at me, Alice." When I met his gaze, I saw a plea in his eyes. "For the sake of our daughter, we must keep her apart from my family, and from yours."

"I would not think of allowing her to be brought up by my parents. I—"

"Listen to me, Alice. Look at me." I had glanced away. "There may come a time when I will ask you to do something," he began. When he was certain he had my attention, he added, "It will, I think, be the hardest thing you have ever had to do. You must walk away from me and both our families."

I could not believe what I heard. "Walk away from all I hold dear? I will not desert my daughter!"

He shook his head. "The king and queen have promised to find a way for you to be with Bella. Eventually. Another foster home will be found—"

"Foster home? Listen to you! How can you bear to send our Bella away? *Our* beloved?"

He closed his eyes for a moment, then quietly said, "When it is safe she will be placed with you in the royal household."

Though his coolness chilled me, I lunged toward that shaft of light. "At least that, God be thanked." I crossed myself. "But walk away from you? Why, Janyn?"

"Isabella has told you as much as you may know. Now, listen. If someone gives you these beads," he held out his favorite rosewood paternoster beads to me, "you will know that it is time for you to walk away. That is your signal."

"Janyn, I cannot! I could never do so."

"I love you more than my own life, Alice, and I mean for you and Bella to have long, wonderful lives. My family foolishly agreed to something long ago that brought them wealth, but at what cost they had not then fathomed. How terrible it would be . . . how it might destroy our family. I do not want you to suffer for it."

"But without you I *will* suffer, Janyn."

"Then think of our Bella."

"What could be so dangerous, my love?"

"Knowledge, Alice. I'll say no more. Never doubt that I love you and Bella. I have been so happy with you."

Trembling with anger and frustration, I backed away from him, shaking my head. "How could you do this to us? What possessed you to pursue marriage if you knew this lay ahead? What right had you to bring this curse down upon me and our innocent child?"

"Hush, hush, Alice, my love." Janyn reached out to me. "I thought the queen mother would live a long life. She appeared hale and hearty."

I was torn between running from him and seeking comfort in his arms. While I hesitated the tears came and he gathered me to him, holding me close as I wept. We clung to each other so hard that the next morning I saw the bruises on both our arms. I prayed to God, His mother, and all the saints to take this burden from us. To bring a miracle to save us.

Within days of our meeting, Isabella, the Queen Mother, insisted on a large dose of the physick she had been taking, and died in peace. We had already returned to London. When the messenger arrived from Hertford with the news, Janyn and Tommasa, who was dining with us, both looked as if he had brought word of their own imminent deaths. Pale and wooden, they received the news with a terrible quiet, so unlike them that the servants looked as frightened as I felt.

WHEN I was summoned to Windsor Castle shortly after Isabella's death, I thought my heart would shatter with the pain of leaving Bella and Janyn. But seeing how my emotions affected them, I forced a brave countenance. I would find a way to reunite my family. Until then, I would strive to treat this as an adventure. I would make Janyn and Bella proud of me.

I had thought Hertford splendid, but it was modest in comparison to the royal couple's grand palace. I was overwhelmed by its vastness, bewildered by the opulence, and spellbound by the magnificence of color and light within. My resolve weakened in the face of such a foreign domicile. In our first days at court, Gwen and I were often lost in the maze of corridors and buildings. When Queen Philippa realized why I was often late to the sewing room or to attend her in her chamber she assigned a young page to me, Stephen, who had been at court long enough to know every nook and cranny. Every night I cried myself to sleep.

Through that first autumn and winter, I lived only infrequently at court, for in the brief time between my meeting with Queen Philippa at the lodge and my joining her household she had fallen from her horse while hunting with the king. She suffered grievous pain in her lower back and hips that kept her bedridden, unable to participate in state occasions, requiring fewer attendants.

Aware that these visits would become shorter and less frequent when my role in the queen's household was firmly established, I lived for my sojourns at home, treasuring each moment with Bella and Janyn. But the tentativeness of our situation haunted me and confused the household. Our housekeeper Gertrude and a new nursemaid helped Janyn with Bella when I was called to court, with Dame Tommasa in attendance as much as possible, and they were loath to change their routine when I was in residence. My sweet Bella, in her second year, was happily adaptable. I was not so fortunate. I hovered about her to such an extent that she grew querulous under my regard.

Things were little better with Janyn. Since Isabella's death he seemed far away. I persisted in wooing him, desperate to have another child, holding firm to the belief that if I were to conceive, I would be released from the queen's household and all would be well in my little family.

My duties at court became more regular in April, when Queen Philippa insisted on taking an active part in the annual celebration marking the Feast of St. George at Windsor during which members of the Order of the Garter gathered for jousts and tournaments. The order had been founded ten years earlier by King Edward after the glorious victory at Crécy. Twenty-six knights companion pledged loyalty to Edward and to one another. They met for a grand celebration each year on St. George's Day, the twenty-third of April at Windsor, where the king was building a new hall for them.

For such festivities all members of the king's and queen's households wore the same colors as their master and mistress, which for the Garter meant accents of azure blue and gold. It seemed frivolous to me to spend so much time and money on special robes, but then I resented everything about court and was in a particularly darksome mood. My darling Bella had just been sent to live in the household of Queen Joan of Scotland at Hertford Castle.

Queen Philippa informed me of this arrangement one morning as I worked beside her in the sewing room.

"And then to Scotland?" I groaned. "So far!"

"Joan is unlikely to return to Scotland with her husband," the queen said, quietly, for my ears only.

I forced myself likewise to speak softly though I was screaming inside.

"Why must she be taken from her home?"

"You know why, Alice. For her own protection, just as your silence about how you come to be here is for yours."

Of Philippa's eight living children, her youngest son, Thomas, was but three years old, not much older than my Bella. Her two youngest daughters, Margaret and Mary, twelve and fourteen, were often in residence, and even the twenty-six-year-old Isabella was a frequent resident. The queen loved her children; she might understand my yearning to have my daughter with me.

"If only she might bide with me at court." I was mortified to realize by the queen's expression that I had said this aloud. "Your Grace, I pray you, forgive my outburst."

"You are here to attend me, not your daughter. It is so with all my ladies." She shook her head with irritation. "A commoner's child being raised in my household—" She stabbed at her needlework. "It would invite gossip. Dangerous gossip."

"Yes, Your Grace."

There were two levels of well-born women in the queen's household, those of us who were of birth status above serving women but yet not of noble blood were her dressers and fetchers, and noble women were her companions and sometimes messengers. Throughout the day I was one of several responsible for assembling the queen's robe for her various activities—gowns, headdresses, jewels, shoes, and cloaks, cleaning and mending as needed, as well as spending time most days doing the decorative stitching on new garments. I was also in attendance when the queen consulted the sempsters, designing her own gowns and the accompanying livery for her household for feasts and state occasions. And in general we attended the queen, serving her refreshments, accompanying her to chapel, walking with her when she had the strength, sometimes reading to her when she was unwell. The duties were not arduous, nor were they nearly as challenging as running a household. In truth, I was bored, which added to my misery.

I had been permitted to bring Melisende with me to court, and escaped to the stables to be with her as often as possible. I dreamed of a time when she might once again reside in my own stables. But I felt that life receding further and further into the past. And the future was a gray cloud. Even my standing as "dame" Alice was taken from me, as the queen referred to women of my status as "mistress."

Overwhelmed by the strangeness of court, confused by its rituals, and unsure what was expected of me, I made mistakes, overreached myself.

I forgot myself one day when Queen Philippa asked my opinion about the cloth spread out before her on the great bed in her chamber. Cloth of gold, richly dyed wools and silks, intricately patterned . . . though it was a more costly collection than I'd ever seen in one place, I felt comfortable with the familiarity of it all. I knew cloth. I asked what sorts of garments she was planning, for what occasions, and then made suggestions.

Too late I noticed the telltale sounds that indicated the noble-women were taken aback by my audacity.

The queen heard them as well and turning to them, declared, "Listen to Mistress Alice and learn, all of you. She is all that I had hoped she would be."

From that moment they were my sworn enemies.

They would sit to one side of the airy sewing chamber, idly plucking at their needlework while gossiping, their elegant headdresses trembling with suppressed amusement or indignation as they leaned closer first to one companion, then the other. Across the tiled floor we lesser women eagerly applied ourselves, delighted to handle the exquisite cloth, the silken thread, even the gold or silver wire that cut our fingers receiving our admiration. We would comment on the quality, and I would get carried away, expounding on the virtues of the various cloths on which we worked, their weaves, dyes, finishes.

"The pattern in this tabby weave is clever, is it not? Every third strand picked out, then every sixth, every ninth, and back to third," I might note with enthusiasm.

"It is all of a color. You will ruin your eyes with such counting," Lady Ann would say with a lazy laugh. The other headdresses shivered in glee.

Admiring a satin border we were sewing on a patterned silk bodice, I might exclaim, "Look how the indigo draws out the blue cast to the red in the patterned silk." I could not help myself.

"Such an eye for color, Mistress Alice," Lady Eleanor would say. "How clever of you. Is that how the mercers coax their fellows' wives into debt, by such subtle description?"

I had not realized that the high born proudly feigned ignorance of such details.

"And what might this blue be called, Mistress Alice? Is it costly? Or might a fisherman's wife afford it?" Lady Mary would ask.

Their amused glances at one another as they goaded me on to reveal the depths of my commoner's mercantile knowledge eventually silenced me.

Among my peers I was considered arrogant. Among the noblewomen I was considered an inferior, a commoner who did not know my place, and I was treated as a servant when not in the presence of the queen. I kept a modest demeanor, praying that in time I might win acceptance.

Their sneers increased my discomfort about Bella's august upbringing far removed from me. I was wretched, terrified that my own daughter would one day be ashamed of me or, worse yet, forget me. When I thought of her cheerful wave as she'd departed with Queen Joan's party the pain left me breathless.

Only Philippa seemed pleased with me. Although her stated purpose in adding me to her household—to be reminded of the practical considerations in which a woman of the merchant class had been trained—had been doomed from the beginning by her own extravagance, she continued to consult me in all matters of dress. She spoke of the merchant class as practical, prudent folk, when in truth it was the wealthier members of that class for whom she yearned, those who had feasted and jousted with her family in Hainault. And so, instead of learning from me how to make practical choices, she taught me instead how to let go of my inhibitions and indulge my desires, my natural delight in all fine things. In my dress I spent lavishly on gowns of silk, escarlatte, and even one of silk velvet, enjoying the way the soft fabrics caressed my skin, and shoes and boots of supplest leather that seemed to lighten my every step.

Janyn encouraged such spending, considering it a sign that I was embracing my new life, and, in truth, it was worth seeing the light in his eyes as I twirled about showing off my latest gowns. He would lift me up by the waist and dance me round the hall, and I would forget all my misgivings about my current situation for the joy of that moment with my beloved. But it was no substitute for his daily company, the intimacy of living with him.

Two winters had passed without my conceiving the child I prayed would reunite my family. In my desperation I consulted a Dominican friar, Dom Clovis, whose name was passed on in whispers among the women of the queen's household. I asked him to concoct a love potion for Janyn and me. Clovis created a charm of holy words and fragrant oil, but it did not ease our estrangement. I could see that Janyn was ever more anxious, yet I could not reach him.

In the midst of all this came the awful news that Geoffrey had been captured by the French. For several weeks I spent hours in church with his parents, praying for his safe release. When word came in March that the king had ransomed him, Janyn and I joined a celebratory feast at the guildhall. Though I was overjoyed at the good news, Janyn hardly seemed present.

O N THE occasion of Bella's third birthday in June, Janyn, Bella, Dame Tommasa, Master Martin, and I spent a wonderful month at Fair Meadow as a family. It felt a precious gift after seventeen months at court. Bella grew close to her father during that time. Janyn presented her with a pony and taught her to ride. I rode with her as well, but she much preferred preening in the admiration of her handsome, adoring father. The weather was glorious, and everyone seemed determined to be out of doors, riding, walking, gardening. At night, much to my surprise and joy, Janyn and I rekindled our love with renewed passion. It was a happy time, giving me new hope. Returning to the queen's household in July was one of the most difficult things I have ever done.

After the happy month with my family loneliness plagued me more than ever, and, though I knew it for a sin, I found myself unable to conquer my self-pity. Even my familiar confessor had been taken from me, Dom Hanneye having been sent to Oxford. My new confessor, Dom Creswell, was a man of the court. He was kind in his counsel, seeing my unhappiness and expressing sympathy while gently suggesting that, as I had no choice in the matter, I could either be miserable lamenting what could not be or learn contentment with what was. I did recognize the wisdom of his advice. Dame Tommasa had urged me to do the same when I had wept in her loving embrace earlier in the year.

I could not deny that I was surrounded by beauty and had only to ask for most of my material wishes to be fulfilled. Music filled my days, as well as poetry, ballads, tales of far-off lands. There was much dancing and I enjoyed learning new steps, delighting in the heady feeling of being swept along by the music and my fellow dancers. There were weeks of feasting, with guests from royal houses and legendary bloodlines, and hunting, hawking, riding, watching jousts and tourneys. In the quiet in between we embroidered with precious threads on the most beautiful cloth and prayed in exquisitely fitted chapels, the servants ever ready with mantles and lap rugs to warm us if we felt chilled.

Still my heart cried out for my sweet homes with Janyn and Bella, and despite our happy coupling in June, he and I had as yet begun no new life. It seemed that God had other plans for me.

IN SEPTEMBER Janyn departed on a journey to Milan. It was to be a brief one, and he promised to send word of his progress via passing merchants on their return to London. But when November arrived and I had heard no word of him, I was terrified for my beloved and all the family, including Bella and myself. Despite his weaning me from him, I had not imagined that this time Janyn might not return.

While the queen's household was at Sheen, so near to the city, I sought leave to go into London to visit Dame Tommasa and Master Martin, hoping to hear some news of Janyn. Surely by now someone journeying from Lombardy might have returned to London and reported seeing him. I caught the queen in a distracted moment, and she agreed as long as household guards escorted Gwen and me.

My page, Stephen, accompanied us to the city, and two guards followed us at a discreet distance. As I approached the Perrers' house I grew horribly anxious, my mind spinning out tales of terror. I paused in St. Mary Aldermary to compose myself. The church was blessedly quiet as I knelt before the lady altar. Gwen covered me with a warm mantle and withdrew to join Stephen on a bench well behind me and away from the drafts. I knelt there for a long while, praying that I would hear good news, any news, of Janyn, praying for my daughter, for my husband, and for all our family.

My heart finally steadied, I felt I might continue to the house. As I prepared to rise, I noticed a drably dressed woman with a baby in her arms standing to one side of the lady altar, quite close to me. As I rose I must have jostled her, for she dropped her prayer beads. Seeing it would be most awkward for her to bend down with her burden to retrieve them, I reached down. My hand froze midway. God help me, they were Janyn's rosewood beads, the ones that were to signal my walking away from him and our families. I felt dizzy as I grasped them and straightened up. I must be mistaken. I had convinced myself that disaster was at hand, and thus I had seen what I dreaded seeing. I held the beads out to her in my shaking hand.

"You dropped your beads."

"You are most kind, Dame Alice," said the woman as she reached out, palm forward, to refuse them, "but you must keep them. Know by this from whom my message comes. He and his mother have safely crossed the Channel. They will not return. He commends you to the protection of the household in which you serve, and prays that you forgive and forget. As you vowed."

"Forgive and forget?" I repeated, staring down at the beads in my hand. "How did you come to have these?"

When I looked up for her response she was gone, and now Stephen, standing beside me, was asking if the woman had harmed me. I shook my head and pressed the beads to my nose, inhaling, hoping to catch Janyn's scent. But they were merely rosewood beads, though now they held such a horrible weight I could not bear to have them in my possession. I stepped up to the statue of the Blessed Mother and wound the beads round her wrist until they blended with the other offerings that adorned her.

"Holy Mary, Mother of God, watch over my beloved." I looked round for someone from the church who might know the woman I'd encountered, but Gwen, Stephen, and I were the only people in sight. "Is it not unusual to have a church in the middle of the city all to ourselves?" I said, more to myself than my companions.

"Do you know her?" asked Stephen.

I felt as if I were trapped in a nightmare. It would not have surprised me had my companions not seen the woman or the beads.

Stephen repeated his question. "I am responsible for your welfare, Mistress Alice. Why did she give you the beads? Do you know her?"

"She was a stranger to me. I had not noticed that I had dropped the beads. I'd forgotten I had them in my hands." I lied, needing time to think, to comprehend what had just transpired. I did not want Stephen and the guards to insist on my returning to the palace without seeing Master Martin. "Let us continue to the Perrers home."

I hurried now, anxious to learn what Master Martin knew, frantic for his reassurance. I did not want to believe the beads signaled my separation from Janyn. But the moment I stepped through the hall door I sensed an absence, a void in the spirit of the place, and knew that something terrible had happened. The servant who showed us in excused himself at once, which was not his custom. He was wont to ask after Bella and beg to hear what wonders I'd seen at court since we last spoke. As I waited I noticed clutter and dust, and the absence of some of the most colorful cloths that Tommasa used to cover tables and benches. The servant returned in silence, and still in silence led me to where my father-in-law sat in a small screened-off part of the hall in which he worked on his business records.

Master Martin rose from his chair with effort, moving as if his joints were stiff. He had a dazed look in his eyes.

"What has happened, Father?" I asked as we embraced. He smelled sour as if he'd already had much to drink though it was not yet midday.

"She is gone. My Tommasa. First my son, now my wife. God in heaven, what am I to do? How am I to live?"

He held me so tightly I could feel each of his fingertips through several layers of cloth. This was Master Martin, always a source of strength and wisdom in my life. To find him like this was a moment from my darkest dreams.

"Father, what do you mean?"

He let go of me and stumbled back. His servant, who had quietly waited behind me, helped his master into his chair and then, after bowing to me, his face solemn, moved out of sight behind the screens. Master Martin covered his face with his hands and shook his head.

I crouched in front of him. "You are frightening me. I pray you, tell me what you mean. What has happened here?"

With a moan he uncovered his face and looked at me.

"The message came. After all these years, I did not believe it ever would. But it came. 'Flee.' And Tommasa said that she must leave at once. Without me. She said that Janyn must have received such a message earlier, or had known it was coming. She thanked God that the queen mother had found protection for you and our granddaughter."

"Flee . . . without you? And Janyn too had received such a message?"

Master Martin nodded once and took a great, shuddering breath.

"What do you mean, 'after all these years'?"

"I had agreed when we wed. I had foolishly believed the day would never come."

Things like this did not happen to my people. We were mere merchants, so ordinary as to be invisible. God-fearing, worthy members of trade guilds. But even as I thought that, I remembered we were no longer ordinary, for we had been cursed by our connection to Isabella of France.

"Did Dame Tommasa not question the message at all?" I asked. "At least her heart must have protested? It cannot have been easy for her to leave you." *Or Janyn me!*

"She behaved as if she had no doubt it was what she must do." He searched my face as if hoping I might know more.

"Who brought the message?"

"A servant, hooded, cloaked. Tommasa said that she did not know him, but she knew that he was the one she'd been expecting."

"How?"

"She said only that she knew."

"And you demanded no further explanation? She is your wife, Master Martin. Did you give her permission?"

He flinched as if I had hit him.

I was only trying to make sense of what he was telling me. I told him what had happened in the church, describing the woman who had handed me Janyn's beads in as much detail as I could. "Does she sound familiar?" I asked him.

Master Martin's eyes filled with tears at the mention of his son's rosewood beads, but he said the woman did not sound familiar.

I told him the significance of her giving me the beads.

"Then you had been warned, as I had."

"Why did you not send word to me, Father?"

He just shook his head.

"How might I find the woman? Perhaps if I learned how she had known I would be there . . ."

"Let him go, Alice. He is gone. They are gone."

"Do you not wonder?"

"It does no good."

"*Where* have they gone?"

"Home. To Milan. Or wherever her family might hide them. *If* they make it to safety."

"I must hie to Milan."

"No, Alice. You must not call attention to them."

"I cannot simply wait here!"

"Wait? There is no waiting. They are gone, Alice. They will not return. To return would be to die."

I stared up at him, momentarily robbed of the ability to speak. I had lived with the possibility that Janyn might someday die on a journey, but I had never thought he might be forced to choose between coming back to me and remaining hidden but alive.

"Tommasa said we should consider ourselves widow and widower, you and I." Master Martin broke down in sobs.

"Widow?" I whispered, horrified by the word.

I rose and moved behind him, absently rubbing his shoulders, his neck, needing to touch another human, to give or be given comfort. I stood at the edge of understanding, terrified to step over, resisting making it real.

"Have you heard anything of Janyn since September?" I asked.

Master Martin crossed himself. "Not a word, not a sign. May God protect them." His voice broke and he struggled to regain his composure. "And may He keep them in His loving care."

I crossed myself and murmured, "Amen," and then regretted saying it, for it seemed like acquiescence. "What will you do?"

"Live as a widower. Thank God for my other son, safely in the Church, and my daughter living in Lombardy. You must forget us, Alice. Find a new life for yourself at court. The son and daughter of our benefactress owe you and your daughter better lives, the best that can be arranged for you."

Arranged. It had all been arranged with great care, Tommasa's other children out of harm's way, and Janyn's wife and child in the care of the royal family. Were their hearts not breaking to be forced to desert their families?

"How could he bear to leave Bella and me? Did he not love us as we love him?"

"They left *because* they love us. So that we might be safe."

"Who did they protect for the dowager queen, Father?"

He shook his head. "I never knew." He had risen and stood now, idly shuffling the parchments and tallies on the table before him as if the movement calmed him. "There was a rumor I heard years ago. Folk whispered of a man our King Edward met on a journey to Rome. He was called William of Wales, and it was said he claimed to be our king's father, the old King Edward, the Lady Isabella's husband whom we all believed had been murdered."

I crossed myself. "What did our king do? Did he have him executed?"

"No. That was the part of the story that gave me pause. The king invited this man to accompany him the rest of the way."

"So it *was* his father?"

"I know not. I could never coax Tommasa into commenting on it. It was as if she feared to say too much." He shoved aside a parchment and stood there watching as it skittered across the table and dropped to the tiles below.

Someone most precious to me. The husband Isabella had so wronged by her liaison with Roger Mortimer, the husband she had forced to abdicate? Might he have once again become "most precious" to her? I could not judge, for I'd come to see the royal family and their baronial retainers as so separate from the people among whom I'd grown up that they were a distinctly different breed, as alien from us as birds from dogs. The royal family lived as if they were already figures in legend. Nothing was too costly, nothing beyond their reach. How the royal family felt about one another, I could not begin to guess.

Master Martin advised me to find a new life among these legends, that they owed me this in exchange for Isabella's curse on my husband. I did not deny that. But I could not imagine any lasting joy coming of such a life.

"Will you stay here?" I asked. "In this house that echoes with their voices, their footsteps?"

Master Martin raked his hands through his thinning hair and looked around, as if seeing the past in every object surrounding him. "How could I leave? This was the setting for all my happiness."

"What of my homes?" I wondered aloud. "Am I entitled to them?" I felt petty for asking, and yet I needed something to grasp, something familiar.

"I—I will find out about your London home and send you word. Fair Meadow was a gift from the queen mother. Perhaps you might more easily inquire about that property at court."

To speak of my homes as properties took the heart out of me. "I cannot believe all this. It is a nightmare. Father, I pray you, tell me it is a nightmare. Shake me awake."

Master Martin's eyes filled with tears and he bowed his head, I thought in prayer, but when he straightened his expression was that of someone who had made a decision and wanted no argument. His eyes, though still swimming with tears, had hardened, his jaw set. "My dear Alice, you must let go of your old life, let go of the dreams you and Janyn shared. My son arranged for your financial security. I will honor all his arrangements." His tone was curt and impatient, as if I had outworn my welcome. "Embrace the opportunity to begin anew at court. You should be grateful for the queen's largesse."

I realized he wanted me gone.

"May God go with you, Master Martin." I stumbled as I rose to leave. Stephen and Gwen steadied me.

"God go with you, dear Alice." Master Martin made no effort to mask his relief.

GWEN HELD my arm all the way to the barge that awaited us on the Thames, but she did not ask what had happened until we were alone that evening.

"How did the woman in St. Mary's come to have Master Janyn's paternoster beads?" she asked then.

I recounted our brief conversation. It was difficult to speak the words. I did not tell her that Janyn had foretold this day, nor did I speak of the doubt taking shape in my heart. "I wish I knew more."

My dear Gwen, more a companion and guardian than a servant to me, draped a warm mantle round my shoulders and poured more wine into my cup. I was grateful for her thoughtful ministrations.

I agonized over whether to confide in Queen Philippa regarding the incident with the beads and Master Martin's terrible news, and decided it was best that I do so. I thought—indeed, hoped—that she had permitted my visit because she had known what I would learn, and might now tell me more.

That evening, as I accompanied Her Grace to the hall, I recounted my afternoon. Her steps slowed as I spoke, and the distress on her face alarmed me.

"Your Grace?"

"We have a spy in the household, Alice. A spy! How else would that woman know you would be in the city today? You shall make no more trips to London. No more."

"But what of Janyn, Your Grace? What of my husband's disappearance?"

She shook her head. "Isabella. That cursed woman," she murmured, looking at her beringed hands, not at me. "You heard Perrers, Alice. You are safe here, you and your daughter are well provided for. All will be well. I shall make it up to you." Resuming her walk, she waved away my attempts to speak further.

I moved through my days in a fog of pain and self-recrimination. I desperately wanted to reverse time, to return to the life Janyn, Bella, and I had shared—a time so brief I feared I might someday soon believe it had been but a dream. In a way it had been just that. Even in the time we had been a family Janyn had foreseen our separation; what had seemed permanent to me had never been so to him. I tortured myself with the thought that he might have refused to leave me behind had he loved me more, had I been a better wife, had I done something more to please him. In faith, I still prayed that God would show me what I must do to deserve my happiness, to bring Janyn and Bella back to me. But I also feared what I might see in Janyn's eyes, not love but calculation. That he had wed to please the dowager queen. That I'd merely amused him for a time.

Meanwhile, Bella and I had only me to rely on now. I was ever more grateful for the friendship of Queen Philippa, for she tried to cheer me by including me in all the evening entertainments, kept me close to her in the sewing chamber, protecting me from the quivering headdresses, and, even more, she asked the king to include me with those of her women who rode out in his company from time to time, hunting and hawking. The forests surrounding the palace of Woodstock made it a favorite for large hunting parties.

I could not believe my good fortune in being so favored. I was determined to prove worthy. I had kept my distance from the king, having rarely spoken to him since I had first met him at Hertford Castle. Now I was both excited and dismayed by the prospect of riding out in his company.

I managed to remain properly in the background until one morning when King Jean of France rode out with us. I was startled when he complimented me on a Lincoln green riding hat with a dove feather that Dame Agnes had made for me. But he soon put me at ease, and we talked of the skill necessary in choosing the appropriate cloth for an article of dress.

King Edward joined us. "Mistress Alice is too modest to tell you of her own skill. Though she has been at court but two years, she has become indispensable to the queen in all matters of her wardrobe. The queen relies on her advice." He smiled on me. "Her father saw her gift and trained her well."

I blushed under the appraising and approving regard of the two kings. That King Edward was aware of how long I had been at court and knew of my duties in his wife's household surprised and pleased me. But they called too much attention to me. Lady Eleanor in particular watched as closely as did the hawk on her arm.

As time went on, King Edward coaxed me out of myself, instructing me on the handling of the hawks, discussing aspects of horsemanship. My delight in both grew as I gained confidence, and the release these activities provided from my constantly guarded behavior elsewhere perhaps made me reckless. Though I followed all the correct forms of conduct, I reveled in my hawk's predatory magnificence and in my bond with such a wild and cunning creature, and exalted in the power and grace of Melisende as we rode. When I applauded my hawk's attack and kill, the king would join in. When I rode hard, I would find him pacing me, and when he caught my eye, I felt the kinship we shared in the power of our mounts. He encouraged the side of me that I otherwise subdued, and I was grateful.

Perhaps I was too grateful. One morning I could not hide the ravages of the tears I'd shed because of a dream in which I'd become a woodbine to search for Janyn. In the dream I willed the vine I'd become to extend from east to west, with tendrils spreading out north to south, growing as my tears watered my roots. In a private moment the king noted the pretty way my hair escaped my green hat, and said that the blush of color in my face all but erased the signs of my sorrow. I found myself describing the dream to him.

He declared himself shot through the heart by the steadfastness it revealed. "I have never encountered such loyal devotion. How did your husband inspire such loving loyalty in you, Mistress Alice? I must know how I might do so." His deep voice caressed me, his eyes drew me in, as if he sincerely wished to know.

I wished I had held my tongue, or better yet avoided the hunt that morning. I had allowed myself to fall under his spell again, as I had at Hertford.

• Christmas 1360 •

THE CHRISTMAS court was at Woodstock that year, with most of King Edward and Queen Philippa's sons and daughters and their families in attendance, as well as King Jean of France. There were so many guests that most of the servants slept in hastily constructed "houses" that were little more than huts, and some, mostly guards and retainers, in campaign tents. Fortunate in Queen Philippa's affection, I was one of the half dozen women sharing her bedchamber in the palace. This was much pleasanter than my usual arrangement in a dormitory with the other ladies. For this crowded Yuletide my living quarter was peaceful on the surface, and for that I was grateful. Janyn had now been gone for almost four months and with all my worry and reliving of all he had said and done my temper was too easily tripped. I also missed Bella. Queen Joan had chosen to avoid the festivities in her mourning for her failed marriage. At least I was spared the dreaded chore of explaining her father's disappearance. I wrote frequent letters, but had not yet the heart to tell her of her loss.

On Christmas Day King Edward entered the chamber of his wife the queen to escort her to Mass before the festivities in the hall, and I almost cried out as I recognized the design on his gorgeous coat. Embroidered in gold and silk thread were two woodbines twisting and twining across the black satin, and in gold thread was written the motto "Seeking like the woodbine."

It was usually the king who designed the themes for tournaments, jousts, and feasts, for he enjoyed devising ones based on moral mottos or tales of Arthur, the long-ago king of England. So it was not uncommon for him to wear a coat bearing a motto. But this one he had taken from me, and without informing the queen so that she might match him.

Discovering me watching him, he mouthed, "Your inspiration," as he glanced down at his coat.

I prayed that the little wine I'd drunk had fevered my mind, but it seemed clear that the woodbine coat was a warning his kindness to me was no longer innocent in intention. I prayed that I flattered myself, that he meant the design to do no more than symbolize his famously happy marriage with Philippa, which had been blessed by many children, and perhaps to honor my faithfulness to my husband. But he had not shared it with Philippa.

I had never sought the king's attention. I was too vulnerable. I feared jeopardizing my place at court, or Bella's in the household of the king's sister, by seeming anything but obedient and grateful to the queen. I had a great affection for her, and did not intend to wound her by flirting with her husband.

I yearned for a confidant, but my old friend Geoffrey was no substitute for a sister or a grandmother to whom I might pour out my heart. I *was* grateful he was safely home. Upon his ransom he'd been sent back into danger, ferrying messages across the Channel between his lord the king's son Lionel and his household. I had long prayed for this reunion. But he danced away from deep feelings.

As he sat beside me on Christmas Day, enjoying the grand feast, my good friend sought to amuse me—and therefore eliminate the threat of my confiding too much to him—with the highlights of an old book that was popular at court, a cleric's explanation of the art of courtly love. It was clever and worldly, not to my taste, but in gratitude for Geoffrey's friendship I feigned interest, seeing that he found it immensely witty.

"No one can love unless he is impelled by the persuasion of love." Geoffrey paused, cocking his head, a silly grin on his face, as if to say, *Dare to refute that.*

It did make me chuckle. "That would seem obvious."

"Every lover regularly turns pale in the presence of his beloved."

Now I laughed out loud. "That is silly, Geoffrey. Of course we know that they often turn quite a deep red."

He bowed in acquiescence. "The essence of the art, according to this cleric, is the love-yearning for someone other than your husband or wife, the never-quite-attainable."

That one disturbed me. "Why do they all wish to live in dreams, Geoffrey, or as players in elaborate pageants? Have none of them experienced the joy of a simple love? Of a marriage between a man and woman who love and honor each other?" *Why does the king toy with me?* He could not be sincere in his flirtation, for I was so far beneath him. He stirred in me feelings he did not mean to satisfy. Nor did I wish him to.

"Was yours a simple love, Alice, your love for Janyn?"

"But he is my husband." I fought tears.

Sobering, Geoffrey caught my hands and pressed them as he apologized. "My tongue too often wags before my wit awakens. Forgive me, my dearest friend. I meant only to cheer you, and look what I have done instead. I wanted only to make you laugh, to suggest to you a way to find some joy, an innocent liaison."

His eyes were so kind and blessedly familiar. I knew that he had merely been carried away by his own thoughtless wit. "I am quick to bleed these days, Geoffrey, but you are the best physick for me this court holds and I'll not deprive myself of your company by nursing some imagined wound."

He kissed my hand.

I smiled and simpered. "Perhaps I should make this playful love to you."

"Me?" He shook his head so hard he almost lost his bright red hat. "I am unworthy. What of the king?" His eyes teased me. "The woodbine— is it not the flower you have been sewing into everything you own? How comes he to embrace it in his new motto? Did you speak to him of the dream you described to me?"

I meant to deny it, but he saw the truth in my face.

"Alice!" He looked confused. "Has he made love to you? Have you ridden out alone? Is that why the court whispers of your special favor?"

"No! He is kind to me, knowing my sorrow."

"Is that all it is? Think again, my friend. You would not be his first conquest since the queen. You know that. All the court knows that."

I did not want to think about it. I had been haunted of late by the story of Criseyde and Troilus, the tale that Geoffrey had first told me, one I'd heard often since at court.

When Troy was besieged by the Greeks the Trojan seer Calchas fled to the enemy camp, leaving his daughter Criseyde in Troy. Troilus, who was the son of the king of Troy, fell in love with her and she with him. But when a Trojan warrior was captured by the Greeks, Criseyde was offered in exchange for him. She vowed to Troilus that she would return, but once she was in the Greek camp King Diomedes, desiring her, told her to forget Troilus and pledge her troth to him. She acceded to his demand. Troilus, learning of her betrayal, went into battle, fighting with such abandon he was eventually killed. Criseyde was blamed and accused of luring him, of pledging her troth and then abandoning him, breaking his heart and his will to live.

Each time I heard it I dreamed of the horror of being Criseyde, of being blamed for her obedience. She had been traded to the enemy and desired by a king whose affections she had not sought. She had obeyed, and for this and her beauty was condemned. I had caught the judgment in the eyes of the courtiers in the king's party whenever he spoke to me, and I understood full well how she'd felt.

I took Geoffrey's hand and looked into his eyes, willing him to be serious for a moment, for he was wont to skitter off into humor at the slightest discomfort. "Do you remember the tale you once told me of Criseyde and the magnificent cloak and silken gown she wore when leaving Troy and Troilus?"

He looked confused. "What has that to do with your woodbine?"

"As you told the tale, Criseyde was damned for dressing so richly as if her purpose were to catch a lover. Yet she was being *sent* from Troy into the camp of Troy's enemies, *traded* for a captured warrior. She did not choose to go—at least, that is not how you told the tale. I very much doubt she had much choice about how she dressed for the mission either. Yet *she* was damned, not those who sent her. *She* was blamed for betraying Troilus. But had she any choice? When Diomedes, a king, told her to forget Troilus, was that not a command?"

Geoffrey shook his head, frowning. "I still do not understand, Alice. What am I to see?"

"The king, all unknown to me, copied my emblem, and you are thinking that I lured him, are you not?"

"Am I?" He seemed to be asking the question of himself.

"Do you see what I mean about Criseyde?" I asked it without censure, just a simple question.

My old friend, in his fashionable red-and-black clothes, holding the mazer of fine wine we shared, surrounded by fair folk eating, drinking, laughing, gossiping, sat utterly still, digesting my words. I felt oddly light, as if my ability to make him see that Criseyde was wrongly accused would change my own fate. I was desperate to make him see, as if once *he* understood, it was possible *all* would. At last he nodded.

"Yes, I see that if it were a story about someone you know it would be a gross injustice to blame her. But it is poetry, Alice, an example of the inconstant woman. A symbol, you see."

My heart sank. "No, Geoffrey, it is not that innocent. She was not inconstant by choice, and I cannot believe you are blind to that. People hear such judgment in tales, and judge the folk they know likewise. I innocently tell the king of my dream, he uses my emblem, and suddenly I am accused of pursuing him."

"Oh. Yes. Yes, I do see."

He looked so crestfallen I almost consoled him, but caught myself before being so foolish.

"I am judged, Geoffrey."

"You are. That is true. And I dare guess that little of it is spoken in your presence. You've no idea what the courtiers say about you."

"I wanted only to be a quiet cog in the wheel of the household, calling no attention to myself. But any little joy I take is noted. I see the censure in their eyes. What can I do? What might Criseyde have done?"

"You cannot confront the king about his indiscreet use of your emblem."

"Of course not. But, Geoffrey, tell me what you have heard."

"As you have guessed, already they believe you seek his eye, Alice. They notice every look between the two of you, every new piece of clothing you wear, whether you are wearing his favorite colors."

"How can I protect myself against illusions? Lies?"

"You cannot, Alice. The court is a dangerous place for anyone who inspires envy."

The daughter of a merchant a target for envy? They were all mad. I would stop riding out in the king's company. "I am too ignorant of court. My dear Geoffrey, you must be my ears in future. Will you promise to tell me what they say?"

Poor Geoffrey. His discomfiture was writ plain on his expressive face.

"I promise, as long as you do not punish me for my observations. Remember that I merely repeat to you what I have heard and that I am not one of the gossips."

"You have only to remind me of that and I will recall any dogs I might unleash on you," I said.

Geoffrey smiled and kissed my hand, then grew serious. "Have you any news of Janyn?"

I shook my head. I dared not speak of him in public, though we were talking so low and the music, song, and conversations all round were so loud as to drown us out. The danger to my family was not worth even the consolation of sharing my story to receive Geoffrey's sympathy. I would tell him all if a better opportunity arose.

Geoffrey was recounting one of his adventures across the Channel when I noticed a quiet falling around us. I'd been clutching our shared mazer of red wine and now I glanced down, fearing I'd spilled it on the indigo gown that had been my last gift from Janyn, but saw no stain. Glancing up, I beheld King Edward standing across the table from me, his expression merry. I stopped breathing. He bowed to me and held out his beringed hand.

"Dance with me, Mistress Alice!"

"Sweet Mary in heaven," Geoffrey breathed.

"Your Grace," I murmured, rising, and at once a page was behind me to help me climb over the bench and move round to the king. I do not know how I managed on my trembling legs. I told myself it meant nothing, he pitied me for the loss of my husband and no doubt felt he owed me some cheer since it was his mother who had brought this trouble on my family. But the woodbine design taunted me.

When King Edward took my hand I felt pierced by heat. I am quite sure I made some sound, some exclamation, but he was waving the musicians to lift the tempo and we were off, hand in hand, rushing to join the other dancers. From that moment the alchemy of the king's touch, of his presence, of his vigor, worked on me, caught me up in his mood. The king, despite his nearly five decades, was agile and light on his feet. I'd never danced with a more skillful and graceful partner.

"Do you like my emblem for this feast?" he shouted, sweeping his free hand across his gorgeous tunic. "You are my inspiration!" His grin teased, but his eyes lingered on my low-cut bodice with a hungry intensity.

"A simple plant, Your Grace, yet you have worked a wondrous alchemy. Gold and silver! But you are unfair, my lord. Forewarned, I might have designed a matching surcoat for Her Grace."

"And forgone my pleasure in seeing your surprise?" He shook his head, laughing.

As we moved close, again I felt his extraordinary power of attraction. I was a young, giddy girl again, wanting nothing so much as to be desired.

I danced as if I had not a care in the world, and laughed and responded to his compliments with an ease that I would not have believed possible. In faith, he had enchanted me. Some might say bewitched me. Most would say that I had bewitched him. The music was all my body needed to cue me to the movements of the dance, but the king's presence added a sparkle that I had not felt since last I'd danced with Janyn. We were part of a pattern of swirling colors and our jewels caught the torchlight and added to the enchantment.

After the dance the king bowed to me and the page escorted me back to my place beside Geoffrey. When I'd caught my breath I glanced round to see all eyes turned toward me as people murmured to their companions.

"I am ruined," I said, dismayed by my own behavior as I woke from the king's spell. I was a moth to the flame of his presence, despite all that I had said to Geoffrey. What in fact I felt was disappointment that the magical, exhilarating moment was over.

Geoffrey, of course, heard only my words, not my scandalous thought. He took my hands in his. "No, Alice. It was but a dance. The king has done far more with many women who hold their heads high here at court. It was plain you were surprised. Indeed, at first your terror was visible, and I saw in his eyes how you pleased him anon by falling under his spell."

Falling under his spell? I had. Oh, God forgive me, I had. But reason reasserted itself.

"The women of whom you speak are of noble blood, Geoffrey. I will be condemned for overstepping my position in the chain of being."

"Yet you did enjoy the dance," he said, handing me back the mazer we shared.

"I did. Oh, yes, Geoffrey, I did. Of that I am guilty."

We shared a frightened, slightly giddy, laugh.

And therein lay my weakness. For I knew in my heart that not only would I not dare defy the king if he invited me to dance again, I would not wish to. It was one thing to hunt in a crowd with the king, occasionally garnering brief conversation with him; it was quite another to touch him, to match steps with him, to share the exhilaration of a dance.

He danced with all the young, pretty women at court, especially this Yuletide, when he was celebrating peace with France, I told myself. And resented the thought. I wanted to be singled out by him. He had reawakened something in me that I had not felt since the happy times with Janyn, a delight in my power as a woman. I understood the danger; I was so lonely, so hungry for affection. Once before I had been a moth to a bright flame—Janyn's. He had brought me to court, set me down close to an even brighter flame. I wondered whether he'd been at all aware of the danger in which he had placed me. But then, had he ever fully considered the risk to me when he wed me? Had he known he would someday desert me? I crossed myself, frightened by my disloyal thoughts.

After the feast I dreaded Queen Philippa's reaction. Could she see how her husband stirred me? How much I enjoyed his touch? Arousing him? I had not dared glance toward the high table to see how she received my dance with the king. But I could not avoid her, for that very evening it was my turn to bring to her the almond milk she enjoyed as she rested in her bedchamber after her feet, hands, and shoulders had been rubbed with warm, fragrant oils. The task involved warming the milk on the brazier in her chamber, and while I stood there the queen would review with me the events of the day, asking for my impressions. I had come to look forward to these evenings. But not that night.

Reclining against an array of cushions covered in bright silks, her large, wrinkled body draped in a loose gold silk robe, a color unbecoming to her but which she loved, the queen appeared to be in a merry mood. She was sharing a laugh with Lady Neville. While I held the cup over the brazier, stirring it, they traded some amusing gossip, and then Lady Neville departed.

"You danced prettily with His Grace," said the queen as I set the mazer of warm almond milk next to her. As she shifted in the loose robe, the fragrant oils on her skin perfumed the air around her.

"You are kind, Your Grace. And so is His Grace. I was deeply honored by his benevolent courtesy."

"Benevolent courtesy?" The queen smiled to herself. I was terrified that she had *seen, understood*.

"He told me of your dream of the woodbine and what it meant to you." Her smile had faded and she grew thoughtful. "He thought it charming, such a testament of loving loyalty. Thought me cruel to complain of your refusal to accept what is. But it is best you do. You must forget your old life, Alice. The old queen left that in tatters with her death, as she did so many other lives. I do not like to speak ill of the dead, but you are my responsibility now and in need of guidance."

"Your Grace, I—"

"I am not finished. Isabella of France controlled us all. She delayed my crowning for so long I began to think I'd never be queen as long as she lived. She rose up against the man who was not only her husband but a divinely anointed king, not merely forcing his abdication but attempting to put her lover in his place. My sweet Edward had to take command so young, so very young. Because of her." She spoke in a quiet, pensive tone, not so much angry as resolute.

"Forgive me, Your Grace." I felt disgraced, and resented her for treating me like a child.

"But be of good cheer. My husband the king and I are allowing you a new life, eh, my pet?"

"Yes, Your Grace, and I am most grateful. But I would be a soulless creature to forget my beloved husband."

"Do not contradict me. I know what is best for you."

An irritated tone now sharpened her voice. I simply bowed my head. I knew how easily she might sever my ties with Mary, Will, and John.

I believed she was sincerely concerned for my welfare. But she was a queen, and before that the daughter of a count, and her view of life was worlds apart from mine.

Evidently pleased by my acquiescence, she smiled and patted the bed beside her. It took me back to my last meeting with the dowager queen Isabella, when she bade me sit close to her on her bed while she told me of the danger to my family once she was dead. What was it Philippa had said? Isabella had left my old life in tatters. It was true that all my pain stemmed from whatever it was that Janyn and his mother's family had done for her.

Once I sat beside her, Philippa took my hands in hers and looked long into my eyes, unblinking, as if testing me.

"You are a strong-willed young woman, Alice, with a backbone that others will not easily bend. I like that in a woman of my household, for you reside in a court ripe with temptations certain to overwhelm the weak. Be true to me and my Edward and we will prove faithful and generous."

I waited for more, but she was apparently awaiting my response. Her swollen hands pressed mine. Her steady gaze unsettled me. I sensed that she meant to communicate to me something of great significance, which I was still unable to grasp.

"I do not understand, Your Grace. Have I done aught to make you doubt my loyalty? If so, I pray you forgive me, for it was done unwittingly."

Philippa reached out and touched my cheek. "I forget you were not brought up to this. For now, try to be happy, Alice. Forget the past, revel in the honor and delight of being at court. You are young, beautiful, and will conquer many hearts. But remember that your first loyalty is to the king and me. That is all I meant. If there comes a choice between us and another, remember who protects you." She patted my hand. "And now you may retire. I am ready for sleep. Tomorrow you shall meet another who has lost her husband. My sweet Joan of Kent."

"Lost? Have you had news of my husband, Your Grace?"

"Of course not. Would I not tell you?"

I was wondering how I might honestly answer that when she continued.

"I raised Joan, you know, after her father's horrible execution ordered by my mother-in-law's lover. Her mother was of no use, stupefied by potions that dulled her wit as well as her grief. Do you know the tale of Joan's marriage? The scandal?"

I knew not to further irritate the queen by changing the subject. "I do. She was secretly wed to Sir Thomas Holland, he went off to seek his fortune, and she was so young—eleven?—that she did not dare contradict her guardian when he betrothed her to his son and heir, Montague."

The queen made a sound between a chuckle and a snort. "Is that how the London merchants perceived it? In truth, Holland was not the match we wished for her, and when her guardians noticed her sulking about and ascertained for whom she yearned, they consulted me and her mother as to what was to be done. We all agreed that she must wed William Montague at once. But Holland was shrewd, we'd no idea how shrewd. Seven years he waited, until he had the fame and the wealth to go to the Pope. Seven years Joan lived as Montague's wife only to be handed back to Holland. Scandalous! The Pope did it to annoy us, we are well aware. I would have sworn that Joan's heart was with Montague, but she has seemed far happier with Holland."

Fortunate woman, I thought.

"Alas," Philippa sighed, "Holland died a few days ago. If love could have kept him alive, he would yet live by Joan's power. They tell me that she is in deep, grievous mourning. I believe now that her heart was his from the moment she saw him in her guardian's household. You will have something in common, both having lost a great love."

At least she understood that Janyn was that. "Yes, Your Grace."

"Were you and your Janyn a love match? Did you go against your parents?"

"No, Your Grace, though I loved him with all my heart."

"Good, good. I count on you to be obedient."

I left her chamber that evening in much confusion.

T HE WARMTH with which Joan of Kent had greeted Queen Philippa and her daughter-in-law, Blanche of Lancaster, rapidly chilled upon our introduction. I did not wonder at that—the countess had good reason to avoid anyone who had been a friend to the late dowager queen, her father having been executed by Isabella's lover.

"Mistress Alice," she said aloud with a slight nod in my direction. "Isabella's creature," she murmured under her breath as she took a seat near the queen.

"Joan!"

"Your Grace?" she said with feigned innocence, her roses-and-cream complexion subtly coloring, her expression warming once more. She had a way of widening her eyes as she smiled, drawing me to smile with her despite her snub. I saw why two such worthies as Thomas Holland and William Montague had desired her.

"Mistress Alice deserves your sympathy, not your censure, Joan." Queen Philippa proceeded to recount my story, how Father had set me against Mother in order to be joined with the Perrers family in marriage, and how Janyn had abandoned me with a young daughter.

The queen knew far more than I had imagined. It was agony to listen to her account of my life. But it was clear she knew precisely how to woo the countess.

"I pray you, forgive my discourtesy, Mistress Alice," Joan implored as she crossed to me and took both my hands in hers. "Let us be friends."

Of course I responded with warmth, though I doubted she would give a thought to me once I had left the room. A pity, for I quite liked her. She seemed more substantial than the other royal women, more alive.

S HORTLY AFTER the Christmas court, in a time of quiet weather, I asked leave to see Bella.

Still abed midday, resting from the festivities, Philippa said, "It was a pity our sister Joan did not attend the court and afford you the comfort of your dear daughter. I have little need of you until next Sunday. I shall arrange it."

"Your Grace, I am most grateful. I have not seen my Bella since early summer, and letters are little comfort."

She touched my hand and looked me long in the eyes. "You mourn your husband and your separation from your child. I am not blind to your grief, dear Alice. Yes, my child, you may see your daughter."

My precious Bella had grown so in the half year since I had seen her that I was all the more aware of being robbed of her childhood.

"Where is Father?" Bella demanded. She looked more and more like Janyn, in coloring and in her dark, luxuriant mane of curly hair. "Why has he not brought my pony?"

I held her tight and confessed that I did not know where her father was, but promised her I was searching for him. She pushed away from me, looking over my shoulder, seeking him. I felt as I had done when forced to wean her, a terrible sense of separation, as if part of myself were no longer there. I feared she might grow to hate me, to see me as I saw my own mother. I needed to know the truth about Janyn, not only for me but for her.

8

> *For of hire lif she was ful sore in drede,*
> *As she that nyste what was best to rede;*
> *For bothe a widewe was she and allone*
> *Of any frend to whom she dorste hir mone.*

—GEOFFREY CHAUCER, *Troilus and Criseyde*, I, 95–98

• Spring 1361 •

IT WAS a winter of burials for the royal couple, and as I witnessed their grief I understood that even they were not immune from suffering. The death of Joan of Kent's husband, Sir Thomas Holland, had been a blow to the king, for despite his impolitic marriage he had been one of Edward's trusted commanders. The deaths of two more of his captains swiftly followed. And then came the cruelest blow of all, the death of Henry of Grosmont, Duke of Lancaster and father of Blanche, wife of the king's third son, John of Gaunt. Both Queen Philippa and King Edward, and indeed most of the barons, had considered the duke the foremost commander of the realm, and he had been a close friend to the royal couple. His requiem Mass was attended by all the noble families, but though it was a magnificent spectacle it was yet solemn. The king himself had contributed expensive brocade cloth for the vestments and livery, including gold brocade from Lucca for the pall. Some murmured that the brocade from Lucca might be infected with the pestilence, for the sickness was rumored to have returned, moving west and north from the Mediterranean as it had before.

I had been but a child of seven or eight when the pestilence first raged across Christendom. Father later told me stories of the time, how we had fled to his sister's home in Smithfield to distance ourselves from the river, rumored to be carrying the deadly miasma, only to discover that she and both her children had succumbed. In the queen's sewing chamber we were all one in our fear, speaking in hushed voices of nightmares filled with the horror of pustules, stench, corpses piled in the streets. For once I was welcomed and included, as we faced a common enemy.

Several weeks after rumors of pestilence reached the palace, Queen Philippa sent for me after morning Mass. In the spacious room known as the queen's hall Philippa sat alone by the fire, none of her ladies in attendance. Blanche of Lancaster sat apart from her near the high casements, petting a small dog and gazing out at a sudden snow shower. A few serving maids were tidying on the far side of the room. The queen nodded to me the moment I entered the hall, patting the space beside her on a wide cushioned bench. Our privacy and the indication that I was to sit so close warned me that she was about to tell me something she did not want others to hear.

I took a deep breath and pulled myself up as straight and tall as possible so that I did not seem so small and alone as I felt while crossing the echoing room and taking a seat beside she who held my life in her hands.

Her eyes were sad, her voice soft, and I prayed that she had not received bad news of my Bella, for it was said that children were particularly vulnerable to the pestilence in this visitation. I crossed myself and prayed for strength.

"We have received a message from Master Martin Perrers." The queen placed a plump, beringed hand on my forearm and fixed me with such a solemn look that her sad eyes pierced my heart. "You must be strong, Alice."

"I pray you, Your Grace, what ill has befallen Master Martin?" But I doubted it was sorrow for my father-in-law that had so softened her demeanor.

"Both his wife and son, your husband, have been felled by pestilence in Milan."

"No," I gasped. "No!"

Blanche of Lancaster rose and brought her stool closer. I guessed that their partnership had been rehearsed and this had been her cue to join us. Her silks rustled, and yet she thought it necessary to cough as if to warn us of her presence. I said something in that space, but my sense was that the heavens and the earth halted in all sound and movement for a long moment.

"Dame Alice, I too grieve," said the lady Blanche. "I have lost my father."

"But how can they both—" I said. "My husband and his dam were both healthy, grown— Children and the ill—" I stopped, hearing how I babbled. My beloved and his mother were dead. It was difficult for me to breathe. A darkness closed in on me from either side as the queen's round face swirled about in the gathering gloom.

I DREAMED I woke in a large chamber densely inhabited by secrets. Up in the ceiling high above me secrets prowled in the corners, flickered in the shadows, fluttered just beyond my sight, and the subtle draft from the pulsing wings of the livelier ones stirred the tiny hairs on my forearm. I sensed secrets murmuring just beyond my hearing. The winged ones teased, as if half-hoping to be heard. The murmuring and shadowy ones were dark, heavy, frightening. Many of these, garbed in gorgeous widow's weeds, were the former queen's secrets. Many were those of the present king and queen, crowned and gloriously robed. Some were from the wider court, and even clerics kept drably robed secrets in this room. Secrets no one must admit to knowing. Inconvenient secrets. Dangerous secrets, delivering death to the overcurious. I tried to shrink into the bed, drop down between the feathers and slip out below and escape. I did not know how I had come to be in such a frightening room. I had no need for secrets, no desire for them.

When I woke from the dream that night it killed sleep, seeming more real than my usual dreams. Nan once told me that dreams we remembered as we awoke as vividly as if they were memories of real events were significant, sent to warn us. I lay in the dark, thinking of church naves and chapels with gargoyles, carved heads, ornamental bosses, statues. I remembered the woman in the church who had dropped Janyn's rosewood beads, and how I had wound them round the Blessed Mother's arm. The dream had twisted these images. My belly felt weighted down with cold, cold stones, and I felt pinned to the mattress, unable to spread my ribs to breathe.

I would trade my soul for Janyn's warm body beside me, for the gift of his presence. The nightmare of Isabella's curse continued. I accepted that Janyn and Tommasa were dead, but not that they had died of the pestilence. They had gone into hiding, they had been in danger. This explanation was meant to silence me, to kill the need for further questions.

Gwen bent over me, my dear Gwen, offering me a sip of brandywine.

"Drink, mistress. Slowly. Slowly."

I sipped.

"Queen Philippa and Duchess Blanche have sent messengers every hour to inquire after you. Countess Joan as well. I— Oh, Dame Alice, I am so sorry!" Gwen's eyes were swollen and red from weeping.

Secrets. Master Martin had spoken of a tale that could mean Isabella's Edward, the present king's father, had survived his imprisonment in Berkeley Castle and escaped, been hidden in Lombardy. Lombardy. Milan. Tommasa's family. Someone dear who was protected. Had Janyn and Tommasa known of this, it might not have been enough for them simply to disappear. Perhaps they had to die. Or at least the king and queen must believe them to be dead. My thoughts tumbled and turned on themselves until I wished for unconsciousness.

All my life I had obeyed those who cared not a whit for my welfare, for my happiness, who loved me not at all. Janyn as well? I had given him and our daughter everything I had to give, and had hoped only for more of my sweet, simple life, a few more children and a gradual aging with my beloved husband, nothing grander. Now I had nothing.

Except Bella. I would not abandon Bella. I had been abandoned by everyone I had loved, and I would never do that to my daughter. I knew that I must gather my strength. I took a good, long drink of the brandywine. And another.

Gradually over the next few days the frightening dreams abated, but my waking thoughts were still haunted. I almost regretted my bed having been moved to a corner of the bedchamber I shared with several women, screened off for privacy but near a wide window so that the fresh country air might cheer me, for the privilege isolated me with my darksome thoughts.

I felt adrift at court, as if the solid ground of my life had been pulled away and I hung suspended above a vast emptiness by strings held by the queen and king. Yet I depended on their protection more than ever.

As I grew stronger I remembered the solemn requiem for the old Duke of Lancaster and felt humbled. I was not alone in my suffering; it was Isabella's legacy that set me apart. I must not succumb to despair. I lifted my chin to receive the gentle breeze from the unshuttered window. I wanted occupation, distraction.

To my immense relief visitors began to appear—first the queen and the duchess, then some of the ladies who had snubbed me but now found me a tragic figure, my husband and his dam victims of the pestilence, and so far away. They came bearing gifts—sugared almonds, dates, exotic fruits.

Most welcome was Geoffrey's arrival. The others had been curious to see how I behaved, how my grief had changed me, and were intent on convincing me that my life lay ahead of me, bright as ever. In Geoffrey's eyes I saw my sorrow mirrored. So far only he and Gwen seemed to comprehend the enormity of my loss, perhaps because they alone knew that my existence at court was far from what I had ever desired. He was by my side at the requiem Mass for Janyn and Tommasa. Queen Philippa had arranged it in the chapel, and she, Blanche, Joan, and many in the queen's household attended. I might doubt the queen's explanation of my loss, but I took comfort in her kind gesture.

"I pray that you will find joy again," said Geoffrey a few days later. "And until then, that your love for Bella will sustain you. I do not want to lose you, my oldest and dearest friend."

He was holding my hand, sitting close to the bed in which I reclined against a small mountain of pillows that Gwen had collected for my comfort.

"I miss him so, Geoffrey. I had held out hope."

I could see on my friend's expressive face how he struggled to find some reassurance for me, but he was not one to lie in order to cheer up a friend. At last he raised his cup and toasted me—"To your courage"—and drank.

Courage. I wondered how far that would support me, whether it could suspend me above the void.

"To your rebirth as a lady of the court."

I felt forlorn after he departed and regretted having wasted so much of his visit in tears. His friendship was precious to me. Bella was precious to me. And Gwen. And Dame Agnes and Master Edmund. My sister and my brothers. There were still many people holding me to this life. The realization heartened me.

I thought about Geoffrey's second toast, "To your rebirth. . . ." Perhaps in passing through the agony of losing Janyn I *had* undergone a rebirth. I recalled sermons describing how sacred such an experience was, and that the reborn had been divinely blessed for a purpose. What, then, might be my purpose? I wondered. Perhaps that was my way forward, to accept that I had been reborn and must now discover the reason. Once the idea took root, I felt an unfamiliar calm.

In chapel I ceased praying that I might return to the past, to life as it had been, and instead prayed, "Holy Mary, Mother of God, I kneel before you humbled and ask for guidance. How may I best serve you?" I opened myself to divine grace. Gradually, over the days I was filled with a sense of peace and imagined the Blessed Virgin's translucent hand resting on my head. I believed that I would be guided by grace.

When the queen commanded me to resume my duties, she made it clear that I was to set aside my widow's weeds.

"I honor your mourning, Alice. My household attended a requiem Mass for your loved ones. I have permitted you a fortnight in which to grieve and pray. Now you must look to the future—to wear weeds would only prolong your clinging to the past. For a time you may wear your simplest gowns."

I meekly agreed, praying that if Janyn looked down from Heaven he would understand.

Upon my return to the queen's chambers her ladies expressed joy at my recovery, welcoming me back with seemingly sincere friendliness. I took this as God's sign that I was on the path He meant for me.

Queen Philippa stood in the midst of benches draped with cloth, ribbon, and strings of buttons, impatiently poking at the various gorgeous piles with her cane and muttering imprecations. Her demeanor softened as she noticed me.

"Come, Alice, we must begin preparations for the move to Windsor for the Feast of St. George. The king wishes it to be a most splendid feast and tournament, to ease the hearts of the mourners and the fears of all about the pestilence. We have a theme to devise and costumes to design. Tell me if any of this is worth my bother." She lightly patted my arm as I joined her. "In the morning we must begin."

As we sorted through the samples, discarding some, putting others aside for further consideration, I relaxed and grew absorbed in the familiar process.

At last, fatigued, the queen sought her bed for a rest before we supped in the hall. "Praise God that you are returned," she said, kissing me on the cheek as I handed her the cane.

WINDSOR WAS beautiful that April, and the festivities defiantly grand and celebratory against the undercurrent of fear the pestilence wrought. Those who were yet in mourning for the great knights who had died the past year wore gorgeous garments of scarlet and black, while the rest of the Garter knights wore the blue-and-gold of the Order.

The queen had much need of me, changing her exquisite attire many times each day. We worked with splendid silks and velvets, many with intricate patterns including garters and fleur-de-lis. I exhausted my diplomatic skills in guiding her choice of patterned cloth. Her plump and increasingly uneven figure required strategic use of draping, layers, and avoidance of many patterns that emphasized her shape, particularly in the more fitted gowns.

At all times six women were kept busy snipping pearls and jewels and exquisite buttons of gold, silver, pewter, some with pearls and precious gems, from one piece of clothing and sewing them onto others, and as ever some of the patterns we had envisioned looked wrong when executed, so work had to be unpicked and redone. We also discovered that the hems of several of the queen's new gowns were quite long, pooling about her feet as she stood, which was the fashion, but in her condition I thought ill advised. I insisted that they be rehemmed, for the queen was too unsteady on her feet to be trusted not to trip. I enjoyed the responsibility of ensuring that our beloved Philippa looked every inch a queen.

When not engaged in dressing Her Grace, I did have opportunities to see Geoffrey, which did my heart good. Knowing me as well as he did, he could tease me out of my deepest despair, though he swore he was losing sleep over his failure to coax a laugh from me. He was not the only man trying to cheer me.

Richard Lyons, one of the executors appointed by my husband, offered to secure Janyn's home in London until such time as I might afford to buy the lease from him.

"I thought you might prefer to keep it, with the courtyard garden you designed. And Bella will like to see it."

I was encountering a gentle side of him I had not witnessed before.

The one person who might most successfully have enticed me back to life, God help me, had notably kept his distance since the news of Janyn's and Tommasa's deaths—King Edward. The deaths of his own comrades-in-arms and the approaching pestilence were the queen's explanations for his frequent absences from court and lack of sporting activity when present, but I saw him walking with an assortment of beautiful young noblewomen and suspected I had simply been discarded. I told myself I was relieved, that his flirtation had always been a misbegotten game, but my heart did not agree.

There was, however, someone who seemed ready to take the king's place in flirtation, Sir William Wyndsor, a man of some reputation in the military, handsome and slightly arrogant. He made it difficult for me to ignore him, the way he devoured me with his wide hazel eyes and paid me compliments whenever we met, which was far more often than mere chance could explain. During the festivities at Windsor he invited me to dance several times.

"Mistress Alice, you are a feast for the eyes. How is it that we have not met before?"

"I trow it is because you have been occupied with making a reputation on the battlefield, Sir William, and I have been safely occupied in the queen's household."

Such was the depth of our conversations, but I thought it admirable that we managed to say as much as we did while dancing. I particularly enjoyed dancing with him when the king was present.

"It is rumored he will be the Earl of Ulster's captain in Ireland," Geoffrey told me after one of my dances with Sir William. "He's already valued by the king, and if he survives Ireland and keeps Lionel alive, may rise at court. In time you might come to think of him as a worthy spouse and father for Bella. You could do far worse than wed William Wyndsor."

I met his comment with a confusion I tried to hide by protesting, "I am in mourning, Geoffrey, despite my lack of widow's weeds."

"Forgive me, I merely point out a potential escape from court."

"Geoffrey!"

He squeezed my hand. "Dare to be happy, my friend. At least dream of it."

"I am not blind to the beauty and wit all round me," I assured him.

Countess Joan joined Geoffrey in encouraging me to find happiness, though her message was less sanguine.

"No matter what you believe about the deaths of your husband and his mother, know that you are safe in Her Grace's household," she told me one afternoon as we walked in the gardens. In befriending me she had told me all about her scandalous past. On that particular day she had begun by confiding in me that while wed to William Montague she had taken care not to become pregnant, though they had lived as husband and wife for seven years.

"You know how to avoid conception?" I asked, having heard of such things, but never having known anyone who had actually gone to such lengths.

Joan had become serious, glancing round to make sure no one could hear us. Seeing that we were quite alone, she said, "You shall soon lose your heart to one of the worthy knights pursuing you, I am sure of it. And happy for you!"

I began to protest, but she raised her hand to silence me.

"What I wish to say is, should you have need of such protection as I did with Montague, come to me at once. You must drink some of an herbal mixture before and some after the act." She patted my cheek. "You have had enough heartache from dumb obedience. Now it is time for you to take control of your life."

I thanked her for her advice, though I did not consider it possible for me to follow it.

She was truly a most beautiful woman and reveled in life, dressing and moving to show off her sensual body, plunging wholeheartedly into the activity of the moment as if tomorrow might never come. This approach to life excited those about her, lifting spirits and creating possibilities where none had appeared to be before. She spoke her mind and made no effort to be nice as a general principle—one *earned* her friendship.

"We women are treated with less courtesy than men treat their horses, dogs, or hawks," Joan told me. "God granted us souls, like men, and minds with which to reason our way to grace, yet we are expected neither to think for ourselves nor to mind being unappreciated and neglected. They consider us domestic beasts and find us annoying if we behave otherwise, if we question their commands or doubt their wisdom. We are to be obedient unto death, and to bear many sons. And, of course, priests and monks fear us because they desire us and have little control over their own appetites; so they blame us and call us sinful, for they cannot admit to their weakness. I do not understand why God does not better support us."

I did not disagree with her, although I had considered my own anger at such things sinful and would never have expressed it aloud. She opened my eyes to the possibility of trusting in my own wisdom, something the dowager queen Isabella had spoken of also; but Isabella had, I believed, gone against both God's and nature's laws in destroying her husband and king. Joan's way of honoring her own wisdom was far more palatable to me. Perhaps I would find joy again. Life at court did much to raise my spirits. Yet I had only to hear someone speak of a child to be overcome with yearning for Bella.

AFTER THE Feast of St. George the king was off to the Isle of Sheppey to consult the masons and clerks of works on the palace of Queenborough, which he was building there for Queen Philippa. To her deep regret the extravagances of the feast had so seriously exhausted her that Philippa canceled her plans to accompany him to the site. She agreed with her physician that the long journey from Windsor to northern Kent was too much for her. But that did not mean she was willing to forgo having a voice in the palace's design, and so was inspired to send me along in the king's party, as a woman whose taste she counted on. I was to travel with the king. My heart pounded at the news. I was to be one of several ladies from the queen's household in the party, but she singled me out, consulting with me at length regarding the details to which I should give my utmost attention.

"Where is your excited smile, Alice? You are to design a palace for your queen. Create beauty. I am honoring you, entrusting you with something very dear to me."

I was, in truth, overwhelmed by the great honor and trust she was bestowing on me. I forced a smile. The queen was ever impatient with any lack of confidence.

"Your Grace, I was caught up in the litany of all we have discussed, committing it to memory. I pray you will forgive me."

I must have divined the right excuse. She smiled. "You are forgiven."

"I confess I was also thinking how much more delightful it would be were we there together."

She pressed my hands, satisfied, and was soon on to other topics—the sad state of her health, the ravishments of so many pregnancies, and since her accident, the lack of activity that seemed to be leading her into a downward spiral. This talk eventually wearied her, and she, apologetically and I think with sincere regret, sent me off to prepare for the journey.

Gwen brought an enthusiasm to the preparations I'd rarely witnessed in her. She took pains to learn as much as she could about the island and the route we would be traveling, ensuring that I would have enough warm clothing.

"It is said to be damp, with thick morning mists," she explained.

"Well, it *is* an island," I noted.

I could see by the set of her shoulders as she resumed her work that my indifference disappointed her.

"I am excited, Gwen, but I am also keenly aware of my duty to Her Grace. I fear I shall crowd out her instructions with details about the journey."

It was true. I prayed that I remained steady, that I would not disappoint the queen and ruin Bella's future.

On the evening before our company was to depart, the queen summoned me to her chamber rather late. Gwen at once began to fret that the trip had been canceled or postponed, and I found myself also praying that we were still to go. For all my dread of disappointing the queen, I did look forward to the journey.

Rising with haste, I succumbed to Gwen's efforts to erase the signs that I'd already been drifting off to sleep and then hurried along the corridor. I slowed down as I saw several of the king's pages standing just outside the door. I did not wish to interrupt a conjugal visit. But a servant knocked twice on the door when he saw me and stepped within to announce my arrival. I heard the queen call out for him to show me in, and the door was opened wide. Inside I found a cozy domestic scene, the king and queen sitting at a table by a brazier, their postures relaxed. Queen Philippa waved me to the vacant chair between them.

"I could not sleep until I was assured that you both understand that you, Alice, are to represent *my* interests at Sheppey," she said. "I daresay you were abed, catching all the sleep you might before the journey." She was looking better than she had in days, her color soft, her eyes clear. Even her voice held more life. "But Edward was delayed by every courtier not accompanying him to Sheppey, asking for last-minute advice, orders, favors, were you not, husband?"

King Edward patted his wife's plump hands, folded loosely on the table before her, but he looked me in the eyes. "Forgive me for the late hour. As you say, my love, the night before a journey the court realizes that they have left everything too long and try to right that before they sleep." He clapped his hands and a servant brought us jeweled mazers filled with wine. Raising his cup, the king said, "Let us discuss what we must before this fine claret calls us to rest."

I rejoiced that we were still to depart on the morrow. But to sit between my king and queen awed me. Fortunately the wine was delicately mulled and heated just sufficiently to soothe. The queen launched into a now familiar list of considerations essential for a beautiful, inviting palace, particularly considering that Sheppey was marshy.

"Alice, when you walk the land with the masons and the clerk of works, I bid you breathe in and pay heed to the dampness. Notice your feet as well. Steer the men away from the worst spots. Keep them on the highest ground. Husband, pay heed to Mistress Alice."

"My love," the king interrupted, "the location of the palace is already set. It will replace the old castle."

"I remember it as an abysmally damp, dreary place, yet I have other memories of beautiful spots in the grounds. You know better than to question my memory for such things, husband."

The king's laughter brightened the room. I felt it warm my blood. But my heart ached to recognize in both their faces the deep, abiding love I had once enjoyed with Janyn.

Philippa had continued with her description of a pretty walled rose garden for strolling and sitting in on warm days, "even by the sea there are certain to be warm, sunny afternoons," and a suite of rooms specifically for her and her ladies that should include a hall large enough for music and dancing, "for though I no longer dance I delight in watching others."

That provoked a hearty laugh from Edward. His was a deep, full-bodied laugh, a kingly laugh indeed.

"My love, I am ever wary of planning aught with you if I have any thought to the health of our coffers! What begins as a simple castle for occasional, brief visits grows to be a magnificent edifice before it is even begun."

Philippa shrugged in a manner that must have been pretty when she was younger, her smile bright and her chuckle light.

"Then do not ask, my love, and you will happily achieve a plain, uninviting, damp, and cheerless castle safe from thieves, for no one will dare leave furnishings there to molder."

They shared laughter. I downed the remainder of my claret and wished for more. In a moment a servant had stepped forward to refill my mazer.

Philippa tapped the table by my hands.

"Too much wine will make tomorrow's journey more tiring."

"But the excitement, my love. Mistress Alice may need the wine to sleep."

They looked at me expectantly.

I forced a little laugh, a pathetic sound. "You are both right. I shall drink just a little more, though it is a pity to waste it."

"Wine is never wasted," said Philippa. "The servants drain the cups before they wash them. You make friends of them by always leaving a little."

The king yawned, the queen patted her mouth to stifle a yawn, and after a few more rather aimless comments the king proposed we all hie to our beds. I stumbled back to my room, a little drunk and missing Janyn so badly I cried myself to sleep.

THOUGH IT was spring the air was damp and chill on the Isle of Sheppey. We arrived late in the afternoon, the chatter of our company overwhelmed by the warring clamor of wind, waves, and sea fowl. The land was so flat and low lying that it seemed the breaking waves would wash over us. Though I had lived all my life in London, in the flat land by the Thames, I had been surrounded by buildings. I had never seen earth and sea and sky joined so.

I slept in the small convent, in a room crammed with cots for the queen's ladies. We were none of us comfortable or happy. On that first night I slipped out of my room and sought the chapel. Though cold, the sacred space was blessedly peaceful. I knelt before the altar and prayed for release from my mourning, for the wisdom to provide a good life for my daughter, and for the grace to fulfill my duty to the queen. I was discovered by a servant just before dawn and shooed back to the crowded bedchamber. I was grateful to be outdoors again after Mass and a simple meal of bread and thin ale.

One of the convent servants led me to where the king and several other men walked near the old castle. In the flatness of the marshy island the men looked like giants, and the king the tallest of all. He moved with head held high, back straight but not stiff. Indeed, he was the very model of grace in motion.

"Your Grace," I cried out, my only hope to be heard over the wind that rushed past my ears and snapped my clothing. I bowed to him.

Much to my confusion, the king reached out a gloved hand to me, and as I bowed to kiss his ring he shook his head and drew me up. "The gale is so strong I fear you might take flight, Mistress Alice," he bellowed with hearty cheer, though the expression in his eyes was quieter, gentle. "My wife would never forgive me if I lost you to the wind and the waves." He took my hand firmly in his. "I shall be your anchor."

His expression surprised me. I felt that he truly saw me, acknowledged me as Alice Perrers, neither a nameless servant nor one of many ladies of his wife's household. For so long I had felt that no one saw me, saw *Alice*. I remembered how before my marriage I had feared that I would lose myself in my love for Janyn.

"Walk with me and tell me what you think my Philippa would be saying."

Though his familiar behavior confused me so that I feared I might dissolve into giggles, the kindness I had seen in his eyes put me at ease. My good memory served me well, and I was able to repeat the queen's priorities, shake my head when the ground oozed beneath our feet, and nod when we were at a higher elevation and the marshy island swept away from us like a sea of green and brown. But all the time my mind was feverishly arguing against the flutter of hope that he had lit within me, that I might not lose myself entirely at court, that I might prove to be of some worth, and that even without Janyn I might find joy in life.

Suddenly the king stopped. We had outpaced the others and were quite alone with the seagulls and the wind.

"What is this frown, Mistress Alice? I will see your smile before the day is out."

"Your Grace," I said, bowing to him, which was awkward on the rocks. "I was thinking what else Her Grace might wish me to point out." I would have sworn that I had been smiling. I kept my eyes downcast.

"Perhaps." Gloved and beringed fingers reached out and lifted my chin. "Sweet Alice, you have much to grieve, I know. But you have all your life yet to live, and I wish to provide you with the opportunity to live it fully, with grace and joy, free from worry. I owe you this, for it was my mother's work that deprived you of husband and mother-in-law. I promise you that as soon as I am certain your connection with that business is forgotten I shall have your daughter brought nearer to court so that you might be with her often."

"My lord!" I could say no more, for emotion choked me.

He tilted his head, studying me. "You are a most beautiful young woman, Mistress Alice. You will find joy with another man."

I was grateful to be interrupted by the approach of the others, spared the need to respond, for I could not find my voice. He thought me beautiful and had promised Bella would be near me.

"Your Grace," I managed to say, as the others caught up with us and whisked us back to the house in which the king and his knights were lodged, where we sat down to a modest meal.

I found it easier to stay in my bed that night, listening to the other women whisper and snore. In the morning Gwen woke me while most of them were yet abed.

"The king summons you for some hawking!" Her eyes were bright with excitement at such an invitation.

I slid out from beneath the covers with happy anticipation.

Outside, the air was chill with the morning mist that swirled in strange colors, lit by the dawn.

"It will be warm today," Gwen said.

"Later, but not now," I said, disappointed. A hawk would not fly in this. But out of the mist came the king and a servant on horses, leading one other. They carried no hawks.

We rode out onto the beach, then sat our horses, as close together as possible, gazing out on the swirling mist.

"Yesterday I said that I understand your grief, your pain," said the king. "I want to tell you a tale of a young man, younger than you, who discovered that the happy dream of his childhood was just that, a dream." He told me of the moment when he understood that his parents, the king and queen of England, were at war with each other. His mother, my old acquaintance the dowager Queen Isabella, had sailed to France, her home, where her brother was king. She was furious with the way her husband favored the brutal, conniving, greedy baron Hugh Despenser over her. She tricked her husband into sending his son, the Edward who now told me this tale, as his representative at her brother's wedding, for she knew that the king himself did not intend to attend for fear that his barons might rise in revolt against him while he was absent from his kingdom. And then she kept her son in France despite increasingly angry letters from her husband, demanding the return of the prince. "And so I was forced to choose between them," Edward said to me now.

"How cruel of them." I thoughtlessly reached out to touch his arm in sympathy and then quickly pulled back, embarrassed by my presumption in almost touching the king so. "And did you choose?" I asked a little breathlessly.

"I told myself that I was not choosing, that I was refusing to choose. But in my heart I knew that I had chosen my mother. I had chosen treason. I had chosen the path that led to my father's violent death, the sacrilegious murder of a divinely anointed king. And I knew that I had done so because I feared my mother, who had the support of her brother the French king, more than I feared my father, and that I hated Hugh Despenser more than I hated Roger Mortimer, my mother's lover."

"Those were dark times."

"They were."

"Dame Tommasa, my husband's mother, told me that your mother endured much, and that she had suffered."

"She did. And in her pain, took a terrible revenge. She never found joy again. Indeed, I could not imagine that I would ever do so, either. But I did. I have found joy and purpose." He reached for my hand. "And so shall you, Mistress Alice, I am certain of it." He smiled. "I insist upon it!"

"I am grateful for your kindness, Your Grace," I said, aware of the warmth coming through his glove. "But I confess that I do not trust to hope for another chance at the joy I had with my husband, our little family. I cannot think that God blesses anyone with such joy a second time."

"My mother cruelly used your husband's family. You have suffered for that. But I pray that you find joy again."

"May God bless you, Your Grace." We sat quietly for a moment, our hands joined in the space between our mounts. "I pray that you do not take this question ill, Your Grace, but it would help me if I knew. Who was it that my husband's family protected for Lady Isabella, the Queen Mother?"

He looked away from me, and I guessed that he did not wish me to see his true feelings about my question. I began to understand he was not skilled at hiding his feelings. "Not now. But I shall tell you someday, I promise. When we are sure of one another." He moved in the saddle. "Come. Let us ride a little."

The fog had begun to thin and the sea stretched out before us, glimmering in the sun, shimmering as the tide rocked it.

The king's falconer rode up to escort us inland, where the fog had lifted and we might hunt. He had the falcons there. We hawked, and afterward the ladies and knights joined us for a long, wine-soaked feast, and then the company walked about the old, tattered castle and talked of how beautiful it would be very soon.

My time alone with the king had been noticed. In the evening the ladies with whom I shared a bed allowed me some more room than they had on other nights and refrained from sending me off on errands. But they were no more friendly. I guided my thoughts back to those moments I'd shared with the king on the beach.

I shall tell you someday, I promise. When we are sure of one another. And he would bring my Bella nearer to court. The king had promised me. It was a beginning, something to cling to, and I hugged those promises to my heart as I fell asleep.

9

He say his lady somtyme, and also
She with hym spak, whan that she dorst or leste;
And by hire bothe avys, as was the beste,
Apoynteden full warly in this nede,
So as they durste, how they wolde procede.

—GEOFFREY CHAUCER, *Troilus and Criseyde*, III, 451–55

• Summer 1361 •

I VOWED TO heed the king's kind advice and find contentment in my life. More easily vowed than carried out, but I was determined to try. To shelter my child from harm I must retain the protection and affection of the royal couple.

THE PESTILENCE undermined King Edward's efforts to reassure his people. Law courts were closed, reopened, closed. By midsummer we were sequestered at Sheen, though the officers of the household were considering the wisdom of fleeing even farther into the countryside. Lionel, Earl of Ulster, had lingered at Sheen after his sister Mary's wedding, and with him of course his household, so I enjoyed Geoffrey's company at many meals. It could be a mixed pleasure, for he was honoring his promise to be my eyes and ears among the courtiers, and from him I learned that I was rumored to be sharing the king's bed. I was not surprised to hear it—since Sheppey the other women had treated me with icy caution—though the fact that I shared a bed with at least one other woman every evening, in a room assigned to six of us, should have proven it false. Perhaps because I was the only one of the six who slept in that chamber every night, I was the only one who knew I was the sole celibate among them. But though I was not surprised, I *was* frightened by the rumor. I could not think what would happen were the king to learn of it, or even worse the queen, my mistress. Would they remember that I had no power to silence the gossips? Would they believe I had said nothing to provoke such talk?

I prayed for guidance as to how I might clear my name, having no one at court to whom I might turn for advice. Hoping that perhaps enough time had passed since the death of the dowager queen that I might be permitted to see my grandmother, one morning I broached the subject.

But the queen pursed her lips and shook her head at me as if I were a frustrating child, willfully stupid. "Even if I thought that you might slip away to see one of your Salisbury kin without endangering them, I would not allow you to risk going into the hot, pestilence-ridden city. No, I do not give you leave. We have sworn to protect you, and we will." She fanned herself with a vigor that heated rather than cooled her. In the humid warmth of high summer she shed layers and replaced them with dry ones numerous times each day and well into the evening. The laundresses grumbled.

I had few companions to distract me. There were two young sisters living in the household, the orphaned daughters of a lesser knight who had been the queen's countryman, with whom I enjoyed spending time, although they were only girls. They had a more easy grace than the other children being fostered by the queen. At all times there were ten or so youth in the household, some to be companions to the royal children, others orphans who had touched the queen's heart. The two girls from Hainault were Katherine and Philippa de Roët, charming and curious and hungry for learning, bittersweet reminders of my dear sister Mary.

My other occasional companion was Elizabeth, one of the queen's ladies, who treated me kindly. We would walk in the gardens, where she would talk of her lost marital joy. Her husband, a knight, had suffered a head wound in battle that had rendered him so helpless he was now cared for in an abbey in the west country. While she wandered through her memories, describing her courtship, her wedding, her hope for many children, I visited my own.

"You are a most excellent listener, Alice," she would often exclaim, "but I should invite you to speak of your lost dreams."

I would shrug and tell her I preferred to listen to her. She would shake her head, ask a few cursory questions, and then resume her own narrative.

A married sister who lived in the countryside near Canterbury wrote long letters I enjoyed hearing.

"But her life is so dull," Elizabeth would protest.

"It is the life I miss. I love hearing of crops, livestock, and household crises. Life at court has no relation to my old, ordinary life."

It was from those letters that I began to appreciate how fortunate I was to be in the safety of the queen's household. Because the law courts had been closed as a precaution while the pestilence moved through the land—all public gatherings deemed dangerous—many suddenly widowed women had no recourse if their liege lord arranged a marriage for them to his own advantage or decided that their property was best protected by his taking it over and seizing the income.

"Oh, Alice, you must have a care," Elizabeth exclaimed in the midst of one sad account.

"That does not seem to be the king's intent for me," I assured her. "No one has prevented Richard Lyons from protecting my London home on my behalf." For that I was deeply grateful. I felt ashamed when I remembered my pettiness about how unattractive Richard was, for he had proved to be a good and loyal friend. Though as the summer progressed and pestilence spread in the city he stayed away, in June he had made a habit of bringing me bouquets of flowers from my London garden. I felt that I had grievously misjudged him.

"What of your country manor?" Elizabeth asked, interrupting my contrition. "Fair Meadow, is it?"

"The king has seen no reason to take it from me. One of his stewards holds it in trust for me, until such time as I might be able to care for it once more. I feel God watching over me, providing me with those two homes."

"You are most singularly favored by our mistress and His Grace," she said with a sidelong glance that unsettled me.

WILLIAM WYNDSOR had returned to court, paying more attention to me than he had in spring, even inviting me hawking in a party that included Geoffrey and Elizabeth, who both teased me afterward about William's inability to keep his eyes on his hawk rather than on me. It was silly and pleasant. William was dark like Janyn, but with fair skin and hazel eyes. He reawakened my passionate nature with his intense gaze and was a wonderful dance partner despite the way he rendered me breathless and too weak in the knees to dance the next set.

John of Gaunt often danced with me as well, as did his elder brother, Prince Edward.

But Gaunt also happened upon me in the gardens, far more often than seemed likely to be the workings of chance. "Do you not find it significant how often we seek out the same walk, Mistress Alice?" he teased me once. He was one of the handsomest men I had ever seen, but he was not only already married, he was as out of my reach as the king himself. I was disturbed by his attentions. In truth, his words often stung, suggesting that his game was not altogether friendly. Once, when I nervously prattled about the various flowers along the path on which we walked, he interrupted me.

"Ah! So you are schooled in the mysteries of gardens as well as costly cloths and clever tailoring, Mistress Alice. You are no common merchant's daughter."

I did not know what to make of him.

It was his father who often inhabited my wistful daydreams, smiling at me as we danced, as we hawked. But since Sheppey I had not spoken to the king, nor had I been in his presence except in crowds. I no longer caught him watching me, and though I prayed for the wisdom to be grateful, I was not. When I saw him walking with a woman other than the queen, my heart tightened with jealousy.

Despite my mourning Janyn, I could not ignore the way my body was reawakening, how it yearned again for the love of a man. Perhaps that is why I was not altogether displeased by Elizabeth's news that William Wyndsor had inquired of her whether I was betrothed. She was thrilled for me.

"I cannot think of a more handsome man—except perhaps John of Gaunt, and as he is already taken, Wyndsor is the handsomest *eligible* man," she said. "Would you have him if he asked Her Grace for your hand?"

Sir William's effect on me suggested we would be well matched in bed, and for me to wed a knight would improve Bella's prospects. But I did not know what was possible, whether the queen would permit me to wed and abandon court, leave her protection. Or perhaps the king and queen had another suitor in mind for me, a thought that could not but make me anxious. And over all these complexities hung both my own contradictory emotions about marrying again less than a year since losing Janyn and my feelings for the king.

To distract Elizabeth from more questioning, I tried to engage her in considering other eligible men. But she kept shifting the conversation back to William. I learned that his father and grandfather had been loyal supporters of Thomas, Earl of Lancaster, who had opposed King Edward II before Isabella and Roger Mortimer had formed their rebellion, and that their families had suffered for it. His was another family that had risked everything by supporting someone who challenged the king, as Janyn's mother's family had done. Perhaps it was not so unusual. Perhaps William and I might be kindred spirits in our unease at court.

I did not fool myself that this was love, but I did enjoy his company and how alive I felt when with him.

The gift of such attention lay in awakening me to the pleasures all around me—my beautiful clothes, the wondrous palaces in which I lived, my Melisende, the music in the hall, and the dancing that sent me to bed happily exhausted. In the garden I drank in the beauty in which I walked. I particularly enjoyed strolling with young Philippa, called Pippa, and Katherine, naming the plants for them, encouraging them to try to remember the garden in their home in Hainault. They remembered little, for they had been so very young when brought to England, but they surprised themselves with tidbits of memories and seemed truly happy when they did so. The queen remarked on my revived spirits, how I enlivened her daily gatherings.

Geoffrey, too, noticed my improved mood and accused me of being in love with William. I laughed so much as I denied it that he smugly declared he was right. I refused either to worry or feel guilty about my heart's awakening.

In August dire news of more deaths from the pestilence was tempered by the exciting rumor that Prince Edward had secretly wed his cousin, the Countess Joan. Being in such close contact with the queen I almost immediately saw that it must be true, for the queen's fury was impossible for her to hide from us. Her body reeked of rage.

"That whore" was how Joan, once so dear to her, came to be known in Philippa's chamber. It seemed that Joan's having been raised at court deepened the offense, for she "should know better." The king's representatives had been involved in negotiations all year for a marriage between the prince and Margaret of Flanders, the young, wealthy, and beautiful only child of the count of Flanders and his wife, the widow of the duke of Burgundy. The betrothal would have bound the Flemings to the English at a crucial time for such a liaison. But we were soon informed that a messenger had gone to the Pope to annul Joan and

Edward's clandestine vows and to grant the dispensations necessary for the cousins to wed formally. As the deed had been done, the king would see it through. Planning began for an autumn wedding.

"Such an extravagance. The bribes to the Pope! The festivities! And she brings no alliance with another royal house," the queen muttered. "That whore."

I had conflicting loyalties, Joan having taken such an interest in me. I was confused to realize that even as she had spoken to me with such anger about men, she had been falling in love with Prince Edward. I watched her now with keen interest, trying to learn how she both loved a man and honored herself.

I prayed for the wisdom to know when to be more like Joan and when to be meek. I felt that in my life so far I had been more the latter— oh, yes, I had expressed my passion to Janyn and Geoffrey and a few others very close to me, yet I obeyed. I always obeyed. And it had earned me only heartache. But I also appreciated that there must be something in me that drew people to me, for in so many ways I was blessed. I felt more accepted among the queen's ladies of late, and Geoffrey was loyal, Richard Lyons was proving a careful guardian of my finances, and Dom Hanneye wrote often with prayers and guidance.

I do not believe I would have had the courage to do what I did next had Countess Joan's influence not fanned a flame within me.

O N A stormy August afternoon a page announced to me that Geoffrey waited to speak to me just outside the chapel, in the little porch. As I took my leave of the women with whom I'd been sewing, I prayed for strength to bear whatever it was my friend had come to tell me. For by his choice of a meeting place where we would not be overheard—the storm would keep strollers away—I knew it must be terrible news.

His leggings were saggy with rain, and though he wore a short garment fashionably padded around the chest there was yet a caved-in quality to his torso that spoke of sorrow. He stood with chin up, apparently studying the carved figures decorating the arched doorway. As I moved closer I saw that it was not just his leggings that were limp and dirty, but that his formerly bright-red-and-sharp-black gown needed to be dried and brushed.

"You've traveled far?"

Now he lowered his head to look at me and I saw the unease in his expressive eyes. "Not so far. To London and back. But I was there a few days."

"Geoffrey—you have been to the city? Risked the pestilence?"

"I was worried about my family."

"Who is dead?" I asked, a question uppermost in everyone's mind when someone arrived from London.

He crossed himself. "I am sorry to tell you, Alice, but your mother, your brother Will, and Master Martin Perrers have all been taken by the sickness."

"So many!" I gasped. I would have fallen to my knees if Geoffrey had not caught my elbows and drawn me to him.

I remember the sound of rain thundering on the porch roof over-head and how cold my feet were from the splashing of the rain on the stone threshold. I had one of those odd practical thoughts that intrude in times of sudden, awful news—when I returned to the hall my tears would look like rain and no one would comment.

"I am so sorry, Alice, so very sorry. I wanted you to know as soon as I heard."

"How long ago?"

"Will died yesterday, your mother and Master Martin a few days ago."

"I will go to Father," I declared into his shoulder. This loss would be a terrible blow to him. I worried even more for my sister, Mary.

He patted my back. "He has your sister to comfort him."

"But who comforts her?"

My head pounded, and as I gasped for breath, sobs rose up and overwhelmed me. Geoffrey held me all the while, though the wind picked up and the small roof above us gave us little protection. When I stopped weeping, he drew me into the chapel and took off his shoes, draining the water from them.

I did not care about my own wet clothes, but knelt to pray for the souls departed, and for the survivors—my brother John, my sister Mary, and Father. I do not know when Geoffrey knelt beside me, or when Gwen arrived to cover me with a mantle and kneel at my other side. But they were both there when at last I lifted my head. Gwen wanted to hurry me back to my chamber to change into dry clothes, but I waved her off.

"Geoffrey, you must tell me all that you know. We can go to the hall and sit near the fire."

"No, I must away to change into clean, dry clothes. If anyone sees me looking like this, they will guess I've been to the city and I'll be sent away. In truth, I do not wish to return to London at present."

"You will not take me?"

He looked at me, as horrified as if I had asked him to swallow a live rat.

"Alice, you cannot mean to go to the city? What if the queen were to learn you had been there? She would send you away. And then where would you go?"

Surely she would understand my need. This was my family. "What of you? You risked it."

"And I've brought you news of your family so you need not go. Besides, there is still danger for you there."

"I sometimes wonder whether that danger has been overstated."

Geoffrey's expression was carefully veiled, but I could see that he no longer doubted it.

"There is some rumor you would keep from me?" I asked.

I watched the skirmish on his expressive face, heart versus head. Heart won.

"Master Martin Perrers dined with guild members the day of his death, and he had seemed quite well then, showing no signs of illness."

My breath stuck in my throat. Another victim of Isabella's cursed secret? "He was murdered?"

"That is the suggestion."

I crossed myself with a trembling hand. "What was the condition of his body?"

Geoffrey shook his head. "I do not know. The dead are buried so quickly."

"Do you think it was the trouble with Isabella of France?"

"Or that he had other dangerous connections. A friend told me Master Martin had seemed frightened of late. He went abroad with two large men protecting him."

"Where are they now?"

"His servants have not seen them since they found their master's body in his parlor."

So much loss. My heart was heavy with grief. "May God grant him peace," I whispered.

"So, you see, you should not go to your father." Geoffrey squirmed in his wet clothes. "Nor would you wish to. They say he is a changed man, sullen, suspicious, unkempt."

I felt my childhood, my entire past, being ripped away from me where I stood. "Is he ill?"

"No. But like so many, he cannot cope with the horror of so much death and seems to have lost his wits, his speech lacking temperance and sense."

"Poor Mary! If Father is so changed, what must it be like for her?"

"She has Nan, does she not?"

She did, I supposed, though even that I could not know for certain. "I pray Dame Agnes takes an interest in Mary." My grandmother might see her duty, yet be too busy trying to keep herself and my grandfather safe to act on it. I yearned to go to Mary, my sweet, precious sister, left all alone.

In the hall during the evening meal I found myself wondering what Joan would do in my place. But she would never be in my place. No one would forbid her to go to a member of her family who was in need. I was poor company to those seated near me.

When I rose from the table William Wyndsor approached me, inquiring about my pale face and sorrowful air. Even in my grief I noticed how elegant he looked in dark green and gold. The colors called attention to his eyes, which now regarded me with affection and concern. I wished I might pour out my heart to him. I thought I might at least tell him enough so that he would not feel as if I were shunning him.

"In faith, I am in mourning, Sir William, for my mother and a brother."

"I knew that I read great sorrow in your eyes and manner, my dear Mistress Alice. May God grant them peace." He bowed his head and crossed himself, and then he took me by the hand and drew me away from the crowd, into a quiet corner of the hall. "Did they die of the pestilence?" he asked in a low voice.

I hesitated to acknowledge the horrible truth, as if it might somehow not be fact as long as I did not voice it. But I needed to admit the truth, to accept it. "Yes, the pestilence took them." My heart clenched.

His sympathetic expression threatened my composure. "Will you go to be with your family?"

"No, I cannot."

"But they are in London, are they not? So near. Surely you must wish to see them?"

It was too much. The tears came and I sobbed, "Yes, I wish to see them, but the queen forbids it."

"Indeed?" His tone turned angry. It was enough to distract me from my self-pity. "The king would have us behave as if there is no danger, but the queen forbids her own household to enter the city?" William had grown quite loud.

I'd heard of his famous temper, but this was the first time I had witnessed it. I did not wish to call attention to myself. "Might we walk out into the air? My head is aching."

We escaped to the castle yard, where the heavy damp heat combined with the smoke from many torches caused my head to pound even more. I led us around strolling couples, clusters of men crouched over games or drunkenly insulting one another, past the armed guards positioned at regular intervals, to a walk that led to a walled garden, the torchlight from the castle yard and light spilling out from the hall allowing me to find the way. William kept a hand beneath my elbow.

Within the little garden I chose a bench near the entrance, as far as possible from a couple farther along the path who were locked in an embrace. The air was fresher now that we were away from the hall and yard, and I breathed more easily.

"When did you learn of your loss?" William asked, taking my hand and gently stroking it.

"Earlier today, after the midday meal," I said. "Queen Philippa is most kind to me. But she fears the pestilence, and with good cause."

William studied me for a long while as I sat mute in my grief. The damp air was not as refreshing as I had hoped, and I realized that my gown might be taking on moisture from the bench. As I rose to feel behind me, William startled me by pulling me into his arms. For a moment he simply held me. I was tempted to melt into the comfort of his strength, the reassuring sound of his heartbeat. But when he bent to kiss my forehead, I pushed out of his embrace.

"I was not asking for sympathy," I said, shaking out the skirt of my gown.

He raised his hands, palms toward me. "I beg your forgiveness if I have transgressed, Mistress Alice. But I cannot help but feel sorrow for your pain. I love you. You cannot be unaware of my feelings. And in loving you, I am sad for you in your mourning."

"Love? We'd not spoken of love." I backed away. I could not trust myself, my judgment, when my mind was so dull with sorrow, but despite his charm, his declaration of love disturbed me. It was too soon.

"Forgive me. I do not mean to take advantage of your need." He took a few steps away, then turned back with an air of decision. "You must see your family in London."

If only it were so simple, to know what I must do and to take care of it myself. "The queen will not have it."

"I will take you there."

My heart leaped, but reason quickly intervened. "I cannot let you risk the queen's anger for my sake."

"It is what you need, and I offer it to you. I am John of Gaunt's man. He will vouch for me if you doubt my intentions."

He was a knight. The queen might see her way to forgive me for going with someone who could protect me. Countess Joan seemed to whisper in my ear, *Take his offer.* I did so, and despite my misgivings about his sincerity, did not ask what William sought to gain by risking this.

EARLY THE following morning we slipped out of the palace, Gwen and William's servant Alan accompanying us. A groom waited for us with three horses—William had not been certain that Gwen could ride, so she climbed up behind Alan—and we made our way downriver to the barge awaiting us. I was impressed by William's having planned the journey in so little time. I could see by Gwen's expression that she was touched by all that he was risking for me, and the care he'd taken to see to our comfort. I was grateful that he left me to my own anxious thoughts as we traveled downriver.

How strange it was to return to my childhood home after all that time. I remember it seemed both wonderfully familiar and disturbingly changed. Of course, it was I who had changed. Having lived in palaces for several years, the courtyard looked cramped, the hall dim and shabby. But all was still precious to me.

Nan burst into tears on seeing me, and Mary, now a beautiful young woman, did likewise. I laughed and cried as I held them both in tight embraces. Father stood at a slight distance, stooped with grief, his eyes dull. I went to him and hugged him, but he merely patted my back once, as if acknowledging my presence and my effort but having nothing to give me in return.

"Margery could not hold on, she would not wait for me. Your mother would not wait for me."

Seeing him so shattered, I could no longer be angry with him for pushing me at Janyn when he knew it would alienate Mother. I saw him for the weak man he always was.

"I am sorry I was not here to help in their illnesses, Father."

"She would not have you in the house, Alice. I wanted to send for you, but she would not have you here."

Mary put her arm round me and led me away. "He does not mean to hurt you," she whispered. "Since Mother took ill he is often confused."

"How is John?"

"He is well. You'll remember that he has a kind master with a big family? I do believe that he will wed one of his master's daughters when his apprenticeship is over. Her name is Agnes, like Grandmother, and she is a gladsome woman who sees to it that he is well cared for." Her eyes were bright with affection.

How happy I was to be with my sister. My heart was a little lighter for being in her dear presence.

"How have you managed since Janyn's death?" she asked. "I wished I could come to you then, to comfort you."

"Bless you, Mary." I kept my voice low, not wishing to share such feelings with William. Gwen had disappeared with Alan, into the kitchen, but William had remained in the hall. He stood gazing out the partly open doors into the garden beyond, pretty even in the rain. "I have managed as well as any grieving widow manages. Mornings are the worst, when I wake and gradually remember why I am sleeping with other women. Janyn and I were together only four years and yet it feels as if we always shared a bed. I do not understand how my heart works. It has its own sense of time."

Mary pressed my hand. "He is handsome, your friend," she said, glancing over at William.

"This is not Janyn," my father suddenly said. He must have been watching Mary.

"No, Father, Janyn is no longer with us. This is my friend Sir William Wyndsor. It is thanks to him that I am here today. He arranged for the barge and escorted me here."

"Who told you of Mother's death?" he asked, ignoring William.

"Geoffrey told me about Mother and Will yesterday."

I did not think Father a suitable guardian for Mary in his diminished state. Nor could I bear to think what it must be like for her, living in that house of mourning, a place haunted by such recent suffering. Conceiving of a scheme to rescue her, I took Mary aside and asked her how she liked her grandmother, Dame Agnes. When she said she liked her very much, I decided on my plan. I would take her and Nan to Dame Agnes and ask her to take them in. Servants could attend Father; Dame Agnes would see to it.

With little more ado all six of us walked the short distance to Grandmother's home.

Dame Agnes had aged also, but with grace, and though she seemed uncertain about how she should respond on recognizing me, soon folded me in her arms and wept with joy.

"You look healthy and so beautiful, my Alice. I have worried about you, suffering so much loss away from your family."

"I have missed you and worried about you as well. All of you," I told her. When I felt I'd answered enough questions to content her for a while I made my proposal.

She nodded. "I have myself considered such an arrangement. I did not like what I saw there." She looked over my shoulder at Mary. "What think you of your sister's idea?"

Mary looked to me for a sign of how to respond.

"I was very happy living here," I said. "I think you could be as well."

Mary's smile was shy. "Then I would like it."

Dame Agnes clapped her hands. "It is settled! Dear Nan shall be both your lady's maid, Mary, and a help to me in managing the household."

I saw in Mary's and Nan's eyes a release from fear, and I hugged Dame Agnes with all my strength.

"And you, Alice," she said, holding me at arm's length and looking deep into my eyes, "what of you? Will we see more of you?"

I explained that the queen still believed it to be dangerous to visit the city, with the pestilence about.

Grandmother nodded and hugged me. "Then I hope when it passes we might see you more often. Perhaps if you remarried?" She nodded toward William, who had quietly settled on a bench near the fire, his long legs extended to the dry warmth. A servant had brought him ale and bread and cheese, and he'd contented himself with that while we talked. "He is handsome. You called him 'sir.' He is well born?"

"I am most grateful to Sir William for risking the queen's ire to bring me here today, but we are merely friends."

"It is a good beginning." Dame Agnes and Mary exchanged glances.

William had not noticed my regarding him, but he did look up as Dame Agnes approached him, her hands outstretched. His guarded expression bespoke his state of vigilance, emphasizing for me the generosity of his gesture in bringing me here, coming among the family the queen forbade me to see. I could not help but wonder again at his motive.

He rose to take Dame Agnes's hands.

"God bless you for what you've done for my Alice," she said, "and for all of us."

"My heart was heavy to see her grief yesterday and to learn that she had been forbidden to come to her family, Dame Agnes. I feel blessed to have witnessed this reunion." He bowed his head to her, and the smile on his face when he looked up again lit the hall.

A knock on the door prevented further conversation.

A servant announced a page from the king's household. He bowed to Dame Agnes, and then the rest of us, and informed us that the king had sent an escort for my safe return to Windsor. The king! I felt weak in the knees, terrified what this might mean. We had not only been discovered, but the king himself had commanded our return. I glanced at William, who simply nodded to me, his expression blank. That did nothing to alleviate my panic.

Dame Agnes questioned me with her eyes, but aloud she offered the king's men some ale in the kitchen while I bade farewell to my sister. William followed the page to see to the men.

"He is very handsome," said Mary again.

"A bit like Janyn?" asked Dame Agnes, seemingly to herself.

They were babbling, pretending nothing out of the ordinary had happened.

I hugged Mary. "Be happy, my dear sister."

My mind was racing, realizing we had been followed, wondering what it meant that King Edward himself had sent an escort. At least I had done some good. I had no doubt that Mary would be in loving, competent hands in my grandmother's house. She was so pretty and good natured, my grandmother would soon be fussing over her as she had me.

Nan held me tight, weeping for the joy of being reunited and the pain of its being for so brief a time.

"I shall try to return," I said, my attention already elsewhere. I feared what the queen's ire might mean for Bella, and cursed myself for taking the risk. Yet I had helped my family, and prayed that would earn me some grace in God's accounting.

In parting from Dame Agnes, I saw that she was moved as well. She stroked my cheek. "You look so well, so beautiful. Master Martin Perrers explained nothing to us. It was your friend Geoffrey Chaucer who finally told me why you never came to us."

I could not imagine what explanation he had made, for he knew how dangerous the truth would be to them. "What did he tell you?"

"How your mother's venom had frightened you away," Grandmother said, nodding as if to reassure me that she understood. "She was a madwoman."

I was thankful for Geoffrey's clever explanation.

William and I had little chance to talk as the king's men hurried us through the noisome streets to the barge, the king's own, anchored where ours had been. Once we were on the river, I quietly asked William what he'd learned from the men while in the kitchen. "Am I to be punished? Sent away?"

"His Grace is not angry with you but with the queen, Alice." William watched my reaction.

"What do you mean?"

"What I said. He heard Queen Philippa ranting about your having gone to your family, how you could not be permitted to return for you would bring the pestilence with you, on and on, and silenced her with some quiet comment. The page says that you are never to be denied the protection of the queen's household." He took my hands, still searching my face. "Am I in competition with the king in loving you?"

"No!" That he should even think so troubled me. "I am grateful for his protection, but I should think his anger with the queen is over something else, and I was—most fortunately for me—a convenient argument." I touched William's hand. "I cannot remember a more loving gift from a friend than that which you've given me today, William. I pray that someday I am able to give you something as precious in return. Bless you for the peace of mind you have brought me."

He took my hand and kissed it, then pulled me into his arms and kissed me on the mouth. It was like kissing Janyn all over again, sending heat through my body and leaving me breathless afterward. William had felt my response and smiled with satisfaction.

"You shall be my wife, Alice. I swear."

It was a most unexpected declaration and too much to contemplate with all the emotions roiling inside me from seeing my family again. I chose my words with care, for I was grateful to William. "As to that, I cannot say. But I pray that God grants you happiness."

I was sorry that his only response to this was a brooding silence for the duration of the journey. Having no distraction, I gave myself over to my fear of facing the queen and king.

When we arrived at the Windsor dock I was escorted to King Edward's private parlor. William insisted on accompanying me, and I appreciated the gesture. Despite what he'd heard from the page, I knew how quickly the king and queen could change their minds.

Regal in red and gold, King Edward rose from his chair to thank William for keeping me safe, and sent him off. Then, with what seemed sincere concern, he invited me to sit with him, share wine and a light meal, and recount all that had transpired. He commended me for taking Mary from that unhappy household and asked if there was anything he might do to ease my mind further about my family.

"Your Grace, I would see my beloved daughter."

"And why not? Queen Joan is not so far away."

My heart sang. "And as soon as you judge it safe, Your Grace, I would also visit my sister Mary more often. She will soon be old enough to wed and I treasure these last years of her girlhood."

Placing a beringed hand on each of my shoulders, he vowed to arrange for me to see my sister as soon as he deemed it safe.

"For I would not knowingly help you walk into danger, but neither do I wish to prolong this lack of a sister's companionship. And I have not forgotten my promise that your daughter will one day abide near you. But why did you not come to me with your fears for your family, Mistress Alice?"

"I did not think it appropriate, Your Grace. I am answerable to Her Grace, Queen Philippa."

"Remember Sheppey, Mistress Alice. I swore there you would be happy." He kissed me on either cheek. I was glad he still held my shoulders, for I feared I might have dropped to my knees had I not been so supported.

A page escorted me back to my chamber.

Gwen met me at the door with a fierce hug and then pulled me into the room and shut the door, leaning against it. I saw by her ravaged face and by the twisted cloth in her hand that she had been weeping and worrying all the while.

"Forgive me, Mistress Alice, but I must know—are we to be punished for disobeying Her Grace?"

"As I told you on the barge, the king defended our action. In truth, he understands." But I was still unsure how the queen might treat me. She had her own subtle methods of punishment. "Have we been summoned?"

"You are to make her almond milk this evening."

A private conversation. I dreaded it.

"And you are to bathe, and all the clothing we wore is to be burned so that we might not bring the pestilence into her rooms. I have already bathed and changed."

After the evening meal I followed Her Grace to her chamber with trepidation. But she expressed only pleasure that I was able to give comfort to my family, and then said no more about the incident. I had expected at least to sense in her some irritation with me, even if she did not speak of it, but I detected no such animosity in her behavior. I found that most strange considering how adamant she had been that I not go into the city to see my family. Even if the king had convinced her of my need to do so this one time, I would have thought to encounter some resentment. But she treated me as if I had not in any wise displeased her. I expressed deep remorse for disobeying her. She said she understood, and spoke of her own grief at the loss of so many friends and relations.

That night I cried for my losses and those of the queen, and relived precious moments with my sweet brother Will, his life so brief.

As if to compensate for such heartbreak, I also dreamed of William Wyndsor, of lying with him, exploring his naked body. The memory of the dream excited and confused me—confused me because I could imagine lying with him and delighted in that imagining, but in the light of day could not see him as Bella's foster father. Something about him did not feel trustworthy enough to share him with my precious daughter. Or perhaps I was still too bedazzled by the king's kindness.

TO MY amazement, from that time King Edward began once more to make note of me, often pausing to speak to me after morning

Mass. He chose mundane topics, such as the weather or the music in the hall the previous night. I responded with modest gratitude, eyes cast down, desperate not to reveal my adoration. I did not need to look at him to feel his eyes upon me. All my senses seemed tuned to him. His attention was like manna to me in my loneliness. I prayed to have the wit not to make too much of it.

In late summer Queen Philippa withdrew to her bed for days after the pestilence took her two youngest daughters, Margaret and Mary. It was a terrible blow to the queen, to have her young chicks, both recently married and launched into their new lives, cut down within a month of each other. She was inconsolable. She had never been close to her one surviving daughter, Isabella, the king's favorite. Margaret and Mary had been her heart's delight.

On the second morning on which I attended Mass without her, King Edward paused in the corridor as had become his habit, but instead of a brief exchange of pleasantries he invited me to go hawking. Our party included only the falconer, two grooms, and the pair of us.

"I did not think either of us would wish for the noise of a crowd," the king said.

I was glad that I had recently taken in the waist on my Lincoln green riding robe as was now the fashion and replaced the old feathers in my hat with new, brighter ones. The king and I spoke little, attending to our hawks and horses, allowing the woodland and the soaring birds to soothe our spirits. I was aware of him watching me as I talked to my merlin, but did not turn his way. Apart from my attraction to him, I felt a bond of quite another sort between us when we rode through the woodland, into the wind, free to shout, to laugh with abandon, to wonder at the perfection of beauty, grace, and unbridled power exhibited by our birds. Away from court we were at ease together without speech, alike in our appreciation of God's magnificent creation. At peace.

The king invited me again the following day, and the day after that, and on the fourth morning, after our hunt, we talked a little of our recent sorrows. I was glad if I might help the king in his grief as he had helped me. We stood side by side in the middle of a pretty meadow. The falconer had retrieved our birds and departed. Only the grooms were with us, and they were off to one side, holding our horses at the edge of the wood.

"In a year I have lost so many men who fought beside me, on whom I depended and trusted without question to defend my kingdom. They were brothers-in-arms and brothers in my heart, my dearest friends. And now I've lost two of my precious daughters, both of them so young."

King Edward's eyes stayed fixed on the trees, as if he could not trust himself to look at another while he voiced his loss.

Without thinking, I took one of his great hands and squeezed it. I do not know what inspired such audacity. He looked down at me in surprise, then gave me the saddest smile I had ever seen.

"I cannot speak my heart to many people, Mistress Alice. Even my queen reminds me that I am king and must not show any weakness."

"No one will know, Your Grace," I promised. "In faith, I do not understand how anyone would think ill of you for grieving for your daughters."

"A commander may grieve for his men-at-arms. No one else."

"I do not understand how God means us to live our lives," I said as I fought for composure. "We both strive to be good, to fulfill our duties. I do not understand His purpose in testing us with so much loss."

The king drew me to him then and kissed me on the lips, a peck, no more, then kissed my forehead, and held me close for a moment. I heard his great heart thundering, and reached up one hand to touch his pale hair. He lifted my chin and thanked me for my friendship, then released me.

"Your Grace, I am your good and faithful friend." I bowed to him even though he was not looking my way, relieved to hear none of my terror reflected in my voice.

He nodded, still not looking at me. I wondered what he was thinking.

"Our horses wait," he said, striding away.

I followed him, my heart swelling with joy. He had kissed me, he had held me. My good sense quickly intervened, shouting warnings. I should not have touched him, for I doubted he would have kissed me, be it ever so chastely, had I not taken his hand. I could not believe I'd actually had the gall to touch his hair. I would be sent from court. Sent from him. I could not bear that. I prayed for a sign from God as to what I should do, how I might avoid further temptation. It was a sin, coveting another's spouse. I could not betray his wife, my queen and mistress. Yet I could not stop thinking of how it felt to be in his arms, to feel his lips on my skin. Every part of me had been intensely aware of him, intensely aroused.

He did not attend Mass the next morning. I told myself it was for the best. Indeed, it was my salvation. I obviously needed a mate, a husband. Perhaps Geoffrey had been right about William Wyndsor—he might do nicely. He might save me from my dangerous, foolish obsession with the king. That evening I looked for him in the hall. I had not seen him since our journey to London, and feared that the only likely reason he might be avoiding me was that he knew of my mornings with the king. I remembered his suspicion when the king's men arrived at Dame Agnes's house. Eventually I learned from one of his friends that William had been sent north to the border near Scotland. He had received his orders the day after our excursion. It was an honorable posting, but unexpected. I expressed disappointment for having had no opportunity to bid him good fortune.

God forgive me, as I left the hall I was almost dancing with relief that William was not there to save me from the king.

10

> "Allas, of me, unto the worldes ende,
> Shal neyther ben ywriten nor ysonge
> No good word, for thise bokes wol me shende.
> O, rolled shal I ben on many a tongue!
> Throughout the world my belle shal be ronge!
> And wommen moost wol haten me of alle.
> Allas, that swich a cas me sholde falle!"

—Criseyde to Troilus, GEOFFREY CHAUCER,
Troilus and Criseyde, V, 1058–64

• Autumn 1361 •

I HAD LITTLE time to brood over my feelings for the king. The queen devoted most of her waking hours and mine to planning the official wedding of Prince Edward and Countess Joan. She was determined to set aside her disappointment in the match and make the best of the situation. As for all such festivities, the entire household would receive special garments for the event so that all contributed to the theme. Green and white were the prince's colors, so although the wedding would take place in October, rather than echoing the autumn bounty and colorful decay, the chosen colors suggested the freshness and promise of spring.

I needed all my wits to adjust and readjust to the queen's imperious demands and shifting moods. She was moved to see her son and foster daughter so happy, but furious that they had been meeting at the home of Joan's former sister-in-law, a woman who had recently made a scandalous marriage herself. The queen seemed grateful for an excuse to lift her spirits and those of the court with an extravagant feast, but resented the fact that here would be no political gain. This was a marriage that would afford the family no new strategic alliances. Whether joy or resentment would dominate at any moment proved impossible for me to predict. I attended the queen's every gesture or change of tone trying to respond in the way that seemed safest at the time. Every night I fell into bed exhausted. But there were moments too in which Philippa expressed her appreciation—and that made up for much. She could be most generous with both gifts and praise.

In late September I was in the royal family's party accompanying the coffins of Mary and Margaret to the abbey at Abington. Although folk came out to honor the solemn royal procession as we rode through villages, their demeanor was solemn and often frightened—plague corpses, no matter how royal, were to be feared. But of course the villagers were filled with awe to see their king and queen, and it was in their eyes as they stared at me too, wondering who I might be in my fur-lined cloak and beautiful leather boots, riding a magnificent horse. I was reminded how those outside the court would perceive my place in the queen's household. Mine was an honored position, and I was fortunate beyond imagining.

I still felt adrift among the courtiers. But I saw the faces of those villagers again when I tried to sleep, and in my imagination they watched me as I lifted the queen's delicately embroidered night shift from the trunk and walked across stone floors strewn with fragrant flowers and fresh rushes. I lived amid beauty and abundance, in comfort and safety. Those faces taught me humility and gratitude.

I had sent a message to Dom Hanneye by a clerk in our party

who was continuing on to Oxford. I hoped that my beloved confessor, whom I saw only occasionally when he accompanied his bishop to London, might find some way to come to me in Abington. To my immense relief he arrived the day before we were to begin our return journey, and the queen gave me leave to spend some time with him.

With each new loss in my life Dom Hanneye grew dearer to me, for he had known all those for whom I grieved. He had lost weight; his once roundly childlike face seemed drawn as if he did not sleep well. At first we reminisced about the loved ones I'd lost. We wept and embraced. Only when the dead had been lovingly honored did I ask the question that weighed on my conscience.

"Do you think God and the Blessed Mother look down on me in disgust as the most ungrateful woman on earth when I have so much here?"

It eased my heart to have Dom Hanneye assure me that anyone in my situation would grieve.

"I watched you with Her Grace in the chapel. You saw to her every need and treated her with respect and love. You fulfill your duties with compassion and grace, Dame Alice. I find no fault in you."

He suggested what he had before, that I seek the path of acceptance, look for contentment in simple joys and offer my suffering to God.

"Much as monks and nuns do throughout their daily tasks," he said. "But in far more comfort." His teasing smile eased the sting.

"I am grateful that you came. Your reassurance comforts me as no one else's. But tell me, how did you receive permission and hie down here in such haste?"

As he paused and appeared to be collecting his thoughts, I saw he had a tale to tell.

"The brief answer is that I had requested permission several days before I received your message."

"But how did you know I would be of the company?"

"Richard Lyons had come to Oxford, arriving a few days before your party reached Abington. It was from him that I heard you were to be traveling in the funeral procession." He looked concerned as I shifted on my seat, murmuring Lyons's name. "I know that you have not always liked him, but he has proven to be a good friend."

"Yes, he has proven most generous. But what did he want of *you*?"

"It was I who had inquired of him whether you might be ready to purchase another property very near your present one in Oxford. I thought it a good opportunity to invest some of Janyn's estate. Lyons insisted on coming to Oxford to see it. I do believe he wanted to ascertain my competence in the matter." He bowed his head for a moment, folding his hands one way, then another.

Dom Hanneye had been caring for my property in Oxford. As my local representative he'd collected rents, arranged for and inspected all maintenance, and developed and handled all monetary transactions. His itemized summary of accounts was always prompt and thorough. I was very grateful, and concerned that others would respect him as my representative. "I pray he did not insult you," I said, seeing his discomfort.

"It was clear he thought a priest could hardly have a head for trade." He shrugged.

"Then he does not know you."

Dom Hanneye laughed. "He does now."

"Good. I would like to see the property," I said.

"You would?" Dom Hanneye looked surprised. "Do you wish to be a part of the decision?"

"I do. I wish to become more involved in my own investments." I was far more at ease with business than with anything else in my current situation, more clearheaded about money than I ever seemed to be about men. "The rents will bring an income to support Bella and me, and add to the dowry Janyn established for her." It was the one area in which I had some semblance of choice, some power over my life. I was frustrated that the king had not yet kept his promise regarding my seeing Bella, but I could see to her future. "I shall ask the queen if I might return to Oxford with you for a day or so."

"Richard Lyons would escort you back to London, I am certain."

"That would suit me."

Unfortunately, it did not suit the queen.

"No, I cannot spare you, Alice. You know how much we have yet to do before the wedding. No, you shall return with me."

I understood her concern about the approaching event, but could not believe that all would collapse if I were delayed by a day. Perhaps it was selfish of me to wish to go to Oxford, but the prospect had lifted me from my dullness of the past weeks. I tried to explain this to her, but she was adamant.

Help came from an unexpected quarter. The queen sent her ladies away in the late afternoon so that she might rest for the journey. Elizabeth and I sought the quiet peace of the garden. We were walking there, talking little as we simply enjoyed the late-September sunshine and the lovely warmth that took away the chill of death, when the king's page appeared.

Had it been the queen's page I would have resented the summons. But the king's . . . My heart pounded as I followed him to the chapel, where he opened the door and bowed me through. King Edward sat on a bench just within, leaning his back against the wall, his legs stretched out before him, a study in ease. I do not believe I had ever seen him so. For a moment he was merely a man, not a king, albeit a large, physically imposing man. Rather than feeling awe, I felt only pleasure to see him and to be seen by him.

"Come, Mistress Alice. Sit with me and tell me about this property in Oxford." His tone was friendly, pleasant.

I took a deep breath and tried to calm myself as I sat beside him.

"Philippa tells me that your former confessor came from Oxford to discuss your investing in a property, and that you wish to see it for yourself. You are interested in owning land?"

"Yes, Your Grace. My late husband purchased a tenement in my name so that I might have revenue from rent if . . ." I was uncertain how to continue, whether it would insult him. "If I should find myself in need." I almost whispered the last part as I kept my eyes lowered.

"Commendable. But he should have known we would not abandon you."

"Your Grace." I bobbed my head in a sign of respect, while thinking that he was as blind to his own inconstant behavior as was his queen and his mother before that.

"My mother, the Lady Isabella, spoke of your cleverness. That your husband consulted you regarding his business."

He shifted a little, and his scent of spice and leather grew stronger. I found it intoxicating.

"He did. And before him my father likewise. Father would have me sit with him in the undercroft while he explained the accounts books, and often permitted me to listen to trade discussions." I stopped myself, realizing I had said more than required. His alchemy was working on me as it did with everyone, drawing me out, and I felt myself trying to please him. And more. It seemed I could not be in his presence and not want more. A kiss, a touch.

"I see that your skill in hawking and grace in dancing are but hints of your talents, Mistress Alice. Beauty and a mind for trade, hunting and dancing—what else should I know of you?"

I felt myself blushing under his regard and was glad that the light was dim and we were side by side, so that he could see little of me.

"Your Grace, I do not know what else I might tell you. I am little but what others wish me to be." I regretted my words as soon as I'd uttered them.

The king drew in his legs and shifted on the bench so that he was facing me. He took my right hand, turned it over, looked at my palm, and with one beringed finger traced the line that ran from between my thumb and forefinger to my wrist.

"So easily I touch you," he murmured as he did so, "so recklessly I summon you, then tease you and take your hand. How thoughtlessly I pluck your strings, as if you are but a lute."

The intimacy of his touch and his voice, the suggestion of playing me like a lute excited me far too much for safety.

He let go of my hand, touched my chin, gently, oh, so gently, while looking into my eyes. I had not intended to look up, but could not prevent myself.

"Forgive me if I have made you feel so used, Alice."

I did not trust myself to speak; my flesh burned at his mere touch.

"Do you forgive me?" he whispered.

"Your Grace," was all I managed.

"Edward. My name is Edward." He spoke in an intimate whisper.

I shook my head, an embarrassingly jerky motion.

He straightened up, the mood between us suddenly changed, the tension discharged. "You must of course return to Oxford with Dom Hanneye. But we depart tomorrow. Had you any plan for an escort back to London?"

I could not so easily shift. How did he? Was I just a game to him? "Richard Lyons is returning to London in a few days, Your Grace," I said, hating how breathless I sounded.

He tilted his head as if considering, then nodded. "He is a trustworthy man. I shall send him a message that his life will be forfeit if anything happens to you." He took my hand and kissed it, looking me in the eyes while still holding it. "That is no jest."

I shivered and withdrew my hand. "I am grateful for your permission, Your Grace."

"Edward." He smiled.

"Edward," I whispered, and I fled the chapel before I did something foolish like kiss him in gratitude. For I understood, at least on my part, that no kiss between us could ever be innocent.

Once again, as when the king had sent an escort for William and me from London, the queen expressed no irritation about my plan to leave her company briefly.

"I am trusting you to return a mere day behind us," she said. "A day and a half at the most." And then she smiled and sent me off to assist with the packing.

DOM HANNEYE and I made the trip to Oxford without mishap, and in the late afternoon joined Richard Lyons to tour both the property I already owned, which I'd never seen, and the one on the same street that I might purchase. The houses and outbuildings were leased out to craftsmen and students at the university, a mixture that commended them to me for I would not be dependent on one class of people for tenants. The buildings were in satisfactory condition, certainly nothing grand.

"You will continue to oversee both of them for me?" I asked Dom Hanneye.

"As long as I am here in the city, I am pleased to be of service to you, Dame Alice."

I noticed that he called me mistress only when others might overhear. This secret sign of respect deeply moved me.

We supped with Richard Lyons that evening, in a private room at an inn near the convent where Gwen and I would lodge for the night. We discussed the properties at length.

"The purchase would triple your income from Oxford," said Dom Hanneye.

"With the addition of a few shops and workrooms to both, they might do more than that," I said.

We discussed what such additions and a few improvements might cost. Richard and Dom Hanneye expressed their satisfaction and looked to me for the decision.

"We are agreed. Arrange the purchase," I declared, "and the additions."

It was with a renewed sense of confidence in my knowledge and skill in trade that I lay down to rest in a small but comfortable bed, my faithful servant and friend Gwen by my side.

I WAS JOLTED awake by a sound, and then the horror of an oily rag being pressed to my face. I could not catch my breath, I was so terrified. I opened my mouth, gasping for air so that I might scream. Before I managed a sound, my assailant shoved the rag into my mouth. He did so with such force I felt a jolt of pain in the right side of my jaw. Panicked and gagging, I kicked at him, thrashed my arms, and clawed at whatever I could reach, but another came to his aid and they quickly tied my ankles, tossed me onto my stomach, wrenched my arms behind my back, and bound my hands. Suddenly all was darkness as a smelly cloth became my shroud. Gwen whimpered somewhere nearby. I made a muffled complaint when I was heaved over a man's shoulder and carried away like a trussed lamb. It was, I think, a doorway unskillfully maneuvered that hit my head. I felt a sharp pain, and then nothing for a long while.

When I came round I found myself lying against soft cushions, much softer than those on which I'd fallen asleep. I moved my foot and pain ran up my leg. My head pounded above my right ear.

"Where am I?" My voice was weak and my jaw hurt so that I mumbled the words. But someone heard.

"She wakes." It was a woman's voice. "I'll tend to her now."

"Let me see to her, I beg you. My mistress will be afraid with a stranger after what she has suffered."

My heart leaped. Gwen was here. She was alive. Her beloved face appeared over me.

"What happened? Who . . . ?"

"Mistress Alice, you are safe. Richard Lyons has proved a good friend, and the king is sending an escort for us." She lifted my head and helped me drink something that tasted of honey but warmed me like brandywine. "Are you in much pain?"

I wondered the same about her—her left wrist was bandaged and one eye was swollen and bruised. I gingerly touched the right side of my head. My hair was undressed but there was no bandage. I felt a tender lump.

"You have a bruise, but there was no blood."

Only then did I notice that both my wrists were lightly bandaged.

"The ropes were old, rough, and bound too tightly," said Gwen. The strength and steadiness of her voice reassured me that we were safe more than any number of words could have done.

A stranger had joined us, hovering behind Gwen. She was a tall woman with dark, expressive eyes. At the moment she seemed eager to observe me. Her hair was tucked into a crisp white scarf, her clothing simple, but she was not a nun.

Gwen noticed me looking behind her and turned.

"This is Dame Juliana, a healer. Dom Hanneye sent for her. She has been very kind."

"God bless you," I said. So few words, but they caused a sharp pain in my jaw. I covered it with my cool hand, which felt most welcome.

Juliana nodded to me. "You will quickly heal, God be praised," she said. "Did they injure your jaw?"

I nodded.

"They shoved a stinking rag into your mouth." Juliana's frown was so fierce it might have been comical in any other circumstance. "I am glad they are dead."

Dead? I looked up at Gwen, knowing she would read the question in my eyes.

"Master Richard's men, Dom Hanneye, and a bailiff caught two men carrying us from the convent and set upon them. Several more rushed out from the darkness," she said. "It was a frightening battle, made all the worse because you lay so still beside me, Mistress Alice, and I could not lean down to hear if your heart was beating."

"You?" I asked.

"My wrist and eye are sore, but quickly healing with Dame Juliana's care. They stuffed my mouth with a much cleaner rag than they did yours."

I was glad. "The others?"

"Master Richard has a deep wound on his left upper arm and Dom Hanneye a broken nose. Four of the men who tried to take us are dead. The fifth is being questioned."

I embarrassed myself by bursting into tears, and once begun could not stop. My heart had been breaking for a long while over the deaths of so many who were dear to me, and this terrifying night had been the final blow. The two women fussed over me for a while, and then all grew quiet except for my sobs. Finally spent, I slept. I woke a few times to darkness, the curtains closed round my bed, Gwen sleeping beside me.

In the morning Richard Lyons and Dom Hanneye came to see for themselves how I was recovering. Dom Hanneye approached first, blessing me and assuring me that although his nose and eyes made him look as if he were in great pain, he felt better with each day.

"I believe I shall have a more interesting face, more trustworthy in its imperfection, when I have completely healed." Though his smile was oddly contorted by the swelling, he did seem to be himself.

"God is merciful," I said. I, too, was feeling better and found it easier to talk than I had the previous day.

Dom Hanneye withdrew to a seat and at once bowed his head in prayer.

With his good arm, Richard Lyons pulled up a chair beside my bed. His injured arm was bound close to his side.

"Mistress Alice," he said, bobbing his head, "God has answered our prayers."

"How is your arm?" I asked.

"It will mend. Are you in much pain?"

"Better today. Who were they?"

"I do not know. I have been told only that the king commends us for saving your life and that of your maidservant, and that the men clearly intended to kill you. Other than that, the king's man says that his information is for your ears only."

His manner was much humbler than usual, and I sensed a mixture of weariness and unease in it.

"The king's man? But the company left Abington for London only yesterday."

"Several days ago, Mistress Alice. You were set upon three nights ago."

Three nights. "I slept so long?" That I had lost so much time was not at all reassuring.

"You slept a day, and they say you then woke for a little while, and afterward slept another day. In that time a messenger reached the king and returned with Richard Stury, his most trusted esquire, and a small retinue. Stury will come to speak to you later."

I crossed myself at this news and prayed for God to watch over me. Stury was an esquire of the king's chamber who had risen from the position of valet by his unflinching loyalty to his master, his cunning, and the fact that his grandfather had been in the diplomatic service of the king's father. Courtiers were uneasy when Stury was about, for he was rumored to spy for the king as his grandfather had done for the previous King Edward. If the king had sent a man such as Stury, he must believe this attack had something to do with his mother's secret, the business that had already robbed me of so much. Would I ever be free from Isabella's curse? I imagined I would have been questioned by my abductors and then, when they were satisfied that I knew nothing, I would have been murdered, as had Master Martin, Janyn, and Dame Tommasa. I had never believed their deaths were from illness.

"You've nothing to fear now, Mistress Alice," said Richard. "You are well protected. We shall return to Windsor Castle with a strong escort."

I might have believed I had nothing to fear had it been my person someone wanted. A man thinking to violate me would now know that I had powerful protectors. But Isabella's secret, whatever it was, seemed to have a power of its own, and I could no longer doubt the danger it had brought me to. I was a prisoner in the queen's household. No matter that my prisons were royal palaces, they still enclosed me.

Richard waited for my response. I felt humbled by the danger in which he had placed himself on my account.

"Tell me what happened," I said. "Who raised the hue and cry? How did you know to come?"

Gwen interrupted, bringing a physick she insisted I drink at once. It was unpleasantly thick and slimy, and tasted of rotten greenery and damp earth. I tried to hand back the cup after a little sip, but she shook her head and would not take it from me.

"Dame Juliana says that a head wound such as yours that cannot be bled must be fumigated with a strong physick. This will restore your strength and your memory. Do you not think that worth a brief bad taste?"

I drank, though it was the most disgusting liquid I had ever forced down my throat. Gwen rewarded me afterward with spiced wine, which did wash down most of the aftertaste.

Richard had waited quietly throughout the interruption.

"In answer to your question, we had planned all along to guard the convent. But, alas, we gathered too late. They must have already been within the walls when you arrived. The moment they appeared in the yard, we fell on them."

"Did you recognize any of them?"

"No."

"What caused you to plan a guard?" Again, this evidence of his courage on my behalf overwhelmed me.

He shrugged with his good shoulder. "Your husband's disappearance, his mother's soon after, the mystery surrounding his father's death, your being taken into the queen's household while your daughter is fostered in the home of the Queen of Scotland—it is plain to me that you married into a family singled out in some way, most likely their loyal service to the Lady Isabella." He waved his good hand at me and shook his head as if I'd begun to tell him, though I'd not opened my mouth. "I confess, I do not care to know more for fear my own life might be forfeit. But for these reasons, Dom Hanneye and I believed we must protect you."

He sat back in his chair and picked up the cup of wine beside him, gazing down into it.

I was grateful for his courtesy, for the chance it gave me to rein in my emotions. Richard was rightly fearful of sharing our secret.

"I pray you do not suffer for coming to my aid."

The blush that spread even to his ears suggested a vulnerable side to him that I had not seen before.

"I thank God I had the foresight to be there, and to include the bailiff in our plans."

My vision blurred then and Richard's voice seemed to come from far away. When next I woke a stranger sat beside me. For a moment I thought he had been conjured from the unholy slime I had obediently drunk. Dark brown hair and eyes, dark cloak, a dull green jacket, and brown leggings and boots.

"Mistress Alice," he said, bowing his head. "I am Richard Stury, King's esquire."

Only then did I recognize him. I feared the physick had worsened my condition, not improved it.

"Yes, I have seen you at court, Master Stury."

For a moment I thought we were alone in the room and was about to ask that Gwen be permitted to return, but she came forward just then, proffering a cup I was loath to accept until she assured me it was merely watered wine, not a physick. She quickly withdrew to a seat near the door.

"Your lady's maid has your complete trust?" asked Stury.

"Yes."

I sipped the wine as he explained how he came to be there, most of which I had already learned from Richard Lyons. While he spoke I studied him. He might have been a clerk with his tall, skinny body and pinched features. His mouth seemed to hold a perpetual grimace, and though I would have guessed him to be no more than ten years my senior, he already had deep creases between his brows—indeed, they remained knitted together even when he uttered a pleasantry or paused to think. He held his hands on his lap as if he were forcing them still.

"I am most grateful for the king's concern," I said. "I know you to be one of his most trusted esquires."

He inclined his head in acknowledgment of the compliment. "His Grace had no doubt that the attackers knew of your late husband's service to his mother, the Lady Isabella. That is why I am here—I am one of only a few in the household who have been entrusted with the knowledge of your family's connection to the former queen."

"Do you know the men who attacked me?"

"I have known of them, though I met them only as corpses."

"I thought one was yet alive."

"He died this morning." In his dark eyes there was not a flicker of emotion.

I crossed myself and said a prayer.

"I would not pray too fervently for his soul, Mistress Alice. It will do little good. He meant to interrogate and then defile you before he murdered you, I have no doubt."

I pressed my hand to my throat, shuddering at what might have happened. "For whom did they work, Master Stury?"

"You do not need to know that. My orders were simply to reassure you that all is resolved."

"Are you mad? How am I to defend myself if I know not my enemies?"

"The king protects you, Mistress Alice."

"It was not the king who saved my life and that of my maid."

"You need fear nothing."

"Why? Are you taking the lives of all my would-be questioners as they become known to you, before they have a chance to attack me?"

Stury rose. "We shall escort you to Windsor in the morning. I pray you, rest before the journey." At the door he paused, then turned to say, "At court they have been told that outlaws attacked your traveling party. Masses have been said for you and for your rescuers." With a curt bow, he departed.

And so I learned the extent of the prison I inhabited. I feared I might now never again be free to move about outside court. And I began to wonder—was I protected or was I the lure? Why did that question suddenly occur to me? I prayed for courage. I prayed for my daughter's safety.

ON THE journey I felt a heaviness, as if I were returning in disgrace. If I could not be trusted with the names of my enemies, what was my worth? I won a small victory, though, convincing the men I would be more at ease on horseback rather than being bruised afresh in a cart. The weather had turned colder and a drizzle kept us all hooded and quiet, so my brooding silence went unnoticed.

Richard Lyons was subdued in Stury's company. He had greeted me in the morning, then left me to make my farewells to Dom Hanneye, who had hoped to return with us to attend the prince's wedding but had received the disappointing news that his bishop wished him to remain in Oxford.

"Are you being punished for defending me?" I asked, gently touching the discolored flesh between his brows.

"To my surprise, I am being promoted to a more significant benefice here in Oxford, on the understanding I will not talk of the recent incident." He bowed to me.

"I am happy for you, though this promotion be a form of bondage."

He shrugged. "I willingly took a vow of obedience. Never hesitate to summon me if you are in need, Dame Alice."

I thought of our silken bonds all the way to Windsor Castle—Dom Hanneye's promotion in exchange for his silence, an imprisonment of the mind, a restraint on speech if not on thought, the protective custody in which I traveled, and, once back in the queen's household, my restriction to the more-than-comfortable palace where all my physical needs were cared for with the best of everything, yet still I was caged. All those I loved were unreachable, untouchable.

WEARY AND disheartened, with a pounding head and throbbing bruises, on my arrival in the inner bailey of the castle I wanted nothing but to go to bed. Gwen and I walked slowly, arm in arm. My head, ankles, and lower back complained, but I was glad to be moving on my own account. In the queen's hall we were met by a servant who led us past the queen's chamber, and far past the one I shared with the other waiting women, to an unfamiliar room that was pretty and private, and just before the doorway to the king's part of the palace.

"Master Adam, His Grace's physician, has been informed that you have arrived. He asks that you send a servant to fetch him when you have taken some refreshment and have rested."

He was gone. A moment later a maidservant arrived with wine, cold meats, and bread. "Do you require anything else, Mistress Alice?"

When she departed, Gwen and I stood for a moment in the warmth of the brazier, gazing around at the wall hangings depicting young men and women hawking, the large bed hung with gold and green curtains, and my best shift laid out on it. A washing basin stood beside a simmering kettle.

"Is this to be your chamber now?" Gwen wondered aloud.

"Surely not. Perhaps we were shown here for the physician's ease— so that we might be alone, and in a chamber near the king's household." But I did wonder whether it signaled I was thought to be in danger even in the palace, and so I was kept close to His Grace's guards. I pushed aside my fear, too weary at the moment to consider it.

"The king's own physician!" Gwen breathed, and I read in her eyes a fear that perhaps I'd been more seriously injured than Dame Juliana had confided to her.

"Do not worry, Gwen. Look how well I rode, and walked all this way."

Indeed, by the next day Master Adam had pronounced me fit enough to go about my usual activities as long as I rested in the afternoon. That evening Her Grace requested that I prepare her almond milk. While I sat with her a servant showed me the clothing for the wedding festivities, and I made suggestions for the finishing touches, an enjoyable pastime. I was grateful I had returned before the festivities.

"I have decided that after my eldest son and his new wife are thoroughly wed and have departed to Berkhampstead, you and I shall amuse ourselves by fitting you out with an entirely new set of clothes," said the queen with an enigmatic smile.

I had brought with me from my married life what I considered to be a gorgeous collection of gowns, capes, headdresses, shoes, jewelry, and other accoutrements suitable for a wealthy merchant's wife, and had added to it in my time at court. "Your Grace, are my gowns displeasing to you?"

"They were suitable, Alice, but now you are a woman of the court."

She seemed about to say more, then waved me away. "To bed with you. I shall need you tomorrow, so you must rest."

"Your Grace, I called for a servant to move my belongings back to my usual bedchamber and he said that I am to remain in the private one. I think there is some confusion."

"There is no confusion. Now off to bed!" She shooed me out of the room.

After my nap the following afternoon I felt much revived. I recounted to Gwen the queen's plan for new clothes for me.

"This chamber, the king's physician, new gowns . . . ?" She shook her head. "It is as if your ordeal has caused the king and queen to examine their parts in unraveling your family, and are trying to make amends."

Our shared ordeal seemed to have removed any last constraint between mistress and maid.

"You are one of my greatest blessings, Gwen," I told her.

Her eyes filled with tears and her smile was uneven. "God graced me when I joined your household, mistress."

After a thorough study of my gowns we conceded that a few had been redone too many times—buttons, pearls, and ribbons removed and replaced so often that the cloth was unevenly worn and holes and pulls remained, despite Gwen's best efforts. At last we stood thoughtfully regarding the pile of clothing on the bed.

"Well, what else?" I asked.

Gwen wrinkled her nose. "Some of the fur is too long dead."

This simple comment inspired laughter.

Later, when we hastened down to the queen's hall, certain that I had been missed, we discovered Richard Stury pacing near Countess Joan, who was playing dice with my friend Elizabeth. The countess was residing in the castle in the last few days before her wedding.

"Mistress Alice, you are to sup with His Grace the King this evening," said Stury. "I shall come to your chamber to escort you an hour earlier. Before the other guests arrive, he would speak with you about your recent ordeal in Oxford." He bowed to me and withdrew.

My heart had leaped at the invitation. To sup with the king. To be so near him! I composed myself as I joined my friends.

Joan raised her eyebrows, a gleam in her eyes. "It seems you are deriving good fortune from bad. A meal in the king's chamber! I'm delighted for you. I wonder who else will be there?" She kicked the fur-trimmed hem of her gown as she turned toward me.

I wondered as well.

Elizabeth studied me hard, her expression finally easing into a smile. "It is good to see you looking cheerful. Much better than I had expected, in fact. I trow you are sleeping more soundly without Jane and Agnes snoring in your ears."

I was not at all surprised that the news of my new accommodations had been quickly passed around the queen's household. "I am." I took a seat beside her.

"You must take this opportunity to ask His Grace to return William to court," Elizabeth said.

"A lover?" asked Joan. She did so delight in anything to do with mating.

"No, not a lover, but a good friend," I said.

Elizabeth wrinkled her nose and gave a little laugh as she shook her head, signaling that I was not being honest. It seemed to me a betrayal of my confidence. I had not seen this side of her before and was hurt and disappointed. I had thought her a friend, but a friend would not have spoken of William when I had not.

"Do you speak of William Wyndsor?" asked Joan.

"Yes, she does," said Elizabeth. I tried to nudge her foot beneath the table, wanting to silence her, but she prattled on. "And he has declared his intention to wed her!"

I was taken aback by that. I had known he'd asked her of my availability, but not that he had spoken thus. And I had certainly not confided in Elizabeth about his vowing to wed me.

Now Joan was very interested, leaning forward to whisper, "Did you speak of your intention to wed him, Alice?"

I shook my head. "No. We are not betrothed, I assure you."

"Alas that it is Wyndsor." A sympathetic frown creased her pretty forehead. "For the king has need of him in Ireland, ensuring that Lionel succeeds in convincing the Irish to behave themselves. Wyndsor is part of the company sailing over to prepare the way for the earl and his household." Joan watched me closely as she spoke. "Are you certain you did not respond in kind? You might be legally betrothed."

"I did not."

"Of course you might wed him and remain in Her Grace's household as long as you were not with child," said Joan.

I assured her that I had not considered wedding Sir William. She watched me with a curious expression.

"Have you dined with His Grace before?" Elizabeth asked in the long pause that followed.

I shook my head.

"But you've often gone hawking with him alone, have you not?" Elizabeth's look, her tone were challenging.

"In the past, but not for a long while." I excused myself and took my leave.

As I passed Joan, she touched my arm and said, softly, for my ears only, "I am your friend. Come to me if you are confused."

I left the hall in a whirl of emotions. Once outside I could not think where I might find ease. I had thought Elizabeth my friend, my only one in the queen's household. But now it seemed she favored me only for what gossip she might glean from me, and I was sorely disappointed. I should have seen the shape of her discourse before this, the searching questions, how she shared just enough to engage me. On a happier note, I was grateful for Countess Joan's kindness. The news of William's departure for Ireland relieved me, too. Indeed, it was his good fortune that we were separated, for since my abduction in Oxford I had become keenly aware of the danger I might bring to anyone attached to me. It had been good of Countess Joan to tell me about him, and very kind of her to offer friendship, even if I could not imagine why she encouraged me to seek her out if I were confused. How could she be my friend, a woman about to wed the future king? Within days she would be *Princess* Joan. Once again I would be alone.

"Dame Alice?" Gwen stood behind me, holding a light mantle. "Would you walk in the gardens?"

"I wish Geoffrey were here. Or my sister Mary." I held out my hand. "Walk with me, Gwen. Be my friend."

We walked and walked while I related the conversation.

"I am sorry that Elizabeth has proved false," said Gwen. "But how kind of the countess."

"I want to think it kind, but do not dare to count on her. She is soon to be a princess, Gwen. Why should she befriend me?"

"Is it not possible that some at court are sincere?"

All too soon it was time to dress for the evening. I chose my prettiest gown, a red fitted bodice and sleeves with a swirling pattern and a skirt the color of dark berries. The buttons on the bodice and sleeves were silver. Gwen dressed my hair in soft loops round my ears, gathered in a silver crespinette and held by a silver fillet.

At the door to the king's parlor, Stury held out his arm to stop Gwen.

"You will wait with me out here," he said. "I shall send for some food and wine, and a brazier to warm you."

Gwen fussed a moment longer with my dress. "Perhaps I should not have accompanied you. Perhaps it is not appropriate."

I squeezed her hand, and then nodded to the page that I was ready to be announced.

Splendid in a short green jacket embroidered in silver thread in a plantagenet pattern, the king strode across the room to me and embraced me, kissing me on the forehead.

As ever, his ready intimacy flustered me. Surely he must perceive how I felt about him, how he affected me.

"My sweet Alice. God be praised." He held me at arm's length. "I heard that it was a terrible ordeal. But you look well. More than well. You are quite beautiful this evening."

"Your Grace, I am honored to be invited to sup with you." I did not dare look into his eyes but stared instead at his long-toed shoes.

He put his hands on my shoulders—no gloves this time—and I felt the heat of them, and of his gaze.

"You shall not be harmed again, Alice. I swear to you. My mother's curse on your life ends now."

He pulled me closer, and bent his head to kiss my forehead again, then, lifting my chin, kissed me on the mouth. Gently. Oh, so gently. But his hands slid behind my shoulder blades and caressed me in a way that was anything but chaste.

"My lord," I whispered when he released me. I still had not dared look up at his face. My head was spinning with desire, fear, sadness. "Your Grace, what are you about?" It sounded too harsh. How dare I question the king? "If it please Your Grace, I am confused."

"Look at me, Alice." His voice was gentle. "Look at me."

At last I did raise my eyes to his and saw great tenderness there, and something else, a yearning. His gaze held me, and I knew great danger. I felt how easily I might lose my self and my soul, how willingly I might succumb to his desire.

"You know what I am about. What we are about. It began with the hawking. We are kindred souls, Alice."

We were, we were—but I felt myself shaking my head. "You are my king." If he had been any other man, I would not be so frightened, would not mind how his touch aroused me.

"But in my private hours I am a man like any other. You shall come to see that."

"Your Grace," I murmured, too confused and frightened to say more. I did not want to be one of his quickly discarded mistresses. He said we were kindred souls, but for how long? Until he discovered a woman who shared some of his other interests—music, perhaps, a singer with a voice matched perfectly to his? And then what would happen to me? Surely Queen Philippa knew of his liaisons. What would happen to Bella if I fell from grace?

Yet I could not help but thrill to what he was suggesting.

"When we are alone, I would have you call me Edward."

I merely nodded, not trusting my voice. If he were not king . . .

He drew me to him once more and kissed me on both cheeks. His hands on my shoulders were gentle but proprietary, his eyes dark with desire. "Alice, do not fear me." Finally he kissed my hands, then stepped away. "Now, before the others arrive, you must tell me all that you recall of that night."

How easily he moved into normal conversation. My mind and heart could not shift so swiftly and gracefully. Stupidly I stared at his boots and worked to calm my thoughts.

"They will soon arrive, Alice." He forced his voice to stay calm, but I sensed his impatience.

"I recall very little." I told him then all I remembered. "My maid-servant was awake during the attack and might tell you much more. She awaits me in the antechamber, with Master Stury."

"Summon her."

Gwen seemed far more composed than I felt as she described the attack and counterattack. Edward asked some questions, which she answered. When he was satisfied he thanked her for her account and for her loyalty to me, and then gave her leave to depart.

I'd dared to look at him more closely than before. I saw the way he'd given Gwen his complete attention. I also noticed fine lines round his eyes and deeper ones beneath his beard radiating from the edge of either nostril to the corners of his mouth. Signs of age. The queen had recently spoken of his being nearly fifty. He might be my father, yet he was nothing like. So alive, so exciting.

"Master Stury told me little. Who were those men, Your G—"

He shook his head, mouthing his name.

"Edward," I said, though it almost caught in my throat. I feared I might have crossed a boundary I was not yet ready to leave behind. I feared my own desire for his touch.

He smiled at my use of his name, but then grew serious. "As was your late husband's practice, I would tell you as little as necessary. To protect you." He tilted his head and regarded me with a look that seemed to say he expected me to be satisfied with such an answer.

Despite my fear, I trusted him. I never doubted his sincerity. But if we were indeed friends, well, then he should know me in all my stubbornness. "As I argued with Janyn and with the Lady Isabella, those who would harm my family have no reason to believe I know nothing. They will come after me again to find out what they want to know. As they did in Oxford."

Edward bowed his head, his hands clasped behind him. I held my breath, waiting for the revelation that would explain my torment of the past years. I feared it would be something far too trivial to have cost so many lives, feared it would be so significant that I would be forced to endure a lifetime of pain.

"In good time, Alice."

I opened my mouth to protest. He put a finger to my lips.

"I will tell you this. Your husband's family was beset on either side, by those who watched that they honored their pact of secrecy, and by those who would coerce them to break that pact. Members of my family and powerful barons are on both sides, as well as wealthy merchants who hope to make powerful alliances. But now that they all know without a doubt you are under my protection, they will desist."

"Is that why my attackers had to die?"

It was a suffocating sensation, having those remarkable blue eyes fixed on me with such intensity. When he suddenly broke the spell and shook his head, I gasped for breath.

"Surely you would not expect me to allow them to go free? What punishment would you have preferred? That they die slowly in a dungeon, deprived of food and water, of sunlight and the sacraments? Was death then too easy?"

"No!" I made the sign of the cross, banishing the horrors he had described. "But I would have preferred to talk to them first, to question them about my husband and his parents."

"That is not your part to play, Alice."

His air of finality infuriated me. "What of my daughter? What if someone were to take her to force my hand? How am I to live with such a fear, Edward?"

"You have nothing to fear, sweet Alice. My sister fully understands the danger to your daughter." He drew me to him. "I told you, they shall not harm you or your daughter. Those who dared harm you died in the attempt; the survivor was executed. That should serve to warn those who would try such a thing again."

This time I did not respond, but merely endured his embrace. I did not understand how I could both thrill to his nearness and chafe under his control. When he released me, I asked if I might withdraw to my chamber.

"No, Alice." He did not say this in anger, but his expression was serious and his tone firm. "I want my household and those I count as friends to know you better."

But what of his queen? To introduce me to his household . . . I was to have no privacy, no choice. Once so presented, I would be forever branded.

Yet, in truth, I was already believed to have taken the king as my lover, ever since Sheppey; had already been tried and found guilty.

I concentrated on breathing through my panic. I told myself that this was what my heart had truly desired, that I might find a way to gratitude and even joy in it.

PRINCE EDWARD and his bride, Princess Joan, shone in green-and-white robes heavy with precious gems and pearls at their wedding feast, and all their households wore the same colors, including Joan's sons and daughters by Thomas Holland. The couple exuded happiness as they danced at the feast. It was a bittersweet day for me, evoking memories of my own joyous wedding, yet I was happy for Joan. And very happy for myself, for Edward had fulfilled his promise that Bella would attend in his sister Joan's company. I had not seen my daughter for months.

The king ignored me during the festivities, not once to my knowledge looking my way. To see him in such an official role, the white-haired king glorious in robes emblazoned with his heraldic devices, conferring his blessing on his heir, I wondered how I had ever thought he might desire me. Surely it had all been but a dream.

My delight rested solely in my Bella's presence, for this time she seemed thrilled to see me and embraced me with all the warmth and love I could desire. Four and a half seemed a charming age. Geoffrey declared her the most beautiful creature in the great hall, and she giggled and twirled and curtsied with delight at his compliments. We shared but a few days, all too few, and then she was swept away once more to Hertford.

TRUE TO her word, as soon as she'd recovered from the royal wedding Queen Philippa devoted herself to planning my new robes, observing my fittings, inspecting the work before it was finished. I argued against all but a few of the silks and velvets, but she overruled me. She chose for me shades of red from rose to purple, as well as deep golds and indigo. I thrilled to the thought of how I would please Edward. My confessions and prayers were filled with my guilty delight in these sensuous fabrics and splendid colors. Dom Creswell seemed amused by my urge for restraint. I did not dare confess to the true sins in my heart, my betrayal of the queen in every smile I gave Edward.

So began a time in which the king and I played an increasingly strange game of cat and mouse. I was included in his morning hawking parties and in informal dinners in his chamber with members of his household. But he did not kiss me, did not touch me. I was intoxicated by his presence and terrified of the enormity of what seemed to lie ahead.

We were never alone together during this time. He was always courteous and complimentary, but no more.

I doubted he noticed my new elegance, though he did send Master Adam to inquire as to the cause of the shadows beneath my eyes and my dwindling weight.

I gave the physician half an answer—I could not bring myself to confide in him my distress over the conflict between my growing infatuation with the king and my loyalty to the queen. My humors were in turmoil. I confined my explanation to the aftereffects of my ordeal in Oxford. For the first time in my life I was sleeping so lightly that the slightest sound woke me, and upon waking I was beset with the fear that strangers were in my chamber. Though my would-be abductors were dead, I yet feared that, as it had happened once, it could happen again. Master Adam suggested a sleeping draught.

"Then I should feel truly helpless."

"You are safe, Mistress Alice. You are in the king's protection." Looking down his great hawklike nose at me, he clearly thought I was a fool for doubting my safety.

"I was in the king's protection when I was attacked, Master Adam." He snorted. I did not take the draught.

Queen Philippa, too, noted my weight loss and that I looked as if I were not sleeping. She'd listened to my explanation with sympathy, then shared with me her own reason for melancholy—that she had so much pain in her pelvis she would never bear another child, and that she and the king now lived as brother and sister, not husband and wife. She declared she would find something to cheer us both.

I had heard previous speculation from the women waiting on Her Grace that her riding accident had ruined her for sexual pleasure, and that shortly afterward her courses had stopped. However, I had never heard her speak of this herself. I felt honored by her confidence, sad for her, and unsettled by a sense that she was absolving me from guilt. The new gowns, this confidence—I became increasingly convinced that I was being groomed to become Edward's mistress, a realization both thrilling and terrifying.

As we prepared for the Christmas court, the queen's inspiration to cheer us both was that we should dazzle the court with light, drawing it to us wherever we walked. She grew quite merry as we discussed, planned, and chose bright, shiny fabrics and jewels. She hugged me often. The women noticed. They made points of small kindnesses in the queen's presence, but left me alone in her absence. Gradually my sleep improved. I do not think it was so much because of the work, though I enjoyed it, but because of the queen's affection. I felt more a part of her life than I had done before, part of her extended family. That went further in reassuring me of my safety than anything else.

But there was still danger of a different sort. Not Isabella's curse but Edward's desire, and mine. One morning in November I entered my chamber to find a length of the most beautiful, soft, richly dyed crimson wool on my bed, with a note from Edward, sealed with a signet I came to know well: *What better color for hawking? E.*

The king was a canny hunter.

So was I.

A T THE Christmas court the queen wore gowns with so many jewels and pearls to catch the light that she indeed seemed radiant.
So, too, did I. Geoffrey told me of the continuous murmuring among
the courtiers about the queen's intentions for me, and asked outright
whether I was being displayed to the king.

His words verified my fear that all at court saw the royal couple's
design for me. Of course they would note that Philippa dressed me
as a younger version of herself. Of course all knew that I attended
Edward's dinners, and that we hunted and hawked, sometimes without companions. I assured Geoffrey that Edward and I were never
alone of late, but that I felt like Criseyde, being dressed to impress
the king. And who was my Troilus? Janyn? Would he look down on
me from Heaven and think me a faithless wife? What I was being
drawn into was sin, no matter how sincere my love for Edward, for he
could never wed me.

Queen Philippa was successful in her unholy goal. Edward seemed
most drawn to my low-cut bodices, and made no attempt to hide the
hunger in his eyes when they dwelt on me. Indeed, he often caught my
attention, and then held my gaze for a moment before looking down
again at my breasts. He knew what he was about. Had he been bold
enough to lift my skirts, he would have found me most ready to yield,
God help me.

Janyn was gone. I believed that now. And I had been too happily
wed and too long abandoned. My body yearned for a man's attention,
and that man was my king.

So on the fateful early-spring day when I arrived at the mews and
discovered only Edward there, I knew where our morning's sport
would lead, and, God forgive me, I was more than ready, I was eager.

On that morning I wore red beneath a short, Lincoln green cloak
lined in gris, but my red skirt was prominent, and my red hat. Blood
red, cut from the escarlatte Edward had given me. He wore a jacket and
leggings of the deep purple called purpura. He wore it well. We shone
like jewels as we rode through the woods to the marsh. It was early
April. We were enjoying our last days at Sheen before leaving for the
St. George's Day festivities at Windsor. An early-morning mist swirled

along the ground, helping me imagine I was riding into a dream, a space outside time.

We hunted with falcons that morning. Mine, when I stroked him, looked sharply into my eyes for a heartbeat then turned to gaze away, ready for the hunt. As always, looking into his eyes, sensing his wildness and the potential damage he could wreak with his beak and claws, I thrilled to the bond between us, two predators who might so easily kill each other, joining to hunt. We could not speak to each other, could not make a pact, and yet we trusted, we touched, we thrilled to the power we shared.

The falconer and a boy had gone ahead to choose the best area of the marsh while another boy and the dogs waited with us. The two returned with news of herons and ducks very near. We were cautious in our approach, the need for silence adding to the excitement. My falcon saw the birds before I did, suddenly leaning away from me. I felt his tension. The dogs flushed out a heron. I held my breath, my heart pounding, as I released my falcon. I watched him climb, then dive. The heron rose, so awkward until airborne, then so graceful. I almost regretted the skill of my bird as he swooped and struck. The falconer sent the best swimmer to pluck up the catch. My falcon returned to my glove, his feathers quivering, blood on his claws and beak. I murmured my admiration.

Edward's bird was now aloft, diving down toward a duck, and quickly afterward his took a heron as mine went for another duck. We smiled and congratulated each other with our eyes. Edward had once told me that the lack of human voices during the hunt brought him a strange peace—strange to find peace in the midst of the brutality of sudden death. But I had understood . . . the cries of the birds, the rush of wings, the panting of the dogs, the sudden baying.

The falconer and his boys were busy with the prey as Edward now moved close to me, his eyes shining. He looked glorious in the purpura, his long white hair wild beneath his hat, his face ruddy with the early-morning chill and the riding, intensely focused, his posture straight and soldierly. He leaned toward me and brushed my cheek— matted feathers dropped onto my lap.

"Blooded," he said as he put a proprietary hand on my thigh and looked me in the eyes as if in challenge.

I laughed, feeling reckless and alive.

"Your wildness draws me, Alice. You know that. When you are one with your hawk, your horse, at ease in the woodland—that is when I most desire you."

Though my gut clenched in fear I slowly smiled, for I could not deny to myself that I liked the way he touched me. I liked it very much.

Seeing so clearly now that I had no choice, that he had chosen, I thought I might at least play with all my heart, as I rode, as I hawked. I prayed that I might also keep my wits about me. We had been approaching this moment for a long while, but in my wildest imaginings the Alice whom the king undressed and caressed was older, wiser, more experienced. I was but myself, uncertain and overwhelmed by the power this man, this king, wielded against mightier folk than I would ever be. In my daydreams I *chose* to lie with him. But I understood, I felt in his touch, his eyes, that the choice was really his, and I saw that he had been luring me for a long while, subtly, patiently, oh, so skillfully.

If there was a way to refuse a king, I had not learned it. Nor would I.

After the hunt Edward simply said we would retire to his chambers. As we rode back to the palace he entertained me with his wit and snatches of song—he had a rich, deep voice. In his chamber he offered me brandywine. It seemed a heady drink for midmorning, and too heating, for though it had been cold on the marsh I felt a sheen of sweat beneath my gown and knew my face was flushed with my body's own heat. But a few sips helped calm my trembling—until he took me in his arms and kissed me with a rough passion that left me weak with fear and desire, in such a powerful and confusing mix that I pushed out of his embrace and turned away from him.

What am I doing? I asked myself in something like panic. The enormity of what this meant, to lie with my mistress's husband, my *queen's* husband, stopped me.

The king had removed his jacket. The linen shirt beneath it exposed white hair on his chest mixed with dark blond. With his long pale hair and beard, he caught the light from the fire and seemed more than human. He reached for my hand.

"I am frightened, Edward."

He put his hands on my shoulders and gave me a gentle shake. "Look into my eyes and say that you do not want me to make love to you."

I looked into his eyes and felt myself drifting down into their depths. I felt welcome, warm. I leaned closer to him despite my fear.

He stroked my throat as he would his hawk. "Alice," he whispered. He dropped his hands and took a step backward. "The motto I first used for a great tournament was 'It is what it is.' I accepted what God brought my way. I vowed to face without faltering all that He presented to me and to find the best way to conquer it. You would be wise to resolve to do as I did. You are a young, beautiful, desirable, wise widow who has caught the heart of her king. Take him and keep him well, Alice. Welcome him into your heart and body, and he will care for you with such devotion and passion you will never regret it. He promises."

"My lord, my body and my heart are willing. Do not doubt it. But I am bound in duty to the queen. How can I betray her in such wise? For this seems the very worst betrayal."

He bowed his head. I almost reached out to touch the silken, silvery strands of hair.

"My beloved Philippa is consumed by pain. To lie with her would cause her such torment that it would be a grievous sin on my part. She knows that I am yet a man, Alice. My queen is no fool."

He reached for my hands, brought them to his chest so that I might feel the pounding of his heart.

His words had reminded me of Philippa's veiled blessing on our union. I had been groomed for this without anyone asking whether or not it pleased me. I was yet a pawn. But looking at the king, seeing his desire, I sensed I yet held some power.

It gave me the courage to say what was in my own heart. "I have a memory of love that is not yet in the past for me, Edward. Can you tell me that you know for certain Janyn is dead? And will you promise me that my daughter Bella will be brought into the court where I may raise her?"

He closed his eyes and made an odd sound.

"Can you also promise that you will not discard me in a few weeks?"

He pulled me close, his hands moving down to the small of my back. "You would bargain with me, Alice? Like a merchant's wife?"

"I *am* a merchant's wife, Edward."

He pushed me away so suddenly I lost my balance and stumbled into a chair. "You are a merchant's *widow*, Alice," he said, his voice rough with frustration. I had never seen him look so angry, his blue eyes pale in his flushed face, his long white hair wild. He frightened me. "Janyn Perrers is dead. You were right to doubt that he died of the pestilence . . . he died by a murderer's hands, strangled and then stabbed through the heart." He spat the words out as if to stab me in turn.

Though I feared him, the manner in which he was telling me what I had begged to hear infuriated me. I rose up and slapped my king's cheek. I slapped it as hard as I could. He grabbed my fist, then scooped me up and carried me through the curtains to his bedchamber, throwing me down on the bed and roughly reaching beneath my skirts. I grabbed his hand. His eyes burned into me.

"My lord!" I cried.

The fire left his face. He let go of me and crossed himself.

"If you want me, take me as a lover. Naked, both of us. As equals in lovemaking."

For a long while we stared at each other, gradually calming.

At last he said, "As equals in love." He smiled and rose to remove his shirt and leggings. His great, strong body was not so beautiful as Janyn's. Scars tugged at his skin, and it sagged a little with age. And yet I wanted him.

I slipped off the bed and undressed, pushing away his hands when he would hurry me, smiling and shaking my head.

At last he lifted me up and I wrapped my legs around him. He entered me easily and cried out as I moved around him. Too soon he came, too soon.

Afterward he lifted me on top of him and gathered my breasts between his palms, sucking and tugging at my nipples with his teeth until I ached so with desire that I cried out. Only then did he enter me once more and possess me.

He had promised nothing but that I would be grateful. But once I had tasted his body I could not turn away from him.

11

Hire armes smale, hire streghte bak and softe,
Hire sydes longe, flesshly, smothe, and white
He gan to stroke, and good thrift bad ful ofte
Hire snowissh throte, hire brestes rounde and lite.
Thus in this hevene he gan hym to delite . . .

—GEOFFREY CHAUCER, *Troilus and Criseyde*, III, 1247–51

• Spring 1362 •

AFTER OUR first lovemaking, both of us riding the powerful waves of passion, anger, and release, I woke to myself. The image of what he had told me of Janyn's death overwhelmed me and I turned away from Edward, sick with grief.

"What is it, sweet Alice? Did I hurt you?" He stroked my hair.

His tender concern melted the ice around my heart and my tears began to flow. *Janyn, Janyn, my first love, my husband. Murdered. His beautiful body bereft of breath and then torn open.* The pain of imagining the agony of his last moments left me breathless.

"Is it what I told you of your husband?"

I cried out, and Edward held me.

"There is no shame in grief for a beloved," he said.

I slept, waking to find those incredibly blue eyes watching me.

"Alice," he whispered, stroking my breasts, my thighs. I moved beneath his touch, and he eased himself onto me. We made slow, gentle love. I found comfort in it.

"I swear that I will not abandon you," he said afterward. We lay side by side, holding hands in quiet contentment. "And when I deem it time, Bella will be with you."

IN MIDAFTERNOON, Gwen was summoned to dress me so that I might move through the palace to my chamber without causing more gossip than had already been stirred up by my relationship with the king. Gwen's hands trembled as she helped me with my shift, revealing her fear. With gentle care she undid my headdress and wrapped it so that it draped about my face and neck, hiding evidence of the king's beard on my tender flesh.

Once back in my chamber, Gwen asked, her voice breaking, "What will the queen do to you?"

"I do not know, but I believed His Grace when he said that he would take care of me." I took off my headdress and sank down on a bench by the little window. There I sat for a long while, a cup of wine in hand, staring out at the birds chasing one another. Somehow the violent details of Janyn's death had renewed my mourning, as if I had held on to a belief until then that he would miraculously reappear. I envied the birds. It was mating season, after all, and I was a hen. I wondered what they did when they lost a partner. It was said that swans mated for life. I had been foolish to think that, like the swan, I had mated with Janyn for life. It had always been likely that I would outlive him, for he'd been twenty years my senior. I had not wanted to think beyond my happiness with him.

When I noticed that as Gwen moved about the room she was casting worried glances at me, I thought it best to share with her the shocking news.

"His Grace told me that Janyn was murdered—strangled and stabbed through the heart. I do not know how I shall ever have the courage to tell Bella how her father died. Or if it would be best to let her continue to believe he died of the pestilence."

I wept then. Gwen joined me on the bench, praying and weeping with me, as if she, too, had held back the full force of her grief until now. We prayed for Janyn's soul, and then we shared memories, talking of his many virtues and graces.

When I rose from our private requiem it was as if my heart had opened and I was able both to mourn Janyn and rejoice in the promise of Bella's return. I hesitated to rejoice in the king's affection. I tried not to imagine more lovemaking, but of course that was exactly where my thoughts wandered, and my body responded as if he were indeed touching me. I felt like a wilting flower that had been watered. I felt a part of life once more.

LATE IN the afternoon the queen sent for me to join her and several other women working on an embroidered altar cloth. Gwen's eyes were like those of a cornered puppy as she dressed me. I was frightened as well. I did not know what to expect.

The queen greeted me with affection. She did not inquire about the signs of tears. I wondered if perhaps she had already spoken to the king and knew that the cause was my widowhood, one of the topics we did not discuss before the other women.

But the others were sympathetic, asking if I was unwell or had received unhappy news. We all feared the return of the pestilence with the spring weather.

"I had a bad dream," I said.

The queen smiled to herself as she bent over her needlework.

I attended her that evening. She did not mention Edward, but she did know that I had been told how Janyn died.

"May he rest in the peace of salvation," she said, kissing me on the forehead. "Queen Joan will of course say nothing of this to young Bella. She will learn of it from you in good time."

That Bella would be told the truth of her father's death by anyone but me had never entered my mind.

"You will wish to arrange for Masses for Janyn's one-year obit here at the chapel."

I felt as if I were outside my body, observing the two of us discussing Masses for my husband's soul. It seemed impossible that it was only nineteen months since he had disappeared. So much had happened, I felt I had changed utterly.

I wondered whether Philippa had just received word of how Janyn had died or whether she had been biding her time until someone slipped and told me.

"What of Dame Tommasa, his mother?" I asked. "Do you know how she died, Your Grace?"

Fussing with her cushions, a signal to me that I was not seeing to her comfort, she said, "I know no more than you do, Alice. Let us talk no more of death. We have festivities to plan."

I bent to adjust the pillows. Her behavior left me unsettled, uncertain whether or not she knew what had happened between me and her husband. Her husband. *Jesu!* I trembled as I sat beside the queen, pretending to look at fabrics and jewels.

As we looked at a red cloth woven in a small, vinelike pattern, she said, quite casually, "You were a vision of ripe womanhood in that red escarlatte riding gown, Alice. We must dress you in red more often. And pearls. Though low born, you are a beauty, and precious to us." She squeezed my hand, but did not look up from the fabric.

She had seen me at some point with Edward. *We must dress you . . .
Ripe . . . precious to us.* I could not believe she meant to reassure me
that I was doing what she wished, but could not think how else to
interpret her words.

ON THE following night, shortly after I'd retired to my chamber,
the king's page appeared to summon me to Edward. Fortunately
I had not yet disrobed.

Gwen was beside herself—how was I to get my rest, how would
she prepare me for bed? How indeed. All this was outside any sort of
life for which I had been brought up. Though excited, I was filled with
unease. Was I now his plaything, to be at his beck and call, with no
life of my own? He had encouraged me to spread my wings, but how
could I? I feared that his own shackles might destroy all he claimed to
love in me.

Servants were arranging cots for the sergeants-at-arms who slept
in the outer chamber. They glanced my way and quickly averted their
eyes. When I was shown into the king's chamber, he was already in
a simple robe, and barefoot. He crossed the room to me, picked me
up, and carried me to the bed. He lay there beside me and guided my
hand to his groin, showing me how his body anticipated the pleasure
to come. He asked me to undress. Slowly. Near the fire, so that I was
not in shadow. When I was naked, Edward came to me and lifted me
up. I wrapped my legs round him, and he slid into me so easily we both
laughed. Wicked, wanton laughs.

"We are birds of prey, Alice my love, with no thought of spiritual
life. There is only the flesh. Our flesh. Our hunger."

In the morning, Gwen woke me. The king had already risen. On
his pillow was a large pearl, and a note: *"The first of many. E."*

IN A few days the court removed to Windsor to prepare for the St.
George's Day festivities. With so many expected, I shared a chamber
with Elizabeth and other higher-born ladies whose husbands could not
be present. They whispered among themselves over the screens placed
round the small bed that I was to share with Gwen—two large beds
would suffice for the six of them, their servants making do with pallets
laid out on the floor after their mistresses were abed.

My bed was close to a small door opening onto a passage leading to Edward's chamber, so that on those nights I was called away, I

might depart without stumbling over the servants' pallets. When I returned in the early morning to dress for Mass the ladies would include
me in their sleepy chatter; none of them, not even Elizabeth, asked
where I had spent the night. That they were so cautious in their looks
and speech emphasized for me the rank of my lover.

While at Windsor Edward and I hawked and dined together, in
company. I found it exciting to catch him watching me. But when away
from him I was beset by doubts and fears, not at all easy in my mind
despite feeling a bond between us that was strong and true.

When Joan arrived with Prince Edward, she summoned me to walk
with her in the gardens. She looked more beautiful than ever, her face
radiant, her clothes subtly revealing that she was with child.

She saw that I'd noticed, and her face opened up into a most beatific smile as she touched her stomach. "With God's grace, I may be
carrying a future king."

She kissed me on both cheeks, then stood back to study me. She
startled me by pressing my belly. "You are not with child, are you? But
then, I think it might be too soon to know."

"You have heard about the king and me?" She had not been at
court since Christmas. But even before she responded, I thought how
foolish I was to think she might not know.

"That the king has taken you for his mistress? Oh, yes, I do. The
two Edwards send messengers back and forth with news of the realm
and their daily activities." She affectionately kissed my cheek. "My Edward's father is like a child boasting about you, Alice. Be glad. Let your
heart rejoice." Then she grew serious. "I must speak to my maid, have
her give your Gwen the recipe for a physick you must take before and
after you lie with him, and one you must take if, despite this precaution, you quicken. You do not want a royal bastard."

It frightened me that messengers carried news of our liaison. I had
hoped that as long as we said nothing, it would remain merely a rumor.
I had begged Edward to speak of us to no one. I must have made a
face, which Joan misread.

She shook her head at me. "You cannot afford to be foolish. Even
with my royal blood, though I have never denied my fleshly desires,
I've heeded the dangers and done all that I could to protect myself. I
would be sorry to see you suffer."

In truth, my heart and my head were at war over the issue. I feared
such precautions would take the passion out of our lovemaking and

might sicken me. And yet I did not wish any child of mine to be a bastard.

Joan patted her belly again. "Of course you are but nineteen and dream of more children. I assure you, such physics will not ruin you for a future husband. I have taken them, and had no difficulty conceiving."

I thanked her for the advice, and guided our talk to the roster of guests arriving for the festivities. I had realized that Joan could not conceive of my being anything but grateful to be chosen by the king. Such was the flaw, the imperfection in our union, that undermined our love—the power Edward held over me.

How strange then that it was he who reassured me on that point. One night after our lovemaking he caught me biting my lip.

"You worry yet you do not confide in me. How can I comfort you if I know not what troubles you?"

"I fear what will happen to me when you discard me."

He drew me to him and kissed my forehead. "Alice, my sweet Alice, why are you so certain I'll prove faithless?"

"It is said that you have discarded women after a fortnight, again and again. I cannot think why I might be different.'

"And you believed the gossip?"

His sad tone gave me pause. I had not thought to question the rumors. I propped myself up on one elbow so that I might look him in the eyes. "Is it not true?"

The skin around his eyes crinkled with his affectionate, reassuring smile.

"I have strayed from my queen before, but seldom. Though I have often enjoyed the companionship of pretty young women, most of them have been disappointed by how chastely we dined and talked. The few to whom I have made love still enjoy my protection and discretion." He dabbed at my tears with the counterpane, then kissed my lips. "You will be ever near me, my comfort and my delight," he declared.

"And when you tire of me?"

"I shall never tire of you."

I wanted so to believe that. "But what if you do?"

"Then I shall find you a husband. Someone worthy of you. But I do not like to think of that." ·

His voice had sharpened and it was that change in tone rather than all his reassurances that made me believe him, or at least accept that he believed he would not tire of me.

"I shall owe you much if that day ever comes, for I feel as if you have returned my youth and vigor to me, Alice. But I would owe you for more than that. I fear I have not been so discreet about our liaison as I have been with other lovers. In truth, I do not wish to be. I have boasted to my close friends how you have renewed me."

I felt sick to my stomach. "Are the pearls part of your penance?"

For each night or day we lay together, Edward gave me one large pearl or several small ones.

"No, they are not proffered as penance," said Edward. "I have told you what I wish." He wished me to wear them on my gowns, my headdresses, my slippers, or in my hair, so that whenever he saw me he would know that I cherished him. "They are not so much gifts for you as for me. And so you must tell me what I might give you for you, what is your heart's desire."

"My heart's desire?" I could not think what to ask for.

"Search your heart, my sweet Alice."

What I truly wanted was to be with Bella and to give her brothers and sisters, legitimate children fathered by a man who was free to wed me. But even as I formed this wish I felt torn, being otherwise so happy with Edward. How could I not cherish his love? What things might I ask for beyond the beautiful clothes and jewels, the hawks and horses, the fabulous surroundings? I owned Fair Meadow, and Richard Lyons held the house in London for me, and though I could not use either home until such time as Edward felt it was safe for me to do so, I felt reassured by knowing I might return to them someday. The tenements in Oxford provided the income to maintain my homes. Beyond that, in order to ensure that Bella had the opportunities that Janyn and I had wanted for her, I needed to build on the foundation he had left me using the training he had given me.

I thought about his emphasis on the acquisition of land. He had believed that though a man acquired gold, jewels, silks, and spices, if he did not own land, if he had no rents, he was merely a merchant. Land brought respect and a voice in civic matters. He had told me that my father's one flaw was his neglect of this part of his potential. If a man did not step into the civic arena, he was irresponsible. Selfish. Although as a woman I had no place in civic affairs, extensive landholdings would provide me with a status that would attract eligible suitors for my daughter. It was essential I achieve a status in my own right that might overshadow any taint from my liaison with the king.

"Property," I said when I was next with Edward. "I wish for more land and city rents in my name. For myself and Bella." Inwardly I cringed at how acquisitive I sounded, but reminded myself of the loss of reputation I suffered from this liaison.

We were lying in Edward's great bed, wrapped in delicately scented silk bedclothes, with a casement wide open to invite within the soothing sound of a spring rain. Now he propped himself up on some pillows and looked down at me. I lay flat, stretching my limbs. He ran his hand from the middle of my breastbone to the soft hair between my legs, then idly stroked my nearest thigh. "I am glad you have given this some thought. You are so young. You will live on long after I am dead, and I want to leave you with a comfortable income, worthy of a king's mistress. I would grant you a life of ease. I had not thought of property, but it does seem precisely what you need. You speak of such things with confidence. I recall your pride in speaking of how much you had learned about trade from Janyn and your father. What else did you learn from your late husband?"

Even at such a moment, secure in Edward's love, I held my breath in anticipation of the pain inherent in conjuring up that happy time, receding now so quickly into long ago. "Before our betrothal I had never ridden a horse or held a hawk."

"Such an innocent!"

"Nor had I been outside London."

"He opened up the world to you."

"He dreaded the time when he'd have no more to show me." A time he'd not lived to see.

Edward took my hand and kissed it. "You loved him very much."

"With all my heart and soul," I whispered.

"I pray that you can forgive me for the manner in which I told you of his murder."

I took a deep breath to steady my voice. "It is the absence of him that tightens my throat, the thought of him suffering, not how it was told me."

We talked into the night then of how my life had changed with my betrothal to Janyn. It was an evening that brought Edward and me closer as friends, sharing food and wine, laughing, even teasing each

other, and for me it was a turning point, lending me more assurance.
I felt it was extra security for me to be Edward's companion, someone
with whom he enjoyed being, both in and out of bed. I believed he
might be more faithful to a friend than to a lover.

"I shall include you more often in my dinners with merchants," he
said. "It will be most helpful to me to hear your impressions."

I began to see how I might fit into his world, and that was a comfort to me. But I also regularly drank the bitter mixture Gwen had
learned to prepare, to prevent conception.

I did not see Edward every day, managing to find a balance, a way
to live what seemed a double life, between the public and the very
private. I noticed others again, paying attention to my friends Geoffrey, Richard, and the de Roët sisters, who albeit tending to silliness
regarding a new obsession with the opposite sex were still refreshingly
candid and curious about everything. Even some of the other women
of the queen's chamber softened toward me as we bonded together to
assist our mistress.

Sadly, it was becoming increasingly plain to all at court that Her
Grace was ailing. It was now more than four years since her riding accident, and her long struggle with pain was visibly taking its toll. As
far as I knew she had never been a beauty, always slightly plumper than
the ideal, with an awkwardness of movement and a voice that creaked
and cracked from chronic coughs and catarrhs. But with clever face
paint and skillfully designed gowns and veils she had always looked
pleasant, indeed often radiant, and never less than regal. Alas, it grew
much more difficult to mask the broken veins on her face, and her halting gait and crooked posture. She was forty-seven years old, two years
Edward's junior, but looked a decade older.

She did not allow herself to be deluded by the reassuring platitudes
and denials voiced by many of her ladies.

"Your pauses emphasize gravitas, Your Grace," Lady Eleanor once
declared.

"Were I not wheezing so loudly I drown out the minstrels," the
queen retorted. "Are you, too, going deaf?"

Queen Philippa preferred to talk openly of her aging. "You will not
be so intent on avoiding the sunny seats in the garden when your joints
are as old and worn as mine," she teased Katherine de Roët.

"But it colors my skin most unbecomingly," Katherine protested.

"Darker skin hides more wrinkles," the queen replied with a teasing laugh.

In fact, she had recently commissioned her tomb, and often spoke to me of her wish to be beautifully gowned and bejeweled to await Edward, who would lie beside her.

This talk of death reminded me of my own uncertain future. I must never forget I was a commoner. Once Philippa was gone, would Edward take another wife, and would she willingly share him with me? I was troubled as well by the specter she had raised of Edward's own eventual death.

Despite her failing health, the queen insisted on attending all the Garter festivities over the days around the Feast of St. George, even those requiring her to walk a distance on uneven ground, to stand still for long periods of time, or to sit on uncomfortable seats for most of the day and well into the evening. Her face would be pale as alabaster when we helped her to bed, and she would cry out or moan most piteously as she sought a comfortable position. Her physician mixed potent drinks to ease her pain and induce a healing sleep. He urged her to have a day of rest. But each morning she would insist that the sleep had worked its miracle. Of course it had not.

Along with all the queen's other ladies I was fully occupied assisting her through that busy time and heard of the arrivals of only those especially favored by my companions and the queen. And so I was taken by surprise when I glanced up from the dais in the great hall where I was arranging cushions on the queen's chair, in preparation for her imminent arrival at a feast, and beheld William Wyndsor striding toward me through the crowd of servants. He hesitated as he reached me. Though he was smiling there was a guarded quality to his eyes. He took my hands.

"You are more beautiful than ever, Alice." He tried to pull me close to him.

I took a step back and attempted to withdraw my hands, but he held fast and stared at me with a boldness I did not like.

"I thought you were in Ireland," I said.

"I have been in the northern marches. But soon I take ship to Ireland. You must say that you will be my wife now, Alice. I love you more than ever. Let us wait no longer."

"That is impossible, William."

He put his hands on my shoulders and searched my face, his frown deepening. "You've been promised to someone else?"

"You do not know?" Was it possible that a man supposedly in love with me would not have inquired, would not have heard about Edward and me? I drew him away from the servants setting out the wine cups so that we might not be overheard. "The king has taken me as his mistress." I thought the clean thrust of the truth would, in the end, afford the cleanest break.

He stood there for one of the longest moments of my life. Then a sound began in his throat, like the low growl of a wild animal, and gradually rose in pitch.

"He has no right!"

"Hush, William, I beg you." Some of the servants were watching us with interest. "Of course he has the right. He is the king. And I love him."

An unwise comment. He lifted his arm to strike me, but caught himself and rushed away, pushing servants out of his path as he went. As I watched him kick over a small table and storm out of sight, I felt a deep sense of dread.

My unease lasted through the evening. I did not see William, nor did I hear anything of him. That night, as I lay watching Edward sleep, I wondered whether I had been a fool to send William away. A husband might take me from court, give me a life no one would censure. William had done me a great favor by taking me to my family during the pestilence, at considerable risk to himself. But even as I thought these things, I knew in my heart that such a refuge was not for me. I loved Edward. I could not abandon him.

Over the next few days I searched the crowds for William, remembering his anger, dreading his next actions. For such emotion seldom gave way to peaceful resignation. For three days I fretted.

I surrendered myself to the full-time task of seeing to the queen's comfort, grateful to have little time to think, for the grandeur of the nobles crowding the castle humbled me, emphasizing the gulf between Edward and me.

In the intimate setting of the bedchamber or on the marshes with our hawks and dogs, Edward and I were a man and woman who enjoyed being together, mutually satisfying our appetites and sharing stories. But the grand processions, the tournaments and jousts, the splendor and the sense of ancient rituals and noble blood surrounding

the Feast of St. George and the Order of the Garter, all this overwhelmed me with Edward's status as a divinely anointed king. I felt
small, common, naïve, alone.

He seemed beyond human as he rode at the head of the twenty-
six Garter knights, his white hair flowing beneath his crown. All were
dressed in the indigo-and-gold ceremonial robes of the Order of the
Garter, but his cloak was the most magnificent, lined in ermine. They
rode in solemn ceremony around the jousting field as family, fellow
knights, archbishops, bishops, retainers, clerks, and servants cheered.
The queen proudly stood in the center of the stands wearing a matching robe of indigo and gold, an honorary lady of the Order of the
Garter. Her surviving daughter, Isabella, and her sons' wives encircled
her, and the wives of the Garter knights stood behind the royal family. I was one of half a dozen of Philippa's ladies waiting in the shadow
of the stands, ready to come to her aid with cushions, lap robes, and
refreshments. The sound of the horns sent shivers down my spine, as
did the answering cheers. I was thrilled to witness such magnificence,
but felt no part of it.

Philippa and her daughters, by blood and marriage, impressed me
as much as the knights on their high-stepping steeds. They stood so
tall, looking so regal from head to toe. Just this morning sweet Blanche
had received devastating news of her dear sister Maud's death. Philippa,
Joan, Isabella, and Elizabeth, Countess of Ulster, had gathered round
the stricken lady to comfort her, sharing tears and memories, and then,
almost as one, had resolved to say nothing of the tragedy until the
close of the Garter festivities.

"Then we shall announce the sad news so that all may pray for
Maud's soul's salvation and mourn her." Queen Philippa promised requiem Masses throughout the realm.

Blanche agreed, ever anxious to bring ease to those around her,
particularly her mother-in-law, and understanding her role. Now as I
stood below, gazing up at her in the stands, I saw how pinched and
pale Blanche was, listless in her gestures, and how often she sank down
onto her seat even though all the others stood blocking her view of
her husband and his fellow knights of the Garter on the field. My heart
went out to her. I was not the only one who suffered in the strictures
of court life. But the royal family knew well how to hide their pain.

I remembered how I had thought them the stuff of legends, and felt
a fool to have imagined one of them might cherish me as his beloved.

Later that day I stole an hour from my duties to be with Geoffrey, who had arrived the previous day in the company of the Countess of Ulster.

"You shall be in Ireland soon," I said, thinking of William, "with your lord."

"Perhaps not. I think it more likely I shall remain here, with those who oversee Lionel's estates." He laughed at my expression of sympathy. "In truth, I am relieved. I am good friends with several of the king's knights-of-the-chamber and have hopes of joining His Grace's household as an esquire." He peered at me closely and added, "I hear say you might also exert some influence with the king? Is it true, Alice? Are you his mistress of the hawks and the bedchamber?"

I bowed my head, my dismay about my naïveté too fresh.

He put his hands on my shoulders and bent closer to see my expression. "You are not happy?"

Unable to escape his curious eyes, I lifted my head. He made a sympathetic sound and caught one of the tears rolling down my cheeks.

"I have been such a fool, Geoffrey. I have lost my honor to a man of whom I could never be worthy, yet I'd flattered myself that he loved me."

"What is this nonsense, Alice? The king must consider you worthy, for he chose you above all other women at court. Are you still thinking of Criseyde?"

"Yes. More than ever." I lifted a sleeve to show him—silk with pearls stitched to form a vine. Edward's pearls. "My magnificent robes."

"Hardly magical. But I do see, I do." To my surprise and comfort Geoffrey held me, silent for once. At least *he* still counted me a friend, and I loved him for it.

O N THE fourth day William approached as I walked in the garden with the de Roët sisters.

"Might we speak alone?"

I could not decipher his tone.

As ever giddy in the presence of a handsome knight, the girls urged me to attend him.

I noticed how travel-worn William looked as we searched for a quiet place in which to talk. We found a seat in a hedge that hid us from view. He studied my face as if learning my features by heart.

"You departed in such a temper," I said. "You left court?"

He grunted. "Riding until I could ride no longer. Drinking until

I could drink no more. Cursing the king. Cursing myself for waiting until we had known one another longer. Did you not understand that we pledged our troth, Alice? That you are my wife?"

"That is not true. I promised you nothing."

His jaw muscles revealed how he worked to control his emotion. "Do you not love me then, Alice?" His handsome face was clouded by indignation. He did not wait for my response. His hands tightened around mine. "Do you truly love him?"

"I do, William, beyond all other men."

His face twisted with emotion and he bowed his head for a moment, fighting for composure. Tension charged the air between us.

I tried to think of a way to end our confrontation but suddenly he straightened, his expression carefully neutral.

"He will tire of you. We've but to wait."

I might have laughed at his inept wooing were I not still aware of the tension with which he held himself. That is what the gallant William had resolved during his riding and drinking—that the king would tire of me. He expected me to be grateful that he meant to wait for me.

"Do not wait for me, William. I release you from that vow. My destiny is in the king's hands."

"I will have you, Alice. You are my wife."

He moved toward me as if to kiss me, but footsteps approaching halted him.

"I am *not* your wife, William," I said as quietly as my frustration permitted.

"I shall tell the king that we are betrothed, and that I will be waiting for you," he insisted.

"You must do nothing of the sort, William." He could not be such an innocent as to think that such a declaration would find favor with Edward. What was his game? Edward had said that if he tired of me, he would find me a husband. But I doubted he would share me with another before that. Nor would I want him to. "His Grace says he will not tire of me. He would not receive your words with pleasure, your implication that he will not be steadfast."

Shaking his head, William chuckled in the cold way of someone who thinks he has caught another out. "He is an old man desperate to grasp at youth, Alice. The first time he fails to complete the act, he will discard you to soothe his pride. But I'll say nothing. You must get a message to me at once when that day comes. You shall always know where I am."

"Do not wait for me, William. Marry another." And God help her.

We parted then. Pippa and Katherine asked so many questions I laughingly told them they made me dizzy, but in truth I was irritated by the exchange with William. He was an arrogant bully. I yearned for a husband—but the man I yearned for was not William but rather the impossible, Edward, free and asking me to wed him. Though I danced with William several times over the next few days—to refuse might have invited curiosity—we had little chance to talk and my feelings about him remained uneasy. He behaved as if he had claim to me, as if he had heard nothing I'd said.

But Edward, my home, my anchor, was soon of more concern to me than William. I began to notice much talk among the royal family of the king's decision to give his elder sons parts of his kingdom to govern. The women believed it to be a sign that, just as Philippa's mind was focused on her imminent death, so was Edward's, though he showed no outward sign of illness.

"Father is old," said his daughter Isabella one evening. "As with our mother, so with him. They are preparing to pass on."

The queen had retired for the evening and the women of her family, as well as many of those of us who waited on them, had lingered in the queen's great chamber, exhausted yet wakeful.

Princess Joan glanced at me with a teasing look and did not join in with the desultory comments about how seldom Edward had danced or how he'd required rest after participating in the tournament. I was deeply troubled by such talk. I had been so occupied with my duties for the queen and dread of William's possible retaliation that I had not noticed my love's condition.

When the others rose to retire for the evening, Joan stayed behind and motioned for me to do likewise.

"Isabella and Elizabeth seem to be unaware that the king lies with you," she said, laughing. "If they knew, surely one of them would have said something, or at least glanced your way."

"What of Blanche?"

Joan rose and warmed her hands over the brazier. "Blanche knows, I am certain, but does not care to think about it."

"My lady, why are you telling me this?"

"For friendship's sake, and do call me Joan when we are alone, Alice. We are friends, are we not?"

"I am honored to call you friend. And Joan."

"Good! It is not true, is it, that the king looks toward his death?"

"I have heard no such talk from him." I tried to speak with confidence, but something in my expression or posture betrayed my fear.

"You must practice to hide your feelings, Alice. The knives at court are sharp and seldom sheathed. Have a care."

"I am out of my depth, Joan."

She poured us both some wine and, sitting down beside me, put an arm round me in a brief hug. "I am fond of you, Alice, and so I wish to give you the advice that you need, not having had the advantage of being brought up in the court. The king has been indiscreet about you. How Isabella and Elizabeth have not heard of your relationship I cannot imagine, but I think soon most of them will know. And then they will envy you. Envy is an ugly emotion. It inspires cruelty. Meanness."

I crossed myself. "Sometimes I am so frightened, I cannot bear it."

"And more often you are delighted to bask in the glow of his love, are you not?"

I nodded, reluctantly. It was true.

"He is a wonderful man, beloved of his people—including most of the court. So is the queen. If aught goes wrong, you are one of the people who will be blamed. Because you have no connections. Because he loves you. And the king is impetuous. I do not say you are the only one they will blame. They will call down one of his sons as well—not my Edward, for he is a hero and the future king."

"What then must I do?"

"Revel in your love, but keep your eyes open. At all times remember who you are, where you are, who he is. Find and nurture a few trustworthy friends. But do not blindly trust them. Nor should you blindly trust the king. He is a man, as William Wyndsor is a man. Your William is angry, I noticed that. He may yet be your salvation if aught goes wrong, but if you wed him, try to keep some of your property secret. Just in case."

God forbid. I did not like her referring to *my* William, but Dame Agnes had often chided me for arguing with someone who was offering useful advice, so I did not contradict her.

"Is this how you live?" I asked.

She sipped her wine, staring out into the dark room. "Yes. I have always followed the love in my heart, but with my eyes wide open. My father, Edmund, was executed for his loyalty to his half brother, my Edward's grandfather. Executed by the lover of Isabella, my husband's grandmother. As a child I heard many refer to my father's shortcomings, especially his loyalty, as if he had been at fault and deserved to die. Most people live according to fear, not love. My father was fearless in his love for his brother. He was also a loving father, always had time for me. He remembered everything I told him." She was close to tears.

"You are safe now, as princess."

She shook her head. "No, Alice, I am not. My dear Edward is a child in some things and has a temper like your William. Like the king."

"He is not *my* William. I have made that clear to him."

Joan shrugged.

"You have given me much to think about," I said.

"Good. It is offered in love." She embraced me again, and then rose and swept from the room with a rustle of silk.

I remained in the chamber, staring at the brazier, thinking about all that Joan had said. The details were new, but not the warning. I had been naïve in praying that I might trust Edward—or anyone—completely. I resolved to follow Joan's guidance.

12

Tho gan she wondren moore than biforn
A thousand fold, and down hire eyghen caste;
For nevere, sith the tyme that she was born,
To knowe thyng desired she so faste . . .

—Geoffrey Chaucer, *Troilus and Criseyde*, II, 141–44

• 1362 •

AFTER THE guests departed we removed to Eltham, where the royal households could rest after the celebrations. On the day after we arrived, an Italian priest, Dom Francisco, arrived. Philippa had us dress her to receive him despite her obvious exhaustion from the journey and extreme pain—she was so unbalanced in her gait that we all feared she had exacerbated her old injury, for nothing now seemed to ease her discomfort and she struggled to straighten up. I shortened her hem in front and we moved her headdress a little farther back on her head to mask how far forward she pitched as she walked. Her dignity and gentle behavior while suffering such pain were an inspiration.

She and Edward were sequestered with Dom Francisco for the best part of the day, and afterward they assembled all the household who might be spared from their work to join them in prayer in the king's chapel. It seemed to be a requiem Mass for a man of the Church, but we were not told who. Edward knelt with head bowed, often covering his eyes with one hand. Philippa was her usual subdued, pious self at her devotions; she did not seem personally moved by the proceedings. Whoever had died, it was Edward who was in deep mourning. The priest alluded to the deceased being of royal blood. It caused quite a stir in both households, but that was nothing compared with my own churning thoughts. For, of course, I wondered whether it was Isabella's precious one who had died, the one for whom so many Perrers had died, someone in Italy, the person whom Edward had once invited to join his traveling party, the one rumored to have been his deposed father. If this were so, I might now at last be free to leave court.

Now that I no longer *wished* to leave court, to leave Edward.

I wished I might comfort him. I had never seen Edward in such distress. I was also desperate to ask him whether he might now reveal the great secret that had destroyed my wedded happiness. It would not bring back Janyn, but at least I might understand why he had died. As Edward passed me leaving the chapel, he noticed the swirl of seed pearls on my sleeve and lifted his head to give me a wan smile. I pressed my hands to my heart, and he did as well, though by then he was past me.

I was not summoned that evening, either by the king or the queen. I thought perhaps I had been mistaken, perhaps the news had nothing to do with my family. But Philippa and Edward must have known that I would wonder and might have afforded me the comfort of some word, some explanation. I slept badly, my dreams fevered and incomprehensible. I woke several times in the night with my heart thundering. At last I gave up the attempt to sleep and knelt beside the bed, trying to pray. But my mind only conjured nightmarish images of Janyn's bleeding body, his agony, his death.

In the morning I saw the king's favored chamber knights and servants in the yard, sumpters loading their packhorses, and several wagons already loaded. As we dressed Philippa she informed us that Edward was leaving for one of his hunting lodges. My fingers were clumsy over her buttons as tears welled in my eyes. I had hoped he might send for me, to allow me to console him—and perhaps to tell me who had died. His departure without a word cut me to the quick. I feared he was taking this opportunity to discard me. I had just resolved to work hard to keep Edward's love, and he had shut me out.

"He requires rest and prayer," said Philippa. "As do we all."

I require answers! I silently screamed. *For pity's sake, let me know all so that I might put this agony of wondering behind me.* But I said nothing, for I saw by the swelling of her face that the queen had taken extra physick during the night. Whatever she had heard had weakened her. Even so, she insisted on dressing and attending Mass. After a simple midday meal, Philippa told me to attend her as she went to speak once more with the Italian priest.

Perhaps at last I was to learn something. My legs shook so that I was grateful that two servants were assisting the queen in her halting progress to her parlor. I tried to distract myself from anxious fantasies by observing how her pale gray silk gown fitted her—badly. In less than a month she had lost weight and height. Yesterday's alteration in the hem of the gown had simply made it safer for her to walk.

The priest was already in the parlor, rising and bowing his respect as Philippa entered. He was slender and graceful, with pale eyes that looked almost milky in contrast to his dark brows and olive skin.

Philippa dismissed the servants who had assisted her. As soon as she introduced me to Dom Francisco, he turned those eerie eyes on me with a discomfiting intensity.

"Dame Alicia." He honored me with a slight inclination of his head. "His Grace the King has instructed me to tell you of my mission, particularly the history of the man whose death is the occasion of my journey."

The queen nodded her approval and settled back, a cup of wine in hand, as if for a long story.

I sat and shivered.

The queer story of a William of Wales being brought to King Edward twenty-four years earlier was now fleshed out. He had been the guardian of a child brought to an abbey outside Milan as an infant. A child who was to be hidden and protected—the son of Queen Isabella and her lover Roger Mortimer.

The precious one had been a child, not the deposed king. The illegitimate son of the queen and her lover. The Perrers had protected their knowledge of this child.

After Mortimer's capture and execution, Isabella had been kept in seclusion through her lying in and churching. This was no mere bastard, but the son of a former queen who could be used by barons or foreign powers to challenge the reigning king—or whom *she* might use. She had taken up arms against her husband; it was not inconceivable she would do so against her son for executing her lover, and threaten to replace him on the throne with her son by Roger Mortimer.

Tommasa's family arranged the baby's journey to Italy, and my mother-in-law was his wet nurse for the journey. Thereafter her family were couriers of messages and gifts between mother and son, and eventually my Janyn had become the primary courier.

"But my father-in-law swore he did not know whom they protected." I had not intended to speak.

Dom Francisco did not seem surprised by my outburst. "That is true. Master Martin had been told, and apparently chose to believe, his wife's journey concerned a family emergency." Janyn's sister, whom Tommasa had still been nursing, made the journey as well.

"You see the terrible secret they guarded," Philippa said to me, her eyes surprisingly entreating. "Lady Isabella rewarded them with property, coin, and patronage, grateful for their loving care and silence."

I doubted that Isabella had willingly given up her child. She had not been a woman to relinquish control of anything important to her. But both the priest and Philippa insisted that Isabella had never considered keeping the child in England. Perhaps it was one of the many things I would never truly understand regarding the royal family, that ready acceptance of their children being reared in the homes of others. I wondered whether they had any concept of how difficult I found my separation from Bella.

"Do you know what happened to my husband and his parents?" I asked when the priest seemed finished with his story. My voice was a mere whisper as I found it difficult to breathe. I feared to hear repeated what Edward had told me, but I also feared to learn that he had lied.

Dom Francisco's pale eyes seemed to be on me, but when Philippa subtly shook her head the priest shrugged and brought up his hands in apology. "I know only the part of the story that involves the abbey. I am sorry."

I did not believe him, but if the queen did not wish me to know more than that, I would waste my time and try her patience by asking any more.

"And now this child of Isabella is dead of a fever, and the secret is no longer dangerous," I said. *Too late. Five years too late.* I felt ill.

"Of course, you understand that you must never speak of this," said Philippa. "Except, perhaps someday, when she is old enough, you might explain to your daughter what a precious secret her father and his family guarded. But you will speak of this with no one else. One never knows how unscrupulous people might seek to use such information."

"I am ever your servant, Your Grace." I almost choked on the words.

The priest rose. "My mission is now complete. *Benedicite,* Your Grace. May God watch over you and all your family and household." He blessed her and then me. A servant showed him out.

The queen had not stirred. Servants entered and set out more wine and some fruit, cheese, and bread. I rose and stood for a while looking out of the small window, forcing myself to remain silent, to wait for the queen to speak. I prayed she would express remorse on the part of Isabella and Edward. My thoughts were wild, frantic. I wished I might rush to the stables. I yearned to ride hard, the wind in my hair, to scream my frustrated anger where it would harm no one. I might ride forever, a ride with no destination, for no one would be waiting for me at the end, no one expected me. No one. A sob escaped.

"Do not think that I am unaware of the pain this meeting has resurrected in you, Alice." The queen's voice pulled me back into the blue-and-gold parlor.

Slowly, focusing on recapturing my breath, I returned to my seat, accepting with gratitude a cup of wine offered by the servant. I took a long drink, trying to steady myself.

Philippa motioned for the servant to leave.

"Your plight touched me from the moment Lady Isabella asked me to bring you into my household. I blame her for your unhappiness. I harbored much anger toward her for the pain she brought to my husband and his family as well, and your situation gave me a cause to champion. But after hours of prayer and reflection I had to acknowledge my own role in this sad history. It was Edward and I who insisted the child be smuggled out of the country and hidden. We made the arrangements for it. And then, until he was brought to us on our journey to Rome, I forgot about him. Poor child, abandoned to utter strangers.

"My heart misgave me when I met him. I had just been delivered of my son Lionel. In that difficult time—when I missed carrying my child within, was easily brought to tears by anything, but particularly the thought of handing over my baby to a wet nurse—seeing Isabella's son at that moment, a boy of seven, a sweet, timid child, I silently prayed for forgiveness for my cruelty toward him and his mother. He spoke a little French, but mostly Italian, so I did not understand much of what he said, and he did not understand my speech at all. He was handsome, looked more like Isabella than any of her other children. I never spoke to her of the visit."

Philippa bowed her head.

I had initially hung mine and only half listened, but as the queen went on I found myself staring at her. She deserved contempt surely for such treatment of a child? But Isabella had done worse, much worse. My anger toward Philippa did not last. She was too ill, and in many ways too admirable for me to hate. Yet as I absorbed the sorry tale of adults fearing the power of a former queen's bastard son, and in their fear using my husband's family as their shields, I found little pity in my heart.

"How did Janyn and Tommasa die? Were they murdered when they would not betray their oath of secrecy?"

"Yes. Tommasa was forced to watch her son tortured and finally murdered. Her captors did not know of her weak heart. Their efforts to force her to speak killed her. Mercifully, I think."

I pressed my stomach, though it was my chest that felt as if it were being crushed.

"I see in your eyes why my husband did not wish to be the one to tell you this," said Philippa. "You condemn us."

I managed to halt an inner vision of Janyn's torture and Tommasa's torment long enough to speak. "I am no saint, Your Grace. I have lost so much. And why? Because the most powerful family in the kingdom feared a baby boy. A saint might see God's plan in this, but I cannot. My dear husband tortured. My gentle mother-in-law forced to watch. Would that Isabella's bastard had died years ago!"

I drank the rest of the wine and rose to pour more. Despite my anger, I served Philippa as well, with wine and food. It helped me to move, to keep my hands busy. Though she was queen and might consider that I was merely doing my duty, she thanked me, the expression on her face vulnerable and fond. Something in this exchange pulled me back from the brink of dangerous recklessness, and I remembered the deference due to the woman before me. No matter how responsible she was for my loss, I was her servant, I depended on her for almost everything, and she had been generous to me. And I was always uncomfortably aware of how, in the eyes of most people, I would be seen as the usurper of her marriage.

"Your Grace, I pray you, forgive my outburst. You have been good to me and my daughter. I am in your debt."

Her eyes held mine as she said, "You may have lost much, but consider what you have gained." She lifted her fingertips to her forehead in a gesture that signaled a headache, but instead of pleading illness, said, "Still, you deserve an apology. I pray that someday you may forgive us."

I dropped to my knees before her. She placed her hand on my head.

"Let there be peace between us." She urged me to take some refreshment. "I have a little more to say. Then you are free until morning." Her speech was halting. She needed to pause frequently for breath. Her physical collapse was making everything difficult for her, even breathing.

"Your Grace," I whispered, rising. I had no appetite, but busied myself quartering a blanched winter apple.

We sat in silence for a while, both of us pretending to eat but merely moving the food about in our bowls. The sound of Philippa's labored breathing inspired in me both shame and relief—shame for supplanting her in the marriage bed and relief to realize she could no longer find pleasure in lying with Edward. I found myself praying that the latter canceled out the former for her. But what if he no longer wanted me? What if, now that I might walk freely, the secret of the precious one no longer a threat to be used against the king, he felt relieved of his duty toward me? I'd be free, but heartbroken.

After a time, Philippa set aside her pretense of eating. "You have proved a skillful and clever sempster, concealing the collapse of my body and shielding me from humiliation. And you have proved a trustworthy and steadfast companion in a confusing and often difficult arrangement. Few could have done so much. As a token of my gratitude,

I would relieve you of unnecessary discomfort by speaking from my heart."

I found myself shivering as I listened to her halting speech. I could not imagine how she might relieve me of unnecessary discomfort. And what was the necessary discomfort? She had paused to sip some wine.

"Your Grace, you must not tire yourself."

She shook her head. "I will not do more than I wish to, Alice."

Though I knew I'd had sufficient wine, I poured a little more to keep myself busy.

"The love of husband and wife changes over time," Philippa re- sumed, "of necessity. You did not have sufficient time with Janyn to experience this." Her smile was sad and kindly. "The year before you were wed, I was delivered of my last child, Thomas. I prayed that he was my last because I thought I might go mad if I found myself again with child. So many months of discomfort, before and after. I selfishly prayed that God would stop my courses so that I might live out the rest of my days in a little more comfort." She crossed herself. "My womb could not complete the next child conceived, and I lost it. Then I fell. That part of my marriage was over. God often works in unsatisfying ways." A bitter laugh, then, "You are taking nothing away from me, Alice. He loves me in all the ways still possible."

She leaned her head back against the chair for a moment, her eyes closed. "To love a king, Alice, is to dance a dizzying dance, spinning toward him, spinning away." After a deep sigh, she said in a strained voice, "Now you must call the servants to assist me to my bedchamber, and you may take your ease until morning."

"Your Grace, thank you for allowing me to speak with Dom Fran- cisco, and—"

"Go now, Alice. We have said enough."

AS EVER when I did not know what to do with my racing mind and tumultuous emotions, I sought comfort in riding Melisende. Gwen insisted on accompanying me. We spent most of what was left of the afternoon on horseback. As I rode I opened my heart and soul to the emotions boiling in my stomach, permitting myself to feel my sorrow, the terror of Janyn's and Tommasa's last hours, and the fury that built within as I imagined all of this. I was furious with Isabella's and Edward's use of my family, furious with Edward for not having the courage to be there when I learned the truth, furious about his heartless retreat. Though Melisende was accustomed to carrying me as I wept or cried out to the wind, that day my emotions were wild enough to make her shy a few times, bringing me back to my senses. I would slow, compose myself, and reassure her. In such wise we rode through many cycles of both fury and calm.

When the groom insisted that my horse must rest we turned back toward the stables. Gwen and I walked then, through the gardens to the river, and at last I confided in my long-suffering friend all that the priest and Queen Philippa had told me. I felt the need to speak of it all just once, and knew that I could trust Gwen to remain silent. I had spent my anger for the moment. What I experienced as I spoke was a desperate yearning for a different truth, a different outcome. Had Isabella's bastard died earlier, my life might have been so sweet. But that child had grown to manhood, and my husband's family had suffered because of him. And now so did I and my precious Bella.

"At least now you know that Her Grace does not intend to throw you out," said Gwen.

"But I do not know Edward's heart." I had thought I did, and then he'd left without a word. "Though he left it to her to tell me, fearing I would despise them." A dizzying dance, Philippa had said.

O N THE following day I received a summons to Hertford Castle to spend a few days with my daughter. When I asked permission of Queen Philippa, she was bemused that I had not guessed at once she had been the one to suggest it.

"With Isabella's bastard dead, you are safe to visit your daughter. There is no longer any secret to protect. We have ensured the news has reached the right ears."

In my rush of joy I could think of nothing more eloquent to say than "God bless you, Your Grace."

She seemed to take pleasure in giving me even more good news, that Fair Meadow was being readied for me and any members of my birth family I cared to invite. It would take a month or so to prepare, and she and Joan had thought it a good idea for Bella and me to have a little time together at once. She would spare me for a few months in summer.

Queen Philippa leaned heavily on my arm as we entered the sunny antechamber in which the ladies had been picking at their needlework in silence in the hope they might overhear what we discussed behind the shut door.

"Mistress Alice will be leaving us for the summer to be with her family," she announced.

The headdresses shivered as the women glanced at one another, their expressions secret codes. They were bursting with curiosity about my private sessions with the queen the past few days. What to make of my spending the summer with my family? It could mean so many things! Either reward or punishment! And what had I done to deserve it? I sensed their minds spinning, and as I settled to my own needle-work I found myself breathing deeply as if I might thus calm us all.

When at last I returned to my chamber to prepare, I hugged Gwen and cried, "I am free, Gwen! Free to be with Bella, free to be with my family without putting them in danger. I will think only of that now, of this modicum of freedom." Not of my fear that Edward would forsake me.

Indeed, my heart was overflowing with joyful anticipation of seeing my precious daughter as we chose clothes for the journey. I fretted about not having time to make a pretty gown for her. Gwen calmly suggested that we take one of my old gowns and that the three of us might turn it into something for Bella while we were together. I said many prayers of thanks that night, quite a few of them for Gwen.

I remember nothing of the river journey except that the countryside seemed to me more beautiful than it had ever been, and it made me cry.

Bella was at an age in which even a few weeks could work great changes. As I approached the castle I feared I might not recognize her. But stepping into the garden where the children were at play, I knew her at once, for her curly dark hair and large eyes were those of her grandmother, Dame Tommasa. She was tall for her age, slender and graceful. She would be five years old in a matter of weeks, yet she seemed more mature to me, more reserved than Mary, Will, or I had been at that age.

Her wide brow crinkled in confusion when I rushed to her and crouched down.

"Mother," she said, with a little bow, then touched the pearls on my sleeves. "Nurse says we can be together again."

"That is so, sweet Bella."

Something shifted in her face and I realized she fought back tears. "My father called me Bella."

"He did, my love, and so did I. Do I."

"Her Grace told me that he is dead. And both my grandmothers."

The fear in her eyes told me more of the climate in the household than I would surely learn if I asked.

"Many more of your kin are alive and will be so very happy to see you this summer. Do you remember the pretty house where your father and I taught you to ride a pony?"

It took a little time for us to be at ease with each other, but then our days together were delightful. We made a pretty gown and head-dress, we planned parties and long rides in the country, and when it was time for me to depart, Bella clung to me and I to her. I swore to myself that I would move heaven and earth to ensure she did not return to Queen Joan's household.

I would be twenty that September, a mature age. I had been a mother for almost five years, a wife for almost six, two changes that had taken me from girlhood to womanhood. I had lived at court for over three years. Yet something innocent in me had remained—or, more accurately, I had clung to a naïveté I now understood I must shed, for my sake and for Bella's. It was time for me to act, to win my daughter back to me.

Janyn was still lost to me, but I felt as if I might find some happiness if I could be with Bella and my family now and then. I had lost so much—years of my precious daughter's life, years of joy with her father, years of my siblings' lives. I prayed that Edward might hold and cherish me for many years to come, for I needed his love now, more than ever, as I closed the door on the past and my former dreams.

III

THE KING'S
MISTRESS

13

"Allas," quod she, "what wordes may ye brynge?
What wol my deere herte seyn to me,
Which that I drede nevere mo to see?
Wol he han pleynte or teris er I wende?
I have ynough, if he therafter sende!"

—Criseyde to Pandarus, GEOFFREY CHAUCER,
Troilus and Criseyde, IV, 857–61

*I*HAD BEEN *holding my breath for two years, half believing Janyn
would reappear, fearing how Queen Philippa felt about my growing
love for her husband. I had found court overwhelming—so grand,
so complexly stratified. I'd found a modicum of steadiness in narrowing
my attention to caring for the queen's wardrobe, being the best companion
to her that I might be, and, of late, in loving my king.*

*I had thought that he might anchor me. But he was, in truth, more
my siren than my anchor. Philippa had said that to love a king was to
be caught up in a dance, toward Edward and away from him. I was
to learn that dance all too well—in one movement being pulled toward
him in heady surrender, in the next being sent spinning away in sad
solitude. I would know moments of exquisite joy and tenderness, feeling
that we shared one body, one heart, and I would know desolate stretches
of loneliness, emptiness, as he became a figure out of legend, unreachable,
untouchable, unfathomable. I must find my own balance in the momen-
tum of that dizzying shift.*

When had I a choice to be other than I was?

• 1362 •

ONE OF the first times I remember Father inviting me down to his undercroft was to meet a merchant from Ormuz who specialized in pearls. He had brought with him a small drill used to pierce them, promising to show Father how it was done, and Father, quite rightly, thought it something I would never forget. At first it was the merchant who fascinated me, so tanned by the sun that his skin looked like well-worn leather with wrinkles fanning out from the corners of his dark eyes into the folds of his white-and-silver turban. He had the whitest teeth I had ever seen, and showed them a lot as he grinned at me. His hands were of two shades, dark leather on top and what I thought of as "skin color" beneath. He wore many beautiful rings. When he moved he perfumed the air with anise and cinnamon and sandalwood. I wondered what it would be like to live in a land where all men smelled so sweet and dressed so richly.

When he picked up a pretty, not quite perfectly round pearl that shifted color as he moved it under the lamplight, I asked him what he had done to the little holes. For everyone knew that all pearls had little holes so that they could breathe underwater. At first his dark eyes grew wide, so wide that I could see that the whites of his eyes matched the brilliance of his teeth.

"So that the pearls might breathe?" he repeated, eyes widening even more. Then his entire face creased and he threw back his head to laugh, a deep-throated, anise-scented laugh.

And his turban did not fall off.

"Alice, who told you such a tale of pearls?" Father asked, clearly embarrassed.

"I thought that it must be so."

The merchant—I do not recall his name—asked me if I had ever seen an oyster. He drew a misshapen gray shell from his pack. Cupping his dark, beringed hands around it, he told me to examine it closely. Bringing his hands nearer to the lamp, he opened them, the shell falling open as well, and in each palm appeared a vessel lined with pearl, as if many pearls had melted and flowed over its rough surface, blanketing it with beauty.

I timidly touched a fingertip to it, expecting it to be frozen like ice around a branch. But it was merely cool. And solid.

"It is called mother-of-pearl," said Father.

The merchant told me that the oyster produced fluid to line its shell. "For comfort!" he said. "Is that not a miracle?" And when a grain of sand or some other rough particle flowed inside, the oyster would cover it as well with the pearly fluid, until it was so smooth it no longer caused discomfort. "It is a gem to us, but a featherbed to the oyster. Or perhaps a featherbed covered in silk."

"Is this not clever?" Father asked me. "And now he will show us how he pierces this pearl."

The merchant brought out a very slender steel drill, driven by a lead wheel and belt, and held the pearl to it. It was simple to see how it worked, though I cringed to watch such a beautiful thing pierced, expecting disaster. But there was only a little dust. He widened the hole using wire and a little sand, and then slipped the pearl onto a silken string.

"God bless the oyster," I said. I do not remember saying that, but Father told the story over and over again. He said that neither he nor the merchant had the heart to complete my education by reminding me that the oyster would have been eaten.

EDWARD APPLAUDED my story of how I learned the true nature of a pearl. We were sitting in a pretty meadow, our horses tethered nearby, and he had just given me a most exquisite comb for my hair, bone overlaid with mother-of-pearl and several disks of lapis arrayed along it, as if it had been splashed by drops of a beautiful blue liquid. He had asked me to remove my headdress and, after showing the comb to me and watching me with pleasure as I ran my fingers over the pearl and lapis, had tucked it in my hair. It was such an intimate, tender gesture after my suffering so much fear that he had abandoned me, I felt my heart might burst.

We had been together at the hunting lodge for several days, and on each day he had given me pearls or items decorated with them. I had not lost my wits, I was well aware I was being bought, yet it was Edward's way and came from his heart. I chose to be grateful for such loving generosity. I understood that his leaving me at Eltham had been a foretaste of how our life would be. Of the dance.

"You are the pearl in my life, Alice, my comfort, my solace, a creature of beauty and light."

I fell into his arms, holding him as tight as I might. I had asked if we might talk at once of Dom Francisco's revelations regarding the great secret Janyn's family had protected. I did not wish to waste our precious days together cautiously circling the issue. Edward was blessedly willing to oblige me. It had been a difficult conversation, but I had prayed over it, and felt God's guidance in my impulse to be honest with Edward, to reveal to him the pain and confusion in my heart. He expressed remorse for all that I had lost for the sake of protecting his kingship but assured me that hiding the child had been the only solution, both for himself and the boy. A child of such lineage would never have been safe unless hidden as a peasant or in a closed community such as an abbey—a foreign abbey.

"Even so, your mother might have given up any contact with her child and spared my family the dangerous journeys," I said.

He nodded. "That was her choice. In all such things my mother thought of herself first, and only very much later, when she could no longer avoid it, acknowledged that others had been affected. She never asked forgiveness or expressed remorse."

"What was done then cannot be undone. For Bella and I to flourish, I must seek the light, not fester in darkness." The relief in Edward's eyes, the subtle relaxing of his body, was my reward for absolving him. I had entertained him then with a description of my happy reunion with my daughter, and expressed my joy in the prospect of being with her, my sister, and my grandparents at Fair Meadow in summer.

He listened quietly, contentedly, and then talked to me of his own children, his plans for his three eldest sons, giving them pieces of his kingdom to keep them busy and content.

"Though I fear my Philippa means to leave this life soon, I have no such intention. Edward is distracted by Joan at the moment, but will soon grow impatient for my crown. He is for the Aquitaine. Lionel to Ireland goes." He believed they would find their new responsibilities challenging. John would soon be invested as Duke of Lancaster; he would be an important power in the North. "I shall then have more time to rest. I should like time to be quiet, to be with you, to talk of small, everyday things."

I, too, wished for more time with Edward. Away from court, alone with him, and no longer afraid of betraying Philippa, I had fallen deeply in love. As I opened my heart to him, he responded by confiding in me and becoming more curious about my dreams, my preferences. Our bond deepened and strengthened.

We spent most of our time in the bedchamber he had ordered the servants to decorate for me. It was filled with silk-covered cushions in jeweled colors, the bed hung with indigo curtains embroidered with silver thread, the ceiling painted like the night sky, with a gorgeous silvery moon, and the walls hung with tapestries depicting the goddess Diana hunting with a bow. We spent many happy hours in that room, making love, talking, playing chess, spinning out dreams of our life together.

When we were not in my chamber, we were riding out in the countryside. On one particularly warm evening, I sighed as we returned to the lodge. "It seems a pity to go within." While I bathed away the dust of the long ride, Edward ordered a tent erected on the lawns. What a wonder it was for me, who had grown up in the city, to sleep outside that night and wake to the birdsong and the dewy morning chill. I did not want that interlude with him to end.

But of course it did. One morning I woke to the sounds of the household preparing to move. Edward had already told me that he would not intrude on my time with my family at Fair Meadow. I looked round my beautiful chamber—already every item evoked a happy memory.

As Gwen saw to the packing, Edward took me out into the garden, where he presented me with a signet ring. The intaglio was an amethyst with the Virgin and child cut into it, symbolizing me and my daughter, and in the surrounding gold were the initials *A* and *E* intertwined.

He put it on my finger and kissed my hand. His eyes held mine as he said, "Within is a charm to keep you safe. Write to me if you have need. All my people will know that a letter with this seal comes straight to me." His seal, a crown twined with woodbine and our initials, would be for his messages to me.

"I should write if I am in trouble?" I asked. "Not simply to remind you of me?"

"My love, I need no reminding. I think of you with every breath." He kissed my hands. "Write only if you have need of me or require counsel. I am determined that we shall not feed the gossips. I trust you to know when you need to write. And I shall reply as quickly as I may."

The ring, the arrangements, all this felt more substantial, more secure, than what had gone before. I was content, yet careful, still taking the precaution of Joan's preventive drink, for I did not intend to jeopardize my position in the queen's household.

. . .

M Y GRANDPARENTS, Dame Agnes and Master Edmund, had arranged for household servants and ensured that my home was readied for occupancy. Fair Meadow. As we approached the manor, memories of Janyn filled my mind. I had expected my former joy would haunt me on my return. But when it overwhelmed me as I rode through a village that had always served as my landmark for being almost home, I discovered that I was not as well prepared as I had hoped. My grief was an ache deep within despite my love for Edward and my renewed joy in life.

That ache would always be there; it was part of me. My heart could hold both joy and grief.

The air was sweet and sighed across the peaceful fields of Fair Meadow. As I dismounted in the house yard, Bella rushed out of the door and I crouched down just in time to catch her in my open arms. Already she smelled of sun and earth, herbs and flowers and horses. I was strengthened in my resolve to win her away from Queen Joan's emotionally barren household. Here she could be a proper child. She would know love, and she would love. We would be a full and happy household—my grandparents, Mary, Nan, Bella, and me.

Hands that know the earth in all its moods know God's wisdom. Grandmother's wisdom was healing to me now. With my beloved Bella and Mary, I planted flowers, especially roses that Grandfather had brought from Dame Tommasa's courtyard. When the house had been vacant after Master Martin's death, my grandfather had slipped into the courtyard and taken clippings from various shrubs.

"I saved them for your homecoming, Alice." Grandfather stood over them with an air of uncertainty. He had led me away from the dinner table to show me. They were arranged in little pots along the windowsill of my bedchamber.

I was moved beyond words. Putting my arms around him, I kissed him on the cheek, then rested my head on his shoulder. "It is the best gift, Grandfather."

Bella slept with Nan in the same room as Gwen and me, and we were seldom apart. She had been timid after her first exuberant greeting. Hanging back, wary, uncertain of her place. On our first night together I woke in the darkness and found my child sitting up, biting her nails and breathing in frightened little gasps. I did not ask why, but simply gathered her in my arms and softly sang to her. Slowly her little body relaxed and soon she slept in my embrace. In the morning I said nothing of it. I asked if she would like to help me plant the roses. Working side by side in the gardens nurtured my daughter and me as much as it did the flowers and herbs we so happily tended.

It warmed my heart to see my sister Mary grown so beautiful and strong. She sometimes spoke of Father, remarried now and busy with an infant and a wife who was too pious to accept an invitation to visit his harlot daughter. Mary tried to soften all that she said of him, but it proved difficult.

"Let him be," I finally told her. "I have fond memories of him from before my betrothal."

Grandmother held herself slightly aloof from me. I sensed it the moment I embraced her. But she behaved with affection, and we worked in the garden side by side as well as measuring Bella for some new gowns. Together we chose pretty silks and wools for her out of chests of cloth that had been sent by Richard Lyons, merchandise he had saved from the Perrers household and my old home with Janyn.

It was an ill-timed comment on my part that at last revealed what Grandmother strove to conceal. Several of Janyn's former trading associates had appeared on our doorstep, saying that they were passing by and wished to pay their respects. On each occasion the talk eventually came round to their having heard of my "favor" in the royal household, and the fact that they hoped I might now support their petitions or recommend their wares and services to the royal purveyors. I endeavored to be gracious in my assurances that I had no such influence in the household, but that in the unlikely event that someone should ask for a recommendation, I would of course put forward my late husband's partners and guild members.

"They all know!" I cried one evening. "I've been such a fool to think my relationship with the king was known only at court. Who will ever believe that I was sent there, that I did not seek the king's favor?"

"What else did you expect when you took up your adulterous liaison with him, and you a lady of the queen's household?" Dame Agnes asked. Her tone was carefully lacking in condemnation but her words stung. She did not look at me.

I thanked God only Nan, Mary, and Grandmother were present. I shook with emotion—she had voiced my shame. I replied as calmly as I could manage, "I am sorry you disapprove of me. For my part, I had hoped that you would understand how little choice I had in this. I beg you, never speak of my relationship with the king to Bella or even allow her to overhear such talk."

I told myself that she would not judge me so harshly had she known the whole story of my need for the royal couple's protection. Nor did she know of the queen's complicity. But I wondered if that would have mattered to her. As she had judged the dowager queen, so she judged me.

"You cannot protect Bella from the gossip," she said, her eyes cold.

"Are you warning me that I cannot trust you?" I demanded.

We both stared at each other aghast, witnessing the pent-up pain between us. I saw in her eyes the horror I felt in my heart.

Mary stepped between us. "Stop this! We are together again at last, something we have all prayed for. Do not ruin it with angry words. You love each other. Alice had no choice in any of this. I beg you, both of you, remember your love for each other." She had caught the right hand of each of us and now brought them together.

Dame Agnes's mouth trembled. She was close to tears as she said, "Oh, Alice, I have been so frightened. You cannot imagine. With Janyn's disappearance, then Dame Tommasa's . . . The rumors of Master Martin's murder . . ."

So Geoffrey had not been the only one to hear of that, how healthy Master Martin had been shortly before his sudden mortal illness. I let go of her hand and put my arms round her. "I know, I know."

"Do you love him? Is he good to you?"

"Yes. I do love the king, and he is very good to me. I did not realize you had been forced to hear of this in public, to feel shame for our family, Dame Agnes. I am sorry."

We sank down on our knees and prayed for our family. Mary joined us there. We came to a kind of peace.

I used my signet to write to Edward, asking if Bella might now live with Dame Agnes or some other suitable merchant family in London. He wrote back giving me permission to allow her to remain with my grandmother until we might discuss it further in person.

Bella, Mary, Nan, and my grandparents rejoiced when I told them that, for the time being, Bella would abide with her family. It made my return to court easier for them, though not so much for me, for I would have her by my side. But the queen had summoned me, and I must obey. It was not only with Edward that I was set spinning in the dance.

. . .

L IFE BACK at court settled into a routine. I remained in daily attendance to the queen before and during feasts and celebrations,
primarily assisting her with dressing. When she had little need for me,
I was free to spend restorative weeks with my family or enchanted
weeks with Edward wherever he was abiding. Queen Philippa seldom
ventured from Windsor, for travel had become far too painful for her.
Edward bided at Windsor only for state occasions, celebrations, and
feast days.

When in November Edward celebrated his fiftieth birthday, I witnessed, as one of his queen's serving women, the investing of Lionel as
Duke of Clarence, John of Gaunt as Duke of Lancaster, and Edmund
as Earl of Cambridge. From the vantage point of Queen Philippa's entourage, I heard the barons and their ladies whispering among themselves about the king's intention to prepare his sons to rule after him.
Much was made of the wisdom of Prince Edward's yoking the Aquitaine with England in his future rule—he would be moving his household, including Princess Joan, to France in late spring. The honors of
the brothers so displayed during the birthday festivities inspired in the
people joyous hope in a glorious, strong future for the kingdom. Only
I did not like to think of that future.

Philippa worried that more than a few in the crowd prayed for Edward the father's swift departure to make way for the glorious Edward
the son.

"I wish my son was already across the Channel," she said, "else his
pride might become so exaggerated by the roars of the common folk
that he will be in danger of stumbling over it." She addressed the top
of my head as I made some last-minute tucks in her gown. "Would that
Lionel were the eldest. He is so much easier in himself."

Though she had a deep affection for all her children, Lionel was
her favorite of those surviving. She believed Edward to be too ambitious and too quick with his temper. "All refer to him as the noblest
of knights, but should not a great warrior take pride in self-control?"
John was too fond of bedding every woman who appealed to him.
Isabella, the eldest daughter, worried Philippa with her continual rejec-
tions of suitors. "If she were so inclined, I would think she intended
to withdraw to a nunnery and take vows. But Isabella is as committed
to the pleasures of the flesh as is her brother John." Philippa's children

were her anchor, as Bella was mine, and she seemed to enjoy sharing
with her ladies some of her concerns and dreams for them.

My conversations with Edward were even more personal, as well
as practical, like the conversations of a married couple. My earlier efforts to learn about the war with France and other matters of the
realm stood me in good stead as he confided in me now. I was honored to have his trust—Edward never expressed any reservation that
I might share what I learned in his household with the ladies of his
wife's household.

He sought my advice in his financial concerns, and in his dealings
with merchants and financiers. I sought his regarding my hawks, hounds,
and horses, for I saw how he enjoyed teaching me about such things.

I hesitated to consult with him about more serious matters such
as the appropriate etiquette regarding my ambiguous position in his
household. Such questions stoked his temper. Once, while we sat in the
hall at Sheen enjoying a light evening meal, I casually asked whether
he was aware that a guest who would be arriving on the morrow had
recently lost a number of teeth and could eat only soft food.

"You must consult with the cook."

"It is not my place to do so, Edward."

"What? Of course it is your place."

He ordered his page to fetch the cook, then declared to those
waiting on us, "Dame Alice is the mistress of my household away from
Windsor. You, and all my servants, shall defer to her."

There could be no argument. I knew full well it was not that simple. I saw their smirks as they watched the cook approach.

"Dame Alice," said Edward, nodding toward me.

The cook looked down at my hands, folded on the table before
me, then met my gaze with such animosity I blushed though I did not
flinch.

"Sir Rupert requires soft foods at present, broths, pottages, the
softest of breads," I said.

"Sir Rupert favors roasts with savory sauces."

"Minced meats, then."

Tight-jawed, he gave me a stiff nod—"Dame Alice"—then bowed
to his master. "I am yours to command, Your Grace."

The servants found subtle ways to insult me. I cultivated a compassionate but firm manner and offered my slights in reparation for my
sins. The higher-ranking officers and the nobles in Edward's household

treated me with respect, but encountered inexplicable delays in carrying out my wishes, for which Richard Stury was most often the apologist.

"I shall look into the matter, Dame Alice. God keep you for your patience."

At court I was far more confused regarding my place. The machinations of court still confused me, and I suspected that they always would, for I was kept at one remove as an unofficial, politely overlooked, member of the king's household in all events away from Windsor, and at Windsor was merely a lady in waiting to the queen. In Edward's household and my own I was "Dame Alice"; in Philippa's, "Mistress Alice." I'm certain I was not the only one who found my status bewildering.

Edward's most helpful and insistent advice to me concerned the importance of developing strong friendships at court.

"You cannot thrive without allies among my courtiers, Alice. Find a few men powerful enough to come to your aid should you have need of them." To aid me and, as I saw with Philippa, to keep me informed about the king.

I realized this was how Jean Froissart, a fawning Fleming, had bought his way into the household in the past year. He had presented Philippa with a history of her husband's earlier victories, and she saw his future usefulness. He had now become a fixture at court, Philippa's eyes and ears, though in private she complained of his overweening pride.

I was grateful that Geoffrey and I were much together of late, as he had been left in England to serve as a clerk overseeing the Duke of Clarence's properties near London, and was also working increasingly in the Duke of Lancaster's household, as Gaunt administered his now extensive properties. Geoffrey was always a reliable source of news.

My other good friend at court was William Wykeham, a cleric who had so impressed Edward in matters of building and the organization of large projects that he was being given more and more responsibility. Geoffrey admired him as well, which further recommended him to me. I had spoken to Wykeham on several occasions and discovered we shared common interests in decoration and the art of balance and proportion. He had taught me that what I had thought purely a visual art was grounded in mathematics. He seemed to enjoy providing me with examples that proved his point.

Now that I had possession of my homes, I took an active interest in managing them—indeed, I took my responsibility as a landholder very seriously, finding it the ballast I needed. It gave me a sense of purpose.

Wykeham proved most helpful in advising me about the improvements
I wished to make on the house and barns at Fair Meadow to the extent
that he even rode out there with me on several occasions to advise
me. I enjoyed his company. He would apologize for his extended dis-
courses on various aspects of construction and repair, and then laugh
with delight when I plied him with further questions.

"But I applaud your eager curiosity, Dame Alice. Too few land-
holders take such an interest."

On one of our excursions he had witnessed my difficulties with
Peter, the steward at Fair Meadow who had been chosen by Grandfather. Peter would shake his head at me, arguing that he had "never
known it to be done that way, Mistress" when I suggested an improvement, and continue to plod along in the old way.

"His duties have moved beyond his depth of competence, Dame
Alice," Wykeham said. "I have had reason of late to employ a man,
formerly a steward on Queen Joan's estates, who is wasted on my small
projects. He would be excellent for your purposes, one who would
blossom as your properties expand." He knew of my resolve to provide
for my daughter and myself through incomes from rents and crops,
and of my interest in new methods of husbandry. I had recently acquired another small manor north of London.

"I agree with you about Peter's limitations, Master William, but as
he is a worthy man, a good, honest worker, I must needs find a steward
who would put him at his ease in a secondary position. It takes a diplomatic character to achieve that, and it must be handled well by the
new steward as well as myself."

"Robert Broun is such a man," said Wykeham. "But do not take
my word for it. I shall bring him along on my next visit, and you may
decide for yourself."

They arrived at Fair Meadow on a sunny late-summer day that had
begun quite chilly but was warming under the cloudless sky. Peter and
I had been arguing about my adding a second groom to the staff. For
weeks I had noticed a boy hanging around the stables when he was not
needed in the kitchen. Seeing how well the animals responded to him,
I told the groom to train him when the lad was finished with his other
chores. Soon he proved himself indispensable. But Peter complained
that there was not enough work for two grooms, and that he did not
have the time to see to the training of the lad.

Wykeham rode up as I was pacing the yard, pondering how to deal with Peter. The stranger with him sat at ease on his horse, obviously enjoying the conversation and the journey. He was fair haired and tanned, a man who had spent most of the summer out of doors. When Wykeham introduced him, Robert Broun's ready smile and specific compliments on what he had seen of the manor so far won my approval. I thought to test him out right away, explaining the disagreement over the groom.

"No doubt he is a one-manor man," said Robert. "As you've recently added a second manor, he is resisting out of fear that he cannot cope with the added responsibility."

I offered Robert the position of steward over all my properties if he managed to make such an arrangement enticing to Peter. Within hours the usually morose Peter was showing him around the property with a beaming, relaxed countenance. I was indeed indebted to Wykeham.

One courtier I counted no ally continued to pursue me from afar, by way of occasional letters. I scraped the parchments, once read, and used them for accounts. I did not trust William Wyndsor.

IN AUTUMN Edward experienced his first attack of gout. His physician Master Adam had consulted several colleagues before making his recommendations. Edward was advised to ride, hunt, and walk more, and drink and eat less. The physicians assured him that gout was nothing his subjects need be concerned about, being a disease responsive to the prescribed changes in diet and activity. But Edward took it as a portent of old age, and was of two minds about what he must do whenever it returned. When determined to lighten his girth and live a long and active life he would keep me close to him, showering me with gowns and jewels, and making love to me as if to prove he could still do it. In truth, there were times when he could not, and those times seemed to be when he had imbibed more than usual.

As was the case that autumn. We had taken advantage of a crisp, sunny morning to ride out with the hawks. Afterward, the hunting party lingered over a considerable feast, then an excellent brandywine. When our guests withdrew, Edward grew amorous. We took turns undressing each other, amid much laughter as the drink had rendered our fingers too thick for the buttons and our balance unsteady, but at last we tumbled into bed, kissing and tickling and rolling all about. Just as we'd both grown quiet, and I'd begun to mount him, Edward moaned and turned away from me.

"What is it, my beloved? Are you in pain?"

"I am unmanned," he growled. "God curses me."

Sobered by his abject tone, I put aside my disappointment. "It is nothing, my love. I, too, am dizzy with wine, and content to snuggle up to your broad, warm back to sleep it off."

Later that night, when I discovered him sitting by the brazier staring at his hands, veined and wrinkled, the knuckles knotted, I swore to him that my love for him was not dependent on bed sport.

But he was of another mind. "I have offended God with my adulterous liaison with you and neglect of my lawful wife." In the morning he sent me away, then hied to Windsor to spend time with Philippa.

So began a recurring dance.

I was frightened by Edward's pain, physical and spiritual. I tried not to feel wounded by his inconstancy, but to understand it.

I threw myself into managing my properties, the one area in which I had some control and skill, and making a home for Bella. With some thought to enrolling her in a small grammar school in our parish in London, where she would become acquainted with other merchant families, I began to ready Janyn's, now my, house in London for longer occupancy.

But no matter how hard I worked, I could not completely forget my anxiety; for I saw these as no ordinary separations but signs of Edward's doubt about keeping me.

When the queen summoned me to work on her gowns for the Christmas court, she noticed my troubled state and gently counseled me to bide my time.

"It is a bit of temper at his own aging body, Alice, nothing more. Be patient."

Patience. Obedience. I tried to calm my mind with prayer and work, and when away from court spent as much time as possible with my family. Bella eased my heart. Dame Agnes and I grew closer again, and my sister Mary and brother John became my favorite companions.

• Winter 1364 •

IN EARLY winter Father surprised us all by announcing his intention to betroth Mary to a member of his guild who had lost his wife the previous year and had three small children in need of a mother. I hated the thought of losing my sister's companionship. Mary, sweet, obedient Mary, was quite obviously unhappy, and yet assumed she must comply. She had met Thomas Lovekin on several occasions and considered him a doddering old man. His children were ten, eleven, and twelve, not so needy as Father claimed.

"But what recourse have I? Had you any choice, Alice?"

Avoiding that painful topic, I reminded her that the Church insisted on both parties freely agreeing to pledge their troth. "Remember that when you are introduced to him after Sunday Mass. Say nothing implying agreement until you know that you might find him acceptable."

Memories of my own presentation at Mass assailed me as Agnes, Gwen, and I worked on Mary's new robe for her appearance. It was a joy to work on clothes for her. With her pale red hair, she looked best in Mother's old favorite colors, light blues and greens. We chose a tabby-woven plaid cloth in shades of green for the overdress, and a fancifully dagged short cape in pale blue to match her eyes. With these she wore a green headdress adorned with a spray of seed pearls and silver embroidery. The embroidery looked so beautiful that we added an echo of it to the cape. She was a vision of beauty in that attire. But so young! Younger than I had been when presented at Sunday Mass.

God was watching over Mary. This Thomas turned out to be the nephew of the man she remembered, only in his early thirties and quite pleasant and presentable. His children were two, four, and five. Mary's heart went out to them. In a few weeks she was betrothed, the wedding to take place in early May, after I returned from Windsor and the annual Garter festivities.

God watched over me as well. As Edward's gouty discomfort lessened, he welcomed me back into his heart and bed with all the warmth that had been lacking during that dark autumn and winter. *Deo gratias.*

A YEAR WENT by most peacefully but for an unwelcome change in Edward's attitude toward my financial independence. Suddenly he sought to control my business activities in subtle ways. One evening during one of my sojourns at Eltham he sent for me after I had retired for the night. I found him pacing in agitation—hardly in an amorous mood.

"I understand that Richard Lyons continues his interest in your business," he began, holding up his hand to forestall my response. "His role as executor of your late husband's estate has surely long been resolved."

"Yes, but I have retained him as my adviser. I do not understand why you have taken an interest in this, my love. And why address it now? Did Richard offend you today?" He had been among the guests at dinner.

"I take an interest in all that concerns you. I know he also tried to interfere when John Mereworth enfeoffed his manor of West Peckham to you and Dom Hanneye. He forgets his place."

It had been an honor I had insisted on accepting, the trust of the knight. Mereworth was an honorable man and had offered a substantial fee essentially for little more than my signature and that of Dom Hanneye. I had been flattered by his choosing me.

"Richard dislikes Sir John, but I prevailed, my love." Richard did occasionally overstep his bounds, often in a well-meaning but mistaken effort to protect me. But I held my ground when I knew I was right. This all seemed a trivial concern, but the time of night suggested that Edward did not consider it such, and that worried me.

"Lyons has petitioned the Pope to annul his marriage. A dishonorable act. I do not like you associating with him."

I was taken aback. This was news to me. But it hardly seemed worthy of the king's notice. Indeed, I wondered how Edward justified judging Richard when he was unfaithful to his own marriage contract. "He has been a good friend and I rely on his advice. We might not always agree, but I learn from our arguments."

Edward remained adamant. I said no more, hoping that it would be forgotten.

A few days later, having returned to London, I was mortified to learn from Grandfather that Edward had issued an order that Richard Lyons should keep the peace with me, and not interfere with my going where I wished on the king's business and on my own. An official order, announced quite publicly and entered into the records, carrying the weight of law. Despite my sincere efforts to impress on Edward what a friend I considered Richard, I felt responsible for this very public embarrassment. I resented Edward's interference in the small part of my life over which I felt I had some control.

I expected to be shunned by all of London for the incident, which would surely inhibit my ability to trade. But I'd underestimated the cachet of my position as the king's mistress and business partner. The guildsmen, merchants, and lesser knights came courting me in even greater numbers. The only one avoiding me was Richard.

As time passed and I did not cross paths with him, I attended Mass in his parish, wishing to make peace. I approached him after the service. He was alone. His expression was guarded, of course.

I simply said, "Richard, I did not know that His Grace meant to issue that proclamation. I knew that he wished me to be free to act on my own account, but I did not know what he had in mind regarding you. I have always spoken of you to him as a trusted friend."

To my relief Richard's expression warmed as I spoke. He reached out, took my hands, and squeezed them. "I am glad to hear that. I could not think how I had offended you and why you had not come to me to discuss it."

I noticed many glancing our way, the wealthier merchants and their spouses, obviously expecting fireworks. They were disappointed.

"I would have come to you had I anticipated the king's action. You have been a good friend to me and my family over the years, Richard."

"I admit that at first I was outraged. It was no small thing to have King Edward attack my honor. But when my temper cooled I realized that I *had* overstepped my position on a few occasions. Thank you for coming to me, Alice. Let us begin anew as friends."

He invited me to attend a dinner for some visiting merchants in a few days, and I happily accepted.

I enjoyed being in London after my sister's marriage. Thomas welcomed me into their home, and I rejoiced to watch her blossom in her love of her husband and stepchildren, and to witness the excitement with which they all anticipated her first lying in. On a rare sunny morning in January she was delivered of a daughter, fair of face and of the gentlest disposition.

Only after Mary's churching did I permit myself to look inward at a fact I'd avoided. In truth, as I'd taken Joan's physick most faithfully, I'd clung to the reassurance that it had never failed her. But my courses had not come in two months and my nipples were suddenly so tender that I gently distracted Edward when he would suck on them to arouse me. Though I had refused to think about it while Mary needed me, I had been haunted by memories of feeling thus about Janyn's attentions when I'd carried Bella. I was not ill in the mornings, but was quite certain I was with child. The king's child.

I was terrified, and in my terror hesitated to tell Edward. I did not know how he might take the news. I feared that he might send me away. At court the accepted practice was to arrange for a hasty marriage for an unmarried woman of good family suddenly with child by a noble, so that their bastards could plausibly be considered legitimate—by all but the new husbands, who would have been financially encouraged to ease the conscience of the true father. I feared that Edward would so dispose of me.

Joan had warned me not to conceive, and I had done my best to prevent it. But my best had not been enough.

Gwen's tender ministrations suggested she knew my condition and was only awaiting my confidence to express her concern. Realizing that I was intensifying my fear by keeping it to myself, I wrote to Edward requesting a meeting. That same evening I told Dame Agnes and Gwen and watched fear bloom in their expressions. Grandmother held her neck, as if imagining a hanging. Gwen gave a little cry and clenched her hands tight until her knuckle bones were visible through the taut skin. Though she had seemed to suspect my condition, to have it confirmed was clearly a shock.

"But the physicks," she whispered. "They protected the princess. I prepared them just as I was taught."

I reached over to press Gwen's hand, reassuring her. "You are not at fault. They protected me for a long while. God must have a purpose in suddenly rendering them ineffective." I fought to retain my composure though inwardly I was as frightened as she.

Grandmother asked, "What will you do?"

"I have sent a message to His Grace requesting a meeting." *And I am praying, praying.*

"He won't come here?" Gwen exclaimed, glancing around as if seeing a hovel.

"I doubt that he would, Gwen, but if he should, I would be proud to welcome him into my fine home."

I spent the next few days endlessly pacing and praying.

Then Richard Stury appeared at my door like a harbinger of doom, glowering in his dark robes. Edward summoned me to Eltham. Stury would escort me. We would depart the following day. And then Stury was gone again, striding through the drifting snow. I was grateful to have so much to do to prepare for my departure that I could not waste time on further worry. Bella must be bundled up and delivered to her grandparents' house, my steward Robert Broun must be told of any business I had not had time to complete, Gwen must pack for us, the servants must be informed. I must go to Mary at her home and find an opportunity when her children were distracted to tell her my news, and that I would be away. I must rest a little.

But it was difficult to rest after my conversation with Mary.

"How will you explain a brother or sister to Bella?" she asked.

I did not know. That was another worry I was glad to have little time to fret about. But Mary pressed me to devise an explanation then and there.

"I cannot think of that now, Mary. I have all that I can possibly cope with preparing to tell His Grace. And Her Grace. What I might say to Bella I shall decide anon." Bella might have more than a puzzling sibling to cope with if things did not go well with Edward and Philippa.

I would surely be banned from the queen's household. How could I not? And then what would become of Bella and me?

"You are wealthy, Alice," Mary reminded me with a little laugh.

"But I am a woman alone."

She hugged me. "Forgive me. I see that you are frightened. I pray the king is worthy of your love and loyalty."

T HOUGH I dressed warmly for the journey in a squirrel-lined cloak, I thought I would freeze to death on the barge. Gwen covered me with a fur mantle and still I shivered. It was not merely the weather, of course. It was fear that chilled me to the bone. Edward and I had never discussed the possibility of a child. I did not know how much men knew about preventing conception, but thought they must be blissfully, willfully naïve else they would take more responsibility in sowing their seed. I had wept the previous night, remembering how different it had been when I knew that I was carrying Bella. Janyn's joy had buoyed me through all the long days when I ached and sickened. It had been a gladsome time, and after her birth I had yearned for another child. Now I dreaded what I might be commanded to do.

Snow softened the woodland and parks around Eltham. It was a beautiful palace, and I had experienced much joy there. But now I approached it as a place of judgment, the place in which I would learn my punishment. Richard Stury had not helped with his stern silence. As if he knew. But, of course, he could not.

Gwen and I were escorted to my usual chamber, already made comfortable with a glowing brazier, heavy tapestries to block out drafts, heated stones ready to wrap and place beneath our feet as we sat to drink hot spiced wine, eat fresh bread still warm from the oven and a stew that was fragrant and hot. It was a moment in which I gave thanks for being the mistress of a king. I took care over the amount of wine I consumed, needing my wits about me when summoned to Edward.

The summons came just as I was casting longing looks at the bed piled high with blankets and fur-lined counterpanes, yearning for a midafternoon nap, a few moments of unconsciousness. I was grateful my escort was a page, not Stury. A moment of grace. I had chosen one of Edward's favorite gowns, red brocade over an azure blue silk under-gown, and the braids of hair wound over my ears were held in place by a gold netting thick with seed pearls. I wore a pearl ring and earrings, and the largest of the pearls he had given me hung from a gold chain around my neck.

Edward had been out riding. His face was red from the cold and his eyes shining and clear. I could smell the fresh air on him as he crossed the room to me and lifted me up by the waist.

"My beloved Alice. Each time I see you, I think you more beautiful than you were before. How is this possible?" He kissed me and set me back on my feet. "I have ached for you for days. Tonight you shall stay with me."

He was my beloved, my dearest Edward, and he loved me. How could I doubt that he would want our child? That he would cherish our child? But he was king, and I was not his queen. Our child would be a bastard.

I forced gaiety. "And you look hale and hardy, my lord. You've been riding in the snow. I can smell the fresh, crisp air on your hair and your clothes." I lifted one of his hands and sniffed. "And your skin." I kissed his palm.

He brought the palm to my cheek, caressing it, and then lifted me, enfolding me in his embrace, warming me with a passionate kiss. He set me down with a laugh.

"You see my hunger! Come, let us catch our breath."

I felt hope kindled in my loins, cradling our child.

We settled by the fire. A servant poured wine, then withdrew. Edward's long white hair glowed brightly in the lamplight and firelight, but now his eyes were cautious.

"So, my beloved, what is so urgent you must see me betimes?"

I took a deep breath. I had decided to speak plainly, quickly, not create additional suspense.

"Edward, I am with child."

He made an odd sound, a little groan or sigh, so soft and fleeting that I was not even certain I'd heard it.

"How long?"

"A few months."

A long pause while he stared at the fire. I had to remind myself to breathe.

"Mine?"

The question startled me. "There is no doubt, Edward. My body belongs to you alone."

He reached out and took my hand for a moment, squeezing it, studying my face. His expression was one of sad affection. My heart raced.

"Who knows?"

"My maid, my sister, my grandmother."

He nodded. "I must think, Alice. I will send for you."

All warmth left me. I rose and withdrew from his chamber, amazed that my legs supported me. Gwen took one look at me and then undressed me and tucked me into bed with heated stones. I did not protest. I permitted myself a large cup of spiced wine and, against all hope, fell into a deep sleep.

"Dame Alice, you are dreaming." Gwen leaned over me. She held one of my hands to her heart. "Quickly, you must rise and dress. You are summoned."

"Is it morning?"

"Just after vespers. You have slept only a little while."

When I was shown into the room, Edward stood, hands on hips, legs spread wide, looking out of a casement window. A kingly stance.

"Your Grace," I said, kneeling to him.

He turned round. " 'Your Grace'? You are carrying my child, wonder of wonders, and you call me 'Your Grace'?" He crouched down to me, not an easy movement for him, and took my hands. "Rise, my beauty. I have a gift for you."

He presented me with a ruby brooch and ring, large stones resembling hearts surrounded with pearls, set in delicately filigreed silver leaves trailing tendrils. Ruby hearts caught in woodbine.

"I had kept it for the right moment, and this is unquestionably that moment."

I wept as he pinned the brooch to my gown and slipped the ring on my finger.

"They are so beautiful, Edward. Heart and woodbine."

"Yes—the blood of both of us will nurture this child, Alice. We are now bound as father and mother. Is that not the greatest of miracles?"

"Then you are glad of the child quickening in me?" I asked, searching his face. I saw only joy there, and love.

"Glad? I rejoice, Alice. Our love has been blessed. God has granted us grace. I am young again. Potent. How could I be anything but glad? I have felt of late your hesitation before lovemaking. I am relieved to know the cause."

So I had worried him. Perhaps that explained his behavior toward Richard Lyons.

We made slow, beautiful love that evening. Later, when I woke to find him stroking my belly and watching me, I sat up, wanting to talk. First he insisted on wrapping me in furs and showing me the snow without, falling softly on the woodland.

"Do you not love the silence of snow in the country?" he said. "Our child will spend all his or her childhood in the countryside. The city is no place for children."

I loved him so much at that moment I thought my heart might burst.

"I did not see the countryside until I was betrothed."

I turned to him and we were soon back in bed making love.

It was morning before I could finally ask him the question uppermost in my mind. "What of Her Grace? When she knows, and how can she not know, she will hardly wish me to remain in her household."

Edward surprised me by smiling and shaking his head. He was wrapped in a mantle of miniver, his flowing white hair and beard wild, his piercing blue eyes pale in his weather-roughened face. He looked as I imagined warlords of old, never happier than when riding to the hunt—or to war. He often spoke of past battles with a catch in his throat and fire in his eyes. He'd gained weight in the past year, an embarrassment to his pride—his favorite girdle had been lengthened by his tailor months earlier, a necessity that still chafed—but he was still a handsome and imposing figure. When he smiled and shook his head at me, I felt very young and not entirely comfortable about his bare foot exploring between my thighs as we sat in bed together.

"You are an innocent in matters of our kind, Alice. Do you think that Philippa was not prepared for this?"

"But I cannot think that any wife would wish to see another woman carrying her husband's child."

"That much is true. Until you are churched, it is best that you stay away from court."

Now that I was there, he wished for me to stay awhile. With the heavy snowfall making riding treacherous, Edward's physician Master Adam forbade me to ride. But my love ordered some garden paths cleared so that we might walk out together in the fresh air.

Another of the king's physicians, John Glaston, appeared at my chamber door on the morning of the day Edward was to entertain some courtiers and merchants at an elegant feast. He was a pleasant man, kind and reassuring. He glanced round the chamber, moving closer to the brazier apparently to see that it was sufficiently stoked. He considered the window, then turned to me. "I am at your service, Dame Alice." He gave me a courteous bow. "His Grace has told me how it fares with you, and has asked that I attend to any discomfort that requires a healer until a midwife is summoned."

"His Grace is most kind. I am quite well. But I shall not hesitate to send for you if I have need of your services."

"Be assured that you are free to withdraw from today's festivities at any time, and that your wine shall be sufficiently watered, your food not too highly seasoned. I shall see to it myself."

"I am most grateful," I murmured.

He bowed again and departed with quiet dignity, his dark gown whispering softly in the draft from the open door.

I was moved by Edward's thoughtful arrangements, though I faced the event with dread. Remembering my beloved's indiscretion regarding our liaison I could not but suppose he had shared the news of my being with child as well.

Indeed, Simon Langham, Bishop of Ely and Edward's new Lord Chancellor, was so attentive at the high table that I was certain he already knew of my condition. Fortunately, since his ascent to the post he had proved a good friend to me. He was a delightful man, a brilliant scholar, and at previous leisurely dinners in Edward's chambers we had found a bond in our love of poetry, music, and hawking. My fear that he would now be offended by my presence proved unfounded. It seemed his affection for Edward outweighed all else. He remained as courteous and kind as he had been from the start.

Also in attendance was a couple I knew only slightly, Sir Anthony de Lucy and his wife, who were also oddly attentive.

I half expected Edward to say something indiscreet, but to my great relief he did not. I had gradually learned to enjoy these small gatherings, watching Edward at ease among friends. But that evening, despite everyone's courtesy, I was painfully aware that I had no right by birth, marriage, or official position to be there among them. I withdrew as soon as I might with grace.

Hours later, already abed, I was awakened by a summons to the king's chamber. A servant took my hand to steady me as we stepped between sleeping men in the antechamber. Even the guards seemed subdued.

Edward apologized for waking me. He himself was already in a simple robe and barefoot, a sign that he had prepared for bed before deciding to send for me. He wrapped me in furs and drew me over to the fire, where he proffered me a jeweled mazer of spiced wine.

He settled in a cushioned chair so close to mine that our knees touched. Leaning toward me, his eyes loving and yet searching, he said, "Now tell me, what was amiss that you withdrew so early? Were you feeling unwell?"

Despite the furs I was shivering. "I am with child, my love, your child, yet I am not your wife. I feared their censure and your unease."

"Alice, my love, you must not be ashamed." He gave a great sigh and pulled me onto his lap. "You are precious to me. Both of you," he whispered into my hair.

I held his great lion-head in my hands and kissed him on the mouth. "You are precious to us."

He put his hands over mine. "You are cold." He reached for the furs and draped them round my shoulders again. "Perhaps Dom Hanneye will attend you as your confessor when you are in retreat for your lying in. Would you like that?"

My heart warmed to Edward's loving care. "I should like that very much. But what is this about retreat? I thought to be in London."

He shook his head. "No, Alice. I've told Simon Langham to look for an appropriate country house in which you shall retire away from court and any who might wish you harm or hope to gain my favor by seeking yours. You need your rest."

"Wish me harm?" I had feared the queen's reaction, but no other's.

"Do not worry. You are under my protection. Come." He led me back to the seat and settled himself opposite me once more. He took my hands. "You carry the child of the king, Alice. A bastard, yes, but a royal one."

"I had not thought . . ."

Edward's face crinkled in an affectionate smile. "I will let no harm come to you, my love. Neither of you."

I felt small, ignorant, and frightened. I had underestimated the significance of bearing the king's child. Suddenly I feared for it. Isabella had gone to great lengths to guard her bastard. People had died protecting the mere knowledge of his existence. I remembered how vulnerable I had felt when great with Bella, my clumsiness, my sudden exhaustion. I was glad that Simon Langham was preparing a sanctuary for me—for us. "Might my grandmother be with me for the birth?"

"Whoever you wish—within reason, of course. When Simon has found the house—somewhere in the fens, we thought, near Ely, where as bishop he has influence—then we shall know how large a party you might accommodate. Be at ease, my love. You are my treasure. I shall take good care of you. You shall be well guarded."

In the end, we spent the night together. But though he warmed my body, my heart was chilled by my new understanding. To bear the child of a king was no small, private matter.

14

Ago was every sorwe and every feere;
And bothe, ywys, they hadde, and so they wende,
As muche joie as herte may comprende.

—Geoffrey Chaucer, *Troilus and Criseyde*, III, 1685–87

• 1365 •

B ELLA, NAN, Dom Hanneye, and Gwen were with me in Southery from the beginning, and Mary would join us in September,
in time for my lying in. Dame Agnes had wished to come but
Grandfather had suffered a fall earlier in the year and injured his back
so severely he might not walk again; clearly her place was with him.
She had suggested that Bella remain with her to attend school, but I so
treasured, indeed hoarded, my time with my daughter that I arranged
for Dom Hanneye to tutor her while we were in the fens.

Nan seemed invigorated by the responsibility of taking Dame Agnes's place in overseeing the household when I was unwell. As I was
now twenty-two, by my reckoning Nan was sixty, yet she rose with the
dawn every morning to make certain that the servants stoked the fires
and that the cook had something warm and nourishing to coax my
appetite and Bella's. Gwen had not come to know her well until our
time at Southery, and now she observed Nan's shrewd handling of the
servants with admiration.

"Nothing is too small for her attention, and the servants have
learned that. They are so well behaved, I would swear they are not the
same staff as when we arrived."

The house had a solar above the hall, but as it was accessed by a
steep and narrow set of ladderlike steps too challenging in my condition, I hired a local carpenter to screen off a part of the hall for Gwen
and me. He proved gifted and enthusiastic, creating an intricately
carved set of screens depicting the seasons and wildfowl of the fens in
a band across the tops. Our makeshift chamber still left ample space for
activities and meals in the hall. Bella and Nan slept in one part of the
solar and Dom Hanneye in the other, with my steward, Robert Broun,
when he was at the manor.

Robert had become a welcome constant in my life, both steward
and friend, proving himself trustworthy over and over again. He carried himself with quiet ease and confidence, spoke with authority on
shepherding resources, and loved the countryside. He was wonderful
with Bella, often inviting her to accompany him on his rides about the
estates. His smile lit up a handsome face—blond, blue eyed, fair.

He spent most of his time on my other properties, seeing to projects, supervising servants, returning once a month to report to me.
Dom Hanneye and Richard Lyons also grew to respect his opinions

and often invited him to accompany them to properties on which we were considering transactions. I wanted to ensure that Bella and the child I carried would want for nothing. I would not simply depend on Edward to see to our child's future, remembering Princess Joan's warning that I would rue the day if I did so. I took her advice to heart, for I understood that she had thought long on the vagaries of love.

THE MANOR house stood on a low hill in the fens, rising just slightly above the water meadows, vast stretches of whispering reeds and grasses. The flatness felt strangely threatening to me. I felt too exposed and did not trust the earth when it would so suddenly give way to marsh. The light had a disquieting, shimmering quality, and water fowl dominated the sky with their wide-winged flight and lonely calls.

But Bella was fascinated by the unfamiliar landscape and drew me out until I grew accustomed to it. She was a constant joy to me, and expressed delight in the long stretch of uninterrupted time together. In observing her with her tutor—Dom Hanneye was proving quite able—and others, I grew to know my child better than I had since she was an infant, and cherished this chance of a new beginning. As to her reaction to the news of my carrying the king's child, she seemed to see nothing wrong in it. That both pleased and worried me. But Dom Hanneye assured me that she was a devout and moral child, simply confident that her mother was a good woman.

Was I a good woman? Dom Hanneye said that God knew I held myself as betrothed to the king, and therefore our union was blessed. God understood that what separated us was man-made and therefore not His law. I knew that my confessor was grasping at slippery arguments to reassure me and keep me from despair. As Edward's wife was yet alive, his argument did not hold. And I feared Queen Philippa's reaction to the news of my condition. Edward had assured me he would time his revelation for a moment when she was most likely to receive it with equanimity.

But on the long summer days with little to do I worried. I had come to love the queen, to look forward to the long hours we spent discussing fabrics, jewels, ribbons, leathers, buttons, veils, feathers. I missed her, how we would giggle like girls and dare each other to new heights of extravagance, gasping at our own daring, and when she was being fitted how we would make a great show of tilting our heads together to appraise the sempsters' results. I had been most fortunate in my mistress. The queen was a wise and pious woman, worthy of all the love her people held for her.

I was less sanguine regarding myself. I would be twenty-three years of age in September, when my child was due, and felt far less responsible for my life than I had imagined I would at that age. It was as if when I'd gone to court I'd tumbled back into late childhood. During my first pregnancy, I'd admitted to Dame Tommasa that what most frightened me was that I felt too young and inexperienced to be a good mother. She had assured me that as my child matured within, so would I mature, and when my child was ready, so would I be. *That is how we become wise, by living each day attending to the lessons God puts in our path.* How I missed Dame Tommasa's calm presence. Once again I was caught up in the fear that I did not have the wisdom to raise the child in my womb, this time because my child was of royal blood, or half-royal blood. Dom Hanneye's attempt to reassure me only raised further worries. He'd said that if the child was a boy, I would have little to do with his upbringing, and if the child was a girl, I might bring her up as I wished, that the king would hardly care about another girl. Either way, it sounded as if this child would bring me sorrow.

IN EARLY summer I was invited to Bishop Langham's residence near Ely—Edward would be there for a fortnight. He saw this as a lovers' tryst and insisted that we share a bedchamber.

Mostly we walked and talked and slept tangled in each other's arms. As we shared the large chamber with sergeants-at-arms and servants, who slept in an anteroom created by wooden screens, we did not indulge in lively lovemaking, although we managed a few stolen afternoons. The mere fact of my conceiving a child by him had cheered Edward and invigorated him.

On our last day together I dared to speak of my fears for the future.

"I do not wonder at your concern, sweet Alice. But Philippa's only comment on the news was to order me to see that you had the best care."

I admired the queen's mask of reserve, and ached to think on the feelings she so elegantly concealed. "Her Grace is most kind."

Edward patted my hand. "While the child is yet an infant, you will not be so much with the queen. You shall have a wet nurse, and any servants you require. When you are with the queen, you must have someone to care for the children in a home in Windsor. When you are with me at Sheen, Eltham, Havering, or beyond, likewise Bella and our child shall be near at hand so that you might see them often. Is that to your liking? You've only to ask for what you desire, Alice."

That you might be my husband, I thought. "Yes, my love." I rushed to cover my imagined complaint with the more practical, realistic plans he'd come to expect, for I was moved by his awareness of my concerns for my children. "I should like to make some extensive repairs to my house in London, and perhaps use some of the street property for shops and tenements to lease. To provide more for Bella's dowry."

He squeezed my hand. "That's my Alice."

The trouble was, I did not like all that he perceived in *his* Alice; I did not like the role of spy among my peers. He would name some merchants he wished me to approach when I returned to London, and asked about others with whom I'd dined in London or elsewhere since we had last had such an opportunity to talk. I took care to tell him all I knew of the former, all I had discerned about the latter, but I felt unclean. I prayed for God's guidance in learning to accept my situation. Edward had his reasons, and he was my lord as well as my lover. I must never forget that.

I was glad to return to Southery and retreat into my pleasant cocoon.

WHEN MARY arrived in September for my lying in, she was bursting with the news that Geoffrey was betrothed to a young lady who had been brought up in the queen's household, the daughter of a Flemish knight.

"How grand! Are you not happy for him, Alice?"

"Is it Philippa de Roët?"

Mary looked disappointed. "You already knew."

"No. But she is the only unwed young lady of Flemish descent in the queen's household at present."

"So what do you think? Is she beautiful?"

"She is lovely. High spirited." Not at all the sort I would have thought to Geoffrey's taste.

"They are whispering that the betrothal has already been consummated, and that she is with child."

I prayed that it was Geoffrey's, not the bastard of the Duke of Lancaster. There had previously been rumors of a liaison between Pippa and Lancaster. The news stirred up too many emotions in me, too mixed, and I asked Mary if we might speak of something else while I thought on this.

I prayed that they would be happy. Of course her connections and noble birth were just what his parents had always wished for him.

IN LATE September I was safely delivered of my first boy.

"A son." Tears filled Edward's blue eyes.

Tears. I had not expected them from him. He already had five living sons.

"Since I sent Edward, Lionel, John, and Edmund out into the world, I have keenly felt their absence. Thomas is eager to follow after them and I cannot hold him back much longer. Now I need not despair, for I have a new son to teach."

"He will be fair like you." I could see it already. Bella had looked darker, furrier. Just as beautiful but different. "Your joy is like a blessed balm to me, Edward."

He'd arrived but two days after our son's birth, descending upon me in my little bower like a god of old, large and bellowing and overwhelming. And then, with the utmost gentleness, he'd lifted our child in his large hands and whispered, "You are a miracle, my son."

I wept and laughed at the same time.

But it was plain that I would not long enjoy my son's company. His godfathers were to be the Duke of Lancaster and John Neville, so his name would be John after the duke. I was disappointed that Edward had ignored my suggestion that my brother John be our son's second godfather. My brother was a fine young man whose company I greatly enjoyed. He had matured into a steady, generous man, and I wished I might so have honored him. But Neville was a northern baron key to border defenses and I understood why Edward wished to honor him. I did have my way regarding his godmother, my sister Mary. But I knew that it was merely a courtesy. Our son would be fostered in a home appropriate to a king's son, and neither Mary nor I would exert much influence in his life. And yet, how could I regret that his father loved him so?

MY FIRST communication from Queen Philippa after John's birth was a summons to the Christmas court at Kenilworth, the palace of the Duke and Duchess of Lancaster. Queen Philippa wished to make the journey for once. Whenever my lady Blanche spoke of Kenilworth, her voice rang with happy memories and her eyes shone. But for my dread of the queen's anger and the pain of leaving John with the wet nurse, I would have been excited about being included.

I escorted my household from Southery to London before I continued on to Windsor and then Kenilworth. I wished I might stay with Dame Agnes, to comfort her, for Grandfather had died shortly after John's birth. But she would find consolation in the presence of her grandchildren. They would soften her grief.

Geoffrey and Pippa were in London, staying with his parents. I paid them a visit before I left for Windsor. The Chaucer home had always been one of my favorite places, pretty and warm and always slightly crowded at meals; Geoffrey's parents both enjoyed a hall filled with people who loved to talk, eat, and drink—his father was a wine merchant, after all. I looked forward to seeing them and divining how my friend fared.

"How goes your little one?" Geoffrey asked.

"John is not so even-tempered as Bella was, but he has captured my heart. And Bella's. She is a loving sister."

"I've heard that the king is most pleased with you. It was clever of you to bear him a son."

"Clever? Is that your word or the gossips'?"

"The gossips', of course. Do you think me such a fool as to believe you could arrange the sex of your child? I presume you are going to the Christmas court?"

"I am."

"Then I feel it my duty as your good friend to warn you to be wary of those who compliment you and seek your advice or support. They see you as their way to the king. He has not kept his promise to you to be more discreet about your relationship and your son." Geoffrey looked most uncomfortable to be telling me this.

I gave him an affectionate hug. "Be at ease, my friend. I already know."

"It is not merely your son. The wording of Richard Lyons's public humiliation was such that all now see you as a business partner to the royal family."

I frowned. "I thank you for the warning." If one could be thankful for troubling news. But I *had* asked him to be my ears.

"How fare you with Lyons?" Geoffrey asked.

"He knows that it was not my doing, that I still value his friendship.

Indeed, I have retained him as an adviser. But I pray you, what do you hear of Her Grace, how she received the news of my son?"

"You dread the reunion with your mistress?"

"I've worn out my paternoster beads praying for peace between us. What hear you?"

Geoffrey shrugged. "Nothing. She is silent on the matter."

I crossed myself.

As Pippa had joined us, I said, "But let us speak of happier tidings. How do you fare with the child?"

She touched her belly and made a face both happy and rueful. "I did not expect to feel so crowded already!"

"That is nothing compared to how you will soon feel."

We spoke of children and of setting up households, a pleasant exchange.

I regretted that I could not stay longer in London. I wished I might crawl back into the womb of Southery, the gentle summer spent wrapped in dreams of my child. But I could no longer delay my reunion with the queen.

THOUGH MY heart had been heavy as I rode from London to Windsor, once I passed through the gate my mood lifted, for it felt a homecoming. I stepped lightly behind the page who led Gwen and me to our familiar chamber, and began to relax as I warmed my hands and feet by the brazier and quenched my thirst with watered wine, eyeing the soft bed. Gwen was warming stones for my feet when a page arrived to escort me to the queen's chamber. My momentary cheer dissolved. It was not like Philippa to rush a weary traveler. I whispered Hail Marys while Gwen dressed me.

"You are so slender, one might forget you'd given birth less than three months ago," she murmured.

"Her Grace will not forget."

To reach Philippa's chamber I must needs pass among the ladies gathered in her antechamber. They greeted me with a variety of nods, bobs, knowing glances, smirks, and wishes for my good health. I was shivering by the time I stepped through the doorway and bowed to my mistress.

"Stand up straight, Alice, let me see you," Philippa commanded as she motioned for the page to withdraw and close the door behind him.

"Turn." She grunted with satisfaction. "You look well. Good. We have much to do."

I turned back to face her, saddened to witness the ravishes of the past half year. Her face, neck, and hands were flushed and swollen, her breathing labored. As she rose from her chair her limbs tangled in the voluminous folds of silk and I rushed forward to assist her servant in supporting her. My face was but inches from Philippa's as she straightened. I witnessed the play of emotions—fear, self-loathing, and then, registering my nearness, regal reserve.

"Your Grace, I am your faithful servant," I murmured. When I felt her gain her balance I stepped aside.

"You see the enormity of the task before you," the queen said flatly.

I hesitated to respond, uncertain what to say, unable to divine her mood.

She lifted a fold of shimmering silk. "The sempsters believe that I am so exalted my feet need not touch the earth. Only you know to hem my gowns." Her face softened into a teasing smile.

God is merciful, I thought as I breathed out. "I shall see to it at once, Your Grace."

"Tomorrow is soon enough, dear Alice." She held out her hand, and I knelt to kiss it.

And so I resumed my role in the queen's household. Philippa's hunched and twisted frame was now impossible to disguise, and Edward's choice of a falconry theme had resulted in gowns layered with feathers that quivered with her intermittent tremors and emphasized her short and wide physique. She looked like a frightened chick, not a queen. I spoke privately with Edward—*you are tall and long of limb, your posture still wonderfully straight, but Her Grace . . .*—and received his permission to render Philippa's emblems of falconry in embroidery and gemstones in colors that imitated those of the raptors' feathers. The drape of her garments was also increasingly important, and the sempsters had cut everything too straight as well as too long.

I worried that the journey to Warwickshire might prove too much for her. When we reached our first night's resting place her face was pinched and her breathing shallow. She offered up her pain in expiation for the sins of loved ones who had died. By the time we arrived at the beautiful palace of Kenilworth Her Grace was in such distress that it was several days before she appeared in public, and even then she was brought to the great hall in a litter and stayed only a short while. My fussing with the drape of her garments proved unnecessary.

In the grace of design and the richness of the furnishings, the palace of Kenilworth outshone any of the grand royal homes save Windsor. And the light! The amount afforded by the long window embrasures in the great hall, even in the depth of winter, astounded me by day. At night a multitude of torches, candles, and lamps pushed back the darkness. The colorful clothes and jewels of the courtiers were dazzling in the brightness, creating a swirling forest of enchantment.

The queen's inactivity allowed me freedom to move about the festivities and enjoy myself more than I had anticipated. My own falconry motif was a feathery headdress that I'd sprinkled with pearls, and a trim of feathers on the dagged edge of a short green cape I wore over either a deep gold or pale green–and–gold brocade gown. Along the spines of the feathers we had attached small pearls and I'd sprinkled pearls all over the bodices of my gowns.

Our hosts, the Duke and Duchess of Lancaster, had greeted me with warmth and presented me with gifts for John and Bella. I had not expected to be welcomed for my own sake, but to be an inconspicuous part of the queen's train. My lady Blanche was kind, sharing her most recent experiences of childbearing and asking after my comfort. Never once did she allude to my child being the king's. My lord John, on the other hand, teased me about being related in some vague degree to the royal family and assured me that young John would be knighted in due course. I should be happy for my son, but with every honor afforded him by the Plantagenets, Edward's family, I felt more anguish that he was one step closer to a foster home where I would never see him. He would be trained and educated to rise far above me.

Yet as I looked round the hall at the sumptuous dress, the proudly scarred men who had fought in France and elsewhere for their king, the elegant women who bore their children and held the families together when their husbands were away, and most of all John's half-brothers and -sister and his father the king, I knew I could never justify keeping him from this destiny to which he had been born, even had I such power. My son was a Plantagenet, though Edward had chosen to have him known as John de Southery. I set my mind to be happy for him.

Geoffrey had been right—as John's mother I no longer had the invisibility I'd enjoyed at such feasts in the past. I was cajoled into dancing when I preferred to sit in the shadows and observe, I was invited to walk out in the air with ladies who had ignored me before. But I was not free to be with Edward, and my heart sank each time I caught sight of him dancing with some beautiful young woman who glowed in the splendor of his smile.

Perhaps it was fortunate that so many courtiers suddenly sought my advice and partnership in business deals, shipping, and land appropriations, for the distraction permitted me to move through the festivities with grace and prevented such a buildup of jealousy as to ruin my next interlude with Edward. I had been taken aback by my possessiveness regarding him; bearing his child had changed our relationship in unexpected ways.

Over the course of the next year, as my son John grew fat and mischievous, I found myself surrounded by courtly suitors—suing for money, not love. Sir Anthony de Lucy, for example, wished to offer me the use of and income from his manor of Radstone for life in exchange for a sum that would outfit his kinsman to make his mark in battle on the Continent. Such deals would have been abhorrent to my father, who looked for solid value in ships and merchandise, but the queen herself recommended that I judiciously choose a few such offers.

"In such wise you create a bond with courtiers who might prove of use to you at some future date. It is how it is done."

Of all the people who suddenly befriended me, the most surprising was Richard Stury, Edward's grim retainer. At first I felt his compliments and small kindnesses, such as a seat closer to a brazier at feasts and information as to the arrivals of friends, were simply by order of his master. But one afternoon he asked if he might discuss a matter of some delicacy with me. I had grown accustomed to his new attempts at smiles, but the deference he showed me in seeing to my comfort and the true delicacy of the situation he revealed to me—a family disagreement over a trust—bespoke a fresh attitude toward me. He was asking for my advice, and I took care over my opinion. He queried me on several points, and then expressed his gratitude.

"I see why His Grace trusts you to go about his business," he said. "You can see the straight path through what appear to be twisting and devious laws and customs, and you have a clear head about you. I am most grateful for your counsel."

"And I am grateful to you for all that you do for me."

I felt as I had as Janyn's wife and Father's daughter when they conferred with me concerning their trade. It was a good feeling, giving me a sense of purpose.

But I learned to be wary of such feelings, particularly when with Edward. He was too quick to act on comments I had meant merely as idle conversation, often in unexpected and unwanted ways. A case in point: I was deeply moved by Geoffrey's grief over his father's death. As soon as I mentioned my friend's mourning to Edward, he decided then and there to offer Geoffrey a commission by which to test whether he would be a useful addition to his household. It had not been my intention to ask Edward to retain him. I was often uneasy with his quick generosity, for I heard the courtiers whispering of how it stemmed from my greed. In this instance it was one of Geoffrey's fellows who congratulated him for childhood friends adept at teasing fortunes out of fond grandfathers.

I thanked God they would never dare say such things in Edward's hearing.

When Edward was ailing he increasingly showered me with gifts beyond the ubiquitous pearls. He presented me with a life grant of two tuns of Gascon wine for my service to Queen Philippa, a most gracious gift that would appear in the household records. He wished to document my devoted service to Her Grace.

More personal was his gift of a magnificent brown-and-white palfrey named Nightingale. "It has long been my wish that you ride with no reminder of my mother's shadow on your heart," he said with such caring in his eyes that I was choked with emotion.

I'd had no idea that he remembered whence came my beloved Melisende. I loved her too well to ever resent whence she came to me. But I had noticed of late how easily she tired, and knew that it was time to allow her to run free in the fields at my country home, where she would be well cared for.

On another occasion he presented me with several falcons and a falconer for Fair Meadow.

"Or the manor of Radstone," he said with a slight, smug smile.

I could hide nothing from him. This was a new game in our relationship that I found discomfiting.

"You know of Sir Anthony's offer?" I forced myself to say it with indifference.

"You are padding your nest well, Alice. Ardington—that is another property at which you might abide from time to time."

"Do you have people watching what I do when not in your company? Do you not trust me? I know that I am offered these properties only for your sake, though I tell myself I am the protectress of widows and orphans."

He chucked me under the chin as if I were an infant, a gesture I disliked. "To demonstrate my love for you, I have recommended your friend Geoffrey Chaucer for a mission that I would not usually entrust to someone untried in my household. But, in truth, you are not the only one with high regard for him. Both Lionel and John have been most satisfied with his service."

As Edward described to me the mission on which he was sending Geoffrey, my heart sank. He was entrusted with bringing back from Navarre English soldiers who had hired out to the wrong side in a dispute between the rightful king of Castile and his half brother. It was a delicate and dangerous mission.

I felt sorry for Pippa.

And for myself. It seemed to me that with every gift from Edward my ears burned hotter with gossip.

DESPITE MY embarrassment and my lingering unease about the subtle changes in Edward's behavior, for a time my life fell into a rhythm that I found comforting. In most ways he and I grew closer as we watched our son develop—John often accompanied me on visits to his father, and Bella as well, for her half brother was most docile in her company.

My role in Philippa's household had also eased once more into affectionate friendship. We were so accustomed by now to each other's preferences and dislikes that we needed little discussion, simply reached for the items that would best suit both of us and smiled in agreement. It had become our custom to design a beautiful litter that complemented her robes, and as her physical stature diminished we added more gold, more sparkling gems, anything that would catch the light and pick out the queen as a glowing presence in a crowded hall. Her appetite for beauty never diminished.

Nor did Edward's appetite for extravagance. Fortunately he was aging with far more grace than his wife. His height rendered his spreading middle insignificant, and glorious robes of cloth of gold with bright, intricate embroidery; cloaks with ermine or miniver linings; and hats sporting ships at full sail or life-sized hawks all simply added to his regal image. With his flowing white hair, white beard, and sharp blue eyes, his was a long-legged form that strode, never merely walked, into a hall.

But the heady days of our love were past. Perhaps Janyn and I would have grown to be more friends than lovers, given time, though I doubt it would have worried me, for we would have been legally bound.

IN THE spring of my John's second year I saw William Wyndsor for the first time in four years or more. He was soon to take up positions as constable of Carlisle Castle and sheriff of Cumberland, and while still in the south of England came to me at Fair Meadow. He was as handsome as ever and made a point of being charming, but I trusted him no more than before. Since his letters to me went unanswered, I did not understand why he still pursued me.

He was biding near the manor, not with me, but even so I made certain that Robert Broun remained on the estate while William was in the area, and included him in the company whenever William supped with us. To be fair, he treated me with respect and made himself useful, offering counsel regarding a border issue with a neighbor and advising me on several projects. Following his advice, I was able to resolve the long-simmering unpleasantness with my neighbor, and for that I was grateful. He was also kind to Bella—when he noticed her. It was plain he'd had little experience with children and often launched into inappropriately bawdy or violent tales in her presence.

But every time he looked at me in that way of his, I grew uneasy. He had been in the area for a week when I received the queen's summons to Windsor to prepare for the Feast of St. George. It was a week earlier than I'd expected, but Philippa often stirred herself up to a pitch that required action long before it was necessary. It was a chilly late-March day. The spring thaw had begun, rendering the countryside muddy and unpleasantly damp, but I did not permit such conditions to trap me indoors when I was away from court. I was glad that Bella had declined the invitation to come with me when suddenly the clouds burst open, drenching me as I rode hard looking for shelter. I found an abandoned shed, and with my horse tethered in one half of the low-slung interior, I took a seat on what had probably been a sleeping platform to wait out the storm. I was considering how I might start a fire for warmth when I heard someone ride up.

William appeared, leading his horse. As he tethered it next to mine, he said, "It was unwise for you to ride out alone."

"Apparently what I thought a solitary ride was not." I did not like that he'd followed me. I did not like it at all. "I needed quiet to plan, for I depart in the morning. I am summoned to Windsor betimes."

"I saw the messenger." He sat down on the platform and suddenly drew me into his arms, kissing my forehead, trying to reach my lips.

"Stop this!" I tried to twist out of his grasp.

But he held me firmly against him. "Come north with me. Let us live openly as husband and wife."

"William, I am not your wife, nor will I ever be."

He kissed me hard enough that his tongue found entry as I gasped and pushed at him.

He laughed. "How do I compare to that wizened, scarred, dithering old man you sleep with? You are young and beautiful, Alice. You deserve pleasure." He pressed me to the platform and fumbled with the bodice of my gown.

I managed to kick him and roll away. "What has possessed you?"

But he was suddenly alert, listening. He held up his hand to quiet me. I heard it as well—a horseman.

A man shouted our names. It was Robert Broun, coming into sight as he called. And right behind him, Richard Stury. My heart pounded.

Stury bowed to us both from horseback. "When I arrived your steward was about to come in search of you with a dry cloak, Dame Alice." He turned to William. "The Duke of Lancaster would meet with you before you ride north. I am to escort you to him. He is near. If we leave as soon as you've gathered your belongings, we will reach there before nightfall." He did not look either of us in the eye.

Nor did Robert. When we arrived at the manor house, Gwen took one look at me and hurried me to my room.

"Nothing happened, Gwen," I said when we were quite alone.

She looked me up and down. "Your buttons, your hat and hair." She shook her head.

"I know. I fear that Edward, were he to hear of this, might not believe my protest of innocence." I fought tears of rage. "That man is poison to me! His impudence could ruin me, destroy what is left of my family and my honor." I sank down on the bed. "I pray that Richard Stury is discreet. It is no accident we've both been summoned this day. How did they know?"

"Are you thinking Sir William intended to be caught?"

We looked at each other askance.

I felt as if a noose had tightened round my neck. When we returned to the hall, Stury and William were gone and Robert had disappeared. I cried myself to sleep that night. I wept for the memory of my early days with Edward that William's passion had stirred. I cursed him.

But I also feared what he was about, praying I was wrong in suspecting that there was a connection between William's dogged persistence and his being Lancaster's man. If his pursuit had been encouraged by the duke, this day might have far more dangerous repercussions for my family than a simple case of a man who could not accept rejection in love.

BACK AT court neither Philippa nor Edward mentioned the incident with William, a silence that I found more frightening by the day. I was relieved to hear from Geoffrey that William had taken up his duties in the north, but the damage had been done. I devoted myself to Edward and Philippa, but though I had learned to ignore the subtle inquiries and insults from the queen's other ladies, my own sense of guilt now taunted me. The whispers and furtive glances worried me far more than they had before, and I had no confidant to tell me what they actually knew.

But nothing happened, and after a few months I began to breathe more freely. Edward and I grew ever closer, despite the waning of our lovemaking. At last he appeared to understand that I loved being with him, no matter what we were doing.

On fair days I would wake him at dawn for hawking or riding—hot spiced wine or a thick ale at the ready, to tempt him from bed. In his fur-lined robe, fur-lined boots, and hat, he would soon warm with the walk to the stables or mews. Our horses and birds were our most trusted friends. We both felt free when riding, our laughter ringing out as we shouted challenges to each other. With our falcons on our arms we enjoyed companionable silences, heads moving in unison to watch our soaring birds, the bells on their jesses a comfortably familiar music. Afterward we often slept awhile or lingered over a light meal, reminiscing about past adventures. These were our happiest times.

Edward often asked to hear of my day-to-day activities when away from him, imagining another life through hearing of my property management, the children, the comings and goings of London merchants—a life free from the cares of ruling a realm. I understood that he cherished me in part because I brought him news from elsewhere, a life he could never experience.

We slept together more regularly than when our love had been more passionate. Even on the nights when he did not wish to make love to me, he insisted that I lie with him, naked and perfumed.

"I need you more than ever, my love. I need to wake to your scent, to feel your warmth beside me."

His need both reassured and worried me. And as trouble darkened his mood, I had the old sense of silken bonds tightening about me.

THE ENSUING few years proved to be a most difficult time for the king, a period of great loss and of grieving. My role was to be his shelter from the storm.

The first family disaster involved Prince Edward, who made an ill-advised promise to support Pedro of Castile in his battle against his half brother Enrique of Trastámara for the crown of Castile. Although Prince Edward won the battle of Najera, the men of Aquitaine who had fought for him could not be paid, for it turned out that Pedro could not hope to raise the sum he owed. Worse, illness swept through the camp, and many died; Prince Edward contracted the illness, and while still very ill was carried by litter in the company of his surviving troops back over the Pyrenees.

The effect that this had on my Edward frightened me. He was furious with the prince, but also in anguish over reports of his heir's weakened condition and the growing alienation of the Gascon lords. Queen Philippa's usual calming influence did little to soothe him.

I tried to understand the significance. "How does this increase the threat from France?" I asked one evening, when instead of eating his supper he was pacing the chamber bemoaning the situation.

"The prince has bled his subjects in the Aquitaine to pay for this war, but the expected replenishment from Pedro is not forthcoming. Now King Charles can bribe them to his service, leaving my ailing son, Joan, and their young sons betrayed and defenseless. I cannot leave them there . . . and yet to call them home will be to give up the Aquitaine, and thus my foothold in France. My son has ruined me! He chose to play the hero when as a ruler he should have been prudent and wise."

Duke John returned with descriptions of his brother's frailty that sent me to the chapel to pray for Prince Edward, Joan, and their sons, Edward and Richard.

My elderly, ailing love began to talk of leading an army into France to reclaim the Aquitaine. I prayed that something might happen to distract him. I listened, I comforted, I prayed. Perhaps I was too successful as his confidante and shield, for Edward insisted on my presence more than seemed wise to me, demanding that I be present at official meetings with his barons or when he presided in the courts. I felt I did not belong in such places. Indeed, Geoffrey reported that I was ever more on the gossips' tongues, not only at court but elsewhere.

For a little while Edward's spirits were revived by the prospect of the coming marriage of his son Lionel, Duke of Clarence, to Violante Visconti, the fabulously wealthy and reportedly beautiful daughter of Galeazzo Visconti, Lord of Pavia. They were to be wed in Milan.

But within a year Edward was in mourning for both Blanche of Lancaster, his beloved daughter-in-law, and his son Lionel, both of them succumbing to illnesses in their prime.

"Are we cursed?" Edward would often rise with that question on his lips in the middle of the night. I would comfort him, pouring him wine, rubbing his temples. Sometimes we made love. Sometimes he found comfort in just holding me.

Once, in one of his darkest moments, he asked me how William Wyndsor made love to me. Asked it bitterly, as if he had been suffering while imagining it.

"He has never made love to me, Edward. I would not have him."

"Not that day in the storm?"

My breath caught in my throat. "No. He had caressed me and expressed his desire, but I refused him. That is what happened."

It was the only time Edward had mentioned that day more than a year past, and it chilled me. Not that he had heard of the incident, but that he had nursed the knowledge deep within where it had festered until it burst from him in a moment of great pain.

"Who told you about that day?" I asked. "Richard Stury? Or William's lord, your son John?"

Edward would not say. He took me roughly that night, as if taking his vengeance by forcing his seed into me. It was not an act of love. I could not sleep afterward, sick with the bestiality of the act. When Edward woke from a slumber later in the night, he said, "John told me.

He warned me to keep William away from you. And I will, Alice, I will. He shall not have you."

"You do not need to be rough to claim me, my lord."

"My love, forgive me." He reached for me, but I moved away. "I love you beyond all reason, Alice," he said. "I was jealous. Jealous and afraid that you yearned for a younger man. My love, let me make this up to you. I swear to you that I will never touch you in such wise again. Only lovingly. Only lovingly."

I curled up in his arms and wept bounteous tears—for my shame, for my fear, for the twilight days of our love, for the sad truths revealed in his apology.

A few months later I knew I was again with child. I prayed for a daughter. John was now three, and Edward often talked of placing him in one of the Percy households. I prayed for a daughter, who might not be taken away from me.

But even with the joy of being with child, I was frightened. As his sorrows pulled Edward down into grief he grew less decisive, more open to the influence of others. Many openly resented me. Geoffrey told me of rumors that I influenced the king in judgments about my friends, that I dipped into his coffers to buy and lease my property. Until now I had been confident that if Edward tired of me, I could retreat with my children to my properties without much ado. But now I saw how vulnerable I was, realizing that my enemies might hate me enough to wish to ruin me rather than allow me simply to disappear. I had no power, not even a man to stand behind me if Edward should send me away, or, even worse, when he died. And my fear of John of Gaunt grew—I could not fathom what game he played, pushing William Wyndsor at me, then telling Edward. Was he trying to undermine his father's faith in me? I would fight him.

I loved Edward, wanted no one else, but I needed a champion. Yet having loved such men as Janyn and Edward, I could not imagine marrying someone simply for security, not after having tasted the exquisite joy of love.

William Wykeham continued to be one of my most trusted friends. He had risen from the post of Edward's secretary to become Bishop of Winchester and Lord Chancellor of England. I believed he was the person Edward most trusted and so sought his advice in all matters regarding the king, barring those too intimate to discuss. He agreed that I must protect my wealth in preparation for the day when either the king died or I lost favor.

"Never believe that you stand on solid ground at court, Alice. We are all at the edge of quicksand."

Even he, exalted to the position of Lord Chancellor, knew that his fortune could change at any moment, upon the king's whim. He believed that it was in my son John's best interest that he be fostered by the Percys. They were the most powerful family in the north of England, crucial to Edward for their protection of the northern marches, particularly against the Scots. John would enjoy the added protection of a bond with such a powerful clan.

"And for your daughter Isabella, a minor knight for a husband or a respectable nunnery. Either should be possible."

But what of a bastard daughter of the king or a second son? I did not tell Wykeham of the life quickening within me as we spoke.

Fear became my constant companion as I suffered a difficult pregnancy. Queen Philippa lay ill at Windsor and I prayed night and day that she would recover. I yearned to go to her, to cheer her with pretty baubles and shimmering cloth, to coax her back to health. But I was in my seventh month and would not flaunt my swelling womb in front of her—nor could I comfortably or safely travel. Edward did not ease my mind, threatening to take ship to Bordeaux and personally lead an army against King Charles of France.

I could not sleep for worry that the aging couple who held my life in their hands were slipping away from me. I obsessed over my fate if Edward should die in Gascony, or if Philippa should die and Edward remarry. Now it was I being comforted by the king, who knew only that I was beset by nightmares.

And then, even with his loving concern, I lost the child. A little son, stillborn a month before his time. Edward and I were both diminished in spirit by the loss. He held me and comforted me. He sent for my sister and my children. In this he knew me well, for all three served to remind me that I had much for which to be grateful.

"We shall have other children, my love," Edward whispered to me in the dark of the night.

He spoke no more of a French campaign in my presence.

ONE WARM but overcast day in July, Edward, Mary, and I were in the stables watching the antics of Bella and John with a litter of puppies. Mary and Edward hoped that it would cheer me. But though I loved my children, I saw in the puppies the promise of new life that I had been denied. It is a most terrible pain, losing a child one has grown to cherish in the womb.

Shouts in the yard drew our attention. Edward groaned as a messenger in the queen's livery approached, breathless and sweaty.

Despite his obvious exhaustion, the man dropped to one knee to deliver his message.

"Your Grace, you are summoned to Windsor with all haste." Queen Philippa lay mortally ill, and the physicians believed she had little time remaining.

Edward had clutched my hand as he listened to the messenger. Richard Stury, who had come rushing out of the palace upon the messenger's arrival, offered to assist him into the house and then make the preparations. Edward's ashen face and hollow eyes frightened me almost as much as the viselike grip that locked me to his side. I had never seen him so. I saw in this terror of his wife's imminent death that he loved her as deeply and completely as I had loved Janyn.

"My love, I shall come with you," I proclaimed.

He shook his head. "No. You are still unwell, Alice. I would not have you risk a journey so soon. You will be everything to me when Philippa . . ." He let go my hand and took me into his arms. "I must know that you are here waiting for me, safe and well."

It was true that I ailed in heart and body and soul, but I regretted that I could not be with the queen in her last days. I mourned for her almost as deeply as for my child. I had learned much about dignity and graciousness in her service. She had also instilled in me self-respect for my own talents. And I had loved her. As soon as Edward departed for Windsor, I withdrew to Fair Meadow and gave myself up to prayer for Philippa, that her passing might be peaceful and her eternal salvation be assured. She had been in pain for so many years, I imagined she was ready to die but for her concern for her husband and her children. Bella joined me in prayer.

As Edward later told me, when he arrived Philippa was anxious that he grant her three requests—that he pay all her debts, which were considerable; that he fulfill all her bequests and gifts to churches and all who had been in her service; and that he be buried beside her at Westminster, that he let no one coerce him into a burial elsewhere. He wept and promised her all that she asked.

He and his son Thomas of Woodstock were with her when she drew her last breath on the fifteenth of August, the Feast of the Assumption, in the forty-second year of Edward's reign.

Requiescat in pace, noble and beloved Queen.

THE QUEEN'S death frightened me. She had given her blessing to my liaison with her husband. If the king were now urged to remarry, I could not hope for such a sanguine arrangement with a new bride.

I wept for Edward, I wept for the realm in losing such a gracious queen, I wept for myself and the uncertainty I now faced. *Deus juva me.*

15

"*For wel thow woost, the name as yet of here
Among the peeple, as who seyth, halwed is;
For that man is unbore, I dar wel swere,
That evere wiste that she dide amys.*"

—Pandarus to Troilus, GEOFFREY CHAUCER,
Troilus and Criseyde, III, 267–70

• 1369 •

I COULD NOT imagine Windsor Castle without Queen Philippa's throaty laughter, her exclamations of delight when sorting through cloth and decorations for her gowns, her almost childlike eagerness as the time approached for a long-planned celebration. I could not imagine the Garter ceremony without her. Indeed, I could not envision how the court would function without Philippa ordering it. Princess Joan was still in the Aquitaine. Though Princess Isabella had returned to court after her husband de Coucy returned to France, in essence deserting her, I could not imagine her presiding over the court.

But more than all this, I feared that a part of Edward might have died with Philippa, and that he was now frighteningly vulnerable. I vowed to protect him, to envelop him in my sheltering love.

W HEN HE had realized that he would be at Windsor for a while, Edward had freed me to go to one of my homes as soon as I felt well enough. On my journey to Fair Meadow I witnessed how Queen Philippa's death had cast a pall over the entire kingdom. Even in the countryside I encountered tradesmen, the local parson, neighbors, my own tenants and servants, all mourning as if the queen had been their dearest friend.

On my occasional trips to London to tend to business, I found the sense of loss so palpable it was almost unbearable. In the churches the priests prayed for the king and all his family, enumerating the losses they had suffered in three years, the death of the queen being the culmination of a long, sorrowful time. I had not thought the common people knew of Prince Edward's illness, but they did, and all feared what would transpire on the death of the king. It seemed that the queen's passing had reminded the people of Edward's own mortality. They wondered how the prince could rule if he did not recover his full strength, but worried that if he died the kingdom would be ruled by a boy younger than the king had been when he ascended to the throne. Had Prince Edward no male heir, the Duke of Lancaster might have ruled. People were uncertain how they felt about him, but at least he was hale and hearty and mature. They counted it unfortunate that Edward and Joan had two sons, still but children, who stood before the adult Lancaster in the succession.

Geoffrey reported speculation about the king remarrying—his grandfather *had* married a second time. I tried not to think about it, arguing with myself that my beloved was too old, that he had sufficient sons. But in the dark hours I lay in bed feverishly planning what I must do to prepare myself for being abandoned, because simply to feel the pain of a possible parting was unbearable.

O N A blue-and-gold day in early autumn, as Bella and I were exploring the gardens at our manor of Ardington, enjoying the warm afternoon and visions of the beautiful garden we were planning, we heard several horsemen approaching the house. I expected no one, and except for Dom Hanneye and my steward, no one knew I was in Berkshire. No one *I* had told.

Anxious to see who had arrived, Bella rushed ahead. I watched her long-legged run, graceful and swift, her skirts held daringly high, and felt a glow of joy. Her beauty mirrored her gentle, loving nature. She was beloved by all, servants, friends, family. Edward said that Bella was the perfect name for her, for she was in all ways beautiful. I could not believe she was twelve years old. It seemed just yesterday that I had first held her in my arms and counted her fingers and toes.

She had reached the servant hastening to fetch me, then raced back to announce, "It is the Lord Chancellor himself, Mother! Himself!" Her dark eyes were wide in her flushed face. She did not ask, but I knew the question in her mind. *Trouble? Another death?*

I grabbed her hand and hurried back to the house with her.

William Wykeham stood quite still in the middle of the modest hall, his dark, serviceable traveling jacket, hose, and riding boots neither obviously those of a bishop nor a chancellor, but rich and well made, part of his heavy gold chain of office escaping from between his buttons beneath the dagged shoulder cape. He'd developed a more elegant style of late, a charming hint of the pride he felt in attaining such high offices in both the clerical and the secular worlds.

"*Benedicite,* Dame Alice, Mistress Isabella. I regret intruding on your peaceful afternoon." His smile was warm, genuine, and somewhat eased my worry about the cause of his visit.

Bella bowed to him. "*Benedicite,* my lord Bishop," she whispered.

I echoed her and added, "Welcome to Ardington. Would you care for some refreshment?"

"You are most kind. Wine is sufficient. I cannot linger." His smile had faded.

Bella slipped away to summon a servant.

Wykeham eased himself down on a chair by a small table and proceeded to remove his gloves with a meditative slowness, as if using the time in which to compose his thoughts. When he had at last set them on the table beside him, he took off his wide-brimmed hat and pushed back his hood, mopping his brow. But he did not remove the shoulder cape, indicating a brief visit indeed. I had seldom seen him look so ill at ease.

"You come on official business, then?" I asked. "Something that you find unpleasant?"

When he met my questioning gaze, he looked apologetic. "I am here to summon you to King's Langley. His Grace the King needs you."

"Now?" I had not expected to be summoned until after the queen's burial, which had been delayed until after Christmastide. "Surely not. It is not appropriate for his mistress to come to him in his mourning."

I could see by the conflict in his eyes that Wykeham agreed, but he said, "And yet it is just so. He is the king and he summons you." He paused to accept the mazer of wine proffered by a servant. "The Duke of Lancaster has also urged me to ensure that you are by the king's side. He wrote that His Grace is best with a woman's gentle guidance, and that at present you are that woman, Dame Alice. The king is at ease in your company, more . . . temperate." He paused to take a long drink.

"*At present* I am that woman." I took a deep breath. "Are there plans for the king to remarry?"

Wykeham grunted. "I pray you, forgive my choice of words. I have heard of no such scheme. It is my understanding that His Grace is content, and his sons see no need for . . . challengers."

"You will tell me if that changes?"

He bowed, hand to heart.

"God watches over me with your friendship, my lord." I put that worry aside . . . for the nonce. "Precisely *how* goes His Grace? What might I expect?"

"Much hawking, much riding, much drinking and gambling. As if he intends to outpace the sorrow that chases him. We pray that you help him embrace his grief."

I watched a bee explore the rim of my own cup, then fly away. I wished I might fly away as well. I had begun to look forward to a quiet autumn working on my properties, enjoying my children, caring for my aging grandmother. Yet I missed Edward. "Someone from the royal family might be more appropriate."

"With the Princess Joan in Gascony and Princess Isabella sulking I know not where, you do seem the obvious choice. You will remind him of happy days." His eyes implored me.

"Of course, I am my king's to command." I touched my heart and gave Wykeham a little bow. "Shall I—may I bring the children?"

"His Grace suggested that they might follow anon. For the moment, he wants only you." He set the mazer aside with a look of regret and rose with a sigh. Only then did I see how exhausted he was. "Richard Stury will come to escort you in two days. Where will you be?"

My possessions were scattered about. "Fair Meadow. My gowns are there. You might rest here awhile, my lord."

He picked up his gloves. "God bless you, I would if I were at liberty to do so. But I have others to see before nightfall."

He kissed my hand, blessed me, and was gone before I could ask how he proposed I help Edward "embrace his grief." I was familiar with the mood he described, and though I had usually been successful at dispelling it for a time, in the present circumstance I did not know what might comfort him.

Bella reappeared before I'd had time to consider how to tell her that I would be leaving again in a few days.

"Will you be going to the king?" she asked.

She took my breath away, my beautiful child, so canny, so quick, so accustomed to her mother being summoned by the royal family.

I bent down—when had she grown so tall I did not need to crouch?—and hugged her. "Yes, my beautiful Bella. I shall send for you as soon as His Grace permits."

"Sometimes I wish he would find a queen he liked as much as you," Bella whispered in my ear. "Then I could have you all to myself."

"Oh, Bella, has he not been good to us?"

"Not when he separates us."

I could not explain to her my need to be with him.

A S I stood in the hall at King's Langley, slaking my thirst with a mazer of watered wine before continuing up to my chamber to bathe away the dust of the road, I marveled at how long I had been with Edward. So long that I was at ease with ordering his household. I told a servant to remove the pack of hunting dogs snarling over a bone to the kennels.

"But His Grace brought them in, Dame Alice," said the young man.

They reminded me of the growing factions at court, snarling over favors, choice posts, hoping to procure as much as possible while Edward yet lived, worried about what changes Prince Edward might bring.

"Where is His Grace at present?" I asked.

"In the bathhouse."

He would be washing for me. Forgetting for a moment that lovemaking was not necessarily his intent, I smiled at the thought of him in the bath and was tempted to join him there. But I remembered myself, and my resolve to attempt propriety during this time of mourning so that no one might find cause to separate us.

"Tell the grooms to remove the dogs, and replace the rushes they fouled."

I waited until the servant bowed and moved off before I climbed to the solar. There I allowed Gwen to undress me, wipe away the dust of travel with damp cloths, and soothe me with fragrant oils. Then I slept for a while.

When I woke, Edward, in a thin linen night shift, nothing more, lay beside me, just watching me.

"I thought you would never wake," he whispered. He knelt and peeled back the covers, then entered me with such ease that I must have been dreaming of just this moment. "Would that my whole body might follow my cock and rest in your womb for all the remaining days and nights of this life," he moaned with pleasure.

I felt the rush of his seed flooding me, and then we collapsed together. Unlike our customary pattern—he would fall asleep and I would lie beside him, listening to his steady breathing—I slept as well, a deep, comforting sleep. When I woke I turned to him and caressed him until he was aroused, and then, though he was only half awake, I mounted him and took him inside me so deep that my bones touched his. We were one, a swaying, breathing, pulsing being, needing no other, nothing more. Afterward, I washed him with a cloth soaked in lavender water, and then he washed me. He was no longer my siren, but now my anchor. He steadied me amid the storms of court, our very human love, our fond familiarity. I caressed his arms and back as he bent over me, my beloved.

We drowsed side by side until dawn.

When his manservant knocked, Edward sighed. "I must attend a Mass in memory of Philippa." He shook his head in wonder. "I thought that a part of me had died with her, but I feel whole again." He kissed my forehead, my breasts. "My love for you never diminished my love for Philippa, my queen. She was my succor and my salvation. She taught me how to win the hearts of all my subjects, from the common folk to the barons and archbishops. She bore me magnificent sons and gentle daughters, and I loved her with all my heart and soul. Now you are all to me, Alice."

"And you to me, Edward." I was in no wise jealous of his declaration of love for his queen. I could never take her place; no one could. I was content to have his love now.

My sense of profound union with Edward, of being his solace and retreat as he was mine, was something that I clung to in the months and years ahead, when it seemed that all the kingdom condemned our love, refusing to accept it as that. I wished I might somehow prove to them our sincerity, but how one "proves" such a thing I did not know.

I was certain that I'd conceived that night, and I was glad. I pushed away Gwen's concerns, her insistence that I drink the usual potion to stop whatever might have begun. If God had seen fit to allow me to conceive from that night of love and union, I felt only joy and grati-tude that soon I might again have the intensely private and miraculous sensation of a child blooming within my womb.

My intuition proved to be right. Happiness brightened my world. I was grateful for the comfort I derived from the beauty surrounding me and the solace of the chapels wherever I abided with Edward, and rejoiced in his delight that we were to have another child.

The most difficult time was Christmastide. John, Duke of Lan-caster, as well as Edmund and Thomas, Edward's youngest sons, joined us at King's Langley. I felt a fraud, a usurper, while present at the table in the hall or in Edward's parlor. I had seldom been with the two youngest sons while Philippa lived. John welcomed me, but Edmund and Thomas were offended by my presence and made no attempt to hide their feelings. Thomas had seen little of me with Ed-ward. Until his mother's death he had known me only as one of her ladies, though he had surely heard gossip about Edward and me. At sixteen, he was less in control of his emotions than his older brother, so his was the most hateful voice and behavior. He made certain that I overheard him telling Edmund that he looked forward to his father remarrying, when I should be unceremoniously kicked out of his bed and his household.

Even worse for me, Bella and my own son, John, had not been invited and so spent the Christmas season with Dame Agnes, a failing Nan, and her replacement as the children's nurse, Betys.

I was rescued from this unpleasant atmosphere by the burial of Queen Philippa. Her entombment had been delayed until the abbey was ready, and Advent and Christmastide had passed. When the funeral procession accompanying her coffin to Westminster departed from King's Langley, I was permitted to retire to London. Richard Stury and a new man in Edward's entourage, William Latimer, escorted me.

My John, now four years old, greeted me with such tearful joy that my own emotion rendered me speechless. Hugs and kisses sufficed.

Bella waited her turn with good grace, then flung herself into my welcoming arms.

That night, as Nan, Grandmother, Gwen, and I shared some spiced wine in my chamber before we all retired, I learned that Henry, Lord Percy had visited with several kinswomen, assessing in which household John might best be fostered. Edward had not told me of the visit, and my first reaction was of fury.

"How dare they come here without my leave? He is my son!" I had known, of course, that John would likely be fostered by the Percys. But to frighten him with the possibility that they would take him while I was away was unforgivable. I could not sit still but started to pace angrily, holding my stomach.

"Have a care," Gwen said, draping a soft wool mantle over my shoulders.

"I did not think they would take him from us so soon." Dame Agnes dabbed her eyes. Since Grandfather's death my little family had become her succor and delight, the beneficiaries of all her needlework and worry.

"I would have warned you had I known it was imminent. And I would have found a way to prepare John." It was made worse by the fact that I did not care for Henry, Lord Percy, nor trust him. He seemed to me a man out to advance his own family no matter who fell before his ruthless advance. Such blatant disregard for both John's feelings and mine was proof of it. But Edward did trust Percy.

"Your life is not yours to order, is it, Alice?" asked Nan. Sweet, elderly, frail she might be, but she still saw what was right in front of her more clearly than anyone else I knew.

"What woman's life is?" asked Dame Agnes.

"But I trow it is worse for the mistress of a king," said Nan. "Is that not so, Alice?"

Her words conjured up memories of my resentment when I'd first gone to court, how I had felt I was treated as a child.

"It is true. I command servants, live in most beautiful houses, own and manage property, and have the love of the king—it would seem that I have everything. But the price I pay is that my own life is not mine to order. The king commands and I obey."

"Women rarely have a say in their sons' occupations," Dame Agnes soothed me, "and many of the wealthier merchant families send their boys away to be fostered in homes with good connections. I did not expect we might be left to raise little John de Southery in London. But I hated to see how disquieted the children were by the proud Lord Percy and his haughty women."

After a fitful night's sleep I asked Bella about the incident.

"They frightened John, picking him up, asking him if he would like to live with them. And they talked about his appearance, his speech, how he carries himself, as if they did not think he could understand. He thought they meant to steal him. He still cries out in the night if he cannot see me or Betys."

My sweet son, when I inquired how he found the Percys, clenched his little fists to steel himself as he declared them arrogant, discourteous. But his bottom lip betrayed him, and then the tears came. I held him close, assuring him of both my love and his father's.

I could not imagine that Edward would have agreed to such treatment of our son. I poured out my anger and frustration to him in a letter, certain he would agree, and sealed it with my signet. I'd sent a messenger with it to him at Westminster before doubt overtook me, doubt that I had a right to demand anything for my son. Then I prayed that I might put the matter out of my mind and enjoy being reunited with my children. This required the cooperation of Nan and Dame Agnes, who were loath to silence their irritation, but both of them remembered that a woman in my condition was easier to live with if she had her way.

One of my new pleasures was to lie down in the afternoons with my son. It began during one of his bursts of anger that were so like Bella's when she had been too tired but too stubborn to rest, and as I stretched out on my bed I invited John to join me. Curled up against me, his head on my stomach, he fell asleep at once. With his calming warmth beside me I was able to set aside my fears for a while, and eventually I slept as well. On the following day he expected we would do the same after the midday meal, and I was delighted to comply. Again he slept, again I fell asleep as well. And so it became our routine.

A WEEK AFTER I had written to Edward condemning the behavior of Henry Percy and his family, a messenger from the king informed us that on the following day John, Bella, and I would be escorted to the White Tower in the city. King Edward wished to show the children the exotic animals housed there, gifts he had received from far and wide—tigers, lions, monkeys, and more. I was delighted for the children, and I was excited as well. Later that day, however, I fell prey to worry about Edward's responding in such an impersonal manner, whether rather than being angry with the Percys Edward might be angry with me. But I was determined not to allow my gratitude for the day's adventure or my own worry soften my stance on the Percy family's high-handed behavior, particularly their scheming to meet John when I was not there.

The White Tower was a tall stone keep surrounded by smaller timber buildings set in gardens along the River Thames. The high, well-fortified walls encircling the entire area prevented any enjoyment of the riverside views, except from some of the upper stories or the top of the wall, but it was lovely within.

"Did they build this so the animals could not escape?" John asked as we entered the inner ward from the gatehouse.

"No, John, this was built long ago to protect the royal family in time of war. The animals came later."

Just then he caught sight of his father and began to jump up and down, waving his little arms. Edward had been frowning at his companion, his son Thomas of Woodstock, but as he noticed us, and his youngest child's antics, his face relaxed into an expression of such fatherly love that my anger eased a little. Thomas, too, came to greet us and then took his leave, exhibiting far more courtesy than at our Christmas meeting.

How I loved Edward as we exchanged greetings now, his eyes warm and welcoming. John clamored to be noticed. When he raised his arms in the hope of being lifted up by his father the king, he was instead proffered a hand.

"Come, my son. You are beyond the age to be carried. We shall walk together." Edward held out his other hand. "And, my dear Mistress Bella, please walk with us. Let us confer with the keeper of the royal menagerie!" He winked at me and proceeded toward the area whence came animal sounds that made me ill at ease.

I followed with the nurse, Betys, who was dumbstruck by the grandeur of the place.

Edward delighted, as ever, in the children's excitement. He was charming to Bella and John, and both were fascinated by the creatures on display, though John chose not to reach into the cage to touch the male lion's mane when the keeper offered him the chance. Bella did stroke it and declared it rough and filthy. Edward roared with delight.

"You speak your mind just like your mother. You shall lead the young men a merry dance, sweet Bella!"

I was grateful that he treated her with such affection. In awe of him, she treasured such moments more than all his lavish gifts. I understood, remembering the day on Sheppey when he had made me feel "seen."

While the children and their nurse talked to the keeper, Edward led me to a bench where we might rest and talk.

"You are beautiful today as always, my love," he said. "Are you well? This is not too tiring for you? You are pale." He touched my cheek.

"I am comfortable," I assured him. Then repeated to him the tale of young John's nighttime fears since the ill-advised visit by Henry, Lord Percy and company.

"I apologize for their behavior, Alice. I thought it would be easier for you if they met our son when you were not present. I am well aware of your reluctance to let him go. I am sorry for that. I love both of you—you know that."

To say I was disappointed that it had been Edward's idea for them to visit when I was absent would be an understatement. "Have you no heart, Edward? Henry Percy *frightened* our son. Does that not anger you?"

Edward chuckled. "He is a loud lout. But what is done is done, and he is impressed with the way you have raised John so far." He kissed my hand.

I was too angry to be charmed. "So even after this breach of courtesy, John will be fostered by a Percy? You might have your choice of noble families."

"He will go with Percy, Alice. John may be a bastard but he is my son and shall be raised as such, knowing his duties to me and the realm, able to move with ease among kings, emperors, archbishops, barons, popes, . . . and Percys." He marked my lack of amusement at his wordplay. "You shall not stand in his way, and that is an end to the discussion." He startled me with the coolness of his tone, the sudden abandoning of my hand.

We said no more, but sat observing the children. I was relieved that Edward did not press us to linger once John grew weary and fretful.

Of course, I had always been aware of two Edwards, one who was king and treated me as his subject, and one who was my lover, who needed me, cherished and protected me. Sometimes this duality so frightened me that I would seek reassurance by cuddling up to him. It often worked, inspiring him to remember his other self and soften. But this was hardly the place to behave so, and I found myself wishing only to flee his presence.

Indeed, for the first time in a long while, I looked forward to being away from Edward. Afterward I wrote a loving, gently apologetic letter, explaining that I had only wished to protect our son. I promised to argue no more against his being fostered by Henry, Lord Percy. Edward expressed his satisfaction at this, sending pearls and a miniver-lined cloak to reward me for my obedience, and agreeing that I might spend the remainder of the winter at Fair Meadow, awaiting the birth of our child.

By Candlemas I was settled at my beloved manor. Sacrilegious as it may sound, I felt as if God had held off the winter snows until I was safely installed, then covered the world in a snowy blanket for several months, tucking me in. John and Bella were with me, as well as Dame Agnes, Nan, Gwen, and my household servants including Betys and Robert. Edward had also agreed that I might choose my own midwife, and I had immediately requested Felice, who had presided over Bella's birth. She would bide with us closer to the time. Content, I allowed myself to become lost in the dream of this happy little household remaining undisturbed for a long, long while.

Robert and I grew close that winter and spring. He had recently lost his wife of a few years and welcomed the opportunity to be away from his home near London where every room evoked memories of her suffering. She had fallen down the stairs in early pregnancy, losing the child and eventually her own life. For months she had lain in bed, barely able to move, speaking little, her mother looking after her. We talked of our lost spouses, and gradually he seemed to have said all that he wished to say of this and turned the talk to the coming child, to Bella and John, and to the work ahead on my properties and on his—he had begun to acquire his own modest estate. I felt I could say anything to him. The children thought of him as their uncle. I thought of him as an uncomplicated friend in whose company I could be at ease. It was a happy time.

While the snows lasted, the dreamy state of my comfortable little household did, too. Even well into the thaw we received neither guests nor messengers. But early in April, toward the end of the Lenten season, a letter arrived from Edward announcing that an escort would arrive for our son John at the royal hunting lodge near Fair Meadow on the eve of Lammas Day. My son would be gone from me in four months.

Another blow came shortly after Easter, in late April, when Nan took to her bed, refused food or drink, and within a few days simply stopped breathing. There was not a soul in the household who did not mourn the loss of her sweet presence.

Bella was the first to notice that Nan had died—pressing her ear to the shrunken bosom, then lifting her hand and finding it cold and life-less. Her cry had brought me rushing to her side. After the burial, my daughter seemed to spend her days in prayer, her lips moving cease-lessly as she performed all her chores. This stopped only when she was at her lessons. Though I had always found comfort in prayer myself, I worried that Bella's piety might result from her childhood pain, my absence while she grieved for her beloved father.

But her example drew me back into the habit of daily prayer, first for dear Nan's soul, later for myself and my family and all in my house-hold. I found myself including Robert in my orisons more and more, appreciating the security he provided my family. And always Bella was with me in the chapel, rapt in devotions.

It should have come as no surprise to me when on her thirteenth birthday in late June she expressed her wish to take vows. But her announcement, coming just over a month before young John was to leave the household, gripped my heart with a terrible sense of loss.

"Is it a vocation, my love, or something else?" I asked. "Have you considered all that you renounce by taking vows? The love of a hus-band? The joy of children?"

Bella was so beautiful it seemed a sacrilege to close her up among brittle old women who had never known life or grieving widows seek-ing safe havens. I was concerned that she as yet had only a vague sense of what she would be renouncing, and of the tedium of such a life if her vocation turned out to be simply an idea with no substance.

She lowered her head and looked up at me with a frown as Janyn had when I did not respond as he'd hoped. "Is it so difficult to believe of me?" she asked.

I wished I was not so large and clumsy with child and could have gathered her up in my arms. "No, Bella, that is not why I ask. I merely—" I stopped myself. I did not want to speak my fear, that my unholy alliance with the king had frightened or shamed her. "I shall honor your wish, if that is truly your desire."

WITHIN DAYS of Bella's birthday I gave birth to another daughter, Joan. A daughter. It was no surprise to me that Edward took a week to come and see his child this time. What need had he of an illegitimate daughter? He came for the day and then departed, leaving gifts of precious gems, silver, and gold for Joan and pearls for me. Beautiful things, of course, but I wanted him. I wanted him to hold me, to hold his infant daughter. Affairs of state called him away, he said. I was uneasy that my silence during the months at Fair Meadow had cooled his ardor. My time away from court had been peaceful and had allowed me the opportunity to become reacquainted with myself. In truth, as our separation lengthened—unlike my last lying in, Edward had neither sent for me nor visited, though he had written to me—I had felt more and more at ease in a respite I'd not enjoyed in the twelve years that the court had been my home. The peace of Fair Meadow had suggested another sort of life, one I found appealing. But I had not intended to push Edward away. I fought back my hurt at his lack of interest in Joan and rejoiced at her birth. She was mine, all mine. There was no danger of her being fostered. I reassured myself I had misread Edward.

My infant daughter was flaxen haired and blue eyed like her father, and I adored her. She also reminded me of her first godmother, Princess Joan. With John's birth, Joan had decided I was not one to take her advice on preventing conception and had embraced the inevitable, demanding to be godmother to our first daughter. Of all the Plantagenet family, she was the most accepting of me, embracing me as a woman who completed her father-in-law's life in a way that was good and necessary for the realm, and as a friend whose company she enjoyed. Her friendship meant more to me than I could ever express, and she was always in my prayers.

The infant Joan became the center of our little world at Fair Meadow. Bella enjoyed helping Betys, me, and the wet nurse, Ann. On the warm afternoons all the women would sit out in the garden and share in caring for the baby. Robert teased us that she would grow up believing she had many mothers.

He regarded her with such tenderness, I wondered whether he yearned to remarry. The thought saddened me, remembering a moment a few nights earlier. I'd stepped out into the cool night air and found him gazing up at the stars.

"God's majesty," I whispered, joining him.

He'd slipped an arm round my waist, and I'd leaned my head against his shoulder, at once at ease, content. We stood so for a long while, watching the heavens in silence. It seemed a moment most intimate.

And then, abruptly, the interlude was over. Edward summoned me to Sheen a week before John was to depart for his fosterage. Bella and Joan were to bide in a house near the palace, and John would be with us for a few days before his departure. I felt an immense relief that Edward still wanted me, and yet I found it difficult to leave Fair Meadow. I had for the first time been able to imagine without terror a life away from Edward.

This quiet time at my manor had inspired a yearning in me for a more ordered existence. Even for a husband. Knowing that could never be Edward, I had fallen to fantasizing about life with someone like Robert, a man of the land with no ties to court, imagining his smiling face greeting me each morning or looking down at me as I nursed our child. I did wonder whether, with a more ordinary family and life Bella might still have felt called to the Church or not.

Nevertheless, I had been summoned, and as Gwen and I sorted through my gowns and began to redo them, I gradually set aside my daydreams. I was not yet ready for that life, not so long as Edward wanted me. But still I felt an unfamiliar lethargy as we worked on the silk, velvet, and escarlatte gowns. Once I had seen my time with Edward as an enchantment, all passion and beauty, but now it was often frightening, and of late he had ceased to anchor me.

I was not comfortable traveling on horseback a little over three weeks after giving birth, but fortunately most of the journey to Sheen was by river barge. I worked with the grooms to assemble a sturdy side-saddle platform with enough cushions to ease my ride to the waiting barge, and we traveled at a slow pace through the countryside. Still confused by Edward's inconsistent behavior toward me, I did not wish to appear weak by traveling by litter on any part of the journey.

Bidding adieu to my son was far more debilitating than the travel. I felt part of myself being torn away as I lost sight of him, riding off with Lord Henry's party.

. . .

B UT I had little time to despair. On my arrival at Sheen I discovered a crisis blooming. The situation in the Aquitaine had deteriorated as Edward had predicted, and Prince Edward and his family were to return to England in the autumn. My Edward was moving forward with a plan to lead a military expedition into France, formulating his request to parliament for more taxes to finance the effort. The barons and archbishops warned of resistance. Landowners had not yet recovered from the devastation of the recurring pestilence, and the Crown's repeated demands for more funds for war were deeply resented. Edward needed a splendid victory to inspire confidence that the money would be well spent, yet he first needed money in order to gather the troops to pursue such a victory. I understood the financial conundrum, but my main concern was for Edward himself.

I did not know how many were aware that the king had suffered from vague maladies all winter and spring, rallying for Easter and the Feast of St. George then collapsing for weeks afterward. Parliament would surely be even more reluctant to grant his request for fresh taxation if they knew of his fluctuating health. I had certainly not known the extent of it, had not understood what strength of will it had required for him to journey to Fair Meadow after Joan's birth. I was thankful that I had not confronted him with my simmering resentments and doubts then. He did, in truth, need me. And he was not in any condition to lead an army into battle.

Loving him as I did, I devoted myself to him. I took it as my role to see that he ate well and drank more moderately than was his wont, and drew him out for walks, rides, and hawking as often as possible. Although he chafed at the extent to which I watered his wine, in general he seemed comforted and restored by my ministrations and encouragement. In fact, those close to him expressed relief at the improvement in his health and manner; some even had the grace to thank me for my part in the transformation.

Geoffrey congratulated me on staying so long away from court that the gossips had forgotten me. "Though they are abuzz with your son's being a bridge between the Percy family and the king, they do not mention you by name, merely that the king's bastard, John de Southery, is to be fostered by Henry, Lord Percy. The king has succeeded in impressing all with his ability still to sire sons. One would think that he had managed not only to supply the seed but also given birth to the boy! You are absolved from all connection." When

I said nothing, he noticed my distress. "Are you not relieved to be forgotten?"

"By the crowd, not by my son."

"Surely you do not believe that will ever happen?"

I did.

On days when my patience wore thin, I would chafe at the way Edward took all credit for our son and remained indifferent to Joan and Bella. We argued about my misgivings concerning Bella's vocation. Edward impatiently ordered me to cease my fretting and settle on a nunnery suitable for her. But in truth even John, had he not been safely far away, would have felt Edward's indifference, for he was impatient with anything that robbed him of my full attention. My life away from his presence concerned him not a whit.

Or perhaps not entirely. He had saddled me with a troublesome wardship that he hoped would eventually provide security for our son. Edward had encouraged the underchamberlain of his household to sign over to me the wardship of the late Joan de Orby's daughter Mary and her estate; Joan had been the stepmother of Henry, Lord Percy. By tradition and law wardships were sources of revenue for the king, for while the heir was in his or her minority, the income from the lands came to the king as well as the fees for eventual permission to marry and any other financial dealings regarding a match, save for the dowry. It was a desirable wardship, and Edward believed that the heiress, young Mary Percy, might be a match for our son John.

I was uneasy, wishing to confer with Robert about the feasibility of adding such a large estate to his responsibilities. I also worried how the court—and even the public—would interpret this boon. And though I called it a boon, it was in fact a business transaction that would cost me a considerable amount if the land had been as indifferently managed as I'd heard. But Edward grew impatient with what he called my dithering and insisted that I accept it without caveats. How easily he spent my money! When I told Robert about it, he assured me that we were quite capable of taking on such a challenge and managed to calm me.

Perhaps sensing that he had pushed too hard, shortly after I arrived at Sheen Edward sweetened the burden with a gift of the dower estates and some other de Orby holdings. "In honor of the birth of our daughter, Joan."

For her sake I was moved by this gesture, but this huge addition to my holdings would be expensive to set right.

Our relationship was becoming confusing, my role in it more and more complex. Until I returned to Edward after Joan's birth, we had been lovers and companions in activities we both enjoyed—riding, hawking, hunting, lovemaking, dancing, music, chess. Our time together had been a refuge for both of us. Now Edward clung to me in the privacy of his chambers, and in public I was increasingly placed in the role of gatekeeper. Before events Edward would instruct me to keep this bishop or that lady from him.

"But how, my love?"

"Catch my elbow just so and pull me away, or whisper in my ear."

"But they are my betters, Edward. I cannot do so on my honor!"

"I ask you to do nothing that Philippa would not do."

"But she was the queen, Edward. I am not."

"You will do this, Alice."

He would accept nothing but my cooperation.

I had no right to assume the roles the queen had played. Nor should I have accompanied him to meetings in which I overheard much to which I should not have been privy. I shrank under the disapproving, indeed disbelieving, stares of others, often the only woman in the chamber.

Playing nurse and protector to Edward made me feel more his concubine than ever before. My presence was too public now. It felt far more presumptuous, and I was certain it put me in much greater jeopardy. Geoffrey had congratulated me on having been forgotten; it did not last long.

IN LATE summer, only a month after I had returned to Edward, we were once again in mourning. Young Edward, the eldest son and heir of Prince Edward and Princess Joan, had died in Gascony. I grieved for Joan; with the prince's ill health, I doubted she would have more children. Their younger son Richard, a child of four, was now second in line to the throne after his father. It seemed cruel that this should happen just as they were preparing to return to England.

In the twelve years that I had been in the royal household Edward had lost so many loved ones—family, friends of his youth, his most trusted commanders—but the death of his grandson, the shining boy previously second in line to the throne, was the weight that sank his confidence in what the future might hold for his kingdom. Prince Edward's long illness and erratic behavior as Lord of the Aquitaine had,

I was certain, contributed to my love's anguish. Of course Edward realized that Joan and Edward were unlikely to produce another heir. Young Richard must duly return to the safety of the royal court.

I sent a messenger to William Wykeham, asking if he might set aside his duties to come to Edward. He was most often at court as the king's chancellor and close adviser, but he was also Bishop of Winchester, a pious and inspiring cleric, and in this time of grieving it was his spiritual gifts I prayed would lift the weight of worry from Edward's shoulders and give him succor. Wykeham hastened to King's Langley and stayed for a fortnight, sitting with Edward long into the night, listening, praying, consoling.

I took the opportunity to confess to Wykeham my own unease about my increasingly public role in Edward's life.

"What matters is that, through you, His Grace finds comfort and ease, which affords him the strength to rule his realm," Wykeham counseled me. "I know that it is not easy for you, but God will reward you for your devotion to the king. I cannot believe He would forsake you."

"You once advised me to remember the uncertainty of my position, how all at court walk on shifting sand."

"That has not changed. But I need not remind you of it. Indeed, I commend you on your diligence in seeing to your future financial security and that of your daughters." There was something in his eyes and in the tension with which he held himself that told me he was not saying all he thought.

"Is there anything else on which you might counsel me, my lord?"

"No. Be at peace."

His counsel did ease me. No matter what my doubts, my duty was clear. Edward, too, seemed restored by Wykeham's visit.

All my children, including John, gathered round me at the Christmas court. Edward showered them with gifts and attention, and I felt truly blessed. It comforted me to see that John was thriving with the Percys, though I was also pleased that he still enjoyed my fussing over him. I treasured that yuletide.

WHILE PARLIAMENT sat that winter, I insisted that I stay in my London home rather than with Edward at Westminster. To finance his battle over the Aquitaine he needed the support of the commons, the very folk most likely to stand in judgment over our liaison. It was better we should remain apart while living in their midst, that they should see me going about my business in London, worshipping in my parish church.

Grandmother and my sister, Mary, fussed over Joan, and I saw to Bella. While at Sheen, Wykeham had suggested several nunneries, the two closest being St. Helen's Priory and Barking Abbey.

"Barking is for the highborn," I demurred.

"Your daughter is the goddaughter of a former queen, Dame Alice, and her half brother and sister have the king for their sire. With a generous dowry, which you have already said you will provide, she would be welcome there."

Wykeham had written Bella a letter of introduction. One dreary January day she and I rode out to the abbey, accompanied by Robert. The beauty of the church and grounds, coupled with the serenity of the abbess and the novices Bella and I met, calmed me, but what convinced me that this was the right place for Bella was her response to the abbey. She glowed with joy there and respectfully asked such pertinent questions that I understood then how much thought she had devoted to this decision.

The abbess, plainly delighted by and impressed with my daughter, suggested that she bide with them for a year while considering whether this course seemed right for her. Bella wished very much to do so. The abbess assured me that Dame Agnes and I might visit her a few times during that year.

My heart was heavy on the ride back to London without my daughter. Robert attempted to distract me with details of his autumn visits of inspection to my properties. His friendship was precious to me.

As ever, my peace was short-lived. Richard Lyons, Geoffrey, and Pippa dined with me a few days later, all abuzz about the clemency shown to the murderer of Nicholas Sardouche, a Lombard merchant Janyn had known long ago. I had not heard of the incident, which had happened in Cheapside, shortly before Christmas. Sardouche argued with a mercer who owed him over £100 sterling. The mercer, joined by two other mercers who claimed not to know him, beat Sardouche to death.

"London mercers against Lombard merchants—it is an old story," said Richard. "Even my fellow Flemings take precautions when traveling in the city at night. The London guilds claim the king unjustly favors the foreigners."

"All three were set free without punishment," said Geoffrey.

"How can the court be so blind?" I asked.

"You have been too long in the king's company, my friend," said Geoffrey. "You forget the angry undercurrents in the marketplace."

"It seems to me they have taken that anger to parliament," said Pippa. "They say the commons have turned on the king."

News from parliament had trickled through the city. The people were excited about it, seeing it as a triumph. The commons blamed the clerical councillors for the failed war effort in France, particularly Wykeham and the treasurer, Thomas Brantingham, Bishop of Ely. In exchange for their agreement to new taxation, the commons insisted the two be replaced by laymen. Edward had bowed to their demands. By the time I was reunited with him, I was agitated beyond wise courtesy.

"You asked William Wykeham to step down? But, Edward, he is your good friend and trusted adviser. He came to you so recently, guiding you through your mourning. You have sung his praises as chancellor to me. I cannot understand why, *how* you succumbed to the rabble's demand."

"Alice, my love, I hardly expect you to understand how a king must rule. Wykeham is still Bishop of Winchester, and he is still my wise counselor. I spoke to him in private. He agreed to this for the sake of the kingdom. As did Brantingham."

Edward's words were brave and matter of fact, but the vein throbbing in his temple and his clammy skin bore witness to his secret disappointment and anger, a frustrated anger. I feared, as had Lancaster when he had sent for me after Philippa's death, that the king's age rendered him increasingly vulnerable. He needed one of his eldest sons by his side. Edmund and Thomas were too untried to advise him.

"Promise me that you will indeed abide by Wykeham's counsel," I implored. I was frightened for Edward. I did not understand this new power of the commons—for power they must have, to have coerced him into parting with Wykeham.

He lifted my chin and kissed me. "I have already said I shall. Do not fret, Alice."

But I did, even more so as further changes came in swift order. Edward made William Latimer his chamberlain and John Neville of Raby, our son's second godfather, his steward. I was not concerned by Neville's appointment, but could not fathom what Edward saw in Latimer. I knew him a little through Richard Lyons and his time at court, and thought him an opportunist more suited to affairs of customs and the mint than the king's household. He could not possibly have been Edward's own choice. My beloved seemed no longer to be in control.

I was relieved to hear that Prince Edward and Princess Joan had landed and were expected at court at any time. I had forgotten for the moment why they had left Bordeaux and prayed they would know how to set things right. But I had my doubts when I beheld them. At the sight of his eldest son being carried into the hall on a litter, Edward sought my hand and clutched it so tightly that tears sprang to my eyes. Princess Joan walked beside her ailing husband, regal and elegant even after the long journey. As soon as she had instructed the litter bearers in the manner in which to proceed, she hurried forward to bow in obeisance to Edward. I nudged him to lift his eyes from his shattered son and attend to Joan.

When she straightened and allowed a servant to remove her mantle, the toll of the years in Bordeaux was revealed. Her beautiful face was fraught with lines of weariness and sorrow, her once lithe body, plump now. Even so, she outshone anyone in the hall, and her kind eyes and bright smile lit me within as she greeted me with sincere warmth. An ally had returned.

Later, after a brief rest, the prince managed to walk from his chamber to that of the king for the welcoming dinner. He leaned on both Joan's arm and that of a page, but made an effort to straighten up and give his father a slight bow before taking his seat at the table. The talk was of Channel crossings and the funeral arrangements for young Edward, which had been left for John to carry out in the cathedral of St. André in Bordeaux. Lancaster was still in France.

Edward wept in my arms that night. "He was the bravest of us all, my glorious son and heir! Now he is a swollen, misshapen creature, crippled by humiliation."

EARLY THE following morning Princess Joan knelt beside me in the chapel as Mass began. It was comforting to have her there, exuding a perfume both flowery and spicy, softly whispering prayers as she fingered her ivory and jet paternoster beads. The king was sitting up above in his private area, warmly wrapped. He had slept little.

After the service Joan asked if she might accompany me to my chamber.

"It has been so long since we talked. I want to hear about my namesake Joan, and how John likes the Percy household. And beautiful Bella—is it true that she is at Barking?"

When I expressed my sorrow over the death of her son, she squeezed my hand. "Let us not speak of my troubles, not this morning, Alice. I must find a way back to joy."

In my chamber I drew out my latest treasure, a long mirror that Edward had recently given me. Gwen had quickly become adept at holding it so that if I turned a little this way and that, for the first time in my life I could see almost my entire self.

I, too, had added some weight of late. Not so much as Joan, but enough to require alterations in most of my gowns. I stood before the mirror and frowned at my own reflection.

Joan laughed. "You are so lovely, Alice, and so young! Revel in your time, my friend." She stepped forward. "Now hold it up for me, Gwen, I pray you."

Joan was beautiful this morning, her gown cleverly fitted to accentuate her breasts and disguise her thickened waist.

"The needlework is excellent, the body shockingly aged," she said with an exaggerated frown. "This is no avenue to joy!" Her silks whispered as she settled down on the window seat and patted the cushions beside her. "Now come, tell me about your darlings."

We talked for an hour or more. I had not laughed so much in a long while. She described magnificent feasts and tournaments, ridiculous lords and ladies, gorgeous gardens and water courses. By the time she left, I felt I knew something of Bordeaux and why she loved it so. Except for the toll it had taken on her family.

TO MY immense discomfort, Prince Edward summoned me to his chamber later in the morning, to glean what he could regarding his father's health and state of mind. It seemed father and son were mutually dismayed by the changes time had wrought in each other.

"My lord, with all respect, it would seem best you should ask such questions of His Grace, your father, and his physicians. I am neither qualified nor at liberty to discuss His Grace's health."

"Who better?" Prince Edward barked, with a loud, brittle laugh. "I wager you are more familiar with his body and his moods than any other in the kingdom! He has planted two children in your womb . . . or is it three?"

I blushed to realize how much the sons must talk of me. Of us. I wished Princess Joan had remained present.

"Can he still perform, eh?"

Can you? I wanted to say, but bit my tongue.

My silence seemed to rebuke him. He shaped his bloated face into an expression of concern. "Forgive me. Discomfort makes me cruel. I pray you, be at ease, and hold it not against me. I count on you to be my ally."

He told me of his long illness, and with bitterness described the gradually escalating disrespect he had suffered from the Gascon lords. In his version it was not his own poor judgment and quick temper that had led to his abandonment by the Gascons, but rather their arrogant dismissal of his authority because of his infirmity—a lord who could not sit a horse on campaign need not be obeyed.

"This must not happen here. My father the king must not appear weak. The barons must never sense that they might gain ascendancy over him."

His swollen face burned with outrage, yet his voice was but a whisper.

"My lord, I have seen no evidence of such dishonor or disloyalty."

"What of this parliament? How dare they question the king's authority to raise taxes in order to defend their own pathetic lives?" His emotion set off a coughing fit. A servant hurried forward with a warm drink.

"My lord, I have no knowledge of the workings of parliament. Perhaps the Bishop of Winchester might better inform you."

"Wykeham?" He growled the name. "His incompetence has brought us to this crisis! Do not speak of Wykeham in my presence."

Then more fool you, I thought. "What would you have me do, my lord?"

"Stay by the king's side as much as you are able. Review his dress. Recommend that he retire and see no one when he is unwell."

"My lord, you describe an invalid. His Grace is by no means that. He rides, he hawks, he presides over meetings with his council."

"Which brings me back to my earlier question, is he still active in bed?"

I had never been fond of the prince, but liked him even less at that moment. Fortunately, his physician had just entered the room.

"Your physician awaits you, my lord. May God go with you." I bowed to Prince Edward and withdrew.

It was one thing to obey the king, but the thought of being the pawn of his sons I could not bear. After I'd worked off my fury on a long ride, I felt ill and took to my bed for the rest of the day. It was not as pleasant as it might have been to burrow down beneath the bedclothes and doze, for my mind was troubled. I could brush aside the prince's bawdiness and bitterness, but not his concern that Edward should appear hale and hearty at all times to the courtiers and the public. Had he not seemed so to his son? As the day wore on I grew more fearful that Edward was in a decline I had failed to see. I felt the deep sand shifting beneath me. I wanted to be his lover, not his keeper. Had that blinded me to the extent of the changes in him?

Yet I knew that I must manage to be gracious to the prince. I could not risk offending him. I must do as he asked, though I felt he saw me as little more than a servant.

But taking on ever more responsibility for Edward's welfare might prove difficult for the next nine months or so. Gwen groaned when I became ill two mornings in a row.

"At least you will cease growling at the mirror," she said. "You know now why your waist is widening. You were wrong about your flux being delayed because the commons' behavior upset you so."

Weeks later, when I was certain enough to tell Edward the news, he bragged to his son that he had once more sired a child.

Prince Edward winked at me.

Princess Joan suddenly suggested that we leave the men to talk. She walked with me to my chamber, sitting on my bed and inviting me to join her.

"My husband is angry at the world these days, sweet Alice. I pray you, pay him no heed. His purpose was not to insult you." She leaned close and smoothed my hair from my forehead, kissing me on the cheek. She smelled of lavender and sandalwood. "You have made the king so happy. He is giddy with pride and reassured of his manhood."

"Do you find him very changed?"

She sat back and tilted her head to study me, no longer smiling. "Are you worried about him?"

"Your husband is." I told her of Prince Edward's suggestions.

Joan took a deep breath. "The king grows old, Alice. He does look much older than when I last saw him, but I expected as much. He has lost Philippa, Lionel, Mary and Margaret, Blanche—the list is endless, is it not? And the Aquitaine." She glanced away for a moment, as if composing herself.

"Then I should heed your husband's advice?"

She shook herself as if emerging from a dream and smiled on me. "Continue as you have been, Alice. I have heard of no one showing disrespect to the king."

This time Edward insisted I remain by his side until a month before I expected to be lying in, and I did not argue. It was as if Prince Edward had lifted a veil from my eyes. I grew more aware of my beloved's lapses. One morning in late summer he woke to no feeling in his right arm. I massaged it and made him perform simple movements until we were both reassured that, whatever had happened, it had passed. But often afterward I would notice that arm hanging limply and would touch it to remind him that it was there.

"You must make an effort to use it more, my love, else it will wither." One of his physicians had so advised us. He thought it was the result of an old wound that had been reinjured while the king was hawking.

"Mother the child in your womb, not me," Edward would growl.

WHEN IT was time for my lying in I moved only so far as a pretty house on the river at Windsor. Grandmother did not bide with me for that birth. Even such a brief trip was too much for her to contemplate. But Felice the midwife was with me, and Gwen, Mary, and Joan.

In November I gave birth to my beautiful Jane. Little Joan was excited to have a companion. Edward was disappointed.

"You do favor the female sex, my love. Perhaps we should consult an alchemist about turning females into males in the womb."

"You have been too much in the company of your son the prince," I said. "Your witticisms lack humor and grace.".

Edward glared at me and departed, but within hours he returned, assuring me that he had been teasing. He showered me with pearls, rubies, and diamonds and insisted I be with him at King's Langley for the Christmas court. John and his new duchess were to be there.

Edward's rejection of Jane both chilled and offended me. Even the arrival of my dear Robert bearing gifts for Jane and me could not entirely warm me. But my steward's gentle presence was, as ever, a great comfort.

16

> *In al this world ther nys so cruel herte*
> *That hire hadde herd compleynen in hire sorwe*
> *That nolde han wepen for hire peynes smerte,*
> *So tendrely she weep, bothe eve and morwe.*
> *Hire nedede no teris for to borwe!*
> *And this was yet the werste of al hire peyne:*
> *Ther was no wight to whom she dorste hire pleyne.*

—Geoffrey Chaucer, *Troilus and Criseyde*, V, 722–28

• Christmas 1371 •

IN GOWNS of cloth of gold and headdresses with ships at full sail—the rigging fashioned from the same gold wire that was the weft thread in my long surcoat and his robes—Edward and I dazzled the guests at the Christmas court. The headdresses symbolized Edward's intention to sail to France in summer in order to win back the Aquitaine. Emeralds and diamonds set in gold powdered our robes and headdresses. The warp of our cloth was green, and the livery of his household was green cloth with gold embroidery. Prince Edward and Princess Joan wore similar robes and headdresses, and many courtiers wore headdresses in maritime and martial themes. Edward and his daughter-in-law Joan both saw the gold and green as the sun on the stormy waters of the Channel; it pleased them to imagine how the assembly might look from the ceiling of the hall—a fleet setting sail across a sun-dazzled sea.

Though I could not deny the effect of our attire was breathtaking, I regretted that Edward had prevailed in the mission, for it seemed certain that it would end in defeat. King Charles of France had proved unexpectedly effective in wooing back the lords of the Aquitaine. Many believed it was already too late for Edward or anyone else to influence events there.

I feared as well the court's censure of my part in the spectacle. Neither part of the royal family nor of noble blood, I should have been less prominent.

"I am the king," Edward argued. "They expect magnificence from me. And you are the mother of my youngest son and daughters. The court dare not criticize you."

He would not betimes have believed the commons would coerce him into asking Wykeham to step down as chancellor, either. His refusal to see how much control he had lost frustrated me. I feared it would prove our downfall. And indeed, in hindsight, this was perhaps our first grievous error.

IN EARLY February, the city of London and all the court welcomed Duke John's new bride, the Duchess Constance. She was dark, angular, not unattractive yet not pretty. There was a stiffness in her movements and her character did not generally please, her dark eyes full of censure.

When I was introduced to her she did not even glance my way but changed the subject of conversation and wandered away. I was shaken by her hostility, unexpressed though it was.

Princess Joan assured me that all felt the sting of her Spanish arrogance.

"You do not need her approval. Duke John is your friend, as is the prince," said Joan. "You know that, do you not? They are well aware of their indebtedness to you for your care of their father."

"I know all this, Joan. That does not mean I am easy in my mind."

She patted my arm and remarked that the king was gazing our way, apparently requiring me by his side. "You look more of a queen than Philippa ever did," she said as I made to walk away.

That chilled me. I prayed that no one else thought so. Joan looked like a queen and it was most appropriate for her. She would make a magnificent queen in due course. I prayed that her husband recovered enough to rule wisely and without the bitterness that had darkened his character of late.

I wondered what would become of me when that time came.

. . .

IN LATE winter, only months before Edward planned to embark for France with the prince and a large fleet, he had several memory lapses so alarming that I begged him to consult his physicians. He resisted my entreaties at first, though I knew he was as frightened as I was.

The first event I had initially taken as a slight to our youngest daughter, Jane. She was in my chamber with me. When Edward arrived, he seemed taken aback to see her.

"Whose child is this?"

"Whose? Edward, this is Jane, our daughter."

He gave me a sharp look, as if I had dared to insult him. "Do not dissemble, Alice. We have a son and . . ." He hesitated, his mind quite visibly confused or blank. "Have we a daughter as well? Yes, I believe— but older than this poppet. Who is she?"

I handed Jane to the nurse and gestured to her to withdraw. Edward, seemingly dressed for hawking, now sat down beside me and began to talk of his plan for new baths at Eltham, a project that had been completed several years earlier. I did not correct him, listening and nodding as appropriate. Suddenly he slapped his thighs, rose, and exclaimed, "Why are we speaking of this? We have enjoyed those baths for a year or more." He glanced around the chamber. "Was Jane here?" He rubbed his temples, then seemed to notice his clothing. "I meant to hawk."

As he left the room I followed, pretending to have some small item to discuss as I escorted him safely to the stables. He seemed more his usual self now, puzzled by Jane's nurse whisking her away before he'd had a chance to greet her. Yet there was a wildness in his eyes.

"I should like to ride out with you, my lord," I said, trying to sound light and ready for an adventure.

"I need no nursemaid," he growled and waved me off.

Though I regretted having irritated him, I had learned that he realized something was wrong and was uneasy, perhaps even frightened. I prayed that would make him more approachable if I suggested he speak to his physicians.

Similar incidents occurred a few days later and a few weeks after that. Fortunately, Duke John witnessed the third occasion and supported my encouragement that the king's physicians should be told of events, in the detail only I could provide.

Edward's shoulders seemed to sag as he listened to our advice and studied our expressions. But I had guessed correctly—he was aware that something was wrong, and grudgingly agreed to do as we requested. Old age, too much wine, insufficient activity, too little sleep, too much sleep, too much food, too little of the food that would balance his humors . . . in the next several days Edward was subjected to so much conflicting advice that he threatened to exile all three physicians, but in the end he chose to heed the advice of the one skilled in soothing his headaches, reasoning that memory resided in the head. His was the diet appropriate for the king's unbalanced humors, with more activity and less wine.

I prayed he was right, but feared that soon Edward must accept a quieter existence, perhaps allowing his sons to participate more fully in governing—as he had planned but not fully implemented. He clung yet to governing his own isle. I urged him to look to his sons rather than Latimer and Neville and several other courtiers and financiers, including Richard Lyons, who crowded around him. Edward found it amusing that I cautioned him against men with whom I myself chose to do business.

I did not in fact do business with all of them, but that was not the point. I did not argue but focused on my purpose. "They are suitable for commerce, my love, not for ruling a kingdom."

When he laughingly disregarded my opinion, I felt I had lost my voice. Long ago I had worried that, in loving a man, I might lose myself. But this was worse. Nothing I said seemed to count anymore. I was chided for expressing an opinion even slightly contrary to his.

Duke John and Prince Edward instructed me to stay by the king's side when neither of them was present, guiding him if his memory should fail, making excuses if he needed a respite from courtiers other than his most trusted men.

"They will resent me. What if the courtiers and barons turn against me?"

"Have faith in us, Dame Alice," said Prince Edward. He had been kind to me of late and far more courteous, at Joan's prompting, I imagined, although it might have been the result of a sudden improvement in his health. "John and I will shield you from harm," he assured me.

Of course they would say so. They would say anything to coerce me into staying. But the truth was, I had no choice.

My life was by no means completely bleak at that time. No matter the troubles and disagreements Edward and I might have by day, our evenings were loving and affectionate, sometimes still passionate, and we often rode or hawked in the early morning. Despite his wrinkles and complaints in his joints, Edward always dressed to look his best, and still sat his horse with elegant grace and command. We played more chess than in the past, and often of an afternoon I would read to him—letters, documents, but mostly sermons and poetry—or we would sit arm in arm, listening to a minstrel or watching a tumbler.

When I could, I went for more challenging rides than those with Edward, setting off without a goal, wishing simply to experience the joy of being one with a magnificent animal, challenging my body, drinking in the air. It helped me forget for a little while my fears for my beloved, and for my own future.

WILLIAM WYNDSOR'S name had been on all tongues at the Christmas court, regarding controversy surrounding his execution of his duties as Edward's governor in Ireland. He had stubbornly enforced an unpopular statute requiring the English landlords to provide for the defense of their Irish properties under pain of forfeiture to the Crown, thus angering the Earl of Pembroke, the Mortimers, the Despensers, and other powerful families. Edward did indeed take many of the lands into custody, which to my mind indicated complicity, for he needed the income to fund the force he was gathering to attack France. But he eventually bowed to the growing clamor among the baronial families, summoning Wyndsor to Westminster to answer to their accusations.

It was Geoffrey who informed me of much of this. Edward and I did not speak of William.

"He is expected to return in spring," my friend told me. "It is good that you did not heed my advice to wed him. He seems to be a man destined to make enemies."

I had been too confident that William would remain in Ireland, for no one else wanted the post. They wanted the glory and plunder promised from a French expedition.

"*Deus juva me,*" I whispered, crossing myself. "I pray that something happens to cancel this summons."

"Why? Surely he has forgotten you."

"No, he has not, and it is partly my fault, my insistence on repaying what I felt was a debt I did not wish to owe."

"To repay a debt is a worthy deed," Geoffrey said, "but I am amazed that you would have risked owing Wyndsor aught."

"He solved a dispute with a neighbor that had long weighed on my mind. Months later he wrote from Ireland seeking my assistance in selling some land he held near Winchester, needing the money. Owing him a favor, I obliged. His letters since have grown more and more importunate. I have ignored them. But coming here . . . I do not trust him. I fear what rumors he might spread."

Geoffrey shook his head. "The gossips have more interesting rumors to digest. They are saying that His Grace has given you the late queen's jewels."

I instinctively touched the jewels on my sleeve, rubies surrounded by pearls. "These were not Her Grace's."

"The gossips say you wore familiar pieces at the Christmas court."

I felt myself tempted to lie. I had never questioned the source of the jewels Edward gave me. Of late he had given me fewer pearls and more precious stones, which he urged me to wear. I usually ignored him. I feared reprisals if I outshone my betters, and told him so. But at Christmas he had insisted that I would ruin his design with my modesty.

"His Grace did insist I wear some of the late queen's jewels then," I conceded. "But I knew they were never mine to keep. What else do they say of me?"

"That you control access to the king, and that his household is now filled with your friends."

"Geoffrey! That is not true." Perhaps the first was, to an extent, but not the second. Those perceived as my friends were the very men I had warned Edward against. "They connect us because we engage in trade."

Geoffrey held up a hand. "I know that, and most other folk do as well. But they prefer to chatter about such nonsense rather than delve more deeply, where they might discover the uneasy fact that His Grace is not the man he once was, and neither is his heir. Prince Edward's son Richard is likely to be the next king, but he is so young—too young— and too much like the late Queen Mother Isabella for their tastes."

I worried for Joan. I, too, had heard this said about her youngest son. "Poor child, already criticized for a likeness over which he has no control."

. . .

EDWARD'S IMPENDING sortie into France loomed over the household all spring, for essentially all the household officers, pages, grooms—all its males—were to embark with the king and the prince. Two men in ill health confronting a wily fox on his own terrain—I feared for our two Edwards. I planned to retire to one of my manors in the countryside with my daughters and Grandmother, if I could persuade Dame Agnes to make the journey. She had been frail and confused on my most recent visits, but I wondered how much of that was worsened by her withdrawal from society. She rarely left the house now, doing so only to cross the square to the church. I also hoped that John would join us for a while; Lord Percy was considering my request to have my son with me for a few months.

All my bustling about in preparation could not drown out my fearful thoughts. Despite knowing how much it meant to Edward, I prayed that something benign might prevent his proceeding. He counted on a victory over Charles to take away his aches and pains, rejuvenate him, right all the wrongs of recent years. But neither victory nor defeat could change the truth that he was an aging king with a troublingly broken heir, and I feared how he would cope with disillusionment after victory even more than I feared how he would meet with defeat.

It had been months since he had been able to make love to me, though we continued to pleasure one another in other satisfying ways. I tried to convince him that we were as passionate and loving as ever. But I knew he felt diminished. One evening he urged me to seek out love potions or spells that might make it possible for him to make love to me again. My arguments that he *was* making love to me in all the ways that mattered only angered him.

"I fear such people as those who dabble in love potions and spells, Edward, my love. What if someone should find out and condemn us?"

"I am the king, Alice. Who would dare condemn me?"

Some questions were better left unanswered, but in my heart I doubted that he was as safe as he thought.

IN LATE July I gathered my daughters and Dame Agnes, to whom the warm days of summer had been kind, and we began our travels with the short journey to Barking Abbey to spend a day with Bella, now a novice. I had seen her earlier in the season, on her birthday, and rejoiced to witness her contentment. As I had hoped, Dame Agnes was comforted by seeing this as well.

We then continued on to the manor of Tibenham in Norfolk. It was part of the de Orby wardship in which I had invested a great deal of money and Robert's time, hoping to return it to productivity. Henry, Lord Percy had suggested that his half sister Mary, my ward and heiress to the manor, might accompany John and revisit the home in which she had spent her earliest summers. She was a few years his junior, and as Edward still considered her a possible wife for our son I agreed, thinking it worth observing them together. The manor was very near the sea. I did not like to journey so far with my frail grandmother and little Jane, who was still very young, but in the end Joan's excitement about seeing her brother won me over.

It proved to be a beautiful house, and Dame Agnes enjoyed sitting in the garden there, feeling the cool salt breeze beneath the hot sun in the late afternoon. I missed the bright mornings at Fair Meadow or Ardington, though. So near the coast, the mornings were often dull with fog.

I was soon distracted by an unexpected visitor. One misty morning as I stood in the hall looking out on what seemed to be a solid wall of gray just beyond the porch, two figures on horseback emerged from the fog. My first thought was fear that something had gone wrong in Sandwich. In June Lord Pembroke's fleet of ships sailing to La Rochelle in Gascony, carrying a small fortune to pay for the military support of Gascon lords and their men, was utterly destroyed by a Spanish fleet. After the initial hysteria, the silence into which the palace sank was more terrifying than all the cries and moans and shouted accusations that had greeted this news. I and many attached to Edward's household had invested heavily in the war as a show of confidence. We were stunned by our loss. Plans for embarking from Sandwich had resumed with a sense of desperate urgency. Both Princess Joan and Prince Edward had impressed upon me how devastating was the loss of our fleet and wealth, and how essential it was to retaliate. They had asked me to go to Richard Lyons to ask for more financial support, which I had done, with much misgiving. The king, my beloved, was not strong enough for such a venture either in body or spirit.

Now I crossed myself and said a prayer that these visitors did not presage ill news. As the men drew closer, a different dread manifested itself—the taller rider on the fine horse was William Wyndsor.

"What is he doing here?" Grandmother hissed behind me.

I had not noticed her there. "I do not know. I pray it is not bad news about the sailing." I turned to her, looking into her gauzy eyes. "But how can you recognize him from here?"

"I smell him, the rat who tore our family apart. Friend to the she-devil!"

She thought it was Janyn. "It is not my husband, he is dead, Grandmother. It is Sir William Wyndsor."

She looked confused.

"From afar his dark hair and his height could fool me as well," I said. Courtesy required I should invite him into the hall. "Shall we welcome him?"

I sent a servant to fetch a groom who then invited William and his companion within. I reached the screens shielding the hall from drafts just as William stepped through them, shaking out his damp cloak.

"God's blood, you are as beautiful as ever, Alice!"

"Is there some trouble?"

"No. I come to thank you for your assistance."

"As I wrote at the time, there was no need to thank me." How could he not know how unwelcome he was in my home?

I sent his page to the kitchen for some food and ale.

Grandmother greeted William with cautious courtesy. Mary Percy, John, and Joan looked up from their play to study him as only children can, openly staring, taking no care to hide their disinterest when he did no tricks.

But William strode over to them and crouched down. "I am William Wyndsor, recently come from Ireland. Whom am I addressing?"

"Mary," she said with a lisp and a finger up her nose.

"Joan."

"John Southery," my son said, scrambling to stand and give William a stout bow.

William expressed delight upon meeting them, then noticed Jane in her nurse's arms as he rose. "And this lovely child?"

"Jane."

"These are all yours?"

How little he knew of my life. "Not Mary. I am her guardian, though she does not usually reside with me. John is being fostered by her half brother, Henry Percy."

William lifted a brow. "The three others are the king's children?"

"Of course." I felt myself blush though I knew his question was most likely innocent, not a suggestion that I had more lovers.

"They all favor him. But where is Bella?"

"She is now a novice at Barking Abbey. Her choice."

"Such a beautiful child."

"Yes, she is. Now come, William." I led him out into the brightening yard, then turned to him and demanded, "How did you know where to find me?"

"Does it matter?"

"Yes, William, I believe it may."

"I asked. Discreetly. I have but a few days, Alice, then I must return to Westminster. I had to see you."

"It is most courteous of you. And now, your deed done, you are welcome to refresh yourself before continuing on your journey."

"You would send me away so soon?"

"Yes. Rest here in the garden. A servant will bring you some food and ale."

"Will you sit with me awhile?"

"I cannot. I must see to the children." I hurried back inside the house.

Robert came to me in a little while to say that William and his servant had departed.

"Had His Grace sent him? Is there news?" he asked.

"He said nothing of Sandwich. He'd come all this way merely to thank me for arranging the sale of that manor—the one you took care of for me. But how he knew where to find me, and to come so far . . . I do not like it. What sort of man persists with so little encouragement? What is his game? Who sent him?"

Robert took my hands. "If he returns, I shall deal with him."

I pressed his hands. "He is not your burden, my friend."

"Nor should he be yours."

I drew strength from Robert's concern. But I was still worried. Edward must not hear of William's visit, innocent though it was. In his frail state his reactions were unpredictable, often rash. I asked Robert to listen for gossip among the tenants. Days later, when he had heard nothing, I finally began to hope that nothing would come of William's unwelcome appearance.

"Your new tenants have benefited from your improvements, Alice,"

Robert assured me. "Even had they noticed anything awry, I doubt they would speak ill of you."

Unfortunately, I soon learned that Henry, Lord Percy knew of William's visit. Not wishing to call more attention to the incident, I did not investigate whether John and Mary had spoken of it as children might, or whether it had been Henry Percy himself who had told William where I would be. I would not have considered the latter but that I knew how ambitious Percy was, and could well imagine his tucking away this knowledge of William's interest in me as possibly useful in future. I could not judge whether my concern for Edward's failing health and his reckless intent to lead an army had rendered me so worried about my own future that I suspected enemies where there were none, or whether I was right to sense ranks closing in round me. For the rest of our sojourn in Norfolk I walked about in a fog of fear and anxiety that dimmed the joy of having my children and Dame Agnes with me in such a beautiful setting.

I did not see William again until I returned to Westminster, which was much sooner than I had expected.

IN LATE summer the weather turned foul. The king, the prince, the barons and all their men, ships, and stores were still waiting in Sandwich for the winds and storms to abate so they might cross the Channel to France when word came that the English-held town of La Rochelle had fallen to Charles's troops. The weather had defeated the two Edwards, father and son. In mid-October the expedition force was disbanded, having achieved nothing, gone nowhere, at great cost. It was a financial disaster, for wars were funded on the understanding that ransoms and plunder would refill the coffers. There was no hope of that this bleak autumn. Worse, the great kingdom of Aquitaine was all but lost—little now remained in English hands but for some strips of land along the coast. Edward's dream of being king of both France and England was dead.

I thanked God that he was back in Windsor, but he returned aged and dispirited, craving escape in lovemaking, hunting, hawking, dancing, yet bereft of the will even to rise from his bed. In truth, he suffered from such debilitating despair that I agreed with Prince Edward that we must protect the king from public view on his worst days.

The desperate financial situation required Wykeham's calm wisdom and Brantingham's practical caution. But Prince Edward denied them both access to his father, saying the two bishops had had their chance to advise the king and failed. All of us at court who had the where-withal once again bought some of the loans, to provide the Crown with immediate cash.

I do not know whether a younger king and a healthier prince might have made the journey to France that late summer. On some days Edward was certain that he had failed his people; if he felt that the prince might better lead the people, he would have stood aside. But the horror of it was that the heir, too, had failed his people. On other days Edward railed against the winds and tides, the inefficiency of his captains, his son's plodding progress to Sandwich.

He began to slip back into the past, talking obsessively about the half brother he had met in Italy, the bastard son of his mother and Roger Mortimer. He spoke of how he regretted never having made the effort to meet him again after that one encounter when the boy was about eight.

"My half brother . . . What sort of man did he become? Was he bitter? Content?"

He also thought much about the rumor that his father had escaped from Berkeley Castle and secretly retreated from the world, living out the rest of his days in peace in a monastery. "Would that I might do so. An old king is no good for the realm."

Gradually a darksome aspect crept into this plan; he began to for-get more and more often that his father had actually died at Berkeley, and that his retirement had been only a rumor. He reassured himself that he would be following his father's "wisdom" in knowing when a monarch should abdicate with grace. I would try to distract him by drawing him out for a brief ride or, if he were not so inclined, at least to the mews to see the hawks. I hoped that being out in the countryside and moving freely would bring him back to the present. I remembered with what anxiety Tommasa and Janyn had witnessed the dowager queen's decline, and how right they had been to fear it. I prayed theirs would not be my fate.

As EDWARD'S health continued to deteriorate through the win-ter, it was increasingly difficult to conceal his spells of illness. A moment I had long dreaded occurred during a feast at Windsor. Ed-ward was seated on the dais in full view when he suddenly slumped in his chair. Princess Joan and I quickly shielded him, pretending to be discussing something about the jewels in his crown. Just as suddenly he opened his eyes, straightened, and commanded us to stop fussing over him. More often he would briefly lose the use of an arm or leg. I grew adept at staying close to him and masking how much I was aiding him in sitting up straight or holding his arm naturally.

I resented the ease with which Joan and the prince would withdraw to their palace in Kennington for a rest, John would disappear to his mistress Katherine or his wife Constance, and I would be left in charge of Edward, night and day. Of course he was surrounded by his household administrators, knights, and servants, but they all looked to me for direction when the king confused them.

When Dame Agnes was on her deathbed, I left John Neville in charge of the king, with two of Edward's physicians seeing to matters of a more personal nature, and worried about him constantly during the weeks I sat with my dear grandmother. In faith, while I watched at her bedside, I imagined sitting so at Edward's deathbed. At thirty years of age, all my thoughts had turned toward the deaths of my elders.

On the rare occasions that I was freed from my duties at court, I would gather my daughters from the home of my sister Mary, send for Robert if he were not too far afield, and we would enjoy a respite in London or at Fair Meadow. I rode as much as possible and sought the comfort of hawking in season. When I freed my hawks from their jesses, I would tell them to soar and imagine taking their place, flying free, enjoying the exuberant rush up, up into the air before returning to my master's glove. But these interludes were brief and seldom.

My time with Edward was now bittersweet, his physical and mental decline reminding me that my days with him were numbered. My heart ached when I thought back on my life with him. In losing Edward, I would lose not only a lover and a lord but a confidant, a keeper of my secrets. I expected nothing from Edward's family once he was gone, except the status he had sworn to give our son John—knighthood in the year of Edward's jubilee, the great celebration of his fifty years of rule in four years' time. He had obtained promises from both Prince Edward and Duke John that they would carry out the knighting if he were to die before that date. As for our daughters, Edward felt certain that the estate I had acquired would provide excellent dowries for Joan and Jane, sufficient for them to wed minor knights or wealthy merchants.

"Why do you love our daughters less than John?" I asked him.

"How can you so accuse me, Alice? I greet them with as much

affection as I do John. And I believe I have given them far more gifts than I've given him."

"But he will be a knight, respected and honored as your son. They will enjoy no such status. Could you not recognize them as yours, Edward? Give them the benefit of noble standing?"

"Were you happy as the wife of Janyn Perrers?"

"You know that I was."

"Why should they not be happy in similar marriages?"

"Because they know they are daughters of the king. Your blood runs in their veins, Edward. They will have your pride."

On this matter he would not bend. And, God help me, I could not forgive his slight to his daughters.

And yet I loved him still, though it was not as before. I felt a tenderness for him, an affection, as I imagine one does in the latter years of a long marriage. His white hair was thinning, his flesh hung slack on his still-straight but often aching frame. His joints swelled with long sitting. He drooled in his sleep. Yet when he rose and was dressed in his kingly robes, he was still an impressive figure of a man, and most days his mind was clear and cunning, his wisdom deep, his love for me constant.

IN THE forty-sixth year of Edward's reign, when Philippa was almost four years dead, my love presented me with diamonds, rubies, and emeralds that had belonged to her. Some were in settings I well remembered—a circlet with fleur-de-lis set with diamonds and rubies, a gold ring in which was set a large emerald flanked by insets of lapis lazuli, a girdle of interlocking gold and silver sprinkled with diamonds, to name my favorites. Others were loose stones to add to all the pearls he had given me—and still did. I remembered Geoffrey's warning about the gossip surrounding my wearing the less identifiable jewels at a Christmas court. How I could wear these there I did not know. Edward was oblivious to the danger of such gifts. It was madness.

ONE OCTOBER morning at Havering, as I returned from a solitary ride, I encountered William Wyndsor in the hall, his shoulders hunched defiantly, his visage turned in on itself in anger. He was coming from the direction of Edward's chambers. Such was his self-absorption he did not notice me until I stepped in front of him and said his name, loud and sharp. Only then did he pause and look up.

Though I would have preferred to have avoided him, I could not, and therefore I put on my cordial court façade. "William, what is amiss?"

He growled, shook his head, and pushed past me, but had taken only a few steps when he turned back. "You've done enough. Leave me be!" he said in the impatient tone he used with misbehaving dogs— and he was not fond of dogs.

Having been blamed for what I did not know, I followed him. Once out in the yard I grabbed his shoulder and demanded, "If I'm to be blamed, have the courtesy to tell me what I've done."

"His Grace has dropped the charges against me and is sending me back to Ireland."

I almost laughed at his snarling delivery of such good news. "I should think that is what you wanted."

"I return as King's Lieutenant, not Governor."

I looked into his beautiful eyes and saw there a spoiled, greedy boy. "Titles mean little, William. You have been cleared of charges and shall resume your post. You should be celebrating, not berating me."

With a look that chilled me, he removed my hand from his shoulder and walked away. I cannot say I was disappointed to see him go, but I was puzzled. And I felt subtly threatened, though I could think of no cause for this. I realized he had not explained what he thought I had to do with such news.

That evening Edward told me of his decision about William. He had been in a charming, amorous mood all afternoon. We had taken a long walk in the gardens, lingered over a delicious meal, rested together—he insisted that I join him—and since waking had sipped watered wine and reminisced about our years together. As he told me about William he seemed oddly gleeful, as if he were congratulating himself for besting someone. William, I supposed. Though I did not like to discuss him with Edward, I could not help myself.

"Forgive me, my love, but I do not understand your mood," I said. "You are happy you did not need to punish one of your trusted administrators, yet seem to feel you tricked him."

Edward laughed, a deep, satisfied laugh. "He claims you are his betrothed—that you've been betrothed for years. I wished him all happiness after I'm dead. For now, you are mine, and he shall remain far from you."

I thought I might choke, it was suddenly so difficult to breathe. I felt more than betrayed by William, I felt defiled.

Still smiling, Edward reached for my hands, looking me in the eyes. "Alice, I love you too much to share you with another man." He kissed both my hands. When he looked up once more he had ceased smiling. "I am protecting you from a man who does not deserve you. He is cunning and greedy, and angry with the world for its imagined slights."

"Edward, my love." I had found my breath. "I agree with all you say about him. I saw through his shallow charm long ago, and I never swore to wed him. I sent him away. I love you. Only you."

"I do not blame you for seeking pleasure with a younger man." He held up a hand to stop me from protesting. "I have known that you have been with another when you are away from me."

I cringed under this blow. He had said on several occasions that his indifference toward the future of our daughters was inspired by doubt that they were indeed his children. I had sworn every oath I could think of that his doubts were utterly unfounded, that it was impossible that they were not his. Indeed, Joan, with her flaxen hair and blue eyes, looked so like Edward that he often swore it must only be Jane about whom he was unsure. Jane favored me, her bone structure softer than his, her hair a little darker, her eyes gray green. These doubts assailed him only on the days when he woke confused. On his more coherent days he sometimes declared he would acknowledge Joan and Jane.

"Wyndsor is my son John's creature, Alice." He chuckled and kissed my hands once more. "I have urged him to marry Wyndsor off to a dark beauty from Constance's household and send him to Castile in some dangerous post, but he makes excuses, pretends to have forgotten. Beware, my love."

Of all the accusations and slights I had endured, this was the most bitter. I had been impeccably faithful to Edward and he did not believe it.

"Why would I have told you how he pestered me had I anything to hide? I have lain with no man but you since Janyn. Did he say we had lain together?"

"He did not need to."

I was furious to find myself both insulted and unheard by this man who had won my heart by making me feel both seen and heard.

. . .

I N SPRING of the forty-seventh year of Edward's reign he named a ship after me, *La Alice*. It was beautiful, and I was touched by the joy it gave him to blindfold me and lead me along the dock. He had greeted me that morning with an air of happy anticipation, and the wondrous vessel before me certainly exceeded all my expectations. But it was far too public an honor, the sort of extravagant gesture that could only do me harm.

When I next saw the Duke of Lancaster, he said, "Give thanks for your moments with my father, Alice, but remember that he is old, he is failing, and when he is gone you shall need another protector, whether a ship rides at anchor on the Thames bearing your name or no."

"I live with a keen awareness of the precipice just beyond my sight, my lord. I am most grateful to have your friendship." I believed it imperative to pretend I still considered him my friend, concealing the fact that I had become ever more wary of him.

The duke looked pleased. "I am glad of that."

This encounter chilled me. Why he had felt the need to warn me, I did not know. There were few at court I felt I could always count on. Indeed, at that moment I could think of but one, Princess Joan. I still had Wykeham's friendship, but his influence was now limited. Despite Edward's advice I had failed to make any deep friendships at court; those I had were all shallow, based on business, not trust.

Lancaster's words echoing in my head, I walked the palace corridors with eyes cast down, avoiding the cool looks, the knowing grins.

I N SPRING of the following year, Edward planned what would prove to be his last great tournament, an event that was to bring home to me how justified was my deepening sense of dread. To be staged at Smithfield in early May, the event would extend over seven days, with jousting, tourneying, and feasting in celebration of the glory of Edward's realm and reign. True to his lifelong delight in devising elaborate themes for such festivities, Edward chose to be the Sun King, and I, his lady of the lists, was to appear as the Lady of the Sun. All such tournaments began with processions through the city, and I was accustomed to playing some role in these, but this time he meant for me to lead the ladies of the court, riding in a golden chariot. I imagined Lancaster, indeed all of the courtiers, watching me with scorn.

"As my Lady of the Sun you shall be as regal and fiercely beautiful as that magnificent bird, Alice." Edward sat with head flung back, watching a falcon in flight.

"Edward, no, it is impossible that I should play such a role. Let Princess Joan be your lady in this."

I had drawn him out to watch the falconer training new hawks, hoping to distract him as I argued against his scheme. We sat on a bench beneath a pretty arbor, the sun warming us.

"You are my queen in spirit if not in title, Alice, and I will have it so." His voice was low, his tone conversational, his eyes fixed on the birds.

"No, Edward, I am not your queen, but a merchant's daughter raised to know my place."

He reached for my hand and squeezed it. "Your place is beside me, my love."

I did not need more enemies. I slipped my hand from his grasp and knelt before him. "Edward, look at me for a moment."

He squinted down at me, his once wondrously blue eyes clouded now with age. "You are so beautiful. . . ."

"Edward, I pray you, listen to me. You must understand that you endanger me by insisting on my being the Lady of the Sun."

"You shall not deny me this pleasure, Alice." He was no longer smiling.

"Princess Joan—"

"No. My son is too ill to take part. His wife would not wish to call attention to his absence by appearing on my arm." The peacock feathers in Edward's hat shivered as his head began to shake, his temper rising. "You must trust me. You must be there."

His health was too fragile to risk an angry outburst. I retreated at once. "My love, my love, please be calm. We shall discuss this later." I rose to sit beside him once more, kissing his hand, his cheek.

Each time I tried to dissuade him, he frightened me with his temper. In the end, I accepted defeat and buried my fears, doing all that I could to ensure that the tournament would be a success.

It was at such times that I most missed Queen Philippa—her enthusiastic encouragement of us throughout the weeks of work, her almost childlike delight in our progress and astonishment at the results. She had lifted our hearts and rendered it all innocent fun. I still took immense pleasure in the sumptuous cloth, the feathers, buttons, and jewels gathered for the costumes, the silver-and-gold wire, the cloth of gold and silver, but I had no one with whom to share my delight. Princess Joan and Edward's daughter Isabella were vaguely interested, but the sempsters and servants working with me were for the most part quietly intent on their assignments, and I did not have the queen's talent for lightening their spirits.

It was Edward who finally engaged their enthusiasm. He took it upon himself to appear in the sewing chamber at the end of each day, to examine our progress. The women would sit with eyes meekly cast down, listening while I pointed out the fine details of their work. He would lavish praise on it and urge me on to more splendid designs, more gold, more silver . . . more, more, more.

"We are proclaiming the glory of England," he would declare to the room at large. "I would dazzle my people."

On the morrow the women would crowd round me, eager to see what I had added to the design, that they might better honor their beloved king, still the king of their hearts. I could not help but be caught up in their excitement.

When all was ready I stood in awe of the robes, the sheer spectacle in which I was to be one of the central figures. My gown, like Edward's, was cloth of gold. The background, or warp threads, were red silk and the foreground, or weft threads, were the most delicate gold wire. Red was for the rubies associated with the sun. Once cut and fitted, our gowns were embroidered with gold thread, sunbursts surrounding balas rubies and diamonds, which were also emblematic of the sun. Even my mantle was of cloth of gold, caught in back to free my shoulders and reveal the lining, the reverse of the gown, gold background with red foreground. From my neck to the low-cut top of my bodice, I wore gold tissue so fine as to be almost invisible, sprinkled with large rubies and diamonds set in gold sunbursts, as if even my flesh were transformed. For once I might feel like his queen as I stood by Edward's side.

On the morning of the procession my heart beat so fast I felt faint, all my earlier misgivings returned. It did not help that the elaborate headdress, of gold tissue built up to create a sunburst around my head, had to be firmly fastened to my hair, which was coiled beneath, to prevent it from taking flight. I felt the pricks whenever I made a sudden movement. Gwen needed six assistants to dress me. My hair, skin, everything, was covered in gold cloth. Finally the women stood back from me, their eyes wide. The sempsters, standing by to make last-minute repairs, applauded.

When Gwen held the long mirror up to me, I did not recognize myself. It was how I imagined the pagan goddesses to look.

Striding into the room, deriving renewed vigor from his own glorious costume, Edward spread his arms wide and proclaimed me to be every inch the Lady of the Sun.

"You are magnificent, Alice, my beloved!"

"As are you, my king," I said, gliding toward him to take his proffered hand. Though my headdress was light enough, my robe was not. But I did not complain. I would not ruin Edward's day.

The ladies of the court simpered over my costume as we moved into formation for the procession, but their eyes were cold. They were to walk behind me, all in silver cloth with simple silver veils held with silver fillets, leading horses on which rode their lords, also dressed in silver. Their only jewels were pearls. Cool moonlight trailing my blazing glory.

Our procession would move through the London neighborhood of Cheapside, not so far from where I had grown up. My golden self and the wake of silvery courtiers followed a goodly distance behind Edward, who had wished for a pure white stallion but had been persuaded to ride in a gold chariot as well, so that he might save his strength for the ceremonial ride on horseback to begin the tournament. Cheering throngs greeted their king, but as he passed and all eyes turned toward my advancing chariot the cheers faded. I shall never forget their eyes, first startled, then dazed, then shocked and quickly outraged as murmurs of protest gave way to jeers.

"Whore!" they called me. "Harlot!"

Though the sun beat down warmly, I was chilled to the bone. The Londoners did not see me as a symbol of England's glory but as the usurper of their beloved Queen Philippa. I made manifest their suspicions that the monies for the war had been spent on the court's excess, an aged king's obsession with his young, greedy, common mistress. Though hot with shame, I held myself straight and proud. But I knew I did not belong in that chariot.

During the entire week of festivities, I felt the threat to me whenever I passed crowds of commoners. No one touched me, there was no need. I shrank from the hatred in their eyes.

"I pray that you will look back on these glorious days with joy, Alice, and remember our love," Edward said as we watched a joust.

I squeezed his hand and gave him my warmest, happiest smile, for I had not seen him in such a gladsome mood in many a day. I could not bring myself to tell him what little joy I felt. That he did not comprehend he had raised me too high in naming me lady of the lists was evidence of his failing mind, his increasingly frequent inability to distinguish between what he might dream about and what was acceptable behavior in a king.

I feared for Edward that he could not see the dangerous mood of the crowd regarding his extravagance. He had thought to fool them with the appearance of being yet the Sun King, the glorious warrior, the young and vital monarch, and me as his young and vital queen. The illusion had failed as I had dreaded it would.

Princess Joan had once worried me by noting that I looked like a queen. Geoffrey had warned me that folk were appalled when I wore Philippa's jewels. But this . . . this went far beyond it in hubris. I remembered his warning to me of long ago about those who fell prey to their own weakness for finery and flattery.

Yet when had I the choice to be other than I was?

As WE withdrew from the banqueting hall the day after the tournament, Edward and I overheard a young cleric reciting to a pretty serving maid the names the Londoners had called me. Edward's head whipped round. I grasped his elbow and called for his page.

"Slanderer! Traitor!" Edward shouted, and with his old strength he broke free of me and boxed the cleric's ears. Never had I seen him attack one of his subjects.

Bishop Wykeham and Richard Stury hurriedly came between them, Stury taking the arm of the whimpering cleric while Wykeham admonished the foolish young man in a voice that reassured the gathering courtiers.

"Come, Your Grace. Let us leave the rabble to their sermon," I murmured as we were surrounded by guards who escorted us to the king's chambers.

When we were safely behind closed doors, Edward kissed my hands, then gathered me into his trembling arms. "They do not know you, Alice, else they would not abuse you so."

"Your love is all I require," I murmured, feeling his agitation.

He retired to bed for several days afterward.

"I must leave court," I told Geoffrey.

"Perhaps Fair Meadow," he said. "The city is the worst place for you. The people say it was you who insisted on parading yourself as Edward's queen."

No champion defended me, for who but the king could do that, and he was incapacitated, beyond caring about the mood of the crowd.

In the end I remained by his side at his insistence, though I felt myself to be a leper at court; all eyes watching me, judging me, all avoiding contact with me. Joan agreed that it had been a dangerous choice to make me lady of the lists and parade me in a robe so much more magnificent than those of my betters, though she had not attempted to convince Edward of his folly beforehand. I wondered now whether she merely pretended to be my friend.

In late summer a party of louts descended on my manor of Finningley in Nottinghamshire, stealing some cattle and mutilating or driving off the rest—destroying crops in their stampede and holding my servants and tenants hostage in the house until they swore an oath to leave my service. The violence of the attack shook me. I thought that if I did not respond with force they would feel free to repeat the action. In truth, I wanted vengeance. But Wykeham advised me to investigate the disturbance without calling too much attention to it. I sent Robert and Richard Lyons to look into the matter and assess the damage.

Edward began to experience his spells more frequently and developed painful boils that at first we feared were marks of pestilence. But his physicians were confident they were caused by something in his diet and his often-agitated spirits. That they remained by his side and cared for him reassured me more than their words had done. After a visit in which Bella proved a calming presence, Edward asked often for her, and with the permission of her abbess she came to help me in the long vigils in his chamber. I, too, found her a great comfort.

As my beloved succumbed to the toll of his years and his maladies, I felt increasingly helpless to draw him back to the present, to clarity. My paternoster beads and my sewing kept my hands busy when I was with him, and when I was away from him I knelt in the chapel or rode until exhausted, my tears a sacrificial offering to the wind, as if I believed the air so mingled with my essence might enter Edward and revive him. I wanted him back with me. I wanted our lives to be as they had been.

My sweet Bella was my succor and delight in those dark days. When

Edward slept, she and I would sit in my chamber and talk of him. Bella wished to know all about our years together, about the joys we had shared. She asked about her father as well. I had always hesitated to tell her the story of his family's loyalty to the dowager queen and the tragedy it had wrought, fearing that she would hate Edward for his mother's part in it and blame me for staying with him. Now it seemed the right time to tell her everything. I spun out the story over the course of several evenings. Her behavior toward me subtly changed during those days. She was watchful, curious, and in the end sympathetic.

When I had completed the tale, Bella reached over to me, putting one hand to either side of my face, and held me gently, looking deep into my eyes. After a while, she kissed my forehead. It felt like both a blessing and an absolution.

"I almost said that I did not know how unhappy you were, but that is not true. I have always sensed an unspeakable sorrow beneath your gaiety," she said. "Why did you never tell me this?"

"I did not wish you to grow up beneath a cloud," I said. "When I saw how frightened you were in Queen Joan's household, I was determined never to send you back and to do all that I could to give you the joy Janyn and I meant you to have."

Bella bowed her head for a moment, the veil hiding her face from me. I feared she was weeping and my old guilt was rekindled. Though I'd had no choice, I had felt then I should have insisted on seeing her more often. But when my daughter looked up, she had regained her equanimity.

"In truth, I have some happy memories of my life there. Few include Queen Joan, not because she was unpleasant or frightening to me but simply because she had little to do with her wards. The household servants saw to us, and most of them were kind. No harm was done by my being there, except that I missed you and Father."

Later, as we lay side by side in my great bed, she said, "It was always painful to be parted from you. I feared you would disappear as Father and Grandmother Tommasa had."

"Was I then wrong not to tell you?"

She rolled over on her side and kissed my cheek. "It was probably best that you waited until the king was so ill, since I cannot find it in my heart to condemn him."

I found the courage then to explore my fears about her vocation. She was now Dame Isabella—she had taken her vows at fifteen. "Did

you choose to take religious vows because of my liaison with Edward?"
I asked.

"No, Mother, I have told you over and over again—I was called,
and have no regrets."

My daughter had grown up to be not only wise, pious, and beautiful, but compassionate, too. I was grateful for it and terribly proud of
her.

"What will you do when His Grace is gone?" she asked.

"I do not like to think of it, Bella. For a while I will allow myself to
grieve—for Janyn and for Edward."

My daughter nestled closer and put a protective arm round me.
"May God grant you peace after all this."

I prayed for the same, but did not dare to hope too much.

I believe Bella spoke to the king's physicians, for without my saying
anything about being exhausted or heavy of heart they came to me as a
group to suggest that I spend some time away from Edward's sickbed.
I resisted the idea at first, but Bella convinced me that I would return
to him with a lighter heart, which might do him good as well.

AFTER A few days of rest at my home in London, I invited Robert
and Richard to discuss the repairs to Finningley and the reparation to be paid to those who had been injured or imprisoned by the
attackers. Robert spoke with confidence about setting all to rights,
but his expression was guarded. When he was finished, he and Richard
exchanged a look. Richard nodded and sat forward, taking his turn to
speak.

"A number of those who worked at Finningley wish to leave your
service," he said. "Some out of fear of further reprisals and some because they have come to believe the lies their attackers have spread
about you."

I had imagined the former but not the latter, having prided myself
on being a caring and responsive landlord.

"What sorts of lies? You can tell me, Richard. I am not so fragile,
and should know what people say of me."

Robert interrupted. "Alice, perhaps—"

I shook my head at him. "Go on, Richard."

It was a long and varied list. I had put a spell on the king and
replaced his counsellors with my business partners and lovers. I'd
prevented his wise counsellors from seeing him. Had weakened his

manhood with fornication. I was blamed for high prices, the loss of the Aquitaine, even the debilitating illness of Prince Edward.

"Dear God in heaven, they believe me to be a sorceress!"

Richard took my hands and waited until I looked into his eyes. "You will survive all this, my friend. We will make certain of it."

I could not see how, but was moved by their loyalty and love. I thanked them and withdrew to my room, where I knelt and prayed that Edward might return to health long enough for me somehow to redeem myself in the eyes of the people. Foolish prayers.

ONE EVENING in London, after the children were abed, Robert found me silently weeping by the dying fire in the hall. He joined me on the bench and put his arm round me. I leaned against his shoulder and took deep, shuddering breaths. With his free hand he stroked my hair, and whether he spoke the words or I just divined them from his heartbeat, I heard his gentle reassurance that all would be well, that Edward could not have found a more loving companion for his last years, that I was yet young and would find love again. I felt my body and my mind released from grief for a while.

When I was breathing with ease, Robert drew his arm away and rose. "Come," he said, "Gwen waits for you above." He held out his hand.

I rose into his embrace.

"God was looking to my welfare when he sent you into my life, Robert," I whispered. "You are my solace and my anchor." Edward had once been that to me but those days were long gone. I remained tethered to him by the ropes of memory and the demands of his sons. But it was Robert I longed to be with now. From depending on him, trusting him, I had grown to love him.

"I will ever be here, to comfort and steady you," he promised.

17

*My lords, we have declared to you and to the whole council of parlia-
ment various trespasses and extortions committed by various people,
and we have had no remedy; nor is there anyone about the king who
wishes to tell him the truth, or to counsel him loyally and profitably,
but always they scoff, and mock, and work for their own profit; so we
say to you, that we shall say nothing further until all those who are
about the king, who are false men and evil counsellors, are removed
and ousted from the king's presence; and until our lord the king
appoints as new members of his council men who will not shirk from
telling the truth, and who will carry out reforms.*

—Peter de la Mare, speaking for the commons,
Good Parliament, 1376 (trans. Chris Given-Wilson)

• 1375 to 1376 •

Throughout Edward's illnesses I remained by his side,
sometimes sending for Joan and Jane, finding comfort in their
company. It lifted my spirits to see the palaces in which we lived
through the curious eyes of my children, to hear their laughter and
shouts of delight echoing down the corridors or wafting in through
windows. My sweet ones were affectionate toward me but wary of their
father, who as often as not thought they were someone else's little girls.

But Edward never forgot that John was our son. When we had seen
him at the Smithfield tournament, John had been warmly affectionate
toward his father. In contrast, though he'd spoken politely to me, he'd
shown no great affection. Of course, he would be most impressed and
proud of his father, the King of England, and it was seemly that a boy
be closer to his father than his mother, but I had hoped he would remember how he had loved to rest with me and listen to the stories I
wove for him on those lazy afternoons. Since he had joined the Percy
household I had seen him only on state occasions or at Christmas, and
gradually he had grown distant. Though friends assured me that it was
the way with young boys, I feared the Percy clan were poisoning him

against me and prayed I was wrong. He was growing into a handsome young man, looking very like his father. Edward had proudly taken him round to his uncles, aunts, and cousins, declaring, "Undeniably a Plantagenet, eh?"

Geoffrey empathized with me, but gently reminded me that it was no small honor that the king was so proud of our son. "And have I heard correctly that John is to be betrothed to Mary Percy?"

"It is true." That had, of course, long been in Edward's mind. But as I now confided to Geoffrey, I had been surprised that Henry Percy had so readily agreed to the betrothal.

"You do not look pleased."

"I would have been a fool to reject the proposal, for the marriage will elevate my son more than I had hoped possible. Yet I do not care for Mary." Being my ward, she now lived in my household as one of my children, as John lived among the younger Percys. "At the moment she is a willful, spiteful, and unimaginative child."

"She is still so young. Surely you might influence her, having her in your care?"

"I can only pray, though she makes it plain she considers us beneath her." Another problem with the betrothal. And they were *both* still young, too young to be so bound.

I also disliked the fact that Henry Percy was one of John, Duke of Lancaster's staunchest supporters. I increasingly felt as though all my life was being arranged by Lancaster toward some unknown purpose. I remembered his warning about my needing protection when Edward died, and Edward's warning that William Wyndsor was John's man. I imagined that my son's marrying a Percy might be part of such a scheme, but did not trust the Percy clan. What sort of protection would the marriage provide? And for whom?

The duke continued to promise that he and Prince Edward would ensure that my children and I would be safe from any harm, and that after their father's death I would be free to withdraw to my estates and live in peace and comfort. It was the frequent repetition of that promise that worried me. And how everyone who crossed my path was so tightly bound to Lancaster.

IN MAY of the forty-ninth year of Edward's reign he would once again approach parliament requesting a tax to raise funds for war. Not only did he need to repay loans made toward his failed attempt at crossing to France and to rebuild the fleet lost at La Rochelle, but he had also inexplicably begun to believe once again that the crown of France was within his grasp and dreamed of yet another mission across the Channel.

"This time we shall vanquish them, eh, Edward?"

The prince and his brother the duke exchanged uneasy glances.

"Fear not, sweet Alice," Joan whispered. "Neither of them could sit a horse all the way to Portsmouth. Nor have they a fleet!"

Her words were little comfort, pointing out my beloved's self-delusion. All who heard this plan would surely wonder at his folly.

In the weeks leading up to the meeting with parliament he was in much better health, the boils having finally faded and his episodes of confusion and weakness having eased. We retired to King's Langley in late April for a brief respite after the Feast of St. George and before the ordeal with parliament. Edward was riding again, and hawking, though he wisely declined invitations to hunt, too vigorous an activity at his age. Even with this wise caution I could not rest easy, too aware that his confusion and weakness could return at any moment. His love was both a blessing and a curse for I lived only for him, to keep him content and calm.

My suggestion that while parliament sat I should go to Gaynes, my manor near Havering, disturbed him. He did not want me away from him so long.

"I need you, Alice. You complete me."

We held each other. I, too, felt that we moved as one when together; I had worked hard to learn to anticipate his needs. That he believed it was the natural outgrowth of our love for each other had been a boon, ensuring the success of his sons' scheme to hide the seriousness of his condition from his subjects. But I craved some peace, some freedom.

I backed out of Edward's embrace for a moment, stroking his gaunt cheek with the back of my hand, kissing his forehead. "How long could parliament sit, my love? No more than a month, surely. It would not be so long a separation."

That night we slept naked together, each affectionately exploring the other's familiar, beloved body. I massaged oils into his joints, his groin. He explored me with his tongue and fingers until I cried out in a bittersweet release. How different was that night from those of our earlier years together. In truth, this felt more like love in some ways than our lust ever had, for we each sought only to please the other, not ourselves.

In the end he agreed to my plan, and though he did not explain why he had decided I was right, his exhortations for me to hie straight to Gaynes convinced me that he, too, had heard the rumors of expected trouble and thought them plausible.

This anxious time would only grow worse. Richard Lyons sought me out after a meeting with Edward to warn me that one of the most powerful barons of the moment, the Earl of Pembroke, was fomenting anger in the commons against what he called the "court party," those of us who had shielded Edward from gossip during his episodes of weakness. Of course, by design few knew why we had shielded the king. Here was the public censure I had long feared. It was of no comfort to me that even Lancaster was suspected of supporting the "court party."

The beauty of the spring garden at King's Langley dimmed for me. "I will bide at Gaynes while parliament sits. It will be good to be free from court." I tried to sound resolved. "Perhaps Henry Percy might allow my son to be my guest for a time."

"Do not count on it. I do not know which barons agree with Pembroke. Or with Mortimer, Earl of March."

I had my own reason to dread any mention of the Mortimer family. Though Edward had never chosen to tell me *who* had shadowed Janyn and Tommasa for the secret they kept for the dowager queen, I had always suspected the obvious—the Mortimers, who would have been thus exalted to the crown family. They were powerful, as William Wyndsor had learned in Ireland, but not as powerful as they would have been in possession of the bastard son of Roger Mortimer and Queen Isabella. Yet as far as I knew, Richard had no knowledge of this, so I wondered—and worried—at his mentioning Mortimer.

"Why should I worry about the Earl of March?" I asked. "He was brought up by Wykeham. He is hardly my enemy."

"He is no longer under the bishop's guidance, Alice. You know that they are furious with Wyndsor over his heavy-handed governing in Ireland. The Earl of March and his friends, who might have been your allies against the commons, will not be looking kindly on you." Richard had never before mentioned William to me. Now he regarded me with interest, apparently curious to see how I would respond.

"Why should they connect me with William?"

"Is it not true that you are to wed him upon the king's death?"

A cold hand clutched at my heart. "No!" I cried out, as if to ward off a curse.

"Ah. I did wonder at that."

"Who said this?"

"Wyndsor. When we met to sign a business agreement. He was insufferably smug."

"I shall never wed him. Never!"

"You know that Wyndsor will be returning soon, do you not? Nicholas Dagworth is to preside over his investigation."

"Dagworth? But he is William's sworn enemy. His Grace knows that." I had cause to condemn William, but yet believed he had been loyally trying to enforce the law in Ireland in order to assist Edward with his war chest.

With a shrug, Richard said, "That is what I have heard."

MY CONSTANT Robert headed our small company departing King's Langley for Gaynes at Upminster in early May. Anticipating my needs as he so often did, he had already fetched Joan and Jane from my sister's home in London. They lent a gladsome mood to our journey down the Thames that spring afternoon. My son John had arrived by early evening and was to stay for a fortnight; Henry Percy had not forsaken me. I felt blessed and comforted by my children, Gwen, and Robert.

I had come to prefer Gaynes over even Fair Meadow. It was a pretty house, with windows that caught all the best light of the day and views of rolling woodland and meadows. I prayed that violence never shattered the calm there as it had in Finningley. Even my son John fell under its peaceful spell, reverting to his old loving and giving self, a delight to his little sisters and a great comfort to me. I still treasure as one of my life's most precious moments the afternoon when he asked if he might rest with me as we had in years past.

Yet however much comfort I found in my children and Gaynes, during that sojourn I often sank into anxiety, sorrow, and fear. From the beginning, that parliament was out for blood—that of William Latimer, John Neville, and Richard Stury as the courtiers, and Richard Lyons as the financier who had advised them in what the commons saw as their fraudulent use of power to fill their personal coffers.

Apparently Pembroke's man, Peter de la Mare, stepped up to lead the commons, and managed to press forward with their complaints. Though Prince Edward, adamantly opposed to conceding any ground to the commons, had been present for the start of the proceedings, he was so ill that he withdrew immediately after that.

I was terrified, fearing that public condemnation of me would surely follow. How I wished I had feigned illness and not displayed myself as the Lady of the Sun! I might lose everything now. I might lose my daughters' dowries.

Blame hung in the air. Working in the gardens at Gaynes, I would interpret birdsong as chiding. Riding out with Robert or my children, I would hear a litany of my sins in my mount's hoof beats. No matter how my family and friends tried to distract me with pleasant activities, I felt as if I were continually examining my conscience in preparation for the sacrament of confession, and was increasingly terrified to take my turn before my confessor.

While I watched Joan and Jane play in the garden, I would read missives from Geoffrey and my brother John. Joan's amusingly imperious voice, instructing Jane in the ever-shifting rules of her games, would suddenly in my mind call out more frightening news.

The commons claimed that the "court circle's" loans were grossly criminal, defrauding the Crown of huge sums owed it, that, in short, we had profited from Edward's financial problems. They claimed that in his dotage the king had been led into error by us, and that we controlled him—conveniently forgetting the strong arms and close involvement of Prince Edward and the Duke of Lancaster.

The accusations against Richard Lyons worried me for both our sakes. It was true that he had benefited from Edward's financial difficulties, but it had been his cleverness in investing that had first attracted the king's notice and inspired him to use Richard as an unofficial member of his council. It was Richard who had taught not only me but all the courtiers now accused how to buy Edward's letters of debt for a low fee and then bargain with the holders of the loans for a lower payment. The debtors had grown less sanguine about their settlements over time. Peter de la Mare was giving voice to their grievances. Even worse, Richard was a foreigner, a Fleming, of low birth, and a bastard; it angered Londoners in particular that such a man was so trusted by the king that he had been made warden of the royal mint and held high civil office in their city.

Richard and I had been raised up higher than our backgrounds would commonly allow, intruders in a class to which we did not belong, fraudulently enjoying the king's favor. I remembered the angry and disbelieving looks as I'd progressed through Cheapside in cloth of gold. God's blood, what had Edward been thinking? The commons hated both Richard and me.

I learned much of which I had previously been unaware, and knew that it would be impossible now to convince anyone I had not been part of the more outrageous profiteering, for I was not without blame. I had accepted Edward's largesse and used it to buy what I'd thought would bring me security.

My brother John risked a visit to Gaynes. We sat on the window seat in my bedchamber while we talked.

"The commons have found fault with Richard Stury's stature at court. They condemn him for the wardships, lands, offices, and marriages with which the king has rewarded him, though they do not suggest what might be done to remedy the matter."

"Even Stury?" I wondered aloud. "There are few the king trusts more than him. He has proved his loyalty and worth for fifteen years or more."

The commons judged Edward's benevolence and gratitude for service as weakness on his part. They had apparently forgotten that all property in the kingdom is in the king's gift, that all rulers use such gifts to reward loyalty—or so Edward had told me. I saw now that I had condemned myself in others' eyes by accepting presents given in love.

I drew out a casket of my most treasured gifts from Edward, primarily pearls, including the comb set with lapis that he had tucked into my hair so many years before, but also the ruby ring and brooch he had given me the night I told him I carried our first child.

"Would you take this and keep it for me, John? These are most precious to me." I would not give him all; if they came for my jewels, they would find only the costliest ones and search no further.

It was uncanny how like Father my brother looked at that moment, the crease between his eyes, the set of his jaw. But his shoulders did not cave in as Father's had in a crisis. John lifted the small casket. "I am glad to be of service to you, Alice. You have only to ask."

By late May orders had been given for the seizure of Richard Lyons's goods and those of other merchants implicated. Richard had reportedly offered a gift to the prince in exchange for his protection, but had been refused. Prince Edward had also reprimanded Stury for soft-ening his daily accounts to the king of the parliamentary proceedings. I was certain that Stury had meant only to protect the king, but the prince was in too much discomfort and his temper too short for him to hold his tongue long enough to consider how parliament would interpret his anger. All walls had ears, it seemed. We must watch our every word.

Everything happened so quickly, I felt unable to catch my breath. It was as if the poison that had collected for years in people's hearts and minds burst out all at once. It seemed as if I had just heard of the confiscation of Richard's goods when I received the terrible news that Prince Edward was grievously ill. His physicians believed he would die within days. The prince had summoned me, intending me to swear once more that I would shield his father when he suffered his spells from the eyes of those who would ridicule him and call for his abdica-tion. My brother advised me to stay away, but I meant to go. John did not, could not, understand my role at court.

While I was arranging for a barge I learned that John Neville was no long steward of the king's household. Even a member of a powerful family could fall, it seemed. Robert and Gwen urged me to change my mind about going to Westminster. The fear in their faces mirrored my own. But I still held out the hope that my heeding the prince's sum-mons would inspire him to continue to support me.

"But if he is dying?" Robert asked. "How then can he help you?"

I had never heard such fear in his voice. My own hands were clammy with dread.

"Robert, I must try. For Joan and Jane." Bella's dowry was safe at Barking. "For His Grace."

"You do not need him. Any of them. I will take care of you and your daughters, Alice, I promise you."

I took that promise into my heart, but could not yet clearly hear and accept it. I felt tied to Edward and his family despite a sense of impending betrayal.

I arrived under cover of darkness on the eve of Trinity Sunday, the feast that Prince Edward held most dear. I was shown to the king's chamber and was greatly grieved to find him looking so lost. I held him in my arms throughout the night and sang his favorite songs as he wept for his son. I knew then that Robert had been right, death was in the palace.

The prince died the following day, past remembering that he had summoned me. I felt cold and numb. But when Edward returned from the death chamber of his heir, looking near death himself, pale and hollow cheeked, I knew that God had meant for me to be there, caring for him.

"My heir now is but a child, Alice. Young Richard stood there, so slight, his eyes too large for his sweet face. The barons will devour him."

"My love, my love, you have many happy years ahead of you before young Richard takes your place."

Edward grasped his velvet hat and slid it down the side of his head, then let it drop to the floor, as if the effort of lifting it off and placing it on the table before him was far too much for him. His white hair now hung straggly and thin, the bald spot more visible than usual with his scalp red from the exertion of his walk.

"Let me undress you and cool you with cloths dipped in scented water."

He sighed and lifted his arms from his sides to allow me to remove his robes.

As I washed his body and then rubbed it with soothing oils, Edward muttered about parliament and how they had robbed him of Neville. His body felt different, diminished, as if some of his spirit had departed with his son's death. I tried to guide his thoughts to plans for a summer interlude at King's Langley or Havering. But he kept drifting back to parliament's outrageous, insulting behavior. Later he grew agitated once more about the danger of having so young an heir.

"I thank God that no one knew of my half brother—a Mortimer on the throne? Never!"

"My love, you have sufficient legitimate sons. No one would have thought to place your bastard brother on the throne." Indeed, from what I had managed to learn, few had ever known of the child. "You must never speak of him. Never. Lest you slip and mention him when others could be listening." They might think him mad.

"Do you doubt me, Alice?" Edward, suddenly lucid, glared at me.

"Never, my love." I knew my role. I must focus on his state of mind, not let him see that I knew he was frail and frightened.

PRINCESS JOAN took some refreshment with us in Edward's chambers that evening, mostly wine. Newly widowed, she looked almost as pathetic as her father-in-law; my heart ached for her. She had been so in love, had shared such dreams with the prince. She would have been Queen of England.

"It is a curse to outlive two beloved husbands," she sighed into her mazer, then tilted her head back and emptied it. A servant stepped forward to fill it once more.

"You will be sick from so much wine on this warm night," I cautioned.

"I shall find no comfort this night, Alice, with or without the drink. It is no matter." She shook her head, the jewels in her crespinette glittering in the candlelight. Her golden hair was dull with streaks of white. This small sign of neglect told me she'd known her husband's death was near, to have neglected the regimen of lotions and sunlight that kept her hair golden. Suddenly she planted her elbow on the table and shook a finger at me, peering at me rather unsteadily. "You, my friend, should not be here. They plan to banish you from His Grace's presence."

Edward grabbed my hand. "No! I am the king. My beloved stays with me."

Joan shook her head. "They intend to sweep all your council into the Thames, Your Grace, though they would prefer to take them down the Thames to the sea and sink them with stones. Alice is too clever for a woman. They do not like the thought of a cunning, beautiful woman whispering in your ear."

The following morning, Edward ordered Richard Stury to escort me back to Gaynes.

"I shall come to Havering as soon as I may," Edward promised me. "Stay there no matter what you hear, my love. They shall not deprive me of your comfort in my grief."

His timing flawless, Lancaster met me on the steps as Richard Stury escorted me to the barge. I shivered, wondering what his purpose had been in intercepting me. I did see on his handsome face, so like the king's, the marks of grief.

"My lord duke, I grieve with you on the loss of your dear brother the prince," I said.

"It is a terrible blow to all the family and the realm."

"May God grant him peace," I murmured.

We both bowed.

"Are you traveling as well?" I asked.

"No. I came to warn you that you may hear reports I have expressed what would seem censure of you. It might be necessary for me to seem to agree with the commons, in order to calm them. If anyone questions you, do not fear the truth. Do not attempt to hide anything. Lies and evasions will only complicate the matter. I promise you that you shall not be touched, and that any separation from my father will be brief. I know that he needs you now more than ever."

His cold eyes offered me no comfort, none of the reassurance that his words would seem to imply.

"Your Grace." I bowed to him and continued down the steps, accepting Stury's hand to steady me. His grip was strong and reassuring. I was surprised to look into his eyes and find understanding there.

As we moved downriver Lancaster's words haunted me—*any separation from my father will be brief.* Was I then to be thrown to the lions and rescued just in time? My future, it seemed, was now in the hands of the duke, a man I did not trust. Cold comfort, indeed.

Once back at Gaynes, I discovered my daughters distraught over the abrupt departure of their brother. Percy had sent an escort to retrieve John in the uncertain climate. I did not blame him. Indeed, I feared staying at Gaynes. My accusers might think it too near Havering, making it easy for me to slip over to Edward under cover of darkness.

SOON AFTER Richard Lyons's goods were confiscated, he himself was arrested and sent to the Tower, as were others. Surely I was next.

I did not know what to do. Lancaster's proposal might be my best recourse, to bow my head in shame before the public, and trust he would uphold his side of the bargain and see to me and the girls on Edward's death. Robert would have me, but though I wanted nothing so much as that, I feared he could not protect me, that I would bring him down with me.

Nor did I have the heart to leave Edward now, so soon after he'd lost his once-glorious heir. Besides, if I did, I feared that in one of his fits of Plantagenet temper he would take our children from me. Definitely John, possibly even Joan and Jane. Though he might not acknowledge them as his daughters, he did love them.

The commons would come after me, for Lancaster said he could not afford to stand by me. I knew why he would betray me: the mighty Duke of Lancaster and would-be King of Castile was cowed by the commons and their disapproval of his love for his mistress, Katherine de Roët Swynford. They cursed him for the good health they would rather he'd bequeathed to his well-loved brother Prince Edward, now dead.

Not long after the death of his father, the young Prince Richard was presented to parliament. They requested he immediately be given the principality of Wales, which had been his father's. The king agreed, and then retired to Eltham. I understood why he did not keep his promise to come to me, but I grieved.

The parliament dragged on to the tenth of July, on which day representatives took barges to Eltham to take their leave of the king. Stury, still adamantly devoted to Edward, came by barge to Gaynes to bring me word of the accusations made against me. Edward had sent him, wanting me to know and be prepared. *Do not let them see you weak.*

Stury had aged since spring, his grim visage worn by the events of the past months. I received him in the small parlor from which Robert and I conducted business, a sparsely furnished room—table, several chairs, a brazier, a cupboard for the accounts—but with a south-facing window that allowed the gift of daylight.

"Dame Alice, I find no joy in bringing you these tidings."

"First tell me, how fares His Grace?"

Stury dropped his gaze to his long-fingered hands and shook his head. "I fear for him. His Grace needs you beside him."

I caught my breath and took out my paternoster beads, something to hold on to. "Tell me my fate, Master Stury."

I was accused of using my unnatural influence over the king to protect my friends and household, and to interfere in the courts in the interests of my retainers.

"But I merely attended His Grace at the courts, and I have no retainers." I had never even considered maintaining household guards. "I must protest."

"You are neither summoned nor permitted in any way to speak in your defense. Truth is not what they seek, Dame Alice, but someone to blame for all the ills of the realm."

I crossed myself. Stury did as well. He was being deferential and kind, for which I was most grateful. And yet it frightened me all the more that he should pity me, the stoic Stury.

I was warned that if I were to be found practicing any form of protection of my "people," such as interfering in the courts or bribing officials, my property would all be forfeit. What most frightened me was the vagueness of the terms of forfeit—for it was not clear who was to judge whether any act of mine might be construed as interference, nor whom they accused me of protecting. It seemed to me a gift to my enemies, an accusation they might pull out of the air to condemn me at any time.

Despite my years of loyalty and devotion, I was condemned for my efforts to secure a good future for my children. Abandoned by those who had sworn to protect me. How had it come to this? What a fool I had been to ignore my doubts about the sincerity of Prince Edward and Duke John. What a fool I had been to follow my heart rather than my head.

My most immediate agony was that I had been officially banished from Edward's side. Stury warned me to stay well away from the king for the nonce.

"You will be sent for when sufficient protections are in place."

So Lancaster had promised. I prayed he would keep his word, but did not know how I could trust I would be allowed back. Lancaster was so changed from the handsome, courteous young man I had met with his grandmother so long ago, who had presented me with Melisende.

When Stury departed I sat staring out of the window, seeing nothing, blind with shock. I feared for my daughters if I were imprisoned. They needed their mother. Robert and Gwen found me there, steadied me, and insisted that I eat and drink and then walk out into the air, assuring me that they would see to the safety of Joan and Jane.

I could not think what best to do. Robert had some property to which we might retreat, but I feared he might be one I was accused of "maintaining." I urged him to go about his duties quietly, and to retreat to his own property at the first sign of trouble. My brother John suggested I hide in the open, where no one would think to see me, in London, at his house. But I feared for his family and Mary's if I were noticed. And what would happen to me then? What of my daughters? The specter of the Tower loomed large in my nightmares.

Help came from an unexpected quarter; Robert Linton, a knight in Edward's household who had always been kind to me, offered me sanctuary at an estate deep in the West Country, where my daughters and I might await rescue.

"They have no cause to connect us, Dame Alice. They will not look for you there."

"You and yours shall be forever in my prayers, Sir Robert," I vowed. His kindness and courage gave me hope in that dark time.

It was a long journey by barge and along rutted country tracks with carts and children, all the while watching over my shoulder for my enemies. But once we arrived without mishap I gave myself over to the beauty of Somerset, devoting myself to my girls and deeply grateful for the respite. On the feast of the Virgin Mary's Assumption to Heaven I attended Mass in Wells Cathedral with Geoffrey, who had come to visit. My one other guest was William Wykeham, riding from Winchester in mid-September to celebrate my thirty-fourth birthday with me. He encouraged me to count my many blessings, though he did not in any way pretend I had nothing to fear.

"The king loves you as his life, Alice. If he is able, he will summon you and protect you."

If he is able. So Edward, too, was caught in the frightening gyre.

I heeded Wykeham's advice, using my paternoster beads to count my blessings over and over, interspersed with frightened prayers for the safety of my family and friends, for Edward's health, for Robert, and for myself.

O N AN ordinary autumn afternoon, as Gwen and I were absorbed in undoing my daughter Joan's latest attempt at embroidery, laughing at the remarkable knots she had achieved—taking care that Joan could not hear our laughter, for she was quite proud to be trusted with a needle—we were surprised by a servant announcing a visitor.

"It is Sir Robert, Dame Alice, Sir Robert Linton."

I traveled from hilarity to terror in a heartbeat, grateful that I was seated, or I might have lost my balance. Our benefactor had been careful to stay away. I could only think he had come to warn me of my imminent arrest. I crossed myself and dared not look at Gwen, for I knew she must be equally frightened.

At first I did not believe the sincerity of the smile with which Sir Robert greeted me as I joined him in the hall. It took a cup of brandywine to calm me enough that I might absorb his news.

Lancaster had found a way to reverse parliament's judgments on his father's proven friends. On January 25 the kingdom would celebrate Edward's royal jubilee, his fifty years on the throne. In honor of the occasion the king would offer a general pardon, a gesture with a long tradition. Considering the enormous number included in the pardon—two thousand four hundred people—the list was already being put before parliament to afford them time to implement it.

"Apparently a 'general' pardon is not what I had thought. Not all crimes are pardoned, not all forfeits reversed, hence the list," said Sir Robert. "Your name is prominently featured, however, for the duke says His Grace needs you beside him. As soon as may be."

I could not believe my good fortune. My prayers had been answered. I was free to join Edward—in fact, Lancaster was searching for me. To that end, and to avoid his discovery of my retreat, Sir Robert had come to escort me to Gaynes.

Gwen lost no time in making the preparations. I would leave Joan and Jane at Gaynes in Mary's care, and join Edward at Havering.

When I was reunited with my sister we held each other tightly and wept. She had been widowed while I had been in hiding in the west, her husband having succumbed to a summer fever. She and her children had moved to Gaynes to heal in the countryside.

"I was frightened for you," she told me.

"Hush now, Mary, all will be well." I forced myself to say the words I needed to believe.

My dear Robert was also there to welcome me. He brought me news of my properties. I had feared more uprisings as at Finningley, but all had been quiet. I was so happy to see him that I forgot decorum and fell into his arms, rejoicing in his warmth and strength. We were a loud and merry group at dinner, and for that one night at Gaynes I could almost pretend that all was well.

It was at best a bittersweet time for me. My daughters remember it as a happy period. They were far too young to understand the crisis we faced.

A S SOON as all were settled at Gaynes, Gwen and I departed for Havering.

On a brisk, clear autumn day such as would in the past have drawn him out into the park to ride and hunt, I found Edward nodding by a fire that sucked all the air from his chamber. Despite the heat and the furs tucked round him, the hand lying beside a forgotten mazer of wine was cold and dry. I knelt to him and called his name.

His eyelids fluttered and he muttered nonsense.

"Edward, my beloved, it is Alice."

"Alice?" Now he opened his eyes and, seeing me, knocked over the mazer as he struggled to rise. I freed him from the furs and helped him to his feet. So frail, so frail.

We held each other and wept as we swore our everlasting love.

"I shall not leave you again, my love, no matter what they threaten," I vowed. Alone in my chamber I cursed his sons for their indifferent care.

I learned that Edward had suffered one of his worst spells the previous month, and had since been lethargic and inconsistent in his memory. His balance was so poor that he could not ride. Nor could he hawk, for he was convinced that the birds had decided in a parliament that he deserved death, and meant to attack him. This last, more than anything else, convinced me that I must remain by his side as much as possible, for he had never before suffered such a severe delusion.

In more lucid moments Edward was obsessed with ensuring a comfortable future for me and our eleven-year-old son. He was stubbornly determined to push forward with John's marriage to Mary Percy and his knighting at the Feast of St. George in April, alongside Prince Richard. I was moved by his ambitions for our son, but expected him to meet with resistance. Once again, Henry Percy surprised me by agreeing that the marriage should be formally celebrated in January. Nor, to my knowledge, did anyone object to John's being knighted. He was, after all, the king's son.

For my future comfort Edward urged me to transfer some of my jewels to a trustworthy friend so that they would be safe in case his enemies tried to attack him through me again. He did not know of the cache of jewels I had already entrusted to my brother, nor need he. This scheme made it clear that at least in his mind the pardon was no guarantee of my safety. I could not decide to whom to entrust my remaining jewels—Geoffrey? Robert? Perhaps Princess Joan?

While I was deliberating, I sent for them and was informed that the Duke of Lancaster had already arranged a custodian for them. This was delivered to me as reassuring news, that he had been so moved by his concern for my daughters as to ensure the security of my jewels. I could only pray I was wrong about him.

Edward's moods left me drained and confused. As he often woke in the night in an agitated state, I fell into a dangerous exhaustion. My only restful nights were on those occasions that his physicians gave him a strong sleeping draft and suggested that I sleep in my own chamber. I did so with gratitude.

I was increasingly anxious about Lancaster's maneuvers regarding the jewels and all else he seemed to control. Shortly after Martinmas I was privy to what was apparently an ongoing argument with his father about investigating William Wyndsor's deeds in Ireland.

"I understand you have not yet issued the order for Nicholas Dagworth to represent you at the Irish council. Why do you hesitate, Father?"

"Dagworth?" Edward shook his head. "My mind misgives. Surely he is not the only possibility. I prefer to send someone known to take no side in this issue."

Lancaster made no attempt to conceal his irritation with his father. "Wyndsor is my man. Do you accuse me of acting against my own man? If Dagworth says that the charges are without weight, all will believe him and the matter will be settled for good."

"And if he finds the charges just? No." Edward swept out his arm, upsetting a flagon of wine. As I reached out to catch it, he growled at Lancaster, "You are wrong in this. It is not reasonable that any man's enemy should be his judge. Dagworth shall not go."

Though I rejoiced to hear Edward so lucid, I shivered for the cold glare with which his decision was received.

After a subdued Christmas at Havering, which included only Edward's children and their families and some of his most trusted friends, Henry Percy and his family arrived with John and Mary. For an eleven-year-old, our son was tall and strong, excelling in martial arts, and a particularly gifted horseman. I saw in him what a beautiful young man his father must have been. Yet there was a sulky aspect, too, like his uncle and godfather the duke. I hoped that it was simply his impatience regarding the negotiation for his coming marriage ceremony. He was as immature as most boys of his age, and lacked all interest in such events.

"Do you not like Mary?" I asked when he had complained of the uncomfortable robes he must wear.

"No. Nor she me. She says I smell of horses."

"You do not like her because she insults you?"

"Is it an insult if it is true? Of *course* I smell of horses. She is proud and dull, and that is also the truth."

I could not help but laugh. I hoped this outspokenness was a sign of John's resilience, for as the bastard son of an aged king, he would need it. I had no power over his future, could be of little help to him. I prayed he would not forsake me.

On the day they took their vows, Mary looked lovely and John remarkably elegant. My sister, brother, and John's wife Agnes all attended, thrilled to be part of such an intimate celebration in Westminster Abbey. The ceremony was brief, with Bishop Houghton of St. David's, now also Lord Chancellor, officiating. Houghton, a kind, gentle man, had agreed to keep the ceremony short to prevent the guests from seeing too much of the king, for Edward was again having difficulty with his right arm and was in one of his more forgetful phases.

Within a few days all the guests had departed, Mary and John returning to their interrupted lives. We had agreed they were too young to consummate the union as yet. They would set up a household together in four years. Until then Mary would remain with me. Edward had wished them to bide at Havering for a while, but his physicians, Lancaster, and Houghton had all convinced him that was ill advised.

He was also disappointed on being advised not to appear at the opening of parliament. He had looked forward to declaring that two thousand four hundred pardons were to be given—an extraordinary number. But his family and physicians prevailed, impressing upon him the dampening effect one of his spells might have on the glorious proceedings.

Bishop Houghton went on to Westminster without Edward. His opening sermon incorporated the charge to parliament in which he made use of the first public acknowledgment of the king's illness while assuring them that Edward was almost recovered and would soon return to public life. He urged them to support the general pardon as a token of reconciliation.

As if Houghton's words had worked a miracle, Edward's mind cleared within days. He began walking round and round the hall to strengthen his legs, and in early February proceeded downriver by barge to Sheen. He wore a magnificent red cloak embroidered with his arms and tiny fleur-de-lis. It was lined in ermine as was his red escarlatte hat and the purple wool robe beneath. I was determined he should not take a chill. He looked in every aspect a king. As the barge passed Westminster, the parliamentarians assembled on the riverbank to cheer him. I was riding in an enclosed area of the barge, carefully hidden from the crowd but able to see Edward. I rejoiced to see him straighten in his seat and acknowledge the cheers with a regal wave. For a moment I allowed myself to dream that all might yet be well.

Indeed, our time at Sheen leading up to our remove to Windsor for the Feast of St. George was a peaceful, happy period, but for news that I tried to keep from Edward. A mob had attacked Lancaster's Palace of the Savoy, damaging the outbuildings and the gate and gaining access to the hall before being stopped by armed retainers. The duke had escaped over the Thames to Kennington, seeking to shelter behind Princess Joan's popularity as the widow of the beloved Prince Edward and mother of Prince Richard. She had calmed the crowds.

It was Geoffrey who explained to me why Lancaster was so distrusted, even despised, by the common folk. "He undid all that the commons felt they had achieved in the last parliament. There is also a rumor that he is behind the omission of the Bishop of Winchester from the general pardon." Though parliament found fault with him as chancellor, Wykeham was beloved as bishop.

That was a topic of interest to me as well, our good friend being so unfairly singled out. I had been shocked to hear he was the one victim of the parliament of the previous year who had not been pardoned.

When I'd asked Edward why he had not pardoned Wykeham, he had said, "He sided with those who attacked the honor of my trusted chamberlain William Latimer."

"He spoke the truth about him," I had said. But I did not remind Edward that Latimer was no longer chamberlain. I was learning that it angered him when I pointed out such confusion, and I did so only when it was crucial.

"We shall speak of it no more," he said. I saw by the set of his jaw that he meant it.

"Is the rumor true?" I asked Geoffrey later. "The decision was Lancaster's?"

He nodded. "He loathes Wykeham, blaming him for all the losses in France. The commons also resent Lancaster's support of Henry Percy using his influence in the governing of the city."

"What else should I know of the duke?"

"I believe you know the rest. I do not know what to think of him these days."

Nor did I, but I very much feared him.

EDWARD OFTEN drew me out of my darksome thoughts, rejoicing in his regained strength. Though we no longer rose at dawn to ride out into the countryside as we had done in the past, we did take short rides together and walked in the garden. In the evenings we played chess or listened to music and song. But I could not ignore the milkiness of his once-piercingly blue eyes, how easily he tired.

One morning, as we walked beneath a rose arbor, Edward paused and took both my hands. The sun shone on his pure white hair and for a moment he was the man I had first glimpsed in the great hall of his mother's castle.

"You have given me such joy in my old age, Alice, my love."

"You have given me equal joy, Edward."

He shook his head. "No. You have suffered much pain along with the joy. I have become a labor. And we began in such tragedy—the death of your beloved husband."

My breath caught at his acknowledgment of my suffering. I bowed my head, unable to think of a response.

"I pray that you remember me with love, no matter what may come." I lifted my head to reassure him, but he continued before I could speak. "I fear you shall face one more labor before you rest, but I pray it may prove unexpectedly happy."

"What labor? What are you talking about, my love?" The apology in his eyes made my stomach ache.

He lifted my hands and kissed each in turn, then let them go and tapped the finger on which he wore the signet ring with which he sealed his letters to me. "When you see that I am gone, remove this from my finger and keep it. Remember me by it, my beloved."

I caught up the hand with the signet ring on it and kissed it. "You are not dying yet, my love." But it was a denial of what I felt to be true. We had little time left together.

"I have also arranged for an account in gold to be opened for you in France. In case of exile. I do not trust the commons to honor my pardon once I am dead. Joan and Jane, take them away. They must not be harmed."

"Exile," I whispered. Fleeing to France with our daughters. "Oh, Edward!"

He drew me into his arms and held me, whispering of his love, but also words less comforting, "What have I done? What have I done?"

I reassured him out of habit, though I shivered with fear. He foresaw exile, danger to our daughters. Would our son be safe?

I put all my hopes and prayers for John into the needlework on the robes for his knighting. At the Feast of St. George, Prince Richard would be knighted and admitted into the Order of the Garter, and our son would be knighted. Princess Joan was helping with the work on her son's ceremonial robes. I was comforted by her presence in the palace. She took charge of the household and of my few leisure hours, insisting that I rest, eat, and pour out my heart to her.

I did not tell her about Edward's fears for my exile, nor did I confide in her my worries regarding Lancaster. I could not tell how she herself felt about the duke, her brother-in-law.

But I did inquire of the duke himself when he arrived at Windsor as to the disposition of my jewels.

He leaned toward me, and in a conspiratorial whisper assured me that they were safe. "They will be there for you when you have need of them. If you wish to add to them, you have only to ask."

I found it difficult to warm myself after that until a long ride brought me out in a good sweat.

I worked on Edward's robes as well as John's. Despite its being his jubilee year there would be no extravagant headdresses for Edward this time, for he was unlikely to remember to hold his head upright. They would besides only call attention to his tremors. I designed robes with gold and silver threads and the most dazzling whites we could find, to give him a beatific glow. We trimmed his long white hair and beard and used some of Princess Joan's lotions to brighten his hair. He enjoyed the fuss.

We had become like father and daughter now, most fond of each other, sharing years of memories. Sometimes we were almost mother and child. It hurt my heart to see him so confused, so impatient with himself, so frightened. My vibrant, passionate Edward was gone. It was as if the glorious shell had cracked open and exposed an infant within. I played the fool with him to rouse a sparkle in his eyes and some weak laughter. I danced jigs, sang the silly songs with which I cheered my children. In the chapel or out riding, I wept. Wept for Edward and for myself. I was losing him. Every day brought subtle changes, a new weakness, another memory gone. His remaining time grew short.

Joan knew, and having so recently stepped into her own grief, she understood when to speak and when to be still. I saw the fear in her eyes that her too-young son would soon be king.

His knighting ceremony came none too soon. It was a glorious celebration. Prince Richard had been well trained by Joan to look every bit the king-to-be, walking straight and tall, his head held high. He was

Plantagenet in all but his stature, carrying his beauty on a smaller frame than Edward and his sons.

I wept to see my own son knighted. How proud he looked, how straight he walked. Sir John Southery. His child-wife seemed impressed by the event, though I had heard her ask rather loudly why the king looked like a magician, not a ruler. Fortunately, Edward did not hear.

As soon as the last guests departed he and I took the barge to Sheen, hastening to have him out of sight of the gossiping court before he succumbed to exhaustion. We were there but two nights when he suffered another spell, this one robbing him of the use of his left arm and leg. In his immobility, he grew by turns irritable and filled with vague regrets.

On a particularly gray May morning, Edward was overcome with remorse for having given some of Richard Lyons's lands to his sons Edmund and Thomas when my friend had been in the Tower. Richard had, of course, been included in the general pardon.

"Richard will accrue more lands, my love."

"He has been a good friend to you and a comfort to your family, Alice. I would do something for him. My sons do not need his properties. If I restore those to him, and pardon the several hundred pounds he owes the Exchequer, would that be of use to him? Would it be enough for him to begin again?"

I called it generous.

As with Lancaster's obvious knowledge of Edward's advice to me to hide some of my jewels, this private conversation became public knowledge and would later be used as proof that I told the king to give Richard Lyons money. I became the hunted, the prey.

DEATH, WHEN at last he stepped forward to take my beloved Edward, chose an exquisite setting in which to claim his dance. Tempted from our reverences in the chapel by the balmy, fragrant air, Edward and I walked out into the May morning, marveling at the explosion of color in the gardens, the sensuous feel of the breeze.

"Let us dine out here today," he exclaimed.

I had agreed and was about to call for a servant when Edward suddenly clutched my hand tightly. Seeing the paroxysm of pain in his face, I called out to the guards to help me return him to his chamber.

"Call for the king's physicians!" I shouted at the servants as we hurried past—Edward still had hold of my hand even as the guards carried him in their intertwined arms. I had never seen such torment on anyone's face.

"My head, my head," he moaned as the guards laid him on his bed. Stury managed to release my hand from Edward's desperate grasp.

I sat on the bed beside my beloved, begging him to look at me, to speak to me. His eyes did not seem able to fix on me. His words became garbled.

I remember little of the days that followed. I stayed by his side as much as I was permitted, but the physicians often sent me away, to eat, to sleep, to walk or ride.

"He will need you," Master Adam reminded me. "You must not fall ill."

Gwen took care of me as I had of Edward. I was at a loss now. I had no role but to care for the shadow of the man I had loved.

Gradually Edward recovered enough to speak a little and sit up for brief periods.

I sent for Wykeham. I did not care what Lancaster thought of that. Edward knew that he was dying and needed someone he trusted to shrive him, someone who loved him.

Edward lived as if in a dream for several weeks, so broken and depleted that in my prayers I asked that his soul be released from the prison of his unruly body. Though frightened what it would mean to me and my children to lose his protection, remembering all too well the terror with which Janyn and his mother had received the news of the death of their protector, I could not bear to see him thus diminished. Death was like a cat, playing with his prey. I prayed for Edward's release.

On the twenty-first of June he suddenly suffered another most grievous pain in his head, shouting for relief. The servant who had watched with me hurried away for the physicians. But within moments, clutching my hand so hard it was as if he shared the pain with me, Edward mercifully let go his mortal prison and was at peace.

I had followed so closely his every tortured breath that when it ceased, so did mine. I imagined Death spreading his light-swallowing robe over Edward, and felt a flutter of panic. I must follow them. Edward needed me. Pain gripped me and I doubled over, at last gasping for breath. All the agony of watching Edward's suffering flamed within me, all the emotion I had hidden from him.

I squeezed Edward's hand, the large, once beautiful, once warm and enticing hand, remembering how his mere touch could melt me. I felt the signet and, remembering Edward's request, forced myself to ease my hand out of his death grip and work the ring off his finger. I did it clumsily, chafing his finger, and wept as I hid the ring in my bodice. When the physicians arrived, and Lancaster and Thomas of Woodstock, they ordered me to leave the room. I threw myself across Edward's body, wanting no one else to touch him, for I knew that once they did, his soul would leave. I was not ready. Master Adam peeled me away. In that uncoupling I felt a terrifying emptiness, a void of echoing nothingness. No purpose, no anchor. Looking round, I saw only anger and condemnation in the men's faces. I stumbled out of the chamber, seeking solace in the chapel.

Princess Joan advised me then to leave, to seek sanctuary and peace at one of my manors. She herself trembled at the thought of her ten-year-old son being crowned.

But there was much to do before I departed. Numbly I went about the palace for several days, managing the servants, advising on the locations of Edward's belongings. I could not leave him. Could not part from my life with him. I completed tasks I had promised to do for Edward, disposing of all signs of his illness, giving presents to his physicians.

Later I heard rumors that I had taken all his rings and hurried out of the palace with them. No one came forward to declare that I had lingered at Sheen for days. No one.

Edward was to be taken in grand procession to Westminster in early July. I would not be in the funeral party. Nor did I stand with the crowds who came from near and far to line the way, straining to catch a glimpse of his hearse, draped in a red silk pall on which were displayed his arms.

I heard that his funeral effigy carried his death mask, revealing to all who saw it the droop of the right side of his face. Edward would have hated having his weakness so exposed.

ROBERT ARRIVED to escort me to Gaynes. Apparently Stury had asked Richard Lyons to find him and bring him to Sheen. By the time he arrived I could not wait to leave the palace, my emotions drained, all sense of Edward gone from those rooms, the corridors, and gardens. Perhaps no one came forth to deny the rumors of my rushing from Edward's deathbed because to all but the servants I had disappeared the moment the king died. All around him, the household, the family, the court had rushed into activity, ignoring me. I had been played out and was now out of the game. I pressed myself back against walls as the courtiers and household and family hurried past. I kept to the shadows in the chapel. As Gwen and a few servants packed my belongings, I took my leave of the bedchamber in which Edward and I had spent so many loving days and nights, lost in our delight in each other. I wondered whether I would ever return.

This room had been decorated with gifts from Edward and everywhere were cherished memories. One cushion held his scent, another a bloodstain from the bouquet of roses Edward had gathered himself, forgetting to trim the thorns. Here was the nick from the mazer I'd dropped as Edward swept me up in his arms. Memories of our love overwhelmed me on every side. I fell to my knees and wept, hugging the cushion that smelled of him.

I could not sleep in the palace. I escaped as soon as Robert sent word a barge was arranged. As I left Sheen for the final time I felt as if I had been stripped of past and purpose, walking naked and bewildered into an obscure future. I had loved Edward with my heart, body, and soul.

BOOK

IV

A PHOENIX

18

It is neither fitting nor safe that all the keys should hang from the belt of one woman.

—Bishop Thomas Brinton, referring to Alice Perrers, sermon delivered in Westminster Abbey, May 18, 1376

Naked and bewildered. I had lost myself. I was yet spinning in the dance, dizzy, seeing but shreds of memories, spinning, spinning, and Edward's hand was not there to pull me out of the gyre. Death had interrupted our dance.

Edward, my beloved Edward, was gone, and with him my life, my purpose. With him died the intimate history of my role at court. The dowager Queen Isabella, Dame Tommasa, Janyn, Queen Philippa, and King Edward—they were now silent. Not even Edward's sons or Princess Joan knew all the story. How could they?

Voices whirled about me but none of them the voice I strained to hear—the voice of Edward, my beloved, calling for me, guiding me to his side. The voices accused me, threatened me, condemned me. I could say nothing, for I was a sinner, though my sins be not the ones they intoned. How might I find my way to absolution . . . salvation? Spinning, spinning, breathless and overwhelmed with grief and remorse. Where had I fallen off the path of righteousness? At what moment had I misstepped? When had I a choice to be other than I was?

• 1377 •

A HAND REACHED out. Robert beckoned me. I knew his voice as if from a great distance, more memory than sound. I remembered. My daughters needed me. Joan and Jane were too young to be without their mother. I must not abandon my precious Bella. And John. My son might need my comfort as he mourned his father.

I strained toward Robert's hand, spinning toward it and away, toward it and away, and at last the sickening movement slowed, I felt warm fingers curl round my wrist, and I was still. I was Alice, sitting in the barge, my hand in Robert's, warm, alive. I saw the riverbank sliding by. Gwen sat nearby.

"I must see my daughters. Are Joan and Jane at Gaynes?" My own voice startled me.

In his eyes I could see that Robert had been aware of my absence. "Yes. Joan and Jane are safely awaiting you at Gaynes in the company of their aunt. But before we join them, would you care to rest at Barking Abbey? I thought you might find comfort in Bella's company."

My heart swelled with the thought of my eldest child. "Bella! Oh, yes, Robert, I would see her first."

That he had suggested something so certain to comfort me helped me come to a decision. I drew out from my scrip Edward's signet. "I entrust this to you," I said, closing his hand over it.

He knew what it was when he saw the intaglio. "Are you certain?"

"I am. I trust that you will keep it safe for my son John. When he is ready, I shall ask for it."

Robert kissed my hand, then looked at me with his steady eyes, blue, but a softer shade than Edward's, grayer, as if he knew the world he looked on would not always be gladsome. "I swear that I will prove worthy of the trust with which you honor me, Alice."

His gaze steadied me.

"I have always believed you trustworthy, Robert."

When we arrived at Barking I went at once to the chapel while a sister fetched Bella. Gwen offered to assist in arranging some light refreshment for us. She who had been with me so many years understood that I yearned to be alone with my grief.

The dimness of the nave after the golden morning sun at once seemed to quiet and cool my anxious, feverish mind. The smoky, spicy aroma of incense mingled with the delicate fragrance of roses and the ordinary scent of candle wax, all familiar smells calling me to prayer. I found myself kneeling before the lady altar without having consciously chosen it. Ribbons, prayer beads, flowers, and jewelry adorned the statue of the Mother of God. With a sob I remembered the woman holding out Janyn's paternoster beads in the church—could that truly be nearly seventeen years ago? I could see it so clearly, feel it so sharply, that it seemed it had been only a few weeks past. I took out my own beads and bowed my head.

This was no time for remembering Janyn. Today I wished to remember Edward. Edward, the king who had loved me. Edward, the man who had satisfied me and filled me with beautiful children. Edward, the friend who had delighted in my achievements. Edward, my companion in riding and hawking, my opponent in chess, the frightened, ill, aged man who had feared little when I held his hand. He had filled me and depleted me, over and over again.

There, in the chapel at Barking, I prayed for release from Edward, from the spell with which he had bound me, for release from the dance. I prayed to reawaken, to remember my family, my friends, my purpose. Work I might now be free to enjoy. At any moment I would hear Bella's voice. I would soon be with my precious Joan and Jane, my sister Mary and my brother John and their children, and my friends. Robert and Gwen would take me there. I could walk and work in the gardens at Gaynes, become reacquainted with my hawks and horses. I reminded myself of all this, of life's continuance, the possibility of joy.

A rustle of silk. The abbess of Barking was highborn and elegant. She took my hand, cupped it in her warm palms, waited until I looked her in the eyes.

"I had not recognized you at first in your widow's garb, Dame Alice."

"I was not permitted to wear it when my husband died years ago, Mother Abbess. Now I am free openly to mourn him and the king."

She pressed her hands together and gave me a little bow. "God grant you peace now, Dame Alice."

"May God protect and guide me."

"Your daughter suggested that you might be in need of her prayers and companionship in your mourning. Would it please you if she were to bide with you for a fortnight?"

I felt a warmth rush through me, the promise of a thaw. "I can think of no greater comfort." I bowed to kiss the hand of the abbess.

When Bella joined me she cried out with raw emotion to see me in mourning.

"For Father?" she asked.

"For Janyn, yes, and for Edward."

"Both good men," she said.

We talked for a while in the abbess's parlor, remembering. I warned her that there would be trouble ahead, at the least a trial.

"I fear that you will hear horrible things said of me. And I fear the outcome." I told her of the possibilities—forfeiture of my lands, even imprisonment or exile.

She held me and assured me that her love for me was unwavering.

THE FOLLOWING morning we continued on to Gaynes—Bella, Gwen, Robert, and me. Joan, Jane, Mary, and her little ones, all came rushing from the hall to greet us, encircling me in love. I gave myself up to the joy of homecoming.

I fell into bed exhausted that first evening at home and slept as one drugged, a blessedly dreamless night. In the pale hour of dawn I placed a statue of the Blessed Virgin and a reliquary containing a drop of her milk on a low table in the corner of my chamber. On a cushion I knelt and began a prayer vigil. For a week I prayed while memories assailed me, tears cleansed me, prostrations purged my soul. Sometime during the first day Bella joined me, and she stayed by my side, a blessed companion, until at last I slept for a day and a night.

On the following morning Gwen helped me dress in one of my simple country gowns, humming as she worked on the buttons, shaking her head a little at how loosely it fit.

"At least I set aside the weeds," I said. "I promise to fill this out by summer's end."

"I shall see to that," she said with a little laugh.

When I descended to the hall, Joan and Jane timidly looked up from their milky bread with wary eyes.

"I am well again," I said, kissing each of them on the forehead.

After breaking my fast with bread, cheese, and watered wine, I went in search of Robert, and together we rode out to see the manor. It was a joy to be out in the air, and with someone I trusted completely. I was ready to see my land and talk of the mundane chores of managing it. Once back at the hall, Joan and Jane, curious to see the contents of the chests I had brought from Sheen, begged to help Gwen and me unpack. They anticipated redecorating my bedchamber with the finery that Mary Percy, now Southery, had told them I must have brought from Windsor. She was unfortunately still living in my household while John was serving as a page in Henry Percy's.

I did not like to dip into those chests, drawing forth memories still raw and painful, but my daughters, at seven and five years of age, were too young to understand my reticence, and I acquiesced.

By evening I was agitated by the memories released in my bed-chamber and loath to return to it. I sat in the hall until even Bella reluctantly left me. Only Robert remained, sitting by the fire opposite me, working oil into the leather of a harness as he had done all evening while the women talked.

"Surely that is the groom's work?" I said, crossing over to him and settling on the edge of the bench.

He looked up at me, his blue-gray eyes warming me. "I find it soothing."

"You are troubled?"

"I am worried about you. Lyons is worried about you."

"I am as well, Robert."

We sat quietly for a time, occasionally commenting on the fire or some trivial event of the day, and I began to calm. My daughter Jane's favorite cat, Willow, a battle-scarred calico with a notch in one ear and one eye missing, curled up on my lap. I stroked her to the rhythm of her loud purr and thanked her for gracing me with her warmth.

After a long silence Robert left the hall, promising to return in a few moments. I waited, gazing into the fire, holding Willow, wishing that I might put all the past behind me and settle into a quiet life. Wishing again that I might be forgotten. Robert returned, standing before me, reaching out to me with clean hands. I could smell the soap he had used to remove the oil.

Willow jumped off my lap and curled up on a cushion near the fire.

"Come," Robert said, "I shall sit with you until you sleep."

Up in the solar, Gwen was nowhere to be seen. She must have noticed us in the hall and guessed we might go up together.

Robert took a turn around the room, admiring the finery, the silken cushions, the tapestries, the great bed. I had thought he might be uneasy there, but he seemed relaxed, curious even, and when he returned to where I stood by the door, simply said, "I have never been in a room this fine."

I smiled at his words and gestured to a chair. "Do sit with me awhile. I do not want to be alone just yet with the memories furnishing this chamber."

He drew me close and held me for a moment, then released me. "Are you certain?" He studied my face, his smoky blue eyes crinkling as he read my expression.

"I am."

He settled on the chair. "I'll close my eyes while you prepare for bed," he said.

Once I lay beneath the covers we talked of crops and boundaries, tenants and livestock, until the chamber felt familiar to me once more and I drifted into sleep.

I AWOKE TO a morning of billowy white clouds moving languorously across a deep blue sky. I had invited Bella, Joan, and Jane for a long walk, leaving their cousins behind for the nonce. The air was warm but with a freshening breeze that lifted our skirts and tousled our hair. I had already decided with Bella that it was time to tell Joan and Jane of the death of their father.

Hand in hand, my sweet young daughters danced along the garden paths, their simple, bright-colored gowns blending with the blossoms. Their hats hung down their backs, secured by the ribbons that had been tied beneath their chins. I could see that they had worn their hats in such wise much of the summer, for the sun had worked its magic on their tresses, lightening them and bringing out the highlights—Joan's hair was almost white in the sun, Jane's a mixture of dark blond and red.

Bella and I walked behind them, laughing as we were forced to move more briskly than we might have liked in order to keep up with the two girls.

"How much do you think they understand?" Bella asked.

"Edward remained rather vague to them. I doubt they will mourn him, particularly because they believe I shall not leave them again—the king can no longer summon me." Even such a simple statement gave me pause, brought a tightness to my throat. I missed Edward so. "They will be sorely disappointed when I am summoned by parliament."

"*If* you are." Bella caught my hand, though she neither slowed down nor abandoned her watch over her half sisters. She knew how frightened I was.

"Joan and Jane are two angels," I said, forcing myself to look to my blessings, not my fears. "As are you as well." I pressed her hand, grateful for her loving companionship.

First we visited the mews, the falconer giving the girls an account of the latest feeding.

"Each hawk believes it is king or queen of the fowls," he concluded.

"Father was a king," said Jane, looking very proud.

"God bless him, he was, and the best of them, Mistress Jane."

It seemed a perfect doorway into the topic I wished to raise. From the dovecote and the stables we adjourned to a lovely spot beneath an oak, settling in a circle on spread blankets to enjoy pieces of cake that Cook had wrapped up for us. When the young ones seemed satiated, I took a deep breath and explained to Joan and Jane that their father had succumbed to the long illness that had made it difficult for him to be with them.

Joan asked, "He was not locked up in a dungeon and murdered like Grandfather?"

"Murdered like Grandfather?" For a moment I could not think who she meant.

"Your Edward's father," Bella whispered.

It was strange, but I had never thought about Edward and Isabella as my children's grandparents. They seemed so far removed.

"No, my loves. I was with your father when he died."

Jane slipped her hand into her sister Bella's and would not look up at me but stuck her other fist in her mouth.

I was uncomfortable pursuing the question of their grandfather's murder, yet as Joan closely watched my face with eyes so like her father's that they made my heart ache, I sensed it was important for me, their mother, to do so. "Who told you that your grandfather was murdered?" I asked her. I could not imagine either my sister or any of the household saying such a thing.

"Mary."

"Ah." Of course, the poisonous Percy in our midst. I quickly countered with a comment on the way gossip ripples through the court, how Mary might have heard such a rumor. "But your father was ill. He suffered from a problem in his head that gradually weakened him. I was with him. He was not frightened. We were walking in the garden and he was at peace when God called him."

"Do you have a problem with your head, Mother?" Jane asked.

I gathered my youngest into my lap and hugged her. "Sometimes I am quite silly, but other than that my head is healthy, my sweet."

Joan laughed. The sound was a great relief, and I was delighted when Jane, then Bella joined in. I felt blessed to have such beautiful, loving, delightful daughters all with me. They had few questions about Edward's death and what it might mean to them.

"I do not think he made much impression on their lives," Bella remarked as we watched her sisters rush off to join their cousins back in the hall. "Far less than my father made in mine."

I put an arm round Bella and rested my head on her shoulder for a moment. "You were blessed with the most loving of fathers, Bella. Janyn adored you. He had waited so long for a child, and you more than fulfilled his dreams."

I heard her breath catch.

R OBERT CAME to me after everyone else had retired and we talked far into the night, so easy with each other that I felt free to broach more personal concerns than I had the previous night. I told him about Joan's revelation of Mary Percy's gossip and allowed him to soothe my fears about my daughter-in-law and my regret that Joan and Jane had not known Edward well enough to miss him.

"There is no grace in regret, Alice," Robert said. "I might spend my life regretting all the petty arguments and slights in my brief marriage, but I do not believe God would bless such a life."

I had not known his late wife, Helena. The few years they had been together I had been busy with Edward.

"Were you very much in love with her?"

Robert dropped his head to his chest for a moment and took a deep breath, as if gathering his energies to speak of her. "We were more like brother and sister than husband and wife. A teasing affection that did not carry as far as our bed. I frightened her with my need, and eventually she closed her mind to me when evening fell. When she lay dying, she asked my forgiveness. 'I was afraid,' she said. 'And I pushed you away. Now it is too late.' I, too, was afraid, afraid to hold her as the life ebbed from her. But I did. I lay beside her and held her until her heart stopped."

I crossed myself. "Janyn died so far away. I would have held him so."

On the third night that Robert came to my bedchamber I greeted him with a kiss, a long, searching kiss, for all the day I had watched him, desiring him. For so long I had yearned for my early years with Edward, as his passion failed him. For so long I had dreamt of this with Robert. It was not like my desire for Janyn or Edward. There was no recklessness, no fear or helplessness in this. I simply wanted Robert, body and soul, and believed we might be happy.

He traced the lines of my brow, my cheek, my jawline, then gathered me in his arms and carried me to the bed.

Our lovemaking was tentative at first. I could not believe my flesh was once more pressed against the warm, muscled flesh of a man I desired, and who desired me. Perhaps he, too, could not quite believe this blessing. As we explored each other's body, our kisses and our touches grew more urgent, until the boundaries between us blurred.

I woke in the night to find the lamp still burning.

"You are so beautiful," he whispered.

I did not answer at once, cradled in the warmth of his presence. For this moment I felt content, beloved, safe. His body delighted me. It was strong and supple, the body of a man active and temperate. He was like Edward in coloring, but more like Janyn in proportion.

I wondered if it was possible that I might be so blessed as to find happiness with Robert. That I might be forgotten by parliament and left free to live out my days in peace and love. I prayed for that miracle.

To wake beside Robert in the dawn light was a sweet experience. He lay on his side, gently tracing the areolas of my nipples and smiling a smile without guile, without secrets. I had no doubt that he loved me. How precious it was to lie with a man I had chosen, a man my heart had chosen.

The days were warm and sun filled. I felt blessed to be surrounded by young ones, being coaxed out to search for a wandering kitten, to see a strange-looking egg, to marvel at the water fowl. Joan and Jane truly seemed to have accepted the death of their father with little ado. Joan had enjoyed the pomp of the court, but Jane had been frightened by the elaborate clothing and loud voices, the confusion of so many adults hurrying about her. Edward's death meant that they would have me with them, and it was difficult for them to see that as anything but good.

I HAD BEEN at Gaynes almost a month when William Wyndsor arrived. I had walked out into the garden to gather flowers. My basket was filled with roses and the pale green blossoms of lady's mantle, sprigs of rosemary and lavender.

"You gathered no such garlands for me." William slouched down onto a bench near where I knelt. The sun picked out the silver threads that feathered his dark hair since last we'd met. Ireland had aged him. Yet he was still a handsome man.

I felt a warning drumming along my bones when I looked him in the eyes, but could not control my tongue. "How dare you show your face here? You told Edward we were betrothed. I cannot fathom what you thought to gain, but you have forfeited any shred of trust I had in you." I thrust a handful of roses at him. "Take these and leave me in peace with my family." *And may the thorns prick your pride.*

He shrugged and looked toward the house. "The king is dead. It is my time now."

I sat back on my heels, dumbfounded. "I wish you to go, William."

A cold laugh. "I have the jewels, the ones you entrusted to the duke."

I did not want to hear what he had said. I stared down at the ground, catching my breath. "The jewels? You? What possessed the duke to entrust them to you?"

William rose up so suddenly that I had no time to back away. He grabbed my arm, lifting me to my feet, flowers and all, and shook me. "You are my betrothed!" he shouted, his face red, his eyes wild with rage. "You dare not deny me!"

From the corner of my eye I saw a movement. "We are observed, William. Be so kind as to unhand me."

He let go, glancing around. Robert was now approaching from the house, two male servants right behind him. I sensed more than saw someone hurrying off in the other direction. My daughter-in-law had been lurking in the garden, gathering gossip, I had no doubt.

Though I was shivering with fear, I lifted a hand to stop Robert and the other men. I hoped to avoid a confrontation between him and William. Turning to the latter, who was now fussing with his clothes, I said as quietly as I might, "Leave me now, William. When we are both calmer we shall discuss the jewels. But I tell you this—I will never consent to marry you. Never."

"We shall see." He managed to walk away with stiff dignity.

I sank onto the bench he had vacated, praying for calm. But I shook so violently my teeth chattered. He had my jewels, my gifts from Edward, my daughters' dowries if my lands were taken from me. I cursed Lancaster.

"May I sit?"

I nodded to Robert. "I was glad to see you there. You gave me strength."

"How dare he lay hands on you?" His voice was taut with controlled anger. "I have distrusted his intentions all along."

"Yes, you have."

"Why did you stop me?"

"I feared that if you were even half as angry as I was, you might kill him."

We were quiet a moment, both imagining what might have happened.

"His is not the manner of a lover," Robert said after a while. "It is your wealth that attracts him. Where was he when you were beset a year ago?"

"In Ireland."

"But summoned here. He might have come at any time. He comes at last when you are no longer under the protection of the king."

I sensed that Robert was speaking of a concern even more disturbing to him than what he had just witnessed. "What have you heard?"

"He has requested a list of your manors . . . their incomes, the livestock . . . as if he considers himself master of your domain."

And he had the jewels. My nerves thrummed with alarm. "God help me." I told Robert about the jewels.

"What will you do?"

"I do not know yet. I must think. I welcome your counsel—once you have calmed yourself."

He nodded.

"I pray you, hold me for a moment."

I wished Robert might hold me always, warming and reassuring me with his strength and affection. But the encounter with William had reminded me of the trouble yet to come. Parliament was not finished with me, and neither apparently was William. Robert and I needed to discuss the danger that still lay ahead.

"We can create a new life, Alice. I shall love your daughters and care for them as my own."

He stroked my hair, then lifted my chin and kissed me.

"I believe you, Robert, and I do love you. But there is trouble ahead, and I know not what form it will take, I warn you."

"I care not."

I moved out of his embrace. Looking into his eyes, I saw the life I wanted. "I have lived in a wonderful dream these past days, hiding from what lies ahead. Parliament threatened me, but in such vague terms I cannot predict what they might do, on what grounds they might judge me. Even here at Gaynes they might have spies . . . Mary Percy, William himself. I pray that nothing happens, Robert, that I am forgotten. That we can be together."

He kissed both my hands. "I pray for that as well. I pledge you my troth, Alice."

My heart pounded. I wanted to complete that pledge, to bind us together. "I am so afraid, Robert."

"Say the words and it matters not, my love. We will be together."

"I pledge you my troth, Robert."

We held each other. It was all I wanted, Robert's arms round me and my children, and I prayed that God was now ready to grant me this quiet joy.

A S I had suspected, it had been Mary Percy who had been hiding in the garden. She was adept at listening from the shadows and understood far more than I had anticipated. She was quick to tell Jane, Joan, and Bella that William Wyndsor intended to be their new father. It might have been a more complicated tale had she waited to hear what Robert and I had discussed, or witnessed our embrace, our vows. So far only my sister and Gwen seemed aware of what had been unfolding between Robert and me.

Bella reassured her half sisters and came to me with the tale.

"So young and such a shrew. Poor John," she murmured. "How will you rescue him? Surely you might think of something to cause her to annul the marriage?"

"It is not a good time to make an enemy of Henry Percy. I am too vulnerable." I brought her back to what I thought was the more important issue. "Tell me, Joan and Jane did not like the thought of William Wyndsor joining our family?"

I watched her pretty face, more beautiful than ever surrounded by the crisp wimple of her habit, as Bella struggled with some decision. I was relieved when she looked me in the eyes and said, "No, they do not like him. Nor do I, Mother. I know it is not my part to criticize your choice of husband, but have you not suffered enough? Would it not be better to find someone quiet and steady? Like Robert."

The wisdom of my child moved me to tears. "I have no intention of wedding Wyndsor, my sweet. I have pledged myself to Robert. But I very much fear what Wyndsor is about." For the second time that day I sank down on a bench, this time in the hall, but now it was my daughter who joined me. She pulled me into her embrace and rocked me gently as I wept.

"God grant you peace," she murmured. "God grant you joy." Over and over she wished me such blessings.

Peace and joy. I treasured what I had of both at that moment, for I did not believe I would enjoy either in the near future.

GRADUALLY, OVER the summer and into the autumn, I became reacquainted with my family, my properties, and myself. It was a happy time, but not altogether peaceful. There were rumors I was to be brought before parliament to answer for my "crimes against the king and kingdom," rumblings from past holders of my properties, hoping to catch me at a vulnerable time and grab back their property without compensating me. Robert, Dom Hanneye, and Richard Lyons were busy assisting me in keeping the wolves at bay.

Because of the unsettled situation, Robert was not so often at Gaynes, and I missed him sorely. Over the summer I had lived for our moments together during the day, our lovemaking at night. When he was away I often brought Joan and Jane to my chamber to sleep with me.

THE RUMORS proved true. In the first parliament of the reign of the young King Richard, I was brought to trial for my "misdeeds." This time the knives came out, well sharpened. The Duke of Lancaster and Princess Joan assured me that no matter what the commons and the court said, what they threatened, I would be safe. They recommended that I remain at Gaynes until actually summoned to appear. When I did arrive at Westminster, Lancaster forbade me to wear widow's garb.

"You are not my father's widow."

"These are not widow's weeds, my lord." I wore a dark, simple gown and plain headdress, without decoration.

"You have never dressed so plainly. You are not to wear weeds." His coldness sufficiently frightened me that I did not argue. I detected neither gentleness nor understanding in his eyes.

I had been assigned a large, beautiful bedchamber in the palace, one that I had never seen before, though I recognized several tapestries, cushions, and chests that had once been mine. Someone had perhaps meant that as a kindness. Gwen found some of my more elegant gowns in the chests, and with a little work we changed the bodices so that I would at the least appear less provocative. I wore no jewels. Those that I still had, I had hidden.

On the morrow, I was ready. Though I did not shed my miniver-lined cloak until I reached the door to the chamber in which I would face my accusers, I'd begun to shiver the moment I left my room. I remembered taking this walk with Edward, knowing that he took strength from my presence. I now took courage in that memory.

For hours upon end I stood before the parliament, trying not to look into their angry faces, trying not to absorb their hatred. I stood exposed, forbidden to speak in my defense, a sinner at the pillory.

Two of the most serious charges against me were lies, but with enough truth behind them that it would be impossible for me to disprove them. I was accused of having used my influence over the king to prevent Nicholas Dagworth from going to Ireland to consider the charges against William Wyndsor, and of having persuaded the king to make reparation to Richard Lyons. Both William and Richard were referred to as my partners in business.

I was tried as a *femme sole,* a woman alone, solely responsible for my actions. Had I not been so terrified, I might have enjoyed the irony, that I was solely responsible for obeying my king and his family.

As the trial wore on the charges against me multiplied. Folk came forward, invited by parliament, to make their claims. The allegations were, for the most part, trivial, people petulantly claiming unpaid debts, kin claiming that I had coerced their relatives to enfeoff land to me that they were furious was now out of their reach—all the usual petty complaints made against wealthy persons. But they were threatening nevertheless, because *invited*. Parliament was searching for enough to condemn me, once and for all.

I heard beneath the trivial accusations that Richard Stury had been right. They needed someone to blame for the losses the realm had suffered in the last years of Edward's reign—so much sovereignty lost in western France after years of costly wars, so much taxation. Of course, no one believed that I had somehow caused the defeats, but they accused me of weakening the king with lovemaking.

We had succeeded too well in hiding his illness from the people, and no one in the royal family was coming forward to defend me. They could not afford to open the discussion to the subject of a flawed king—that had led to armed rebellion in the time of my Edward's father. Such talk would be dangerous with a boy now on the throne.

My very soul seemed to be on trial. In an attempt to prove that I had cast a spell over King Edward, they sought out and arrested the Dominican friar, Dom Clovis, whom I had consulted so long ago.

I heard Lancaster ascribe to me Edward's arguments about the inappropriateness of relying solely on Nicholas Dagworth's biased judgment regarding William's service in Ireland. A half dozen former officers of Edward's household whom I'd counted, if not friends, certainly not my enemies, exaggerated my influence over the king.

How they could speak such lies in my presence, I could not understand. I had always treated Edward's household officers with respect. With each new condemnation I stood taller, refusing to hang my head in the face of such lies. But my courage left me at night. Then I was haunted by nightmares of being taken to the Tower, of being beheaded . . . such horrors every time I slept that I took to pacing my chamber rather than closing my eyes.

All the while the trial dragged on I screamed within, *I am powerless! How can you fear me? Why do you need to encase me in walls six feet thick? I have never had a choice except to do what I could to protect my chicks.*

I had benefited from my liaison with the king, yes, of course I had. I did not deny that. But so had he benefited, and through him the realm. And what of his children? My children? I feared what would become of them if I were imprisoned or exiled.

After a great deal more, on which I was forbidden to speak out in my defense, parliament's judgment was thus: the property I had accrued as gifts from the king *or through my own means* during my liaison with him were forfeit; parliament took care to state that only in my case was it waiving the laws that protected enfeoffments and other property transactions, fearful lest any of them might so forfeit their own property in due course. Apparently I was a uniquely undeserving landowner. All the jewels they could seize from me were also forfeit. The worst of this was my pearls. They confiscated what they believed to be all the pearls Edward had given me—twenty thousand according to their count. That was the punishment that cut the deepest. Those gifts of love . . . even those were taken from me. Confiscated as well were the jewels entrusted to Lancaster. Even the gold Edward had intended for my support in exile had been discovered. How parliament had known of all this I could not fathom except that either the duke or William had been indiscreet. Though to what purpose, I could not understand.

The crowning punishment was my exile. Exile! I was forbidden on English soil, on pain of imprisonment in the Tower . . . or worse. All I could think of was never seeing my son John again—or my sister and brother. And Bella! My faithfulness to Edward had cost me everything. I swore in my heart that I would at least take with me my precious younger daughters. I would not be parted from Joan and Jane.

I stood there before the hate-twisted faces in the ornately carved, painted, and gilded hall of Westminster, feeling stripped of all honor.

And I was forbidden to speak a word in my own defense. Inwardly I demanded to be heard. *Listen to me! I obeyed the dowager queen Isabella, Queen Philippa, King Edward, Prince Edward, the Duke of Lancaster. I obeyed them in everything. What do you gain from destroying me?*

Ah, but that was the key, of course. They gained property, they gained a fortune in jewels. I wondered to whom the spoils would be presented. I cursed them all.

WHAT OF the promises Princess Joan and Lancaster had made? It was after my appearance before parliament, after my fate had been determined, that I was escorted back to the palace of Westminster to meet them. Unbeknownst to me, another guest had been invited: William Wyndsor. I had not spoken to him since that afternoon in the gardens at Gaynes when I had refuted him.

That evening I learned of a condition regarding their reassurances of my safety about which I had not been informed, plainly because I might not have cooperated in shielding Edward from the gossips had I done so. My beloved Edward, his sons the prince and Lancaster, and William Wyndsor, had made a pact regarding how I was to be made docile after I was no longer needed to attend the king. My exile would not be enforced so long as I lived under William's rule as his wife. I might live peacefully with my children so long as I acknowledged that he was my husband.

I had stopped breathing while I listened to this. My mouth was so dry that even after I remembered to draw breath, I could not speak for several long moments while everyone waited for my humble submission.

"Might live with my children?" I managed at last. "Do you threaten to take Joan and Jane from me if I do not agree?"

"They are the daughters of the late king," said Lancaster. "As his son, I am responsible for them."

Bastard! Changeling! I hissed inwardly, cursing him. My worst nightmares had not touched this depth of betrayal. I would rather be beheaded than live with no hope of seeing my daughters. But I knew that nothing I said would matter to them. My fate had long since been decided. I was the scapegoat. I simply sat there, in a thronelike chair, a jeweled mazer before me, facing those three I had counted as friends from time to time—particularly Princess Joan. Lancaster I had long distrusted. But I had believed in her friendship.

How had I not foreseen this? William's persistence, his thick skin.

Edward had planned this. I remembered his words in the garden the day he told me to keep his signet ring. *I fear you shall face one more labor before you rest, but I pray it may prove unexpectedly happy.* How could he think so? What a pawn I had been! But, of course, he had not been in his right mind then. Lancaster had taken advantage of his father's confusion, had tricked him into agreeing to this travesty.

"A marriage is not valid unless both parties agree," I declared, looking at Joan for corroboration. She averted her eyes, fussing with a sleeve.

Lancaster coughed, no doubt hiding a chuckle. "Dame Alice, you have lain with Sir William many times. You would find it difficult to convince Archbishop Sudbury that you were not willing."

"I have not! Never!" I looked to William, who stared at a spot on the table. I was nauseated. I loathed him.

"It is this or exile?" I asked.

Lancaster gave the subtlest of nods, as if not entirely approving of his own inhumanity.

"And my lands?"

"Those we cannot save for you. But, in time, Sir William might win them back."

I cursed William then and there. Cursed him and vowed that he would never enjoy the wealth I had so carefully accrued for my daughters.

Joan reached out to me then, gently covering my hand with hers. She explained that the people would forget me as soon as they knew I was safely under the control of a husband, and one with strong connections to the great ones of the land. William was known as a fierce guardian of the law. A man of martial skill, a respected knight of the realm.

I was aghast. "It is you who have kept him adamant about our having pledged our troth?"

"Not me, my friend," said Joan. "I have only this past week learned of this agreement."

But William had told Richard Lyons of it long before. And Edward had told me. I had willfully ignored the warnings. I cursed myself for having been so blind as to think it was passion that drove William when it was anger, his sense of being robbed of his due, that had always been the fiercest of his emotions.

"How can you trust him to keep me safe? He failed you in Ireland. Why William, of all men?"

Lancaster was unmoved. "He is my man, Alice. He has always served me well."

But not Edward, not his king. No, that was not true. William had earned him the money to fight in France. He had a thick skin. Perhaps he enjoyed playing antagonist. I must remember this.

"Is this your wish, William?" I asked. "To wed a woman who does not want you?"

He had sat all this time with eyes trained on that spot on the table before him. While I had questioned his trustworthiness he had finally moved, clenching his jaw. He looked at me now, his eyes assessing me, as if he were sizing up a filly for purchase. "Alice, my love, surely by now you should have no illusions about marriage." He reached for my hand but I withdrew into myself. "In time you will want me, Alice. You will."

Never, I shouted inside. *Never. And I shall never forgive you, any of you.*

MY PUBLIC ordeal was not yet over. I was commanded to present myself at a public Mass in Westminster Abbey, so recently the scene of my son's wedding. To the Archbishop of Canterbury I was to confess my sins and humble myself, begging forgiveness. For this I stubbornly wore my widow's weeds. Archbishop Simon Sudbury raised an eyebrow, but said nothing.

I did all that was demanded of me. I had no choice. I was ordered to accept responsibility for all that I had achieved as well as all that I had humbly done in obedience. It was not enough that I had lost

Edward, that his family had robbed me of Janyn and the comfort of my own kin for so long.

And to add to the insult, though I wanted neither William Wyndsor nor Mary Percy, I was shackled with both.

At least for the moment, until I could gather my wits about me. I had said nothing of my betrothal to Robert. At least I might protect him.

I could not sleep as long as I resided in the palace. I veered between anger and anguish over what Robert and Bella would say—I could see the sympathy in Gwen's eyes, and the disappointment.

The fetters, so lately slipped from my ankles, were back, but now without even the sweetness of my love for Edward to soothe their restraint.

I hated them all for the regret I now felt for loving him.

19

> *Hire face, lik of Paradys the ymage,*
> *Was al ychaunged in another kynde.*
> *The pleye, the laughter, men was wont to fynde*
> *On hire, and ek hire joies everichone,*
> *Ben fled; and thus lith now Criseyde allone.*
>
> *Aboute hire eyen two a purpre ryng*
> *Bytrent, in sothfast tokenyng of hire peyne,*
> *That to biholde it was a dedly thyng . . .*

—Geoffrey Chaucer, *Troilus and Criseyde*, IV, 864–71

• January 1378 •

I WAS GRANTED a few days' grace at Westminster, and made use of the time to send messages to Bella, Robert, and Mary, who was at Gaynes with the children, warning them of the impending change in my status. That cold, practical phrase was more suitable for my situation than "marriage." The messenger was given a letter for each, the longest one going to Robert. I vowed my steadfast love for him, telling him that it was only so that I would not be parted from him or my children that I would acquiesce, and begged him not to interfere. I hated that I could not speak to the three of them in person, and prepare Joan and Jane.

But I was effectively a prisoner in Westminster Palace. Though preferable by far to the Tower, it was still a prison, and a cold one at that. Princess Joan and young King Richard were not in residence, nor was Lancaster.

When he had forbidden me to use the few days' grace I was granted to return to Gaynes and prepare my household, I had asked the duke what he feared I might do if permitted to travel.

Elegant in a dark robe that accentuated his fair coloring but also the shadows beneath his eyes, a sign of ill health or at least poor sleep that I had rarely seen on him, Lancaster lightly touched my arm as we stood by a window looking out at the wintry Thames. "I would protect you from taking some unwise action while your mind is in turmoil, Dame Alice, such as fleeing the country with my nieces. That would be regrettable, for it would render impossible our plan for your peaceful, comfortable withdrawal from the center of controversy. You have had a great shock in the judgment brought against you. Such condemnation while still in mourning would shake the most courageous knight to his core. I admire your strength throughout my father's illnesses, his death, the vindictive attacks of the commons."

His expression of concern served only to nauseate me. In my mind I retorted, *Surely you would prefer that I escaped with my daughters. You would then be rid of me and have all my properties, jewels, money. Even Sir William to wed to another you seek to control.*

But I said none of that, nor did I tell him that I was already betrothed. He might look vulnerable, but he was the wealthiest, most powerful man in the realm, and I dared not antagonize him. I feared what he would do to Robert.

When he left I sent away the servants and paced the corridor, spewing all the venom inside me. My booted feet pounded the wood planks while I hissed and shrieked the curses I had so long held within. I wept, I tore at my hair and pounded my breast until I was spent. Let the servants and the guards whisper and cross themselves, I did not care.

The palace now felt like a mere shade of the Westminster I had known with Edward. To a person, the servants seeing to our needs behaved indifferently toward Gwen and me, though many of them had been accustomed to seeking our advice when Edward was unwell. We avoided talking to them when we might, the contrast being too painful. And I had frightened them with my fury, I knew. They, in turn, were stingy with food, drink, and fuel for the braziers. I yearned to go to one of my own homes, in truth to be almost anywhere but in one of the royal residences, fraught as they were with painful memories.

Gwen fretted over my cold hands and feet, my lack of appetite. "I almost preferred your mad rage," she said.

I assured her that I would thrive once I was able to ride and hawk, once I was home—for it seemed I would be permitted to keep Fair Meadow and the home in which Janyn and I had lived in London.

"Will Sir William agree to bide in one of your homes?" she asked me.

"Agree? I should think it his most fervent wish. Why else would he cooperate in this farce but to acquire all that is mine? No one ever speaks of *his* residences, Gwen. No doubt they are barely adequate."

Indeed, William was not in residence at Westminster, but reportedly occupied in readying his home just north of the city for our wedding night. He had sent a message inviting me for a walk in the palace gardens, but I had begged a headache and heard no more. Robert had been right—William did not behave like a man in love. I was simply his current mission for Lancaster. A page had brought a wedding gift, a gold fillet set with diamonds and emeralds, nominally from William though it, too, smelled of Lancaster.

Long ago Princess Joan had warned me: *They will envy you. Envy is an ugly emotion. It inspires cruelty. Meanness . . . If aught goes wrong, you are one of the people who will be blamed. Because you have no connections. Because he loves you. . . . Keep your eyes open. At all times remember who you are, where you are. . . . Find and nurture a few trustworthy friends. But do not blindly trust them. Nor should you blindly trust the king. He is a man, as William Wyndsor is a man. Your William is angry, I noticed that. He may yet be your salvation if aught goes wrong, but if you wed him, try to keep some of your property secret. Just in case.*

Joan had claimed that she had learned of the pact only the previous week. How then had she warned me so long ago?

I requested a meeting with her. She arrived with servants bearing gifts for me—jeweled mazers; several silver spoons; fat cushions covered in silk and velvet; a generous length of escarlatte in a rich gold hue; another in brunette; a soft, patterned wool in shades of red; and a small casket filled with gold and silver buttons inlaid with mother of pearl. Wedding gifts.

"You must believe me, Alice, I knew nothing of this until shortly before you did. I had intended these gifts to cheer you and the homes you were permitted to keep, or else your abode in exile if the worst happened. I had not known of this arrangement with Sir William, I swear."

Whether or not I believed her did not matter to me at that moment. I was desperate for advice. "I cannot wed him, Joan. I cannot love him."

"You must try, Alice. For the sake of your family. Think, my friend—for once you shall be free to live with Joan and Jane, and be near Bella."

My heart quickened at her mention of being near Bella. Gaynes was near Barking Abbey. "Is Gaynes not forfeit?"

Joan shook her head. "Gaynes is yours, so long as you wed Sir William. You once found him pleasing, Alice. Is not this far better than exile?"

It was a fair question. I considered telling her of Robert. She of all people would understand, having been forced into marriage with William Montague when she was secretly betrothed to Thomas Holland. But I no longer trusted her with information she might let slip.

"I shall be grateful to remain close to my son and my daughter Bella. But for them, I would have preferred making a new life with my two youngest children in France or the Low Countries. I might eventually have felt comfortable in my life there, at peace. I cannot imagine ever being so as an unwilling wife."

"Neither John nor his brothers would have permitted you to take their nieces out of the country, Alice."

"I find it strange, that though they were not recognized by their father, their uncles have acquired them. To what purpose? They will not suddenly give them the Plantagenet name or find noble husbands for my girls. The duke does this only to tie me to William, so that he might reward him with my properties."

I could see from her beautiful, expressive face that Joan had no counter to that. It had been of so little interest to her, she had not wondered why the brothers were suddenly so keen to keep their bastard nieces close to them.

She held out her hand to me. "You look so pale."

So did she, I noticed, though her hair was once more brightened, the white that had been evident at her husband's death hidden with bleaches and oils. She also looked swollen, as if the weight she had gained in the last years in Bordeaux and then lost once back in England had returned. She seemed to eat when worried. I regretted having argued with her. A little.

"Let us walk in the garden," she said. "It is fair and mild for January, a gift we should not squander in chilly, dank, echoing chambers."

As Joan and I walked in the deserted gardens, she spoke not of my coming marriage but of her fears regarding her son, so young to be king, and her inability to sleep through the night since Prince Edward's death.

"It is not as if we had slept in the same bed every night. But somehow my sleeping self knows that he is gone, that our son is vulnerable, and I wake with my heart racing."

I was relieved to be distracted from my own worries and anger for a while. Joan had lost far more than a husband. She had lost a most magnificent future and the time her son needed to grow into a young man suited to rule a kingdom.

But soon she turned the conversation to my distrust of the duke.

"John is fighting to keep a delicate balance, Alice. My husband charged him with protecting the realm for our son while Richard was too young to rule on his own. John knows that there are those in commons and among the barons who suspect him of wishing to keep that power for himself. Such a rumor would only grow if he challenged it, and so he trusts that by acting impeccably on Richard's behalf, he will convince the people that to rule this realm is not his intent. Like you, he is condemned for taking a lover to whom he is not wed, and for having children with that lover. In his liaison with Katherine, he understands you better than anyone else in the family."

I sighed with impatience.

Joan gave my arm a little shake. "He means to save you, Alice! Marriage to Sir William is a way in which he might calm the temper of the crowd, safely settle you with a knight. John intended to *honor* you with such a noble connection."

"I wish I might believe all that you say of him." It would be so much easier to welcome this marriage. But I distrusted it. And I loved Robert, not William. I drew my squirrel-lined cloak up under my chin.

"Come, you are chilled. Let us withdraw to your chamber and some hot spiced wine." As we hurried along the garden path Joan said, "I pray that joy surprises you, Alice. You have done so much for this family, and I wish you happiness."

When she had departed I spent a long while in the chapel, praying for the wisdom and grace to behave as if I accepted my lot. I also prayed that Joan was right about the duke. But it was difficult to push aside thoughts of flight.

WILLIAM AND I were wed in a simple ceremony in that same chapel in Westminster Palace in which I had prayed so earnestly for acceptance. Archbishop Sudbury, he to whom I had humbled myself days earlier, presided. I wore a dark gold brocade gown and blue-green undergown. Gwen had sprinkled the brocade with the buttons Princess Joan had given me. I wore over my coiled hair the diamond-and-emerald fillet from William. He wore a slim-fitting jacket of deep indigo embroidered with silver thread that swirled into the shape of a swan. A hat of lighter indigo sported a peacock feather. His leggings were dark brown. We were a handsome couple, so elegant we would not stoop to revealing emotion. The guests were fortunate, for were we to do so, I would scream, and William, most likely laugh.

For the sake of my children, I vowed to do all in my power to find peace in this hateful situation. But I would never give William my heart. That was Robert's.

As we rode to William's home north of London I forced my thoughts to a neutral topic. I was now the wife of a man of more modest means than either Janyn or Edward, albeit a knight, and prepared myself for a small, plain dwelling. It turned out to be a sizable house and quite new.

"In summer the oaks surrounding it must give pleasant shade," I remarked. "And is that a pond farther down?"

"A fish pond, well stocked when I am in residence."

We had exchanged few words all day, swept along on the falsely cheerful chatter of our "sponsors," as William referred to the duke and the princess. In a peculiar gesture, my father and his wife—whom I had not previously met, being such a danger to her soul when I was Edward's mistress—were invited to the ceremony. Knowing nothing of my feelings about the union, Father wished me all happiness. When his wife would have added her simpering congratulations he drew her away, no doubt apprehensive of my response.

"You said little to your mother," William remarked.

"My mother is long dead."

My stomach clenched at the prospect of years of this empty civility.

His household greeted me warmly. The hall was modest and simply furnished, tidy and inviting, especially the fire in the center fragrant with apple wood. I complimented William on the fine meal set before us and attempted to converse about safe topics, for the moment we had arrived at the house he had begun to quaff brandywine. By the end of the meal, which he hardly touched, he had consumed copious amounts and seemed hungry for an argument.

He began a litany of slights—my sending him away from Gaynes, my refusal to permit him to stay at Tibenham many summers past, my leaving his letters unanswered, and my insulting him in front of Lancaster and Joan. When he reached the end of his litany he began again. I said little. Neither Janyn nor Edward had ever behaved so, and I was unsure what would make him even angrier.

"I am here now, William," I reminded him when we finally withdrew to our bedchamber. I sat down beside him on the bed. "Might we not be courteous to one another?"

He grunted. "That would suit you, would it? Coax me into forgetting all your insults and pretend we have just met?"

"What are we to do? How do you propose we live?"

He lurched to his feet and stumbled toward the door. When he was almost there he turned. About to lose his balance, he flung up a hand and caught hold of a rafter to steady himself, took a deep breath, and blinked, as if trying to clear his mind and vision. "How can you not know that from the moment I first saw you, I vowed you would be my wife?"

So I had not been wrong in believing that long ago. I rose and approached him, reaching out to steady him. "Come, William, come to bed." I wanted any spies in the household to report that we had slept together.

He slipped one hand behind my head and pulled me close, kissing me on the mouth. I managed to disentangle myself sufficiently to lead him to the bed as he pawed at me, undressing him while being partially undressed myself. But I had no sooner eased him under a pile of blankets and coverlets than the drink overwhelmed him. He went limp and proceeded to snore.

When I was certain that he was deeply asleep I called Gwen in to help me prepare for bed. I lay awake, imagining how I must behave in the next few days and weeks to win William's trust, wondering if that was possible. I prayed we might come to a mutually satisfactory agreement.

I woke to find him kissing me, and as he sensed me stirring he gently entered me. His breath smelled of anise and his skin of some exotic perfume—he had washed and prepared himself for me. Though he was considerate in his lovemaking, I did not respond. Afterward we lay side by side, eyes averted from each other, as if wondering whether we dared communicate further.

He turned back toward me and lifted my shift to gaze on my body. "Well, my silent Alice, be assured you shall be so awakened as often as I can manage. I cannot think how I would wake beside this body and not be aroused." His smile was lazy and sensual as he eased himself on top of me once more.

I did not pretend to do more than endure, and he did not seem to care. I prayed that he would soon tire of my unresponsiveness.

Later in the morning, after we broke our fast in front of the fragrant fire in the hall, William and I talked. It was clear that I was not the only one who had spent some time considering how to make the best of our marriage. He vowed that if I accepted his apology for our arranged match and gave him a chance to prove himself a loving husband, he would work through the courts to clear my name, revoke my exile, and reclaim the property I had purchased in my own name.

I agreed in principle. Silently I vowed to secure what I could of the properties I had purchased in partnerships by working once again with my old friends and business partners. I had not forgotten Robert's warning about William having demanded information about my properties, nor Joan's about keeping some property secret.

For several days we both made great efforts in courtesy, but it was plain that it would require constant vigilance and restraint on my part. William managed to forgo too much drink the first few evenings in his home, and I tolerated his sexual demands. It was strange to me, to be sickened by a man's touch. When we talked we chose safe topics such as the household, his other properties, what items he intended to take to Gaynes. But on the fourth day he drank too much at the midday meal, and by evening was alternately vicious about my passive demeanor and morosely silent. By the time we made our way to the barge at Westminster staithe, we were eyeing each other warily. I dreaded the homecoming ahead.

Though Princess Joan and the Duke of Lancaster were granting me safe passage home, there were inevitably those in their retinues and that of the young king who might seek praise and advancement by capturing me. After all, I had been exiled, which would not usually entitle me to a life spent in England, much less the use of a royal barge. William and I had been warned to dress simply and remain well covered.

As I watched the familiar riverscape slip past, I was overcome by memories of ferrying to and from my homes and Edward's palaces. My body remembered my excitement, my heart my expectations. Then the royal bargemen and guards had treated me with respect; now all eyes were curious, and most cold. I tried to avoid the memory of a more recent journey home with Robert, when I had thought myself a free woman.

I hated the fact that I'd been unable to prepare him and my family for this latest development, and that Joan and Jane, and possibly my son, knew nothing of my marriage to William. My youngest children had been happy to have me living in the same house with them, without a man insisting on my undivided attention most of the day and all of the night. I anticipated tears when they realized that William would be sharing my bedchamber and my life. I tried to reassure myself that at least he was not a stranger to them. They had met him before, and he had been, though distant, never mean to them. He would do well to remain so, for my children would always be first in my heart.

But Robert . . . my beloved, true husband. My letter to him had been clumsy for I'd found it most painful to write. The look on his face when he met the barge was one of betrayal and shattered hope. But he quickly gained control of himself and welcomed William. I, however, felt as if I might be sick and dared not meet his eyes.

Joan and Jane were confused, but William greeted them with such hilariously exaggerated courtesy that for days he had but to bow to them to reduce them both to giggles. For that I was grateful. I had not expected such sensitivity. Mary Percy ignored him, but that was her wont. I had recently agreed to her having her own lady's maid, and the two of them gossiped and simpered in a corner of the hall as they bent over their embroidery and other stitching most of the day. I counted it a godsend that she was thus occupied.

Gwen was very quiet. We had been through so many changes together, but this one seemed the most difficult for her to accept. As she tidied my bedchamber the first night at Gaynes, I asked for her thoughts, for she seemed sad.

"I cannot bear to see you so unhappy when—" She pressed her fingers to her lips for a moment, her expression embarrassed. "Forgive me, Dame Alice. I forget my place."

"You are one of my oldest and dearest companions, Gwen. You are welcome to speak freely whenever we are alone."

"In Master Robert you have found a husband you love and respect and enjoy being with. I fear what will happen now. How long can you play the role of Sir William's wife? How will Master Robert bear it? How will you?"

"I do not know what will become of us, Gwen. Each time I believe I am free, I am shackled anew."

She sighed and latched the chest she had filled, pressing her hands to her lower back as she rose. She would age someday, and I would lose her—if I did not go first. I could not imagine my life without her.

"Perhaps Sir William will surprise you," she said, without conviction.

Nor could I imagine it. On his best behavior, William drank moderately the first evening at Gaynes. We began it in pleasant conversation, and ended it in a rough coupling. But the following morning I woke to find him gone. The servants said that he had ridden out early.

I sought out Robert in the fields. His sun-bleached hair, the way his skin wrinkled about his eyes when he squinted against the light, the way he held himself . . . it was all familiar and dear to me. But his greeting was too formal. I talked over it, told him all that had transpired at Westminster. We walked along the hedgerow he had been inspecting while I talked, then paused in an old shed, sitting side by side on a wobbly bench.

"They have no right," he said, staring at the mud floor.

I put my hand over his. "It is I who have no rights, Robert. It seems I never had. My father arranged my marriage with Janyn, and Janyn bound me to the queen's household."

"If you might choose . . . ?"

He had turned to look me in the eyes. As he did so my side of the bench gave way. He caught me in his arms, lifting us both to our feet.

"I *have* chosen you, Robert. Surely you can see that in my eyes?

Surely I made that plain during our nights together, and in pledging my troth?"

We kissed long and tenderly, pressing ourselves against each other.

"God may yet set this right," he whispered.

"I do not dare to hope, but I pray William will quickly tire of the pretense and leave us in peace."

"Until then, I shall watch over you, Alice."

I did not like those words, *until then*. "Robert, we shall be together when he is away. Surely we need not deny our love?"

He shook his head. "I cannot share you with him, Alice."

I felt panic rising. "Robert, do not punish me! I am doing this for us. Protecting you, protecting my children—" I broke off, hearing Janyn telling me he had arranged my summons to court for my safety, for Bella's. "What have I done, Robert?"

He took my hands and stared at them, kissed each in turn, then looked up at me. His love for me was writ on his face, and also his pain. But he managed a crooked smile. "You have done what had to be done. I could not love you as I do and believe for a moment that you would be able to bear a separation from your children."

"No, I could not." I took a deep breath. "What will you do now?"

"I will stay away from you as much as possible, travel to our distant properties, oversee them." He kissed my forehead, my cheeks, my lips, gently, tenderly, then backed away. "This is how it must be, for now. I cannot stay, Alice. I would do him violence."

We parted there. Later that day he rode off to a distant manor.

Gradually, after much prayer and thought, I calmed myself and strove continually to be grateful for all that I had, to push away the yearning for what I had not.

In the next few weeks we entertained a stream of guests—Richard Lyons, Dom Hanneye, Geoffrey, Pippa, and their son Thomas, my brother John and his family. I had urged William to allow us some quiet in which to adjust, but he wished all to congratulate us. He wanted to know my family and friends. As I observed him with our guests, I realized how little we knew of each other.

On the first morning of Richard's visit I proposed we should all go hawking. It was a mild February day, and Joan and Jane had asked if we might. My daughters were utterly entranced by the hawks and all the ritual surrounding hunting with birds.

"A tedious pastime." William was slumped on a bench near the fire circle in the hall, staring into it as if conjuring spirits. He did not even look up to pronounce his opinion. With a wave of his hand, he added, "Be gone if you will. I shall find other occupation."

Even Mary Percy showed more interest, though her participation began with much simpering about how the various birds should be assigned, according to the status of the hawker, with insulting references to Geoffrey, Richard, and myself being unworthy of our falcons.

"Your poor son," Richard whispered in my ear, "he will be wanting a gentle, sweet-natured mistress within days of setting up household with that shrew."

The guest in whom William took most interest was Pippa Chaucer, hungrily eyeing the rounds of her breasts accentuated by the cut of her gown. At first she shamelessly flirted with him, to Geoffrey's discomfort, but she cooled on him one evening when he asked too many questions about her sister Katherine, some of them crude. His thin veneer of courtesy was easily dissolved by brandywine.

"Being Lancaster's man, I should think you see far more of my sister than I do," she said curtly, and moved away to talk to Richard.

William chose that moment to launch a volley of insults my way. As he had referred to Katherine as Lancaster's concubine, he called me the king's. I'd "not had the wit to find a real husband after Janyn's death, but fell into the aged king's bed with no thought to the future."

I'd encountered drunks before, but none with the power so to sting me, to twist the knives that plainly protruded from my still-grieving heart.

I glanced at Geoffrey's face, livid with anger, and shook my head.

"My friend, do not engage him in argument. He is beyond reason when in his cups."

THE FISSURE between William and me yawned wider as our guests departed. He was not accustomed to life in a country manor. He had no patience for accounts, less interest in plans. He belittled me for gardening—"peasants' work"—and I berated him for his increasing nastiness toward the children, not only Joan and Jane but my nieces and nephews, too. I thanked God that I had taken precautions not to become pregnant. Mary spoke of finding somewhere else to lodge, and I eventually agreed that she was better off in my home in London. Of course, then William, too, wished to remove to my home in London, to "see to business."

"You have a home so near London you've no need to stay in mine."

"Ours," he reminded me.

"Janyn's," I countered.

He withdrew to his own home north of London for a few months. I rejoiced at the peace that settled over the house.

Even more wonderful was the afternoon Robert reappeared. I greeted him as my steward and friend when he arrived, and invited him to walk out to a far paddock to inspect a drainage problem. When we were safely out of sight of anyone who might report to William, I stopped and took his hands.

"Robert, does this mean . . . ?"

I managed to say no more before he had silenced me with a long, passionate kiss. When at last we stepped apart, we stood for a while looking into each other's eyes, needing no words.

"You were right, my love," he said as we walked on through the fields. "When he is away, we shall be together. It is how it must be for now."

We planned with care how we would manage our nights together, and agreed to speak of William as little as possible.

"It is not as I would wish it," he said, "but it is far better than being without you at all."

Our mood was so light, our hearts so full, we found it difficult to return to the mundane topic of drainage, and somehow our discussion of the boggy ground provoked much laughter between us.

Robert went away again when William returned in the summer to plague me. He attempted a reconciliation, sleeping with me a few times, but our arguments began anew and he dived into the brandy-wine to fortify his venom, afterward sleeping where he fell. I ordered the servants to prepare a small chamber for him and told them to ensure he was there when they woke. I did not want my daughters to find him lying in the rushes when they came to the hall to break their fasts.

I learned to listen to William just long enough to know when to agree or disagree, to nod or shake my head.

In early autumn we moved to the manor of Crofton in Wiltshire, ostensibly to meet William's family—they had property within a day's ride. His parents were both long dead, but cousins, siblings, and the younger generation lived there about. I found his nephew John Wyndsor, who had expected to be William's heir and still was in his will as it stood, an ignorant lout of a man, but William's sister was a lovely woman with whom I enjoyed talking about children.

The family had been scandalized by our wedding. I felt them covertly examining me, this infamous woman about whom they would love to hear more scandalous details. How perverse of such a well-favored figure of a man, who had so valiantly and nobly served King Edward and the Duke of Lancaster, to settle for a merchant's daughter with three bastards, no matter that one was a knight wed to a Percy. In truth, they were all too careful to say such things in my presence, but my daughter-in-law Mary made certain to repeat all that she had gleaned by listening behind tapestries and at partially closed doors.

Mary was too self-centered, and perhaps too young, to realize that I prompted her to repeat to me what she regarded as hurtful comments. She was only too delighted, and I was grateful to learn the lay of the land. I must know as much as possible about William in order to protect myself from him. I maintained a courteous demeanor toward him in public, and, on those increasingly rare evenings when he had not overindulged in brandywine, tried to be civil in private.

My efforts in the latter eventuality were seldom completely successful, leading me to wonder whether he was as unhappy as I. One evening I dared ask him. I could not help but hope he had a mistress with whom he would prefer to bide.

"Unhappy with you, wife? What cause might I have? That you insulted me in front of the Duke of Lancaster and the mother of the king? That you refused my affections until you had no choice? That you still refer to *our* properties as yours—or, worse, your first husband's, that Lombard smuggler?"

And this on a night during which he had, I thought, drunk little.

"Why, then, do you stay?"

"To torment you."

It was a kind of power, antagonizing me, forcing me to submit. I realized with dismay that it might be true, and if so, there was little hope that he would walk away for good.

DESPITE THE hostility between us, in October, before a new parliament, William fulfilled his promise to begin working toward restoring my forfeited properties. He made the claim that I had been his wife when tried as a *femme sole* the previous year, and therefore my forfeited property was *his* forfeited property; as he had been accused of nothing, his property had been unlawfully taken. This would also render many of the private petitions enrolled against me null and void, for they named me and not my husband. It was legal sleight of hand that we hoped would work in our favor.

I dreaded any and all news of the proceedings, wanting to be quit of that life as much as I wanted to be quit of William himself. I felt cursed. But it was important for me to know how things stood, and so I listened to William's and Geoffrey's reports.

My impression of the petitions in general was that people accused me of having accepted gifts proffered in exchange for my efforts to obtain a favor from the king, the chancellor, or the chamberlain, and when they received no satisfaction, accused me of having made no effort on their behalf. I had seen such complaints made against all in Edward's household and on his council over the years, and knew full well they were seldom credited. One might work diligently on behalf of another, but if the king or his officers refused to change their judgment, there was nothing more to be done. When I wondered aloud why few had made such complaints about me before, yet now so many came forth, William told me the petitioners had a common refrain, "But I did not dare pursue my rights, for it was well known that no one dared touch the king's mistress"—or words to that effect.

I felt a great fool. Far from the giddy glamour of court life and the safety of Edward's love, I was angry with myself for my naïveté. Now that I was back in the circle of London merchants among whom I had been raised, once more influenced by their practical approach of luxury without prodigality, I did not understand my own hubris at court. I had known that what was legal for a man was rarely so for a woman, likewise a noble versus a commoner. Had I been more modest in my ambitions for my daughters, had I refused more of Edward's gifts, I might now be free to live openly as Robert's wife. Remorse ate at me.

William sensed it and goaded me by reciting petitions from memory when he was in the mood for attack. But when one afternoon he found me weeping in my bedchamber, he relented.

"I promise you I will speak no more of this, Alice. You have been cruelly used, and I would make it up to you."

He often made such pretty speeches, but seldom kept his promises. This time he did. For a while we enjoyed a fragile peace.

His petition was taken under consideration, but no decisions regarding my lands came out of that parliament. Because of William's argument that I was a married woman, I was henceforth required to do business as such, which compounded my difficulties, for William's credit was poor. And despite letters from the Duke of Lancaster stating that I and all who traded with me were under his protection, merchants were wary of trading with me because my sentence of exile had not yet been officially revoked.

Once again I was fortunate in my friends. Richard Lyons and Robert smoothed out the ruffled feathers of those merchants I most needed to deal with.

ROBERT AND I lived for the times when William would disappear for a fortnight or longer. Wrapped in Robert's arms, I dreamed of freedom.

My daughter Joan seemed to have fallen in love with Robert as well, becoming suddenly vain about her dress and following him about the estate, hoping to catch his eye, hanging on his every word. He was most gallant with her. Jane was obsessed with animals, and her appearance—feathers, hay, mud, and blood adorning her, badges of honor— was the opposite of her sister's. Caring for my daughters absorbed me, nurtured my ailing heart.

IN THE parliament held a little over a year later William and I were issued pardons for my not going into exile and for William having sheltered me all that time. But I was not yet fully exonerated, nor were my forfeited lands returned.

William went to Lancaster for advice, and was encouraged to volunteer for a campaign that was to be undertaken in Brittany the following year under his brother Thomas of Woodstock, now Earl of Buckingham. Lancaster suggested that if William not only took part in the campaign but agreed to bear some of the costs for the contingent, he would gain King Richard's favor, which could very well lead to the restoration of my forfeited lands. I exhorted Richard Lyons and my merchant friends to finance William's part of the campaign; not one of his own kinsmen contributed. The plan worked. Within months, long before he departed for Brittany, the majority of my forfeited lands were restored—but to William, not to me.

When he informed me of this, I could not believe it. I had done everything Lancaster demanded of me. I had cared for his father when I might most reasonably have taken my leave of court. I had given up everything for the royal family, yet still I was punished. Now I had been used to provide William with a lordly living, just as I had suspected on that fateful evening at Westminster when he was presented as my betrothed.

I rushed out of the house, seeking shelter in the church. *What do You want of me, Lord?* I asked over and over. *What more do You require of me before You allow me peace?* I prayed for deliverance.

L IFE WITH William grew ever more intolerable. We spoke hardly a civil word to each other and rarely slept together—at least that was a blessing. He fed my resentment by insisting not only that he was right but also demanding I admit to being wrong. Which I refused to do, though I also refused to argue unless it had to do with my children, which infuriated him. I saw how his unyielding insistence on being right, on never considering the possibility of being otherwise, had led to his downfall in Ireland and elsewhere. It was this tendency of excessive pride in him that caused problems with our tenants and the shopkeepers leasing my properties in London.

His nephew John was adept at feeding William's appetite for antagonism. During one visit he had been particularly busy. William returned from John's home in a quiet mood, the sort of quiet that alerted me to stormy days ahead. He was coldly polite if asked a question, vague about his time away; and his eyes wandered continually between his surroundings and me, as if he were reassessing our life together. As the days wore on he grew sullen and rude, treating me like an inconvenient guest whom he'd been irritated to find ensconced in his home on his return. The one night he came to my bed I refused him, calling loudly for Gwen, for he was drunk and had gripped my wrists as if he meant to rape me, not make love to me. I had already suffered this behavior on a few darksome occasions, and had no intention of submitting to it again. The following morning, he at last confronted me.

"You lied to me about the king's rings."

"Rumors, William. I kept only the signet he had told me to keep."

"They've not found the rings."

This was old news. "I know, and you are well aware that I have told them all I know of it. Why are you bringing this up?"

"Where is the signet now?"

I fought to show no emotion. "In a safe place. I shall bequeath it to my son John." I was grateful I had given it to Robert for safekeeping. But I also worried that somehow William would find out that it was in his possession.

"What of Queen Philippa's jewels?"

I grew hot with the nerve of him. He already had the costliest jewels Edward had given me.

"The Bishop of Winchester has vouched for me that I never possessed them, though I had worn them. You know all this, William. What is your intent?"

"Walsingham has told my nephew much about you and your whoring ways."

So John Wyndsor had been to St. Albans. It explained much. Thomas Walsingham, a monk at that troublesome abbey, wrote with a pen dipped in venom and spoke from a soul filled with hatred for the Duke of Lancaster and for me.

"Tell your nephew to have a care. If Lancaster should hear of his friendship with Walsingham, he might lose favor. Bereft of the duke's patronage, your nephew might find life difficult."

"Until he inherits from me," William snarled.

I could hold my tongue no longer. "You already have my lands and jewels, why stay if you despise me so?"

"You are my lawful wife, Alice. We are bound till death do us part."

"We need not live together. Release me from this false marriage, William. Grant us both some rest."

"It suits me to stay."

I lived for midsummer, when he would leave for the Brittany campaign. He did not expect to return until late autumn. As the time drew near for him to leave he became more civil, however, and seemed to look upon the household with more affection.

One evening he had been most courteous, even charming, at dinner, entertaining our guests with stories of his previous time in Brittany and in Ireland, providing amusing imitations of both sides on the battlefield and in negotiations. I had never witnessed this talent of his. The last tale had been of a skirmish in Ireland that had been particularly bloody and was won by a clever ruse. Such talk had excited him, it was quite clear.

"You have a passion for soldiering," I said after our guests departed.

"I do. I feel most alive in arms, riding to challenge the enemy. That is why I have advised your son to take up arms likewise in Lancaster's service."

The pleasant glow I had been enjoying after a successful evening abruptly dimmed. "What? You advised John? When did you see him?"

John had not stayed in my home since my marriage to William. I had not seen him in more than a year, and then but briefly at an inn near where he was biding for a few nights. Although I had never gleaned a clear reason from Percy as to why my son had not been at liberty to visit, I had assumed it had something to do with his dislike of William, who had antagonized so many of the nobles with properties in Ireland. To learn that William had seen John was therefore a cruel shock.

"I have met him often in the company of the Duke of Lancaster."

I waited for more of an explanation, but William rose from his seat and moved toward the stairs with a yawn and a stretch, as if to retire for the night without explaining himself further.

I hurried to block his way. "Why have you never mentioned this?"

His expression was one of slightly drunken indifference. "I thought it best not to. I knew you would feel slighted. But these were official meetings, nothing to which you might reasonably have been invited." He patted my forearm.

"Except as your wife."

"You were not with me at the time."

Life as a battle was to him a good life. All I wished for was peace, and to be with my children.

"You know how I've ached to see John. Why does he not come here? Is it Mary, his wife? Does he avoid her?"

"Ask him yourself."

"I do not like to quiz him in letters."

He shrugged. "I am weary of our arguments, Alice."

"So am I. How might we mend the situation, William?"

He sniffed. "What more do you want? What needs mending?" He pushed past me.

I grabbed his arm. "William!"

He shook off my hand. "If you want to talk, look to your beloved Robert Broun." He stalked off to his chamber.

I lay awake long into the night, so heavy of heart I could not even weep. So William knew about Robert. I wondered how long he had known, whether my unfaithfulness was why my lands had gone to him—whether he had informed Lancaster, and the duke had informed the king. The lands I could somehow come to live without. I would find another way to provide for my daughters. But my son! I was furious that William had kept his meetings with my son from me, but even worse was John's silence on the matter. That defection was a terrible blow. I did not know how I might learn to live with it.

20

> N'y sey nat this al oonly for thise men,
> But moost for wommen that bitraised be
> Thorugh false folk—God yeve hem sorwe, amen!—
> That with hire grete wit and subtilte
> Bytraise yow. And this commeveth me
> To speke, and in effect yow alle I preye,
> Beth war of men, and herkneth what I seye!

—GEOFFREY CHAUCER, *Troilus and Criseyde*, V, 1779–85

• Spring 1380 •

WILLIAM DEPARTED shortly after that night, refusing to enter into further discussion regarding either Robert or his meetings with John. He behaved as if our conversation about them had never taken place. I held my breath while he remained with me, watching for any signs that he knew precisely how close Robert and I were, thinking he would surely enjoy destroying our happiness if he knew of our love. I tried to engage him in further conversation about my son, asked again if he knew why John did not make more effort to visit, or why Percy did not permit it—for if it was not to avoid William, I worried that John meant to avoid me. William said that if my son wished for me to know aught, he would tell me himself. I could see no way through William's armor against me, polished to a sheen with painful resentment and reinforced by hatred. In my son he had found the surest weapon against me.

Even after he left, I worried. He was not departing for Brittany until midsummer, but said he had much to do on his own estates first. I imagined him whispering in Lancaster's ear, and half-expected the duke's men to come for me at any time.

I decided to move the household to Gaynes, where I hoped to live peaceably at my favorite manor through the summer and into the autumn. I had much to think about, the sort of thought that required solitude. I had written to Henry Percy to inform him of the move, and requested that John might pay me a visit there. I prayed that my son would wish to be with me and that he would dispel my concerns by openly talking of his meetings with William.

The flurry of activity necessary before a move kept me blessedly distracted, but not so much that I missed an instance of uncharacteristic behavior. My young daughter-in-law Mary was usually the most irritating member of the household at such times, insisting on more than her share of space in the carts. But this time, while Joan, Jane, Gwen, and I rushed about, filling chests with clothing and household furnishings, Mary and her maid quietly saw to their own preparations and expressed indifference as to the household's plans. Always alert to her moods, I was troubled by her lack of interest. A few days before our departure, I received a messenger from Henry Percy who quickly explained my daughter-in-law's behavior. She was not to accompany my household to Gaynes.

The message was delivered by one of Percy's retainers, who had been sent to escort Mary to a manor belonging to his lord. As he sipped wine in my hall, armed as if expecting his reception to be less than cordial, the man informed me that Mary had appealed to the Pope in Avignon for an annulment of her marriage with my son. Lord Henry felt it proper that she should remove herself from my household during the papal investigation of her accusations.

My stomach clenched. "What are these accusations?"

"I beg your patience, Dame Alice, but I was provided with no details." The messenger fidgeted on a bench as he spoke. "You will duly be receiving word from the cleric appointed by the Pope to examine the case."

I was quite sure by his discomfiture that he had the information but preferred not to anger me by sharing it. He was wise to avoid antagonizing me further, for I already fumed from the insult. Mary was but twelve, so I had no doubt she'd had assistance in arranging the request.

I imagined Henry, Lord Percy wished to marry her off to someone of higher standing, someone who might help his own advance to power.

Since her marriage Mary had lived with me for three long years and in all that time had never once spoken of an annulment.

"What of my original request for my son's company?"

"Sir John Southery has been sent to study in the household of the Bishop of Exeter. My master has forwarded your request to the bishop."

I said as little as I might, wishing to provide Percy with no indication of my reaction to such evidence of meticulous planning. Indeed, the elegance of his moves left me shaken. The long period of preparation for the Brittany campaign had allowed Percy time to arrange this betrayal strategically so that William was not there to support me. Though he would not have done so for my sake, he would have seen it as an insult to our status, and that would have infuriated him.

When summoned, Mary entered the hall garbed in an elegant gown, her expression smug and sickening to me.

"Praise God that my family is relieved of this canker," I said under my breath, that only she should hear. For the others, I smiled sweetly.

"And I am relieved of a whore's son," she hissed.

"A king's son, you ignorant child."

She inclined her head toward the others, bidding them a chilly farewell.

I detected nary a tear among the servants or my little family as Mary and her maid departed. Jane, who had held my hand as we observed the procession of servants carrying Mary's possessions to the waiting cart, gave a sigh as it at last rolled away.

I looked down on her with concern. "What is it, my sweet?"

She met my worried gaze with merry eyes. "Joan and I can talk as loud as we please now."

"Mary did not like you to speak loudly?"

"Oh, she liked it very well, Mother, but we did not like her telling our secrets to the servants, especially the grooms."

Joan agreed. "She bought special treatment with gossip."

For the moment, I rejoiced in the gift of peace for all our household. It would be an immense relief to have the deceitful girl out of my house, out of my family.

But peace did not last long. I knew that no matter what he privately thought of Mary, my son John could not but feel the insult of her defection. I prayed it would not widen the wedge between us, the one that William had already begun to drive home with his talk of my being unwelcome at court.

Within days of our remove to Gaynes, I learned that Thomas Arundel, the current Bishop of Ely, had been assigned by Pope Clement to find the truth of Mary's case.

I was grateful that Robert arrived before the interview with Arundel's clerk. I felt stronger with him by my side.

"Mary Percy claims to have been held in your home against her will, Dame Alice. That is her argument."

I fought down the anger that rose in me at such a bare-faced claim. "Lord Percy and the late King Edward arranged the betrothal and marriage of Mary and the king's son, Sir John Southery," I stated without emotion. "What is the substance of her petition, other than this false claim?"

"That your son is not of noble birth, and she would have children with a man of noble blood."

I did not respond at once, feeling a dagger wound to my heart at such an insult. This would wound John as well; it could not help but do so. I fought for calm.

"Granted, I am of common though respectable birth, but my son's father was the King of England. There is no more noble blood in the realm; not even Percy blood is so noble."

The clerk coughed and colored as he was forced at last to declare that John was a bastard.

"Yet knighted by his father, the king."

"I am merely the messenger, Dame Alice."

It was fait accompli, this interview a mere pretense of courtesy. Why they bothered I could not imagine, being only the harlot who had borne the bastard. Such ugly thoughts. I bowed my head and prayed.

"I pray you, forgive me, Dame Alice," said the clerk. "I would not cause you such pain."

Robert showed him out. The clerk would bide with the parish priest while awaiting our formal response.

My consolation was that John came east to Westminster in the party of the Bishop of Exeter and then continued on to Gaynes. For his part, he had been grievously insulted by Mary's petition and was ready to protest to the Percy family, as I had expected. That did nothing to dampen my joy in seeing him—he was almost fifteen now, as tall as me and looking so like his father, from his piercingly blue eyes to his long-fingered hands and shapely legs. My heart swelled with pride and love. But we needed to talk at once. I invited him to accompany me to watch the training of a new falcon, a gift from one of Janyn's old friends.

As we walked through the spring garden, the beds tidy and hopeful with fresh shoots, I asked him how he liked the bishop's household.

"It is pleasant enough, but I shall not be returning. I am now in the service of the Duke of Lancaster."

I sought for a way to express surprise without appearing false. "So you did not care for Exeter?"

John quickened his stride for a moment, then paused as I laughingly begged him to consider the limitations of my skirts. He turned a flushed face to me—it is the bane of the fair to wear their emotions so brightly.

"If Mary wins her annulment, and you know that Henry Percy will spare no expense to ensure that she does so, I must find a way to erase that dishonor, Mother. My skill in arms should do that. The duke has promised that I shall take part in a major military expedition within the year."

"John, you have a comfortable estate from your father."

We had resumed our walk to the mews, but at a more leisurely pace. My son, who had been remarking on how lovely everything looked at Gaynes, was now focusing on the path before him, looking neither up nor around, and had clasped his hands behind his back—both characteristic signs in his father that he was ill at ease and choosing his words with care. I yearned to prompt him by letting him know what William had told me, but stopped myself before destroying my chance for reassurance. I needed John to tell me in his own time. I needed to know he meant to tell me.

"It is not my comfort but my honor at stake, Mother," he said, frowning at the pebbled path. He cursed the Percy family for being so eager to own him before parliament had ruled against me and now so ignobly rejecting him. "I hate what they are doing to you. You have suffered enough."

His loyalty to me gladdened my heart. "I have found much peace in being here, John, away from the city and far from court." I sought to reassure him a little.

"I mean to protest the petition."

I was certain that would be a waste of time and money. Unless he was disappointed in love, something I had not considered. "John, do you love Mary? Do you desire her?"

"Love her? No. Desire her? In faith, I have often wished to feel her breasts." He grinned, a good sign that he was relaxing a little. "But I'd as lief kiss a braying ass as kiss Mary Percy."

We laughed together.

"Yet you would fight for her?"

"It is a matter of honor, Mother."

"We shall find you someone much more to your liking, eh?"

"That is not what angers me. You have reached a settled state in your life. Sir William is a good husband; he is fighting to reinstate your properties and status."

He, of course, did not know the truth of our loveless marriage.

"And now you have been grievously insulted—and I know you will worry about my losing the de Orby lands."

Those extensive lands Edward had urged on me, Mary Percy's inheritance. I had invested a great sum in them to make up for years of poor management.

"They would have brought you considerable income," I said, "but you already have enough. Your father provided a goodly estate for you. Has Lancaster said aught about Mary's petition or your inheritance?"

"As far as I am aware, my half brothers have no quarrel with my inheritance. Sir William assured me that the Duke of Lancaster is pleased with all he hears of me. As, of course, he must be to accept me in his service."

The last statement was said in a rush as John tried to distract me from his comment about William. But it was precisely what I had been listening for.

"Sir William?"

John ducked his head, suddenly commenting on the state of the mews, which we were approaching.

"John, when did you speak to William?"

His shrug made my heart race.

"John!"

He stopped and turned to me, his blue eyes imploring. "I saw him at the duke's residences when I was included in Lord Henry's party. Sir William counseled me to say nothing to you, fearing you might be jealous. He believed you were not welcome in court circles."

Of course I was not. I was an embarrassment to them, the scape-goat who should be safely in exile where I might fade from their notice.

I gently touched his forearm, looking into his eyes. "I am glad to be free from court; you know that, John. What troubles me is this secrecy. I would that you had spoken to me of it. We must have no secrets from one another."

He pecked me on the forehead. "No more. I am glad it does not trouble you."

We resumed our walk.

"How often have you seen him?" I asked.

"Several times a year."

I worked hard to hide my distress. "What do you talk about?"

"Nothing that should worry you."

"John, why are you so uncomfortable about this?"

"Because I was not to speak of it. I promised."

I relented at that moment, too stunned and angry to pursue my son further. But over the next few days he grew more talkative, eventually confiding in me that the only complaint William made of me was my obsession with his will and dislike of his nephew.

"That seems an area of deep distrust between you," he said.

"Is it any wonder, John? As my husband, William seeks to restore my properties to himself, not me, and has not rewritten his will to include Joan and Jane. The properties I accrued for the future comfort of your sisters will otherwise go to a lying, scheming nephew who despises me."

John had begun to look sullen. "He claims Joan and Jane are the daughters of Robert Broun, and that Robert should provide for them."

For a moment I forgot how to breathe.

"Mother?" John touched my forearm. "Are you unwell?"

I found a bench and sank down onto it. "It is a lie! I never betrayed your father. Never. You've only to look at Joan to see that she—like you—is pure Plantagenet. Jane looks more like me, true, but they are both your full sisters. Both!"

John sank down beside me. "I did not want to believe you had betrayed Father."

"William tried hard to lure me into his bed while your father lived. He, of all people, should know how fiercely faithful I was to Edward."

John put his arms around me and held me close. "I will try to change his heart in this, Mother, I promise."

It was a loving gesture, and I abandoned my ire as best I could so that I might enjoy this precious moment with my son, now so grown that I could rest my head on his shoulder. But I knew full well William would not relent.

"I beg you, John, do not let him poison our affections for one another."

"No, Mother, never," John said.

My years at court had trained me well in the art of hiding my feelings. For the remainder of my son's visit I struggled to keep my outrage to myself. I was too grateful to know now of the secret liaison, too relieved that John had relented and confided in me, and that he seemed to believe that I had been faithful to his father.

Though I held my tongue in an effort to keep the peace, a procession of family and friends tried to dissuade my son from military service, but he was adamant.

We had one additional, difficult conversation.

"I want you to know that I would never have believed what Sir William said about Robert had I not known of your love for him, and his for you," John said one afternoon.

It was my turn to blush. "It was Robert who comforted me when your father died. You are old enough now to know the truth, John." I explained to him how I had come to wed William, that our marriage was a façade. But I did not tell him the whole truth about Robert and me. I did not dare let down my guard, even to my beloved son.

We had been reviewing items he might wish to take with him. At that moment we were in the stables looking at Janyn's fine saddle, one that male guests often used. As I had spoken about Lancaster's ultimatum and how it had dashed my hopes of happiness with Robert, John had run his hands over the leather again and again. He had neither looked at me nor spoken. When I had finished, the silence lengthened. I could see that I'd failed to move him.

"Italian leather, very finely worked and tooled," I remarked to ease the tension.

"Sir William said you were bitter toward him. That you would say cruel things to turn me against him."

I gently touched my son's chin, drawing it up so that his eyes were level with mine. "John, I've told you nothing but the truth."

"He is a good man. But for him, I would be stuck with the Bishop of Exeter."

"Oh, John, that is not true. The duke is your half brother. You'd but to ask him yourself for anything you wished."

I saw a flicker of doubt in my son's eyes, but he was young and confused, and doubted himself most of all. He simply shrugged.

"How do you know about Robert? We tried to be so careful."

John grunted. "How could you hope to hide anything with Mary Percy living under your roof?"

Without Robert's solid and loving presence, what I had learned from John might have inspired reckless behavior—an attempt to annul my marriage to William on the grounds of my prior betrothal to Robert, or something equally risky to my family. But he steadied me. I would do nothing to provoke exile—though I held my breath when I considered what William was waiting for. If he truly believed Joan and Jane were Robert's daughters, why then had he not exposed us? I wished I might safely ask John how much he knew, but could not risk his reporting to William that I was anxious.

My longed-for peace was shattered.

IN LATE winter of the following year John announced that he was to take up arms under the command of Edmund of Langley, my Edward's second youngest son, on a mission to Portugal. Lancaster still sought to recover the Castilian throne. The Portuguese were his greatest supporters in the region, but were now beset by the forces of the usurper, Enrique of Trastámara. Remembering the catastrophic consequences of the late Prince Edward's campaign in the region, I feared for my son. But I knew his father would have been proud of him.

In the weeks before joining Langley, John begged me for tales of his father. Joan and Jane also loved it when I described my life with Edward, especially while the girls and I hawked or rode through the countryside, knowing these were some of the king's favorite activities. On those winter evenings my children and I sat by the fire, and I regaled them with descriptions of the glories of Edward's court, his prowess in arms and the hunt, his way with the falcons, the heady joy of dancing with him, his magnificent singing voice.

One evening, after the girls had gone to bed, I gave John his father's signet ring, which I'd retrieved from Robert earlier.

"It is time you had this, my son."

He slipped it on his finger, wondered at how well it fit him.

"A little wax will keep it secure," I said.

His eyes shone with pride. "I shall wear it with honor, Mother."

"I know that you will."

John's properties provided sufficient income for him to be smartly fitted for the expedition, and I was grateful that he welcomed and appreciated my advice and assistance in planning. We had become close again, though neither of us mentioned William.

But William would soon return, and he would be in an even fouler temper than usual, for the Brittany expedition had proved an embarrassing failure. He erupted into our sweet household like a sudden squall on a quiet day. Robert departed, and Gwen gave instructions to Betys to keep Joan and Jane away from William as much as possible. He was furious to have thrown good money—albeit not his but mine and my friends'—after the incompetent Buckingham. This unfortunately rendered him ripe for a temper tantrum. When he discovered Mary Percy gone and learned that the marriage would very likely be annulled, he flew into a fury and swore that he would make it right. He would petition King Richard for his support.

Now quite happy at the prospect of finding a more suitable mate, John said he was content. I watched his puzzlement as William ignored him and ranted and raved until drink silenced him.

When John returned from carrying him to his bedchamber, he asked me how to prevent such interference.

"The king has far too much on his mind to become involved in this case, John. Be at peace. William will find no remedy. Your father would have left such a petition to his trusted clerics. So will King Richard." I had found that advice couched thus, in terms of how his father might have acted, carried much authority and usually reassured John.

Joan and Jane were fascinated by his accumulated gear—the armor, the horses, the weapons. But when the day came for his departure, Jane was dismayed to overhear a servant wishing him God's protection in battle.

"Battle?" she asked, her little hands fluttering as if she might fend off the possibility. "No, John, you must not fight!"

Her elder sister took her aside, quietly explaining what it meant to be a knight. Jane was inconsolable for days afterward. So was I.

My only comfort was that the day after John rode from the yard, William departed for his own home in London.

· · ·

IN SPRING all the countryside was alive with rumors of an uprising gathering in Essex. King Richard and the parliament had so overwhelmed the people with the poll tax of the previous year, following close on one a year earlier, that the money had proved exceedingly difficult to collect. Thousands of taxpayers had evaded the collectors. Now, a year later, new commissioners were sent out into the shires, intent on finding the tax evaders and collecting from them by whatever means they saw fit. My old friend William Wykeham, Bishop of Winchester, sent a message advising me to move the household to a manor near Winchester.

I invited my siblings and their families, but Mary and John chose to stay and protect their homes and businesses. Richard Lyons refused to be intimidated also. Geoffrey's family had already departed for Lincolnshire, leaving him, apparently happily, in the city, where he intended to stay. All of them relayed tales of William's drunkenness and whoring there, and assured me he showed no sign of wishing to flee the city.

The violence quickly spread from Essex through the southeast, moving toward London. As the number of rebels swelled, so did their anger. They blamed not only the commissioners but the Lord Chancellor and others on the king's council, particularly clerics, who to them represented the greed of the Church; but it seemed they blamed Lancaster most of all. The duke was held responsible for all that had gone wrong with the French wars as well. Knowing from experience the danger he faced, having seen the damage the rabble had inflicted on his palace of the Savoy a little over four years earlier, Lancaster fled to Scotland.

Had it not been for my fear for my friends and family in London, I might have felt relieved—Lancaster would forget me for the nonce.

As the uprising spread into Kent, closer and closer to London, King Richard and his mother, Joan, as well as many barons, withdrew into the Tower of London. The mob were committing vicious acts—beheadings, hangings, the desecration of churches and abbeys.

All my household listened in awe to a report of young King Richard's courage. He rode out to meet the rebels and calmly inquired what they sought. They demanded the heads of Lancaster and an assortment of others they had decided were to blame. He did not capitulate and the rebels swarmed into London, freeing the inmates of the Marshalsea prison and this time not stopping at damaging Lancaster's Palace of the Savoy but razing it, and destroying much else in their path.

Eventually they reached the Tower and accosted those within. When it was over, the chancellor and one of the council had been dragged out and beheaded. Nothing like this had happened in Edward's time. But I remembered the hatred on the faces of the Londoners who had beheld me as the Lady of the Sun. I had not doubted that a crowd moved by such festering hatred might erupt into madness, and now they did.

One morning Wykeham rode into the yard and joined Robert and me as we walked toward the stables. He was unshaven and haggard, his color so chalky beneath the flush from his exertions that I feared he might be ill.

"My lady, I bring terrible tidings. Our friend Richard Lyons . . ." His voice broke.

Robert put his arm around me as I grasped Wykeham's hand. "Dead?" I whispered.

"Executed. Three dozen Flemings have been brutally murdered. Richard—he was dragged from his home, beaten, and beheaded."

"Beheaded?" I cried out. "Why? Why Richard?"

"May God grant him rest." Robert bowed his head and crossed himself with his free hand, with the other pulling me close.

But I broke away and knelt to Wykeham, pressing my head to his ring, weeping and praying for Richard's soul. My good and loyal friend . . .

Later, as the three of us shared a flagon of brandywine, I broke the mournful silence. "Why had he not fled?" I asked of no one in particular.

"His fellow Flemings in the city looked to him for leadership," said Robert. "He felt responsible for them."

"We all live with our own guilt," said Wykeham. "We played a game of chance, profiting from the war in France. It does not matter that it has always been so; we knew we were taking a risk."

I shook my head. "I cannot accept this was in any way just."

Wykeham halfheartedly patted my hand. "Pray God we learn from it. We have a choice how we live."

After Wykeham departed, slumped in the saddle, his spirit depleted, as was mine, Robert led me to my bedchamber and sat with me as I wept for my loyal and loving friend, and feared for the others in London. He assured me that Geoffrey and my family would be safe.

"They have nothing to single them out to the crowd. But I will go to London to seek news."

I clung to him, forbidding him to leave me and ride into danger. I could not bear it if I lost Robert.

WHEN THE king's troops had put down the rebellion and London was quiet, Robert and I left the children in Winchester and rode to the city to see to our families and friends. My siblings and their families were blessedly unscathed, although Mary's in-laws' home had been damaged. Geoffrey was subdued, leading us round the city to view the destruction. It was as if a mighty fist had come down on the Savoy and then swept its rubble into the Thames. Even a week later, debris floated in the water. Bloodstained pillars and posts were visible in the streets where Flemings and other foreigners, including Lombards, had lived.

Geoffrey joined Robert and me at the requiem Mass for Richard Lyons.

The morning after the service, as I woke from a troubled sleep, Gwen greeted me with the unpleasant news that William was in the hall. I had heard nothing of him since returning to the city.

He was dressed more elegantly than he had been of late and wore a badge indicating he was in the king's household.

"What is this, William?"

"I wished to show you that I am still appreciated. That I have not come to ruin over our failed marriage."

"I am glad, though I never thought you would come to ruin on my account. You have lived apart from me most of your life, with every appearance of success." I hated the coldness of my own voice, but I felt nothing for William and would not pretend otherwise. I did invite him to share some wine and tell me his news.

He continued to find favor with King Richard, receiving modest gifts from the king, much as I had when first in Queen Philippa's household—some property, rents, a few wardships.

I thought perhaps he might now consider revising the provision of a trust for his nephew in his will, so that my former properties might go to my children, particularly my daughters.

"I do not ask this for me, but for them. You have a sufficient estate of your own to leave your nephew."

He laughed. "Always scheming! You get a pinched look when you scheme, Alice. It does not become you. Had you given me a son and heir, John Wyndsor would have been forgotten."

"You should have told Lancaster to command me to conceive a son, William. But I do not recall that being a part of the arrangement explained to me at Westminster."

He was still laughing as he departed. I did not see him again for more than a year.

L IFE HAD settled into a comfortable pattern. Joan and Jane attended school in the city in autumn and winter, making friends with the children of my childhood friends and many others. My daughters had a way about them that endeared them to their peers. Bella did as well, having recently been encouraged to assist the infirmarian because of her ability to calm those in distress. I felt my old guilt about leaving my children so often in the care of others begin to melt away. Except for John. Except for my son.

Memories of my notoriety seemed to fade from the London community. Any criticism of my family now concerned my absent husband's bad behavior. Gwen and I were free to stroll through the markets, taking up the life we had lived before our days at court.

During the long winter nights Robert and I made most delicious, affectionate, passionate love, and in between bared our souls to each other. We disproved my old belief that no person ever shared their entire being with another—though I understood that it was only through experience and pain that we had arrived at such a miracle.

In spring we retired to Fair Meadow and Gaynes. It was bliss to have Robert by my side. But ever I worried about John. I heard vague rumors that the expedition in Portugal was disappointing.

When he returned the following summer, John was quiet and withdrawn. Though delighted to have their big brother home, Joan and Jane tiptoed in his presence. At twelve and ten they were mature enough to discern his need for privacy and reflection.

Unfortunately, before John had recovered sufficiently to confide in me, William appeared. I silently cursed him for returning after more than a year to ruin this time with my son, but I could not turn him away. He was legally my husband, and it was his right to bide in the house. His presence sent my mind and heart into shadowy places filled with hateful imaginings and robbed me of my anchor in Robert. Worst of all, I feared his influence on John.

On William's first morning in my home I was awakened by his shouts down in the hall. I hurriedly dressed and went to the top of the

steps to listen and assess what to do. I was accustomed to mitigating
the effects of his ill temper on the household.

"You ungrateful wretch!" William was shouting. "I arranged your
post and you disgrace me like this? I placed you in the service of the
Duke of Lancaster and you rebel against his brother? You have ruined
me, you graceless, arrogant bastard!"

I hurried down to them. Considering the hour, I felt anxious to
discover my son sharing a tankard of ale with William, both looking as
if they had been drinking through the night.

I pounded my fist on the table to prevent another round of cursing.

"I remind you, William, that you are speaking to the son of the
former king, Lancaster's half brother. You might have fooled him at
fourteen into thinking he needed you to approach the duke, but he
knows better now. In his veins flows royal blood."

John reached out to grab the tankard from William, but I inter-
cepted, removing the temptation.

"What a sorry sight you both are, and so early in the morning. Get
back to your rooms before Joan and Jane see you so."

For a week John retreated into silence, taking long walks or lying
on his bed staring up at the ceiling. William disappeared. I sought out
Geoffrey to learn the truth of the matter.

"It seems John is in disfavor with Lancaster. He led a near mutiny
in Portugal, against Edmund of Langley, his commander," said Geoffrey. "Word is just beginning to circulate on the streets now that the
men have come home."

"A mutiny? How did I not hear of this? Surely at court—"

"There you are seen as the mother of the mutineer—not a person
in whom to confide."

"I might have interceded." I was frightened for John, knowing all
too well what a formidable enemy Lancaster could be.

Geoffrey put his hands on my shoulders and looked me in the eyes.
"I shall investigate the matter fully and come to you."

On the day my friend sent me word that he had the information,
I requested that John be present for the report.

"You have made it plain since your return that you do not wish to
explain your situation to me, and so I shall hear it from Geoffrey. But
you must hear it also, learn what people are saying of you. You must
know where you stand, John. The longer you hide, the harder everything will be."

By some alchemy William appeared at the door at almost the same moment as Geoffrey.

We sat, an unhappy foursome, in my parlor, away from the servants' ears and the curiosity of John's young sisters.

Dressed in dark, quietly elegant clothing, his hair and beard freshly trimmed, Geoffrey served a stark contrast to William's fiercely bright garb but disheveled self and to John's diminished flesh in clothes sagging now because too large for him.

Geoffrey began addressing me, describing the situation about which I had heard so little. How Edmund of Langley's troops had grown restive over his indifferent leadership and their lack of pay for almost a year. His knights accused him of keeping the money for himself and the King of Portugal of betraying them. Among themselves, the knights proposed bonding together into a brotherhood under the flag of St. George, and becoming such nuisances that Langley would have to heed their grievances.

"John was chosen to be their leader, no doubt because he was half brother to Langley." Geoffrey nodded at my son.

John sighed, never lifting his gaze from the floor. And how could he resist such an "honor," I thought, when his purpose had been to win back the honor of which Mary Percy's insulting petition had robbed him.

The knights had set off under their flag, with the battle cry "For Southery, the valiant bastard!" to make war on the King of Portugal. Oh, my son! I could not look at him while Geoffrey spoke of this. They were saved by the intervention of more experienced English knights who convinced them of the folly of battling the king thus. Instead, they urged John to present their grievances to his half brother.

"John countered Langley's claim that the war was not his but the King of Portugal's with the proposal that, if it were so, the knights would simply take their wages by overrunning the country, each man taking what he might. Langley reminded John of the consequences of mutiny, and the dishonor he would thus bring on his cousin the King of England."

I turned to John. "I can imagine how proud you must have felt to be so trusted by your fellows, my son. I am not condemning you. I wish to know only what was in your mind. Hear your account of this."

At last he looked me in the eye. "I had come to my senses even before Langley reminded me of my duty . . . of the honor I owed you and the king. It was the heat, the thirst, the tedium, that had robbed me of my good sense. I made a fool of myself."

"No, not a fool. You are but seventeen," I said.

"The king is two years my junior and would never behave so."

"John is courageous!" William cried, applauding him, apparently forgetting he'd earlier called John a disgrace. "Langley then sent knights to treat with King Ferdinand, and the men received their wages."

"And Ferdinand then made a treaty with Castile, rendering the entire expedition pointless," Geoffrey said. "And now the king has assigned a commission to arrest the mutineers. Nineteen have been named."

My heart ached at the pain in my son's expression. He bowed his head.

"I know," he said. "His Grace addressed me with much anger, but as I am family chose to believe that the others had put me forward to treat with my half brother against my will. King Richard made me out to be but a child, easily led."

"I hardly believe he could think that," said Geoffrey. "Froissart says that when Langley gathered the men together to pay them, you said, 'Now see if this mutiny has not served its purpose! He who is feared fares well.' "

I was dismayed to hear that the Fleming had included this incident in his chronicle. It would haunt John for life now.

"And still I am pardoned while my brothers-in-arms are punished," he said.

Geoffrey met my gaze and shrugged.

"He proved himself a bit of his mother, a bit of his father, eh?" said William. "Greedy for his money, brave as a fighting cock."

"Be still, William, you embarrass yourself," I said, rising. "John, we shall discuss this more anon. Come out to see the tenements and shops I have built, Geoffrey."

Better to leave William alone to drink himself into a stupor or disappear to a tavern where the women were more pleasing to him. I prayed he would soon depart. I yearned to have Robert beside me again.

But John did not recover from his shame. How I wished his father were still alive. Edward would have known how to turn this around, would have known how to save his son, and John would have listened. He needed his father. He had been deprived of him too young. Now I could find no way to reach him. Nor could his sisters, nor Robert, nor Geoffrey. He eventually took up drinking, and I shuddered to think what else, with William.

I tried to focus on Joan and Jane, on Robert, but a sense of dread that I had failed my beloved son so weakened me that I fell sick with fever. I was so afraid for John. Bella came and cared for me for half the autumn. And in that time my son used the excuse of my illness to take up residence with William.

He returned at Christmas, William in tow.

"We are a family, Mother."

John looked older than his seventeen years—his complexion poor, his eyes glassy, as if feverish. I went from being nursed to nursing, coaxing him to eat, to ride out into the fresh air.

That winter William obtained the keeping of the castle and town of Cherbourg in Normandy. He was to have all ransoms and gains of war by land and sea, and the king would provide his shipping, food, weapons, and an annual fee of £4,000. It was a more lucrative honor than William had expected.

"Will you go to Cherbourg?" I asked when he announced his boon at the dinner table.

"In time. But to begin I shall send a deputy." He turned to smile at my son.

The expression on John's face, of delight and pride tempered with a hint of guilt, bespoke an agreement long kept secret from me.

My heart stopped. "Why John?"

"It will be a fine opportunity for him."

"If it is such a fine opportunity, why send a deputy? Are you not man enough to go yourself?"

"I want to go, Mother," said John. "I am grateful for the chance to prove myself to King Richard."

"Why not send your beloved nephew and heir, William?" I asked. "Why waste your benefices on my son?"

William smirked.

"Why do you risk my only son?" I demanded.

John came to sit beside me. Putting an arm round me, he said, "You will see, Mother. You will be proud of me."

"I *am* proud of you, John."

On my knees before bed I prayed God's forgiveness for allowing

my son to become a battlefield between William and me. I tried to accept that John was doing what he truly wanted. "Grant him peace and
joy," I prayed. "Even if it means he is far from me."

In late winter he departed for Cherbourg.

On his last evening at home he had talked of making a name for
himself so that he might find a wife who respected him for his accom-
plishments, not for being the late king's bastard. As I had feared, it had
been gnawing at his heart all this time.

"Your father was proud of you, John, so very proud of you. That
you were a bastard diminished you in no way in his eyes. He insisted
that you be knighted." I did not mention his insistence also on the
betrothal to Mary Percy, the seed of all this anguish.

John gave me back Edward's signet. "Keep this for me until I have
earned it."

My heart bled for him. I had not fully appreciated until now that
being Edward's son was both a gift and a curse.

And in my mind I raged at William.

"If he makes me proud, I shall change my will in his favor," he'd
said during one of our more amicable meals together.

Damn William Wyndsor, the bane of my fine, noble son!

All through that spring and summer I felt as if I were treading on
unsteady ground that might open up and swallow me at any moment.
My sister thought perhaps I was praying too much and not spending enough time out in the sun and air. Bella understood that I was
doing penance for my own part in John's unhappiness, and urged me
to remember that all God's children were blessed, no matter what their
parentage, and that my son's despair or imagined shame was his burden
to bear or to shed.

"That is his path, Mother, his cross. You cannot take this burden
from him."

Nor could any of my loved ones lift my burden from me. And it
only grew heavier. For in late summer, the ship on which John was sailing home to meet William and the king in order to discuss the problems at Cherbourg vanished in a sudden storm. Frantic, I waited and
waited, praying for word that it had safely berthed elsewhere.

I thought I might go mad. Lost at sea . . . John might yet live.
A boat might have plucked him from the waves. He might lie ill and
bereft of memory somewhere. I had nightmares linking his disappearance to Janyn's. I shunned sleep. Robert held me through the night,

praying, singing, talking of my other children, anything to pull me from my darkness.

William, pale and hollow eyed, came to beg my forgiveness. "It should have been me."

"Would that it had been! Or your hateful nephew. Not one of my precious children." I could not be troubled to comfort him. "Are you happy now? You have done your worst. You have torn out my heart."

He replied that he had loved John as well, but I could not bear his presence.

"My son had a good heart, but you poisoned him with your bitterness."

"You *made* me bitter."

"I take no responsibility for your crabbed heart, William. Go. Get out of my house!"

But I did blame myself for not better shielding John from him. I agonized over what else I might have done—whether I should have told him all the truth about my marriage to William from the beginning, not waiting until the damage had been done, or risked Edward's ire in refusing to betroth John to such a changeling as Mary Percy. There must have been something I could have done to save my son.

It was Gwen who tried to wake me up to the fact that I was neglecting Joan and Jane in my grief. "You must accept that John is gone and see to your daughters, Mistress. They are inconsolable. John was their beloved brother, a handsome, gallant knight, a last reminder of their glorious father. They have lost him as well. They need you to hold them, to show them how they must accept their loss, pray for their brother's soul, and find peace."

I saw the wisdom in her words. That very night I invited them into my bed, and the three of us wept until we had no more tears to shed.

HENRY PERCY came to the requiem Mass that King Richard arranged at Westminster Abbey. He spoke of what an admirable young man John had been, and expressed his regret that Mary had annulled the marriage. Well he might say that now he need no longer fear my son's contamination. Lancaster also attended, as my son's godfather, half brother, and lord, speaking of his martial skill, his honor. Princess Joan embraced me and wept with me for my beautiful son.

William swore that he would change his will, that John's death had shaken him to the core. "I have been cruel and do repent, Alice. All I ever wanted was to live with you as your husband, and I have poisoned my chances."

I wanted nothing to do with him. He showed me a new will he had signed leaving my properties to Joan and Jane. I thanked him for that, but could not bring myself to forgive him. Though my son had been free to refuse William's suggestion that he be his deputy at Cherbourg, I blamed him for making the offer, and he knew it. We could not find a way to cross the chasm that divided us.

He stayed away for a long while. Robert helped me heal, pick up the pieces of my life, and move on. Joan, Jane, and I planted oaks at each of our homes to remind us of John, how tall and strong he had been. How he had blessed our lives.

I N LATE summer, almost a year to the day after John's disappearance, William came to me in London, deathly ill of a fever. All through the autumn Gwen and I nursed him; Robert saw to everything else. This time he did not need to leave. With illness in the house, I arranged for Joan and Jane to board at their school. William rarely spoke, never looked me in the eyes, ate and drank as little as possible. It was clear from the first that he did not intend to recover.

He died shortly after Michaelmas. We mourned the passing of a life, but all the household seemed to breathe a concerted sigh of relief at the possibility of moving forward. I prayed for the grace to forgive William and allow him to rest in peace.

But I could never forgive his nephew John. Upon William's death, John Wyndsor produced a copy of the old will, favoring himself. I searched everywhere for the one William had shown me, but never found it. I swore I would fight John Wyndsor in the courts until I won back all that was rightfully mine. This was my poison, my purgatory, my inheritance from William, the last lingering resentment. It was the only thing that ever came between Robert and me. He could not understand why I allowed that one thorn to continue to infect my soul.

In the same month in which William died, I petitioned parliament to withdraw the judgments against me. William had been clever, focusing his petitions on the reclamation of my properties in his name, refraining from any attempt to clear my name.

Eventually I did forgive him, and even mourned him. How strange that in his death, without the noise of our arguments, I remembered how he had initially charmed me. I mourned my brief dream of the handsome, exciting knight I thought had loved me. I mourned my dreams for my son John. I mourned all the dreams that had been destroyed by my tie to the house of Plantagenet.

Now I abandoned the old dreams and reached for peace.

AFTER WILLIAM'S death, Princess Joan invited me and my daughters to Kennington for a fortnight. Though my sentence of exile had been withdrawn, I had not been in a royal palace since my marriage in Westminster. At John's funeral I had kept to the abbey grounds, avoiding the palace. It was strange to be back in a royal household, strange to have occasion to wear my jewels and grandest gowns.

The once renowned beauty had grown fat and walked with a cane—albeit an exquisitely wrought cane with silver chasing and a mother-of-pearl handle. Her gown was resplendent with jewels, as ever, her hair still pale gold, though years of ensuring that color had left it looking brittle. I learned that she suffered from gout and seldom rode, never hawked.

"Let me inspire you to move about. You know that is the cure for what is ailing you," I offered. There was a time when we had talked so, encouraging each other.

She shook her head. "If gout were the sole cause of my decline, I would have fought it with all my will, Alice."

One afternoon when we were alone, the children on an expedition with some of Joan's wards, she looked me in the eyes.

"You have been so good, listening to my woes. Now I must ask yet another favor. I must beg your forgiveness, my friend. It is time I confessed to you that it was I who betrayed you regarding William Wyndsor. I mentioned his passion for you to my husband Edward, never dreaming he would use the information. I am certain he told his brother John."

I had blamed Henry Percy, or sometimes Geoffrey—he did so love to gossip. Never Joan, though I had suspected she long knew of the agreement that I would wed William.

"You might have saved me a great deal of pain had you kept your counsel," I said. Yet I saw how easily it might have happened.

"They used you, Alice. Edward and John protected you as long as they needed you as their father's caretaker, and then they sold you to William. I am sorry. I wish that there were something I might do. If you have need of me . . ."

I excused myself and went out to walk off my anger. She was aged, she was weak, and in her proud way she was apologetic. *I am sorry.* How easily that was said, how little it did to comfort me. *I will walk on burning coals in penance. I will tear out my hair.* Those words might begin to express how she should suffer for what she had done to me. But she had not intended me harm. As I tired, I abandoned my wish that she might suffer. She had not foreseen such use of her gossip. How could she? But I would use her in her turn.

I told her of my petition to parliament, of the contested will.

"I shall speak to Richard," she said. "But do not expect too much. He does not hold the hearts of the barons as his grandfather did. Or parliament."

"When you speak to him, remember that I might yet have had my son to hold to my heart, Edward's glorious son, had William and I not been forced together in unholy matrimony."

"I did not know until the king's death what they planned," Joan whispered, her eyes haunted.

As I departed from Kennington I sensed that I would not come that way again, that Joan, like William, would surrender soon to eternal rest. Sad, aching, disappointed.

Yet I felt a lifting of a curse from my shoulders, the curse of Isabella of France and her love child. At last I was free. I felt I owed Edward's family nothing, and they could do no more to me.

21

> For I sey nought that she so sodeynly
> Yaf hym hire love, but that she gan enclyne
> To like hym first, and I have told yow whi;
> And after that, his manhod and his pyne
> Made love withinne hire for to myne,
> For which by proces and by good servyse
> He gat hire love, and in no sodeyn wyse.

—Geoffrey Chaucer, *Troilus and Criseyde*, II, 673–79

• 1384 •

WIDOWED A third time—for in my heart I was Edward's widow—at forty-two years of age I prayed that I might at last order my own life. I had been with Janyn for almost four years, two of them happy; with Edward for roughly fifteen years, many of them happy, many unhappy; I had endured seven years of William, my time with him unrelievedly painful, but with Robert's love supporting me.

Not all of my unhappiness had been caused by others—I was only too aware of my own sins, of my passions, my weaknesses. I'd misjudged the value of my security in worldly goods and neglected the importance of strong alliances. I had not stood up against my son's betrothal to a young woman I'd known to be devoid of compassion and honor.

At last, however, I was free to choose how to conduct the rest of my life.

My first choice was to give my daughters a long winter of my undivided attention. Joan was now fourteen, Jane thirteen, and I wished to enjoy them, for in a little while they would be wanting husbands, and we would be caught up in the excitement of courtships and celebrations. Bella visited often. Her abbess was a woman with a kind heart. My daughters were my salvation, lifting me from my sorrow, my regrets. How could I regret having birthed these magnificent creatures? One of my favorite pastimes was turning the gorgeous fabrics of gowns I no longer wore into pretty clothes for Joan and Jane. To watch their delight rekindled in me an appreciation for the beauty all round me. Though I wore dark colors in memory of Janyn, Edward, and William, my headdresses were of silk and my gowns fashionably cut and powdered with the pearls and gems my brother had saved for me. I played my part of grand lady of the manor and benefactress of the parish. My daughters loved to see me so, as did the friends who visited often. Robert and I remained discreet in our arrangement for a while.

We both most enjoyed one surprisingly regular houseguest, Geoffrey. He came and stayed without Pippa—indeed, they were now seldom seen together. "We are not so fond," he said in response to my concern. "It is as it is."

I must have winced when he said that.

"Is it not the truth, Alice?"

" 'It is as it is' was one of Edward's mottos."

Geoffrey pressed hands to heart and made a little bow. "Forgive me. I'd forgotten."

"There is nothing to forgive. Your gift to me is your willingness to listen to me. I am grateful to have a friend in whom I can confide without fear of lectures or censure." Each night after my daughters and Robert went to bed, Geoffrey and I would sit and talk—or rather I would talk. I revealed my heart to my old friend, my loves and hates, my dreams for my marriages and my children, my regrets.

He claimed that being in my home inspired his poetic endeavors.

"And I am much admired by His Grace and the queen, so I must provide them with fresh verse."

He was often invited to read at court, a great compliment.

One afternoon as he made notes to himself on his ubiquitous wax tablets and bits of parchment in between staring out of the open door to the courtyard garden, he suddenly paused and asked, "Do you remember the story of Criseyde that so troubled you?"

"I have never forgotten," I said.

"Your arguments have been much on my mind."

"Are you writing of her?"

By the inward expression on his face I guessed that he was. But he said only, "Would it trouble you to know that your story inspired me to wonder how it might have been for Criseyde?"

"I am honored, my good friend."

"I understand now; they hated you for showing them that their king—he with the power to heal with his hands, he with the well-being of the realm in his care—was yet human."

"More so at the end than they were ever permitted to see."

"I would show how alone Criseyde was upon her father's defection, how vulnerable and without guidance. How her uncle used that to his own end. But I cannot make her so worthy of love and admiration as you, my friend. Nor so tragic. In that story, Troilus is the tragic player."

Worthy of love and admiration? "You do me great compliment, Geoffrey. But as for the tragic, not all has been tragedy for me. I have experienced much joy, and have much yet to live for."

WHEN AT last my little family returned to Gaynes in spring, Robert invited me to ride out with him. The freshly ploughed fields smelled rich and loamy, new leaves softened the hedgerows and the trees that followed the line of the river. We paused in a meadow where a fallen tree provided seating for two.

Robert took my hands in his and looked me in the eyes with such determination that I feared bad news.

"My love, I believe that at last it is our time. Would you be content to bide with me as my wife? Would you take me as your husband? For I would have you as my wife, if you will, to cherish and to love through the rest of my days, as long as God grants me."

Relief flooded me with warmth. I looked into Robert's steady gray-blue eyes and saw love, comfort, laughter, and companionship. Everything about him was dear to me, his crinkly smile, his broad shoulders that had supported me through so much sorrow, his scent, his deep voice and quiet laugh that was more movement than sound. I loved him for never forsaking me, never failing me. I loved who I was when I was with him.

"I take you as my husband, Robert, willingly, with all my heart and soul."

His kiss warmed me to my core and set my heart strumming. When we paused for breath, I glanced round. Seeing that we were quite alone, I rose, taking his hand.

"Shall we seal the pact, my love?"

On the horse blankets we lay, our coupling slow and yet passionate as we made use of all we knew would give pleasure to the other. There was no need to hurry, no one who would have any cause to creep up on us. Afterward we lay in each other's arms, drowsing, until the afternoon chill prompted us to continue our ride.

Joan and Jane observed us closely during the evening meal. Robert had a different air about him, comfortable, already settled. As if he'd practiced this in his imagination for a long while.

As the table was cleared, he leaned toward my daughters and asked, "Would you permit me to wed your mother?"

Jane frowned a little, tilting her head to one side as if considering. Joan poked her in the ribs and with a dazzling smile asked, "Could we call you Father?"

"I would be honored."

"I shall call you Robert," said Jane, "but I do give you my blessing."

He reached for my hand beneath the table. "And you, Joan?"

"I would rather you wed me. But if you have already lost your heart to Mother, you have my blessing."

That evening, as Gwen brushed my hair, we spoke of our first weeks together at Dame Agnes's, preparing for my marriage to Janyn, the beginning of my liaison with Edward, how frightened we had been, and the frustration of my marriage to William.

"You deserve happiness, Mistress. I pray that God blesses you both. I am so happy for you. You have loved one another for so long. At last your hearts are one."

O UR OLD friend Dom Hanneye witnessed our vows in the church at Upminster. We invited only family to the wedding, and Geoffrey. I wore a patterned silk gown in deep, rich hues of blue and green, the feather pattern picked out in seed pearls on the bodice and sleeves. Robert wore a red velvet jacket that I had lovingly made him, with matching hat ablaze on his fair hair, and leggings of indigo. I so enjoyed dressing him, for he had never given much thought to his appearance and was startled to see himself in his new clothes. I imagine we were the most elegant couple ever to take their vows at the small church. But what I loved most was that it had not mattered whether or not we fussed with our clothing; we had no one to impress but each other, and our love transcended all that. Life away from court—I embraced it with all my heart.

Through the spring and summer Joan, Jane, Gwen, and I worked to re-create at Gaynes what I could remember of Dame Tommasa's garden in London and the one that she had helped me plant at Janyn's and my London home when I carried Bella. Robert brought clippings of the most unusual plants from our other manors, and I brought clippings from the garden in London. By late summer, when I discovered that I was with child, the garden was truly taking shape. I had worried that I might not conceive after taking potions to prevent it for so long, and considering my age, but Robert and I were blessed.

"I am the most fortunate man under heaven," he whispered, one ear to my swelling stomach.

Joan, Jane, and I all blossomed that summer. Joan met another Robert much to her liking, a young lawyer from Kingston-upon-Thames, Robert Skerne, whom we had retained for some property transactions. They were a handsome couple, and I found myself praying that he would return for her when he considered himself capable of supporting a household. Jane proved a passionate and creative gardener, and I left much of the planning of Tommasa's garden to her. I had never been happier. Walking, hawking, plunging my hands in the earth and creating a garden I expected to enjoy for years to come, strolling across the fields or along the streets of London on Robert's arm, spending an afternoon sewing with my daughters and Gwen . . . all these simple pleasures were a constant delight to me.

I WISHED I might forgo William's first-year obit at Windsor, for though I was not very great with child yet I no longer enjoyed riding. Nor did I wish to be reminded of my unhappy marriage. But I could not forget William as he was at the end, so lost, so disappointed, and could not refuse to pay him that one last honor. Fortunately most of the journey would be by barge. My daughters and Gwen put much effort into designing a silk velvet surcoat to hide my swelling stomach. Although Robert escorted me to Windsor, he did not attend the Mass. Geoffrey escorted me in his place.

Sir Robert Linton, the friend who had offered his home in Somerset as a haven for me and my children in my darkest hour, had come to pay his respects. He asked after me and the children.

"We are well. Thriving. I shall never forget your kindness in my time of need."

I saw several old acquaintances from court—Richard Stury made a point of speaking to me. He was not so grim visaged as in the past, his hair now snow white and his smile more relaxed and sincere. He found he enjoyed retirement.

"Quietly stalking the wildfowl, deer, and boar on my estates, becoming acquainted with my wife at last—I should think it about time I knew the woman who bore me five children!" He chuckled at his own words, something he had never done in my presence. "And you, Dame Alice?"

"I feel blessed to be free at last to enjoy my daughters, my lands, and my memories, Sir Richard. God has been good to me."

John Wyndsor I ignored, and he ignored me. We were locked in litigation, though it was no longer entirely by my choice—Joan and Jane wanted to see me vindicated in this.

This time I did enter the palace, with great trepidation, and walked about in the company of ghosts, my eyes finding it impossible to alight on anything in Windsor that did not conjure a memory, particularly of my dear Queen Philippa. I had not expected to feel my grief over her death still so poignant. For me she still ruled the castle. I could still hear her merry laughter and exclamations of delight, could smell her evening almond milk. And Edward—his striding steps sounded just ahead, his scent was in the air. Suddenly I lost my courage, rushing back through the hall and out into the yard, grateful to breathe air untainted by shades of the past. I prayed I need never return.

Nor did the gossip around us inspire regret in me that I was no longer at court. Indeed, as I listened I grew increasingly eager to withdraw again to my quiet life. Princess Joan was not in attendance; she had retired to Kennington in August with a vague malady and had died within days, some said of a broken heart. Poor, beautiful Joan, who might have been queen.

WHEN JOAN, Jane, Gwen, and I stepped onto the river landing on our return to Gaynes, Robert, who had gone on ahead to alert the servants, awaited us with our horses. We rode home along lanes made colorful with falling leaves. We were all quiet from the solemnity of the occasion and traveler's weariness. As usual, within moments of arriving home Joan and Jane were off to the stables, the immediate lure the litters of puppies and kittens, anxious to see how much they had grown in a week.

"They will be out for a long while," said Robert, taking my hand and leading me into the garden.

Now the flowers were mostly spent and going to seed, the saplings almost bare. But it held promise of more to come in another spring, and I found it beautiful.

We sat on a wooden bench, on a prettily embroidered cushion that Joan and Jane had presented me on my birthday. "For your bench in the rose arbor," Joan had said. "Bella told us that Dame Tommasa always made cushions to fit the garden benches."

"So she did." The cushion they had given me was embroidered with the moon and stars, and reminded me of the surcoat I'd not thought my mother-in-law would dare to wear, silver and gold moons and stars on a dark background. "Bless Bella. Bless you angels for this."

In February I gave birth to a sweet, fair-haired daughter. Her godmother was my brother John's wife, Agnes, and Robert and I called her Agnes Joanna. As she grew into a beauty like her namesake Princess Joan, we soon forgot her first given name. I had come to understand that Joan had been as good a friend to me as she could.

A year later, our son Geoffrey was born. My old friend Geoffrey

Chaucer was of course his first godfather, and made much of the fair-haired boy.

After Geoffrey's birth I knew that I had passed my childbearing years and I did not mourn for that. Though I loved my children above all else, even Robert, I had not forgotten how utterly my life had changed when I reached childbearing age. It was good to move beyond that. I had been most fortunate in my children. I had lost only two before birth, and lost only one who had lived and thrived. Four beautiful daughters and one adorable son survived.

It was then that I began to write this history of my life, or in truth dictate it to my dear Bella. I felt my years and worried that death might take me before Agnes Joanna and Geoffrey might have a chance to know me, to hear my story from my lips. I did not wish them to hear only the gossip about their mother, but to know all, and then be free to judge the truth of it.

Joan wed the lawyer Robert Skerne when she was seventeen. He *had* returned for her. Jane wed a wealthy merchant, Richard Northland, and made the journey to Italy with him that I had so yearned to make with Janyn. She saw Milan, and many Perrers, but learned nothing more of the fates of Janyn and Tommasa. She found the family unwilling to speak of that trouble.

Joanna was an imp of a girl, always courting laughter with her japes. She was a freer spirit than any of her sisters, always surrounded by family, especially her doting parents, and knew no fear. She adored her brother Geoffrey, who looked so like my long-dead brother Will that my sister Mary often forgot and called him that by mistake. He was a dreamer, a lover of animals like Jane, always nursing a wounded or sick wild creature. I took care to see him not as a replacement for my dear John but as his own wondrous person. Robert envisioned him as a conscientious landholder, reviving woodlands, enriching the fields. To our great sorrow, Geoffrey died of fever when he was but six years old.

On my last visit to Kennington, Princess Joan had said of the loss of my son John, "Perhaps it is a blessing he did not live long enough to disappoint you as my sons have disappointed me."

I would gladly have suffered any disappointment to watch my son Geoffrey grow to manhood. Though with a father like Robert guiding him, I do not believe he would ever have disappointed either of us.

. . .

MY DAUGHTERS and I continue to fight John Wyndsor in the courts. In my will I have stated that all my manors and advowsons other than Gaynes I leave to my daughters Joan and Jane, including all "those which John Wyndsor, or others, have, by his consent, usurped, the which I desire my heirs and executors to recover and see them parted between my daughters, for that I say, on the pain of my soul, he hath no right there nor never had." Sometimes I wish that William had never shown me the revised will. I pray that my daughters win. Gaynes I have bequeathed to Joanna. And I have no doubt that Robert shall be generous to all my daughters in his will.

We are all of us horrified by the overthrow of dear King Richard by Lancaster's son and heir, who calls himself Henry IV. Joan's fears for her son's reign have proved tragically prescient. Geoffrey does not care for Harry, as he calls him. Nor does Harry care for Geoffrey; censure is his favorite instrument of rule, and Geoffrey's poetry has been judged dangerous. It is Harry's loss, for Geoffrey's poem of Criseyde is a true rendering of a torn heart.

Sometimes I fall to brooding over the past. Should I have been more selfish, more stubborn, more rebellious? Have I been too compliant, too quick to give the men in my life what they thought they wanted? Am I a fallen woman, or am I an obedient handmaiden? And ever I return to the puzzle: When had I a choice to be other than I was?

I count myself blessed, all in all. Loving Robert as I do, I no longer yearn for Janyn. But I have not forgotten the passion and the pain of that union, nor the heady honor and deep sorrow of my liaison with Edward.

In the early morning, when Robert and I move out into the fields with our hawks, I often feel as if Edward is with us, as if I can hear his deep laughter just ahead. I always wear red when hawking. And pearls.

Author's Note

I WROTE THIS book to satisfy my curiosity about Alice Perrers and to give her a voice, to allow her to speak through me, a feminine psyche. I have a dyspeptic monk to thank for my fascination with Alice. My first encounter with her was in Thomas Walsingham's *St. Albans Chronicle.**

> [T]here was a woman in England called Alice Perrers. She was a shameless, impudent harlot, and of low birth. . . . She was not attractive or beautiful, but knew how to compensate for these defects by her seductive voice. Blind fortune elevated this woman to such heights and promoted her to a greater intimacy with the king than was proper, since she had been the maidservant and mistress of a man of Lombardy. . . . Even while the queen was still alive, the king loved this woman more than he loved the queen. (p. 43)

Walsingham used his "history" as a weapon for executing a vendetta primarily aimed at Alice Perrers and John of Gaunt, but in the process he grossly insulted the beloved King Edward III as well: "O King, you deserve to be called not master, but a slave of the lowest order. For since slavery is the obedience of a broken and shameful spirit that lacks a will of its own, who will deny that all who are fickleminded, all who are lustful, in short, all who are shameless are slaves?" (p. 59) This was rant, not reason.

And yet Walsingham's description of Alice has long been considered only slightly exaggerated.

---

*All citations in author's note are from *The St. Albans Chronicle: The* Chronica maiora *of Thomas Walsingham, I, 1376–1394.* John Taylor, Wendy R. Childs, and Leslie Watkiss, trans. and eds. Oxford Clarendon Press, 2003.

I never found plausible the underlying assumption that she had so grossly manipulated the king—that a commoner had been in any position to *choose* to be King Edward's mistress and that she had somehow bewitched him. Nor could I see the logic in condemning her for staying with him in his last illnesses—an opportunist would have taken the fabulous gifts and wealth she'd accrued and disappeared at the first signs of Edward's flagging power. Alice must have seen the handwriting on the wall, yet she stayed.

I am grateful to Walsingham for his outrageousness—it inspired me to delve further into the records. I also owe him thanks for a small detail that began to work in my subconscious—his mention of a daughter named nowhere else: "In the mean time the king grew weaker, and the doctors began to despair of him, though Alice and her daughter Isabella would spend the whole night with him." (p. 63) It was this "Isabella," a daughter unremarked in any of the histories I'd consulted, who inspired my connecting Janyn Perrers with Isabella, the dowager queen.

Regarding the tumultuous period following Isabella and Mortimer's rebellion the most famous rumor was that King Edward II had not actually been murdered as reported, but that the story had been concocted to allow the deposed king to withdraw into a continental monastery. But I was more intrigued by another rumor, that Isabella had been pregnant with Mortimer's child when her lover was accused of treason and taken into custody. She supposedly miscarried almost at once. I decided to explore what might have happened had the child lived, had it been the child rather than the deposed king who was spirited away to a monastery. Janyn Perrers's death less than two years after the dowager queen Isabella's death, according to a claim against his estate naming Alice as his wife and executor, led me to wonder whether those who had protected all knowledge of the child would have lost their protection once Isabella was dead. And so the story began. . . .

I've mentioned the source for Alice's daughter Isabella; most historians count her as having had two daughters, Joan and Jane. Whence came the fourth, Agnes Joanna? I thought it interesting that in her will Alice specifically left "to Joane, my younger daughter," her manor of Gaynes, in Upminster, and then "to Jane and Joane, my daughters," all other manors and advowsons. Of course this might have been simply an awkward repetition for legal purposes, but I like to think that Alice had at least another child by her third husband, a man I have a hunch existed—something about the picture of lady of the manor her will evinces suggested to me that she'd remarried after Wyndsor's death. Robert Broun's name appears in many of her land transactions, along with John Hanneye. Robert's becoming Alice's third husband is my invention. Her will identified her as "Alice, widow of William Wyndesor, Knight," and, of course, she was, whether or not she was also the wife of someone yet living. A woman did not always take her husband's surname.

Geoffrey Chaucer was Alice's contemporary and of London merchant stock. Several disproved theories have attempted to connect them in various ways, but I've used none of them. I simply thought that as Londoners, finding themselves in court circles, they might very well have been friends. From my first reading of Chaucer's poem *Troilus and Criseyde* I have been moved by the psychological depth and emotional complexity he infused into the tale and have suspected he based his portrait of Criseyde on someone he knew well.

I shaped a life for Alice. I think she might be pleased with it.

Further Reading

Bak, János M. "Queens as Scapegoats in Medieval Hungary," in *Queens and Queenship in Medieval Europe,* ed. Anne J. Duggan. Boydell Press, 1997, 223–233.

Beardwood, Alice. *Alien Merchants in England 1350 to 1377: Their Legal and Economic Position.* Medieval Academy of America, 1931.

Bothwell, James. "The Management of Position: Alice Perrers, Edward III, and the Creation of a Landed Estate, 1362–1377," in *Journal of Medieval History* 24 (1998), 31–51.

Dodd, Gwilym. "Crown, Magnates and Gentry: The English Parliament, 1369–1421." Unpublished D.Phil. thesis, University of York, 1998.

Given-Wilson, Chris. *The Royal Household and the King's Affinity: Service, Politics and Finance in England 1360–1413.* Yale University Press, 1986.

Given-Wilson, Chris, and Alice Curteis. *The Royal Bastards of Medieval England.* Routledge and Kegan Paul, 1984, 136–142.

Harbison, S. "William of Windsor, the Court Party and the Administration of Ireland," in *England and Ireland in the Later Middle Ages,* ed. J. Lydon. Dublin, 1981, 158–162.

Holmes, George. *The Good Parliament.* Oxford Clarendon Press, 1975.

Lacey, Helen. "The Politics of Mercy: The Use of the Royal Pardon in Fourteenth-Century England." Unpublished D.Phil. thesis, University of York, 2005.

Mieszkowski, Gretchen. "The Reputation of Criseyde 1155–1500," in *Transactions of the Connecticut Academy of Arts and Sciences* 43 (December 1971), 71–153.

Mortimer, Ian. *The Perfect King: The Life of Edward III, Father of the English Nation.* Jonathan Cape, 2006.

Myers, A. R. "The Wealth of Richard Lyons," in *Essays in Medieval History Presented to Bertie Wilkinson,* ed. T. A. Sandquist and M. R. Powicke. University of Toronto Press, 1969, 301–329.

Ormrod, W. M. "Alice Perrers and John Salisbury," in *English Historical Review* 123 (2008).

———. *Political Life in Medieval England, 1300–1450.* St. Martin's Press, 1995.

———. *The Reign of Edward III.* Tempus, 2000.

———. "The Trials of Alice Perrers," in *Speculum* 83, no. 2 (2008), 366–396.

———. "Who Was Alice Perrers?" in *Chaucer Review* xl (2006), 219–229.

Taylor, John. *English Historical Literature in the Fourteenth Century.* Clarendon Press, 1987.

Taylor, John, Wendy R. Childs, and Leslie Watkiss, trans. and eds. *The St. Albans Chronicle: The* Chronica maiora *of Thomas Walsingham, I, 1376–1394.* Oxford Clarendon Press, 2003.

Vale, Juliet. *Edward III and Chivalry: Chivalric Society and Its Context 1270–1350.* Boydell Press, 1982.

Vale, Malcolm. *The Princely Court: Medieval Courts and Culture in North-West Europe 1270–1380.* Oxford University Press, 2001.

Acknowledgments

M Y DEEPEST thanks to Patrick Walsh, my agent and good friend, who has believed in this project—indeed, kept nudging me on—from the beginning, and the talented team at Conville & Walsh.

Kate Elton, Georgina Hawtrey-Woore, and Suzanne O'Neill for their enthusiasm, encouragement, brilliant editing, and absolute support.

Joyce Gibb for being far more than a first reader.

James Bothwell, whose paper on Alice's properties set me on the right path, who permitted me to use his map of Alice's properties as the basis for the one in this book, and who encouraged me to contact Chris Given-Wilson.

Chris Given-Wilson for opening up his files containing years of research on Alice.

RaGena DeAragon, who accompanied me to St. Andrews to guide me through the complexities of the primary source files in Chris's collection in the brief time available and to provide translations, whose expertise on medieval women guided my reading on the subject, and whose feedback on my papers and ideas was invaluable.

Mark Ormrod, who shared with me his discovery of Alice's first marriage and has continued to share his ongoing research on Alice. This book would have been quite different without Mark's generosity.

Laura Hodges, who shared with me her expertise on fourteenth-century clothing, provided immensely helpful suggestions in the first-draft stage, and answered questions all along the way.

Gretchen Mieszkowski, whose monograph on the reputation of Criseyde inspired my interpretation.

Anthony Goodman for sharing his research not only on Alice but also on Joan of Kent, and for lively discussions of the period.

The White Hart Society at the Western Michigan University International Congress on Medieval Studies and the Fourteenth-Century Studies group at the Leeds International Medieval Congress for providing the opportunity for me to present papers on my ongoing research, which reaped a bounty of information and feedback.

The scholars on Chaucernet, so many of whom I count as friends—especially the Thursday-Night Ladies.

Candace Robb for sharing her research with me.

Charles Robb for insightful suggestions and the beautiful maps.

And all the friends and family who have cheered me on.

For this bounty of generosity and camaraderie, I am grateful.

A Conversation with Emma Campion

Q. What inspired your research into Alice Perrers?

A. The more I researched women in the fourteenth century, the less sense the old version of her life made to me. I've used the metaphor of tumbling down the rabbit hole after Alice in several papers presented at academic conferences, first in jest to catch people's attention, but eventually I truly felt as Alice did, that everything was topsy-turvy. The old story was that as the strong, charismatic King Edward aged, he allowed a teenage girl from the countryside, an orphan with no powerful patrons, to take over the reins of government and particularly to control access to the king; despite Edward's living heir being the immensely popular war hero Edward of Woodstock, the Black Prince, and despite the wealth, ambition, and power of another son, John of Gaunt, Duke of Lancaster, who many believed manipulated his father behind the scenes. I could not rectify Alice's reputation with the political reality, but bits of the story did suggest that Alice Perrers was someone the prince and the duke found useful. And that intrigued me, so I started digging.

Q. And as you began to dig, you learned of newly or recently unearthed facts that changed Alice's history. How did that feel?

A. At first, I was simply thrilled—learning that Perrers was Alice's married name explained why centuries of researchers hadn't come up with a satisfactory genealogy for her. But, of course, it also brought home to me how fluid our understanding of history really is. These petitions had sat unread in the Public Records Office for so long—what else was lurking in some dusty corner? What facts would be revealed only after I'd finished the book? That aside, I felt grateful (for once) for my procrastination in actually writing the book, for lingering so long in the research phase. And truly grateful that I hadn't skipped the conference session in which this information was so casually revealed.

Q. Was there anything you learned about Alice Perrers that you were tempted to ignore?

A. I wanted very much for Alice's marriage to William Wyndsor to have been a happy one. But scholar Mark Ormrod convinced me with his carefully reasoned analysis of the facts that Wyndsor used Alice, or, more appropriately, the Duke of Lancaster used Alice in a way that benefited Wyndsor. And Wyndsor never changed his will to include either Alice or her daughters. Still I argued! But in the end I couldn't ignore the evidence that was right there in front of me. That's the rub of writing about an actual person—I could not justify turning that marriage into a happily-ever-after when the facts screamed otherwise.

Q. Why did you write *The King's Mistress* in first person?

A. I didn't intend to. I prefer to write in multiple points of view to afford a wider perspective of the period, but every time I sat down to write, I would hear Alice's voice telling the story. Gradually I saw the wisdom in writing this particular book in the subject's voice because Alice has had such a bad rap for so long and my purpose in writing this book was to present a more plausible story of her life based on other women's lives in the period. I gave Alice a voice. That's also why I dedicated the book to her.

Q. What are the challenges of presenting the life of a fourteenth-century woman to twenty-first-century readers?

A. The greatest challenge is being true to the psychology and the realities of the time. For example, the rituals of the Catholic faith would have been an integral part of a woman's life, no matter what her station or sexual conduct. Young women understood their duty either to marry or to enter a convent for the sake of the family. No matter how much this might raise my feminist hackles, it's fact, and to have Alice specifically rebel against a woman's place is, for me, anachronistic. It's also difficult for us to imagine the narrow frame of reference most people had in the fourteenth century. As a commoner, Alice would know nothing of court life, so the world into which Janyn thrust her would have been frighteningly alien.

My passion about medieval history is all about my own curiosity, wondering what it might have been like to experience that period. Alice Perrers was remarkable in her time, and it's my challenge to show why the people of fourteenth-century England found her so.

Q. What was the most difficult aspect of writing this book?

A. My inner power struggle between historian and novelist. I was surprised by this, but in hindsight I can see why it happened: all along I thought of this book as a fictionalized biography. I wanted to show all of Alice's life, and that's simply too much ground to cover in a novel. My struggle came not in changing history, but in leaving out people, events, political issues in order to move the story forward and not overly confuse the nonspecialist reader.

Q. You portray Alice as dedicated to her children. What brought you to this idea?

A. Several things. One was the offhand mention in Walsingham's character assassination of Alice that she stayed by the ailing king's bedside day and night with her daughter Isabella. Setting aside my fascination with this daughter who's mentioned nowhere else, and my realization that this cannot be one of Alice's infants, the simple domestic picture this provided made her so human. *With her daughter.* And then there's her long battle against her second husband's nephew, John Wyndsor, regarding her properties. William Wyndsor had left Alice and her daughters out of his will, leaving all the properties forfeited by Alice but recovered in Wyndsor's name to his nephew. As King Edward had not officially acknowledged his daughters by Alice, it was up to her to provide for them. Her daughters needed dowries in order to marry well, in order to overcome their illegitimacy and their mother's reputation. Records show that she continuously went to court to turn around the will. By the time she wrote her own will she was comfortably abiding in Upminster. Yet she still angrily wrote that Wyndsor had no right to her properties. I just knew that it was all about her daughters. Else why bother with this old pain?

The

KING'S
MISTRESS

Reading Group
Guide

1. Alice's early interactions with Gwen and Dame Agnes teach her crucial lessons in being the mistress of a household. What would you say she learned? How does her relationship with Gwen develop over the course of the book? With Dame Agnes?

2. Despite the rift it causes between Alice and her parents, her marriage to Janyn Perrers brings her great joy. How does Alice mature during her years with Janyn? What aspects of her role as a married woman and a merchant's wife does she most appreciate? If you were in her shoes, how would you feel about being summoned to court as one of Queen Philippa's ladies?

3. The patronage of Isabella, the dowager queen, is profitable to the Perrers family, but at great cost. Do you imagine that Janyn's family had much choice in their relationship with Isabella? How do you feel about Janyn's marrying and starting a family despite the risks? Do you believe he comprehended the danger he might bring to Alice and Bella? Had Janyn confided in Alice once they were wed, do you think things would have turned out differently? How do you think you would feel to have such a third party in your marriage? Would how powerful the person was make a difference?

4. Dom Hanneye, Richard Lyons, and William Wykeham, Bishop of Winchester, prove to be Alice's loyal friends. What is it about her that inspires their loyalty and respect? What does she give them in return?

5. King Edward takes his time luring Alice. What is it about him that attracts her—the compliment of his attention? His power? Do you think she loves him? Was there a point at which you thought she should leave him?

6. Anya Seton depicted John of Gaunt, Duke of Lancaster, as a

romantic hero in *Katherine,* but he was the subject of much animosity in the kingdom. Why does Alice distrust him? Do you find his behavior toward her when she's up against parliament understandable?

7. William Wyndsor's attentions toward Alice are nothing out of the ordinary—mere court flirtation at first. But Alice grows wary of him. Why? Some might have thought his attentions wonderfully, romantically persistent. Why does Alice question his motives? Why is she so angry about his relationship with her son?

8. Joan of Kent offers Alice friendship and advice on survival at court. Why do you suppose she befriends Alice? Do you think that she is sincere when she tells Alice that Prince Edward and John of Gaunt are her loyal friends? Do you feel Joan remains loyal to Alice? Do you feel she is to blame for John of Gaunt's "solution" regarding Alice's marital status after King Edward's death?

9. King Edward relies on Richard Lyons and Alice Perrers to advise him on business and finance. Queen Philippa says she wishes Alice to teach her about merchant society in London, remembering the very close connection between the wealthy merchants and the aristocracy her parents had found crucial for their political strength in Hainault. Why, then, are Richard and Alice so distrusted by parliament? Alice herself doesn't figure this out until it is too late—what is it that she comes to understand about their resentment and distrust? Why is she so hated by the people of London for her role as Lady of the Sun?

10. The king increasingly depends on loans from Richard Lyons and other foreigners to finance his war. But the London merchants resent the foreign merchants—why? During the peasants' revolt, why are Richard and other Flemings singled out by the mob? Why would the monk Thomas Walsingham, in his chronicle, choose to insult Alice by claiming she was the mistress of a Lombard?

11. Telling a story in first person creates a relationship between the narrator and the reader much like that in actual conversation. As

with anyone telling you their story, you must decide for yourself how candid they're being, how reliable a narrator. As Alice tells her story, what do you feel she leaves out? Do you feel she holds back her emotions, her anger? If so, why do you think she would do so?

About the Author

Since doing her graduate work in medieval history and literature, EMMA CAMPION has been engaged in bringing to life the rich culture of the period, from the arts to the politics. This book is the result of her long fascination with Alice Perrers and the serendipitous discovery of new clues about Alice's early life. Her research on Alice led her to question the accepted reputations of other prominent medieval women, whose lives she plans to explore in future books.

Emma lives in Seattle.

A Note on the Type

The text of this book was set in ITC Galliard, which has its origins in matrices designed in the sixteenth century by Parisian-born type designer Robert Granjon while he was working in Antwerp. The characters he created then are the foundation upon which Galliard was built by Matthew Carter for the Mergenthaler Linotype company about four hundred years later. Carter set out to "make a serviceable, contemporary, photocomposition typeface based on a strong historical design" rather than an exact replica of Granjon's designs. ITC acquired exclusive rights to Carter's Galliard in 1981.